What people are saying about …

Crossing the Lines

"In *Crossing the Lines* Richard Doster takes the reader beyond racial stereotypes and reveals the extraordinary nobility of those willing to fight and sacrifice so all Americans can enjoy equality and justice."
Robert Whitlow, best-selling author of *Higher Hope*

"Richard Doster's poignant novel deftly combines the compelling life of journalist Jack Hall with the stirring history of the civil rights movement. Rich and insightful, *Crossing the Lines* nimbly tells a story of historical depth recalling a time in America's past we must never forget."
Stephen McGarvey, executive editor, Crosswalk.com and Christianity.com

"Richard Doster has done it again. *Crossing the Lines* grabs readers on the first page and takes them to the intersection of America's history and today's headlines. It's a richly told story of deep relevance for anyone who's both a culture-watcher and a lover of fascinating yarns."
Carolyn Curtis, author, speaker, and founding editor of *On Mission* magazine

"I found reading Richard Doster's deeply satisfying novel, *Crossing the Lines*, to be an experience that felt akin to being transported in time. With his narrator I watched—often horrified yet hope-full—events unfold that shaped America. I listened with rapt attention to Martin Luther King Jr., and brainstormed with Flannery O' Connor. I was right there. What an amazing journey!"

Claudia Mair Burney, author of *Zora and Nicky* and *Wounded*

CROSSING THE LINES

CROSSING THE LINES

Richard Doster

A NOVEL

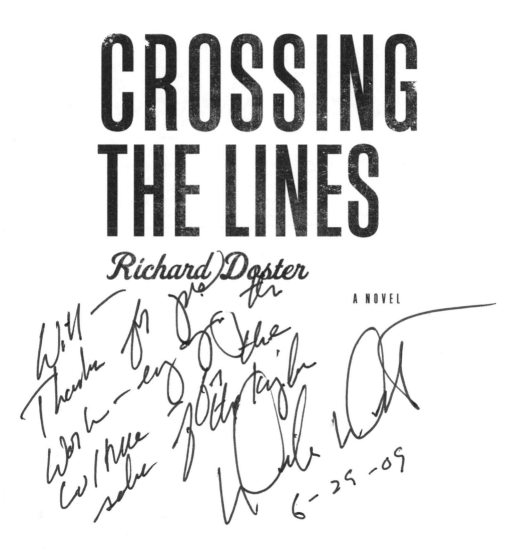

David C Cook

transforming lives together

CROSSING THE LINES
Published by David C. Cook
4050 Lee Vance View
Colorado Springs, CO 80918 U.S.A.

David C. Cook Distribution Canada
55 Woodslee Avenue, Paris, Ontario, Canada N3L 3E5

David C. Cook U.K., Kingsway Communications
Eastbourne, East Sussex BN23 6NT, England

The Web site addresses recommended throughout this book are offered as a
resource to you. These Web sites are not intended in any way to be or imply an
endorsement on the part of David C. Cook, nor do we vouch for their content.

This story is a work of fiction. All characters and events are the product of the
author's imagination, although some are based on real-life events and people.

All Scripture quotations are taken from the *Holy Bible, New International
Version*. *NIV*. Copyright © 1973, 1978, 1984 by International Bible
Society. Used by permission of Zondervan. All rights reserved.

LCCN 2009924470
ISBN 978-1-4347-9984-5
eISBN 978-1-4347-0030-8

Published in association with the literary agency of Alive Communications, Inc.,
7680 Goddard St., Suite 200, Colorado Springs, CO 80920

The Team: Don Pape, Steve Parolini, Amy Kiechlin, Jaci Schneider, and Karen Athen
Cover Design: The DesignWorks Group, Jeff Miller
Cover Photos: Record image is Shutterstock, royalty-free;
Civil rights image is Corbis Images, Bettmann Collection, rights-managed

Printed in the United States of America
First Edition 2009

1 2 3 4 5 6 7 8 9 10

040609

*To Sally, who's been quietly building
the "beloved community"*

A note from the author

This is a story about how a contented Southerner grows uncomfortable with his region. It is a book about how attitudes—individual and collective—were changed, not only by events, but by the flesh-and-blood humans who transformed the Old South into the new one.

This book isn't intended to provide a detailed history. It was written to paint a picture of men and women in the midst of transformation. It was written to entertain readers, to inspire their admiration for courageous people, and to encourage them—in their own neighborhoods—to bring Martin Luther King Jr.'s vision of the "beloved community" to fuller fruition.

Please make sure to read the AfterWords section of this book to find details on what is fact and what is fiction and what books and resources I used to write this novel.

Part 1

Make it your ambition to lead a
quiet life, to mind your own business
and to work with your hands.
—1 Thessalonians 4:11

Chapter 1

There was a time when I aspired to only three things in life: to enjoy my work, to love and care for my family, and to take pleasure in the company of a few good friends.

I never coveted fame nor craved fortune. My proper place, I felt, was adjacent to the fray, but never in it. As a reporter I gathered facts and presented them well. With nouns, verbs, adverbs, and adjectives, I ushered readers to a ringside seat; I put them front-and-center where they could—without obstruction—witness the drama of life in the world around them.

I prowled at the fringes, hovering where I could keep an eye on the men who moved the world. Like a hummingbird, I flitted from one story to the next, extracting what I needed and then quickly moving on in search of more.

In a perfect world, I thought, I'd do my job and then go home. And there I'd savor the last hours of each day with my wife, Rose Marie, and our son, Chris.

But it's been some time since the world was perfect.

Our ambition, the Bible says, is to live a quiet life, but none of us will ever know one. If we're awake in this world, if we breathe in and out, if we put one foot in front of the other, or so much as encounter one other human in the course of a given day—then there's not much hope for more than a few hours' rest.

God has set this goal before us, and then placed it beyond our reach. And that's a mystery that tangles up my mind. If He is good (and I believe He is), then why does His world conspire against us? And if He loves us (and I'll grant that He does), then why does everything get stirred up into one mess after the other, depriving us, every day it seems, of the peace we are meant to have?

I suspect that you've had doubts too; that you've seen the evidence as clearly as I have. And that we've all, in the midst of grief or confusion, built a case against Him, that we've proved, at least in our own minds—and way beyond a reasonable doubt—that God has lost control of this world. Even the dullest among us can point to war and communism, or to hurricanes and tornadoes. And God Himself surely knows we've had our fill of polio and cancer and tuberculosis.

But the testimony that's even more disturbing is what we see two feet in front of our own faces. It's what I have seen up and down Peachtree Street; in Montgomery and Little Rock and Nashville; and even in the hearts of the people I love.

There was a time when I rarely yearned for more than a peaceful life, when I was content with a backyard barbeque, a good ballgame, cuddling with Rose Marie while we watched Ed Sullivan.... And for years the world spun my way. Month after month, life provided more than I asked—until the summer of 1954, until the night my home was bombed, until the lives of my wife and son were threatened, until—in the pitch-black hours of a brand-new morning—our comfortable existence was shattered, and every good thing that I had taken for granted was—in the flash of that single explosion—gone.

Ever since, I've been nagged by the thought that God Himself has been plotting against me; that He has—for reasons He hasn't deigned to share—mined my path with the worst of the world's problems. There've been days that I even thought He hovered above, just waiting for the pieces of my life to come "this close together," and then *Wham!* He dusts off some favorite calamity, hurls it my way, and watches as life peels off into some new wreckage, forcing me to sort out some mess I never made.

It's ridiculous, I know, to think that the God of the universe would trifle with the likes of me, Jack Hall. And trust me, I've spent the opening hours of a thousand mornings wondering, *Why me, Lord? Why, when there are so many deserving creeps in the world, me?*

To date, God's felt no obligation to answer. And by His silence He sets before me the same question He posed to Job: "And exactly who are you, pip-squeak, to question Me?"

Fair enough, I suppose. But like Job I've been wounded and forever scarred. An event like that lingers—it's always there, lurking, and I'm not sure I've known a sound night's sleep in the past six years.

What is it, exactly, that drives a fellow human to so much malice? By what logic does one conclude that a bomb—thrown through the window of a quaint, three-bedroom home—is the wise and sensible course of action?

The answer to questions like these is rarely simple, but I'll do my best to explain:

We lived in Whitney, once the world's most beautiful town, and a place that felt more like home than anything ever built by human hands. But in 1954 we tore the place in two. With bitterness and violence we slashed it along the seam where black met white—and I bore a share of the blame.

I'd been the sportswriter for the *Whitney Herald*, and I had, in an effort to salvage the town's struggling baseball team, engineered the signing of a Negro player, the now famous Percy Jackson. But white fans and most of the city's leaders shuddered at the thought of mixing races, anywhere or for any reason. And night after night Jackson felt, and heard, a full measure of the town's wrath.

We might have survived that. We might have outlived those first bursts of outrage, just as the Dodgers had with Jackie Robinson. And who knows, we may have flourished. But, in the midst of our experiment, the Supreme Court fielded one of its own. Nine black-robed justices outlawed "separate but equal" schools, and Whitney's mothers and fathers came unglued. Our bankers, lawyers, and merchants panicked. Our city councilmen scurried for cover, shielding themselves behind a chorus of defiant proclamations. Our pastors joined the battle too; white and colored both, they stormed to their pulpits and exhausted every ounce of the moral authority they had, urging their congregations to either comply or resist, deepening the wound that had gashed us.

The presence of Percy Jackson, living and playing in the midst of white teammates, was more stress than Whitney could bear. In a Negro ballplayer, my friends saw the looming threat of racial integration. When they watched him play they faced the unbearable truth that a Negro was better than the white men around him; it was a chilling glimpse into a dreadful future, and the threads that had held us together frayed.

As colored folks inched forward, as they crept—ever so scarcely—into the fabric of everyday life, their white neighbors scurried to block the path. And we all, in pursuit of the society we craved, ran ourselves right out of Eden.

Percy Jackson and I became the flesh-and-blood faces of one town's trouble. He and I—a colored kid and a white reporter—personified every last drop of Whitney's strain. And on a summer night in 1954 my home, and then his, became the bull's-eye of our neighbors' rage.

As I faced the aftermath an old college professor had called. And it is there that this story begins.

He had heard from the sports editor of *The Atlanta Constitution*, Furman Bisher. "I knew him when were both at the *Charlotte News*," my teacher explained. "He's looking for somebody who knows baseball, for a guy who's just itching to cover the Atlanta Crackers and the Southern Association. You'd be perfect," he said. Then he chuckled—a little too sadly I thought—"and besides, Ralph McGill, the editor down there, he's probably the one guy who won't hold all that Percy Jackson garbage against you."

My heart thumped audibly at the sound of the words "Atlanta Crackers," and my salivary glands oozed. The Crackers were the New York Yankees of minor league baseball, the best team ever assembled in a Southern city—and that made this the best sports job south of Baltimore. "Who else is Bisher talking to?" I asked. "How long's he been looking? When's he going to decide?"

My friend chuckled. "I think I was his first call," he said. "So if I were you, I'd hang up on me and call him. He's expecting to hear from you."

Furman Bisher had been in Atlanta for three or four years. I'd seen his work and I knew he possessed a first-rate talent. I remembered him from a few years before—it might have been 1949 or '50—when he'd snagged an interview with Shoeless Joe Jackson. There wasn't a sportswriter alive who wouldn't have killed to swap places. It'd been thirty years since the Black Sox scandal, when eight Chicago White Sox players, including Shoeless Joe, stood accused: of conspiring with gamblers, of throwing the 1919 World Series, of profiting from their team's loss. They'd been banned from baseball, and the world had yet to hear from its fallen hero. An explanation was overdue, and when the time had finally come, it was Bisher who got the story.

The man wrote sports like Thomas Wolfe wrote novels—vividly and with elegance. He took his readers where they most longed to go—to the sixteenth green at the Augusta National, where the air was thick with just-bloomed azaleas; to Churchill Downs where the ground shook under the pounding hooves of Native Dancer; to Ponce de León Park where, as they read Bisher's words, they would, within the expanse of their own imaginations, crane their necks to follow the path of a long fly ball drifting back, back, back … and just clearing the left-field wall.

There wasn't a game he didn't love: baseball, basketball, football—he devoured them all. And he looked the part too; a sportswriter straight out of central casting: curly black hair combed straight back, a boxer's nose, thick, dark brows that arched above playful black eyes.

He was rough and old school, but his words were always refined and perfectly mannered. And every time I read his work, I envied the talent he'd been given.

• • • •

I lingered outside his office. It was 9:51 the Tuesday morning before Thanksgiving, 1955. A reporter leaned over the desk, both hands planted squarely on top, waiting. Bisher read; he tapped a pencil, his eyes racing left to right and down the page. A moment passed, and then another. And then I heard the dreaded sigh. "What the—? What is this, Bill? The lead's hobbling around like it's crippled; there's no drama, it might be nice to see a verb somewhere...." There came another words-fail-me huff, then a crumpling sound, and then a ping into a distant trash can. "Do it again," Bisher snarled. "I need something in a half hour."

The reporter turned and stomped away. He was hunched low like a middle linebacker who'd tear your head off and know nothing but glee for the effort. He trudged fifteen feet down the corridor and punched the wall. At twenty feet he muttered furiously and unintelligibly. "Son," "cram," and "stick" were the only words I actually heard, but everyone within fifty feet got the gist of what was on the man's mind. Ten feet farther and he disappeared around the corner, still grumbling, the back of his neck now tinged with bright red rage.

Swell timing, I thought. I took a deep breath, poked my head into the office, and rapped on the door. "Look, maybe it's not a good time," I said. "But—"

"Hall?"

"Yeah. We had a ten o'clock appointment, but really if it's not a good time—"

He glanced at his watch, scowling. "Good a time as any," he muttered.

I eased into a coffee-stained, lopsided, and threadbare chair. Bisher tossed his pencil onto the desk, sat back, and opened with the only cliché I'd ever hear him use: "So, tell me a little about yourself."

Our conversation began, and I have loved Furman Bisher from that day to this one. I told him how much I had enjoyed his work, and how on the day we first met he'd been kind enough to say some nice things about mine. We talked about the Atlanta Crackers and the Georgia Bulldogs. He described what it was like to follow Bobby Jones at the Masters. And I rendered a picture of what life was like covering minor league baseball. I told him how it felt to trail a flock of ugly-duckling farm boys who dreamed of waking up one day—transformed—and standing at the plate in Yankee Stadium ... honest-to-goodness ballplayers.

We talked about coaches and athletes and the writers we most loved to read. We talked about the most thrilling sporting events we had ever actually seen. We talked about why we loved the newspaper business. And we had talked for the better part of two hours when Bisher caught sight of the time.

"Geez, it's nearly noon," he growled. He stared up at the ceiling. Then he popped up from his chair and grabbed a wrinkled blue blazer. "You hungry?" he asked.

"Sure," I told him. "I could eat."

"There's a little cafeteria down near Tech...." Bisher motioned for me to follow him. "Skillet-fried chicken's terrific down there."

We rode down Marietta to Luckie Street, made a right, skirted the Georgia Tech campus until we came to Hemphill Road. The Pickrick restaurant was white with black trim. Four large windows sandwiched a pair of glass doors, and two small billboards—one advertising Dr Pepper, the other 7UP—were posted along the fence at the far side of the building. Inside, the placed swarmed with businessmen, carpenters, plumbers, and college kids—everybody shoving trays down the line, choosing from sweet potatoes, black-eyed peas, chicken, and pork. From the back side of the counter Negro servers heaped mountains of food onto glistening white china—all of it cheaper than anything you'd ever find in Whitney. From the moment I crossed the threshold, my mouth watered at the blended scents of the fresh-cooked foods.

The owner was easy to spot. He was a sunny, bald, round-faced man wearing thick black-framed glasses. He skimmed from customer to customer like a bee in a flower garden, calling his friends by name, asking about their kids and their work and their wives—working the room like a small-town mayor—smiling, backslapping, and joking with every human who had a heartbeat.

This guy would've been a perfect fit in Whitney, I thought. *Homespun and natural, a man in his element, presiding over a room that was filled with friends, all sharing delicious conversation, and where everyone felt at home.*

Bisher and I huddled over a tiny Formica-topped table, and we dreamed out loud about the future of Atlanta sports. It wouldn't be long, Bisher thought, before Atlanta lured a big-league team to town.

"This place is booming," he told me. "There's so dad-gum much money pouring in here...." His eyes filled with thought of it. "Town makes Fort Knox look like a welfare case." Bisher devoured the scene, savoring our rustic surroundings. "Take a good look," he said, grinning. "This right here ... this is the capital of the New South."

He shoveled a forkful of fried chicken into his mouth. "I'm not kidding," he went on. "You take this job and it won't be long before *you* get a shot at the big leagues. There's already talk about a new stadium; won't be long after that."

I held out my glass for a refill. "Sounds promising," I said. "But can I tell you something?"

Bisher glanced up.

"I'm real partial to the stadium you got."

A smile rippled across his face. "You've been to Ponce de León?"

"Yeah," I said. "Once or twice."

"Nothing like it in the world," Bisher replied. "That old magnolia up on the terrace ..." he tipped his glass toward me. "If that old boy could talk, now there'd be some stories to tell."

"Somebody told me that Eddie Matthews hit a ball into the tree. That true?"

"It is a fact," Bisher proclaimed. "And he was just a kid at the time—nineteen maybe?" Bisher stabbed at a mound of green beans. "Story goes round that Babe Ruth put one out there too." He tossed back a who-knows smile. "I can't confirm that one."

"It's a great place to watch a game," I said. "Don't get me wrong; I'd love to cover the big leagues—that'd be a dream come true. But there's a piece of me that'll hate to see Ponce de León go."

Bisher's head bobbed. "I know what you mean," he replied, his voice lilting to the wistful side. "Place has got more memories than my wedding album."

We joined the line at the cash register. Bisher fished for a couple of bucks, and I had just reached for a toothpick when a neighborly clap slammed down on my shoulder. "Hadn't seen you in here before." The owner of the Pickrick reached for my hand and shook as if we were distant cousins at a family reunion. "Lester Maddox," he beamed, "the proprietor."

"Jack Hall," I replied. "Food was great."

"That's what we like to hear," Maddox said, still pumping my hand warmly. "We want to see you back here real soon, and bring your family next time, you hear?"

I raised the toothpick into the air. "I'll be sure to do that," I promised.

He angled his head toward Bisher. "Now this man right here," he said, "he puts out the best sports section in United States of America." I heard the wink in his tone.

"Yeah," Bisher growled—he handed the cashier a five—"but tell me something, Lester: Which is better, my sports section or your fried chicken?"

Maddox tossed me a sly nod; he slapped me on the back and said, "Well listen, you boys hurry back, you hear?"

Bisher laughed and the two of us ambled outside, visoring our eyes against the midday sun. "Seems like a nice guy," I said.

"Yeah ..." Bisher stretched one syllable into four. "He is a nice guy. But he's got this weird love-hate thing going on with the paper." Bisher reached for his keys. Over the roof of the car he said, "And he and McGill—let's just say they're not on each other's Christmas card list."

I twirled the toothpick between my lips. "And why would the editor of *The Atlanta Constitution* have a problem with this guy?"

Bisher climbed into the car; he leaned over to unlock the door. "No need to get into the details," he said, "but Lester's been running these cockamamie ads for years; runs 'em on Saturdays when the rate's cheaper, and he runs 'em in the *Journal*; he won't put anything in our paper." He shot me a quick glance. "And I don't believe we'd take 'em anyway."

"Because they're 'cockamamie'?" I asked.

"Yeah," Bisher said. "He's turned them into these bite-size editorials. He carries on about politics mostly; hardly ever says much about the food. But it's funny, the ads actually work, and the truth is, old Lester's got a following that most columnists envy." Bisher cut his eyes at me again. "He's actually given their Saturday circulation a pretty good bump; people go out and buy the paper just to keep up with what 'Pickrick Says.'"

"McGill can't be jealous," I insisted.

"No," Bisher chuckled, "let's just say that Lester's politics don't jibe too well with Mac's." He swung the car onto Forsythe Street. "We can probably leave it there for now."

Back at Bisher's office, I began to gather my things—wondering in earnest what it'd be like to work here. My eyes toured the room, watching people scurry from point A to point B. Phones rang. Typewriters clacked. Copyboys raced from reporter to editor to composer. This was a different world than the one I'd known. The place surged with energy. People rushed with purpose. They were driven by deadlines and competition—by a hounding need to have their words read and admired.

Being there, standing in the midst of the clatter and chaos, I felt like a drunk in a Budweiser brewery. The sights and sounds stirred something inside, and it wouldn't be long before I'd have to have at it.

Bisher tossed his coat onto the rack. "You mind hanging out for another minute?" he asked. "I think Mac wants to say hello."

I snapped out of the trance. "McGill?"

"Yeah, if he's got time. Just sit tight for a second, I'll be right back."

I grabbed a copy of yesterday's paper, wondering why Ralph McGill would even bother. This was low-level stuff, and Bisher could make the hire. But I was happy to have the chance to meet him. McGill was famous; I'd read his articles in the *Saturday Evening Post* and *Atlantic Monthly*. He was quoted in the *New York Times* and *Chicago Tribune*. He had even been on national television, dubbed by the Northern media as "the moderate voice of the New South."

McGill was one of those guys you either loved or hated. And Joe Anderson, my old boss at the *Whitney Herald*, groused about him fifty-two times a year. "Pompous ass," Joe'd complain, shaking his head and making this tsking sound every time McGill's name was mentioned. "Ain't his job to get people all riled up; that's what the politicians do; good newspaperman just gives 'em the facts," Joe'd mutter. "People want to get riled up about 'em, that's their business."

Five minutes later Bisher ushered me into Ralph McGill's office. He sat behind a humble and cluttered wooden desk. To his right, on a gray metal stand, sat an Underwood typewriter, a page cranked halfway down and paused in midsentence. A rolltop desk was behind him, nicked and scarred and worn with age. Piles of papers were littered across the top of it. In the back corner, a coffee mug was crammed full of dull-edged pencils. Manuals and reports were stuffed in the overhead slots, and across the top a dozen books and binders slumped to the right in sloppy formation.

McGill stood and waved me in. "Make yourself at home," he said. He looked at Bisher, "I'll send him back as soon as we're done."

McGill was shorter than I'd imagined, paunchier, too. But there was an air about him—an aura, I'd guess you'd say—of grand ideas and purpose.

He reached for my hand. "I've read your work," he said. "It's good."

He motioned for me to sit and then dropped into his chair. He threw his legs over a corner of the desk, and then, as if he'd read my earlier thoughts, he explained: "The sports page has always been important to me. When I started in the business, sports was the battleground. It was where a paper won or lost the circulation war. When I came here...."

I could practically hear the memories churn. He sat back, lacing his fingers behind his head. "When I came here," he continued, "we were in a helluva fight with the *Journal* and with Hearst's old paper, the *Georgian*. Sports was the front line."

"Yes sir," I said, "I know. And if I remember right, that's why Ed Danforth brought you here." I held McGill's eye. "I've read your work too," I said, "from when you did sports."

A smile slipped across McGill's face. "I hope you haven't gone back that far. It's been ... I don't know, fifteen, sixteen years since I did anything on the sports page."

I made no attempt to stifle a grin, certain that he knew better than that. "There's not a sportswriter alive who hasn't read your work," I said. "You, Damon Runyon, Grantland Rice, Ring Lardner ... you guys made sports a place for writers, a place to tell stories. We all went to school on you guys ... we all dreamed of writing like you did."

He brushed away the compliment. "Different era," he said. "But Bisher ..." he pushed his chin out toward the hallway. "He's as good as any of us were; he's the guy who's taking sports to the next level."

I trailed a finger along my lower lip, pondering the company I'd kept that day. "I don't mind telling you, having you and him in the same place at the same time, that's a little daunting."

McGill's smile lingered. "You'll do fine," he said. He picked up a copy of the *Whitney Herald*. "This is solid work; you're ready." Then he sat up straight, he leaned forward, stretching as close to me as his body would go. "I want you to know something, Jack: This is the best place in the world for an up-and-coming writer. This town, the South ..." he held his thumb and forefinger an inch apart. "We're just this far," he said. "We're right on the dad-gum brink of—" He suddenly stopped. He turned back to the old desk and asked, "You know what that is?"

He'd caught me by surprise; I wasn't sure, exactly, where he wanted the conversation to go. "The rolltop?" I asked.

"Yeah, you know who that used to belong to?"

"No," I shrugged.

"That was Henry Grady's desk. Grady had my job seventy years ago. He started talking up the New South back in the 1870s."

McGill made a quarter turn and crossed his legs. "The guy was shameless," he said with a grin. "He loved Atlanta and he had this grand vision of a resurrected South. He pushed like hell to bring Yankee money down here—wanted to develop railroads and industry. You ought to read him sometime; his stuff's still down in the morgue. He had this bold, direct style—subject-verb—never got much fancier than that—but he was good. And the thing about Grady … the guy had guts. He used this paper to persuade anybody who'd listen that Atlanta was the place to put their money; he'd tell 'em flat out, every chance he got, this was where they needed to invest their lives."

McGill reached for a bottle of Coke, wondering, I suspect, about Grady's legacy and how, one day, it might shape and color his own. "We've got a chance to build something special, Jack. We're about to make the New South an honest-to-goodness reality—a little different than Grady might've imagined—but even better." He took a sip and dropped his feet to the floor. He pulled his chair forward, resting his arms across the desk, narrowing his gaze. "But let's get back to you." He flung his hand toward the *Whitney Herald* and said, "Tell me what happened over there. What was going on with that colored ballplayer?"

I expelled a dismal breath. I told him about the last year of my life. I explained that my motives had been pure, and that baseball had been the only thing on my agenda. I had hoped, I said, that a Negro player would draw new fans and that they'd keep the team alive. But the effort failed. Percy Jackson had been run out of town, he'd been forced to move north, to the Triple-I league. And then I flipped every card I held: "Look," I said, "my reputation's shot over there. I've been called a nigger lover and a communist; I've been called names I never heard before." I looked up; McGill's eyes were locked on mine. "To be honest, they've run me out of town too. I've got no choice but to move on."

McGill stroked his chin as he listened, and when I'd concluded his smile dripped with grace. "You know, I think somebody called me a communist the second or third day I was here," he said. His chair creaked as he settled back. He tented his fingers beneath his chin. "I'm sorry you had to go through all that, that your family had to suffer. But you know ..." a gleam came to his eye. "I think you did the right thing. And if you'd have done it here, I'd have been proud."

I turned my head, an appeal to hear more.

"The race situation in this country ..." McGill shook his head, despairing. "We got politicians squawking all over the place about separate but equal, separate but equal.... But we all know what's going on. The governors and mayors, they know good and well there's nothing equal about it. You and I, we know. Our neighbors know. And it ain't exactly a secret in the colored neighborhoods. The thing is ..." his voice was suddenly edged with irritation, "if we don't face up to it, it's going to ruin us all—white, colored—it won't matter. If we don't deal with it, in the schools or on a baseball field, well then, the rest of the country'll just pass us by." He looked up, scowling. "And I'll tell you something, they'll be laughing as they go." He sat quietly for a moment wondering, I think, how it'd feel to be the butt of a national joke. Then his countenance eased, and he said, "So this ballplayer, Jackson, is he a good kid?"

"Yes sir," I replied. "Comes from a solid family too."

McGill twitched an eyebrow. "You know his family?"

"Yes sir," I said. And then I explained that Rose Marie, Chris, and I had become friends, of sorts, with Percy, Walter, and Roberta Jackson. I told him that our lives had gotten tangled up with theirs, that we'd suffered through the same bad season, that we'd been victims of the same violence, that one family had come to the other's aid, and that through it all we'd come to care for one another.

"Hard to believe," he mumbled. "You have had a heck of a year, haven't you?"

"It's been different," I granted.

"Well, you did the right thing," he assured me. "You put the problem out there, put it where nobody could look away, where they'd be forced to think about it. That's good," he said. "It's progress." And you know what else?" He looked at me straight on. "It's part of the job. It's what good newspapermen do."

I smiled back at him clumsily. "Well, thanks," I said. "I s'pose there's some consolation in that."

He eyed his typewriter and then his watch. "Well," he rapped his desk and stood, signaling that our meeting was over. "You do what Bisher tells you," he said. "He's good. You follow his lead, and you'll do just fine." He reached across the desk and shook my hand. "There's a lot going on around here, Jack. And you'll have one of the best seats in the house."

I thanked Ralph McGill for his time and left, not knowing that this was the first of a hundred meetings we'd have; not having the slightest notion that this man would become my mentor, that he'd change every idea I had about the South and the press and what it meant to be a writer. I left his office that day with no clue that as a direct result of this brief encounter, the direction of my life would change forever.

• • • •

That night, Rose Marie was up and on the lookout. She rushed out to my car, wrapping her robe tightly against the chill, and peppered me with a thousand questions that had been simmering all day: "How'd it go?" "Did you like them?" "What was Bisher like?" "Did he offer you the job?"

Before I said a word, I drew her close, and through a fatigued, yet relieved and contented smile, I let her know that our lives had taken a promising turn. "Let's grab something to drink," I said, "and I'll tell you all about it."

I tossed my keys and wallet onto the kitchen counter and pitched a copy of the *Constitution* on top of the pile. "Thought you might want to flip through this," I said. "These guys do six full pages of sports—on weekdays."

We moved into the living room. Rose curled into a corner of the couch; she snuggled under a blanket, her eyes alert with the promise of good news. "All right, Hall, I want to know everything," she said, "from the second you pulled into the parking lot."

I sipped from my drink, scrolling through the day and pondering where to begin. Then I grinned at her like a kid on Christmas morning. "Well, I start on Tuesday the third, right after New Year's." I leveled my gaze with hers. And then, slowly, I told my sweet wife: "And we just got a twenty percent raise."

Radiance flared from Rose's eyes, her smile glittered like a sparkler on the Fourth of July, and at that moment, her heart and mind—and even her body—were suddenly freed from the grip of our relentless bad fortune. She raced over and threw her arms around my neck. "Maybe things are finally turning around," she said. "Maybe we're getting back on track."

I put my hand on top of hers. "Maybe so," I said.

Rose moved back to the couch; she drew her knees to her chest and said, "So, you felt comfortable there? Like you'd fit in?"

"Yeah," I said, loosening my tie, "I think so. It always takes time, but I liked everybody. And I liked Bisher a lot." I sipped again, picturing Bill, red-faced and muttering as he stomped down the hall. "He's tough and he'll break you in two—I got a firsthand look at that—but he's good and he cares about the work and he wants everything to be right...." I sat quietly, wondering for a second if I was up to this job; if I was good enough to play in Bisher's league. Then I cut a glance at Rose. "I met McGill, too," I told her.

"Really! What was he like? Were you nervous?"

"Yeah, a little," I said. "But he's a pretty regular guy. And since he used to write sports I think we hit it off okay."

"That's got to make you feel good," Rose said.

"Well, it can't hurt," I replied.

Rose Marie straightened her legs and yawned. She made a quarter turn, resting her elbow on the arm of the couch, cupping her head in her hand. "What about things here?" she asked. A trace of wariness lurked behind the question. "Did they ask what happened? About why you're leaving?"

I swirled the ice round the bottom of the glass. "They already knew," I said. "And Bisher just stayed away from it. But McGill was curious; he wanted to talk about it."

Rose tucked her lower lip beneath her teeth. "And …?"

"It was interesting," I said. "He thought I had done the right thing." I glanced away, thinking back on the conversation. "For him, all the mess we've been through might have been a plus," I said with a chuckle. I tilted my glass in Rose's direction. "It sounds weird, but I actually think it helped me get the job."

Rose took a deep, almost shuddering breath. She raked her fingers through her hair and said, "If that's true, then God works in some mighty frightening ways."

I opened my hands and shrugged. "Don't ask me," I mumbled. "I haven't understood much of anything since 1953."

I did not tell Rose that a similar thought had occurred to me, that I had, for five solid hours, stared at a yellow-and-white-striped highway struggling to puzzle together the meaning of the last twelve months; that I had labored over thoughts about where the events of the past year were leading. I did not tell her that I had wondered how these events had changed us; about how, over the coming years, they'd recast our view of the world, of each other, of our new friends and neighbors. Nor did I mention my last and most disturbing thought of all, which was this: If one event prepares us for the next, if, in fact, we learn from our past—then what lay ahead? And what did that portend for Rose Marie and Chris—the woman and child who were mine to protect and provide for?

I looked at Rose, detected the glint of hope in her eyes, and I wanted to believe that life had taken a good turn, that a fresh start was ours, served up on a silver platter and there for the taking. But once you've been burned, once your life has been so cruelly shattered, you can't help but wonder: What else is out there, crouched and waiting?

Rose stood and came beside me. She put her hand on my shoulder and said, "I'm glad everything went so well. I'm going to miss it here, but I'm glad we've got a good place to make a clean start."

I tilted my face up to her. "I'll be honest with you, Rose; I don't know where any of this is going. And I could not be one bit sorrier for where we've been. But I'm glad about one thing: I'm glad we're going together."

She bent down and kissed the top of my head. "Wherever you go Hall … I go."

I grinned and said, "In that case, I'm going to bed."

The next morning I stood in the bathroom, toothbrush in hand, clearing a spot on the steam-fogged mirror. Rose wandered into the bedroom. She held the Atlanta newspaper, folded down to a quarter page.

"Have you seen this, Hall?"

"I haven't seen any of it," I mumbled. "I just grabbed it on my way out."

She propped herself on the edge of the bed. "I can't believe this," she mumbled.

"What?" I asked.

"The Sugar Bowl," she called. "I can't believe you didn't hear about this."

I stepped into the bedroom, bluffing concern. "Last year you were pretty miffed about the Cotton Bowl, weren't you?"

She peered up, showing no sign of amusement. "I'm not kidding, Jack. Do you know who's playing?"

I frowned, dropping both hands to my sides. "Excuse me?" I said, as if she asked me to name the president.

The Pitt Panthers had received an early invitation, which, to tell you the truth, surprised me. I couldn't remember the last time a team with three losses had been to a major bowl. But two of them had come to top-ranked teams: Navy and Oklahoma. They'd finished the year strong, upsetting sixth-ranked West Virginia 26-7, breaking the Mountaineers' eleven-game win streak. And then they'd knocked off Penn State. I had to admit that they were, at the very least, interesting.

A week later Georgia Tech, with an impressive win over Georgia, had secured the second bid.

"It ought to be a great matchup," I told Rose. "Everybody over there's got to be pretty excited about it."

"Not everybody," she stretched the words into a singsong, foreboding sound.

I headed back to the sink. "What do you mean?"

Rose stood and marched into the bathroom. She slapped the paper down on the countertop: "Look at this."

I saw the headline and glanced at the lead. "Oh geez," I groaned.

Marvin Griffin, the governor of our soon-to-be home state, was steamed. He wanted the game canceled, not because Pitt was a lousy team, but because Bobby Grier, a Pitt safety, was colored.

"We're not going to have our kids playing mixed teams," Griffin had ranted at a hastily called press conference. "Not down here, not in our own backyard. It's an insult and an abomination." He was furious with Blake Van Leer, Georgia Tech's president. "He should've consulted me before they accepted this invitation," Griffin complained. "He's overstepped his bounds, and now he's threatening our state's most sacred traditions." He'd concluded the meeting by telling reporters: "I'm calling on the university regents to put a stop to this game. We can't have our boys on the same field with Negroes, not down here, not in the South."

The sparkle had dwindled from Rose Marie's eyes. She stared at the paper. "This is going to follow us wherever we go," she said. "Every sport, every season—this'll be hanging over us.

Chapter 2

Rose Marie needed to see the lay of our new land. She needed a feel for what was in store, and she needed it, she told me, "Now!"

Three days later we found ourselves with Carl, the same real estate agent Bisher had used a few years before. Rose and I drifted through a pair of houses Saturday morning. Chris played outside with Slugger, our seventy-five-pound mutt, who, he insisted, "should see the houses too." For some reason—one that had prompted Rose to roll her eyes and mutter, "you've got to be kidding"—I'd gone along with the boy's logic. I'd held the dog's head in both hands, looked into his trusting brown eyes, and explained to Rose: "He's got to live there too."

The houses were nice, and both, we agreed, were possibilities. But neither sparked much in our imaginations. "We've got about an hour before we're due at the next one," Carl said. "Why don't we grab a sandwich and I'll tell you about what's left on the list?"

"Yeah," Rose agreed. "I could use a little break."

I spun toward Carl, "Any chance we're near a place called the Pickrick?"

He nodded, pointing off to his right. "It's just a mile or two west of here," he said. He sketched a map on the back of his business card, "Tell you what, I'll run by the office and pick up some paperwork; that'll give you folks a little time to talk privately. I'll catch up in fifteen minutes."

Lester Maddox lit up like a flare when we made our entrance.

He hurried out from behind the counter, reached for my hand, and said, "How you doing there, chief?" Then he took Rose Marie's hand and mussed Chris's hair. "We're glad to have ya'll here," he said. "Come on in; ya'll come on in and help yourself to the best food in Atlanta, Georgia."

We sat near the window, where Chris could keep his eye on the dog. Rose plucked a stray newspaper from an abandoned table; she flipped through it, scanning headlines and photo captions, trying to get a feel for what life was like in her new hometown. She turned the page for the third time and folded the paper in half. "Well, here's something different about big-city living," she mused.

"Tell me about it," I said.

"The building inspector wants to arrest people for burning trash; he says it causes smog and that 'weather can be induced by man and make a permanent mark on our town without the vigilance of the proper authorities and the cooperation of the citizens.'" She peeked up and said, "Not a problem we talked much about in Whitney."

I looked out at the unblemished sky. "I think we're going to be all right," I said, "at least for today."

Rose turned another page, pausing here and there to read a few lines. Between bites of chicken and black-eyed peas she turned the page a fourth time and then a fifth. And there, something grabbed her. She shook the folds out of the paper, gulped down the words once, and then a second time. She pushed the paper across the table. "Look at this, Hall." Her finger was pressed to a headline: "Regent Head Declines to Make Issue over Pitt Negro Player."

The story explained that Robert Arnold, the chairman of the University Board of Regents, had declined Griffin's request. Playing against a Negro, Arnold said, "was nothing new." And as far as he was concerned, nothing for the regents—or anybody else—to get worked up about.

"This is good news," I told Rose. I scanned the lines, picking out a few key words. "Everybody just wants the game to go on; they don't care if a colored kid's on the field or not."

"That's not exactly a unanimous opinion," she replied. "The governor cares. According to this, at least eight other politicians care. Where I come from that'd be just shy of 'everybody.'"

"Well, okay," I conceded. "But the team wants to play, the coaches want to play, the administration says they're going to honor the contract...." I browsed down the page a little further. "The students want the game to go on...." I glanced up at Rose, eyebrows angled optimistically. "I don't see a huge rush to Griffin's side here."

Rose reached for the paper. "You don't get to be governor if nobody's on your side, Jack." She glanced at the article again. "It looks like the regents are split right down the middle—there's plenty of time for this to get ugly."

"Yeah, but I don't see the groundswell for it. Nothing here makes me think there's a mob off smoldering somewhere behind the scenes."

Rose smirked. "I don't think we've been looking in the neighborhoods where mobs smolder."

Lester walked up, a pitcher of tea in one hand, a sweaty pail of ice water in the other. He held the pail out to Chris. "I bet the old dog could use a drink; what do you think?"

The boy smiled gratefully. "Yes sir," Chris said. "I believe he could." He grabbed the pail, thanked Lester, and hurried out to tend to his dog.

"What do you make of this, Lester?" I tapped at the paper. "About this colored kid on Pitt's team?"

Lester pulled up on the pitcher. In a soft and somber voice he said, "Griffin's right; we ought to stop it. We ought to put an end to it right now." He set Rose's glass down. "I'm telling you, Jack, you start letting mixed teams play down here, you let 'em play on Southern soil...." Lester's forehead creased with the thought of it. "We'll mourn the day," he said. "I'm telling you, we will mourn the day."

"What do you hear round here?" I asked.

"Nobody likes it," Maddox replied, "and they all know what Griffin's trying to do. But sitting this close to campus, with everybody all excited about the game, there ain't a lot of people willing to speak up." Lester reached for Chris's glass and poured. "I think they're all figuring so long as nobody's wantin' to integrate our schools they'd rather have bragging rights than protect our state's rights ..." He set the glass back down. "But they're making a mistake, and if you ask me, Griffin's right: We're standing at Armageddon. The classroom and the playing field—there ain't a lick of difference."

Rose sipped her tea and stared outside—at Slugger lapping up the cool water, Chris kneeling beside him. Then she glanced at the paper again. "The Pittsburgh coach says the team won't play without this boy, says they're all coming or none of them are coming. He's going to travel with them, stay with them, play with them.... It's an all-or-nothing deal." Rose peered up at Lester, then to me. "You need to stay clear of it, okay? Stay as far away from this as you possibly can."

• • • •

Four more houses were on our agenda, and first thing that afternoon we explored a contemporary split-level—a beige house trimmed in green—in a subdivision that still smelled of fresh paint and just-cut lumber.

Rose eased from the foyer into the living room; she wandered into the family room, kitchen, and dining room. And then, after a quick tour, Rose Marie was back where she'd started. She twirled slowly, imagining the rooms around her with pictures and new furniture. "I like this one," she told Carl. "It's different; I think it's sort of cool."

I turned, startled at the tone of Rose's voice. For the first time in months I detected humor—a trace of the sassiness I had always loved.

She wandered again, floating through the house, her eyes roving everywhere. "So what do you think, Hall?" She pushed her chin up in the air coyly. "Could we make a home out of this?"

"If you're with me, I could make a home in a pup tent," I said.

She tossed Carl a tickled frown. "Writer's answer," she groaned. "But a pretty good one."

Rose was warming up to the place, to the idea of moving, to a fresh start in the big city. She prowled now, catlike, sizing the place up, a glint in her eyes. I stood back and marveled, thinking to myself: *The Rebirth of Rose Marie Hall.*

"Can we afford this?" she called to Carl.

"It's been on the market a little while," he said; "I'm pretty sure they'll come down." Carl looked at me, pinching his chin between his thumb and forefinger, thinking. He could have sold me that house right then and there. But instead, Carl strolled into the living room. He buried his hands deep in his pockets and said, "Before you settle on this one, I'd like you to see one or two more."

Rose bobbed her head a few times, cool and detached. She took a long, last look around, dragged her fingers through her hair, and said, "Sure, it can't hurt to look."

Our next stop, Carl explained, was a smaller home just a couple of miles away. We traveled north on Peachtree, deeper into the forested suburbs. We veered onto a narrow side street that looped through the pines, curling up and down gentle hills past small, distinguished homes. A half mile later, I pulled in behind Carl along the curb. Instinctively, I glanced to the right, toward the house. A chill ran a quick lap around my nervous system. My eyes settled there, captivated by the small building's charm. Without turning I said to my son, "Nice house, huh, pal?"

Chris and Slugger and I hurried out of the car. We joined Rose Marie and Carl at the foot of the driveway. The three of us—and

Slugger, too—were drawn to this place like horses to a favorite barn. The wide front steps reached out like open arms, extending an invitation to rest and to make yourself at home. The lawn sloped gently to the street, propping the house on a small, majestic rise. The grass was thick and as green as a well-tended fairway. Azalea bushes were everywhere, so thick and full that even I—a guy who's as comfortable in a garden as he is in the beauty parlor—could imagine how glorious they'd be five months from now. A thicket of dogwoods stood between the carport and the house. In the midst of a million pines they were snuggled in the company of rhododendron and camellias, and they'd all, in due season, add a splash of brilliant color.

"The owners've got a knack for landscaping," Carl mentioned.

"Oh, really?" I said.

He laughed. "They put a bunch of money into all this."

"It's magnificent," Rose gasped, her eyes trying to guzzle it all down. Slowly, she lifted a hand, pointing to her right. "Those are forsythia, aren't they? And over there, those are butterfly bushes?"

"I'm not much of a gardener," Carl confessed, "but I think that's right. There's hydrangea round back, and maybe three or four kinds of holly bushes. Come springtime, this place is prettier than the governor's mansion."

"It's gorgeous now," Rose whispered.

Carl placed a hand on my shoulder, gently guiding me toward the house. "Why don't we have a look inside?" he said. "Then we'll check out the back; got a few more surprises for you there."

We paraded up the driveway, along the liriope-bordered walk, up the steps, to the front porch. Carl unlocked the door. He stepped away, and with a grand, sweeping motion, showed Rose inside.

Slowly, almost reverently, she crossed the threshold. She stood in the foyer, eyes drinking in a thousand first impressions. And then her pace quickened. She roamed from room to room with barely a word to anyone. In the silence I could hear her thoughts swirl, imagining the couch here, a bookcase there....

The master bedroom was half again the size of the one we had in Whitney. There was a small niche for a desk, for her, and a jack for a second phone—her headquarters for conducting household business.

The kitchen cabinets were paneled with rich dark wood. And the view from the breakfast nook—it looked as though we hovered in midair, suspended in the midst of the forest and variegated gardens.

Rose's face rekindled at every turn. She stood at the breakfast nook's bay window—hands on top of her head—gazing at the trees, bushes, and still-blooming flowers. And then she drew a sharp, almost fragile breath. Her smile glowed a hundred watts brighter; she turned to Carl: "Is that a creek?"

"Yeah," Carl said with a grin. "That's the surprise I mentioned."

Chris and Slugger bolted. They raced out to the deck, down the stairs, scurrying toward the sound of rushing water. Rose and I followed, not running, but our minds, nevertheless, bursting with the same childlike abandon.

Carl moseyed up behind us. "The owners tell me that at night, when the windows are open, it sounds like it's three feet from the house. Makes a soothing end to hectic days, I bet."

The creek rushed along the property line, slicing through a thin forest of pines, willows, and river birches. Gray and brown boulders flanked it on either side, and the whole scene pleaded to be explored by wonder-filled boys and their faithful dogs. Chris shed his shoes and socks. And even though it couldn't have been more than sixty degrees, he and Slugger waded calf deep into the water; Chris enthralled by the congregation of sounds and shapes around him; Slugger at his side—panting, alert, and wagging the entire back half of his body.

I watched and thought: *This is the place where those two belong.*

"I see why you wanted this to be a surprise," Rose Marie said.

"Something, ain't it?" Carl replied.

I stood at the creek bed trying to absorb all I'd seen in the last few minutes. I turned a slow circle. "In the spring this place is hidden, isn't it?" I said. "I mean, when the leaves come back the houses disappear behind them. It's just you and the forest and the gardens."

Carl nodded. "When you're back here you're all wrapped up in a world of your own. You can sit on the deck and watch the birds and squirrels—never see another human." Then he smiled, "But you got lots of nice neighbors when you want 'em."

I looked at my wife. "So, what do you think, Rose; could we make a home out of this place?"

She leaned on one of the boulders; a tear pearled in the corner of each eye. "You know what, Hall? I believe we could."

Carl stood at a distance. "Couple of more on this list," he said. But his voice lacked conviction.

"I s'pose we should look," I replied. "See if you're still holding out on us."

Carl smiled. "Next one's not far," he said.

I called to Chris. "Ready to go, pal?"

He skimmed a flat stone off the creek's surface. "Do we have to?"

"Yeah, I'm afraid so; got two more houses to see."

His gathered his lips to a frown. "I don't know why," he muttered. "We already know we're going to buy this one."

We raced through two more houses, then regrouped at Carl's office.

"Why don't ya'll have a seat in here?" he said, showing us into a small conference room. "Take some time to talk, just the two of you. I'll be down the hall; I'll check back in a few minutes."

Rose swiveled round to face to me. We sat knees-to-knees; she bent forward, taking both my hands into hers. She peered up, her eyes livelier than I'd seen in an epoch. "I want to be in that house for Christmas," she said. She squeezed my hands, leaving no doubt about her determination. "I know it'll be hectic. I know we won't get everything put away. But it'll be good for us. We need to be some-place new, and that house is better than perfect." She leaned closer, her eyes never straying from mine. "That's going to be our new home, and that's where we need to wake up on Christmas morning."

I traced my thumb along the back of her hand. "It'd make a great first memory, wouldn't it?" I said.

She gently bit her lower lip and nodded.

I am not the most perceptive guy on the planet, and I'm rarely fine-tuned to the subtle shifts in my wife's emotions, but even I could see that Rose needed this: the house, the new project, the fresh start. She sat before me, longing to move on. She sat there, caressing my hands, as bright and beautiful as I'd ever seen her. And right there, in Carl-the-real-estate-agent's office, relief washed over me. Then and there, when I saw the eagerness in her eyes, when I heard the yearning in her voice—I felt as though I'd been acquitted of the crime of ruining this woman's life—and I would—one way or another—give her anything she wanted.

I called Carl into the room. We made an offer, the seller countered, we replied, and then scheduled the closing for the following Thursday.

On the drive home, Rose and Chris jabbered endlessly—about his new bedroom, the den, the creek, and the park that was just down the road. Rose turned in her seat to face him. "It's going to be so much fun ..." she couldn't contain the giggle. "You and Slugger'll have a ball down by the water, your new school's just a short walk away...." She reached over to scratch the dog's backside. "You guys are going to have the best time," she said.

Chris scooted forward and grabbed the back of the seat. "You think we could build a tree fort down there?" he asked. "Down by the creek?"

"That'll be one of the first things we do," I promised him. "We got plenty of trees down there with good sturdy limbs." I spotted him in the rearview mirror. "And I betcha we could build a ramp for Slugger, so the two of you can spend the night up there." The big dog drew his head inside the car and swished his tail, joining the delight.

I studied Rose out of the corner of my eye. I glanced in the rearview mirror at Chris and Slugger. For the first time in months my family was content. For the first time since the worst night of our lives, I dared to think that life might be good again.

• • • •

The house in Whitney began to hatch taped-and-labeled moving boxes; they popped up everywhere, like eggs in a coop full of fertile chickens. And our lives—the memories and mementos of birthdays, Little League games, art projects, and anniversaries—gradually vanished from the walls, shelves, and drawers of the house on Pine Cove Lane.

Late Friday afternoon I was packing books and sorting through old files. The phone rang. I heard Rose's muffled voice in the distance and I knew, from the rhythm of her phrases, that the call was for me. The phone clunked down on the kitchen counter; there was the click-clack of hurried steps across the kitchen floor, and then, from the foot of the stairs, an urgent whisper: "Jack, it's Ralph McGill. He needs to talk to you."

I stepped into the hallway. "McGill? Really?"

"Yes!" she cried. "Pick up the phone, Jack, he's waiting!"

Ralph McGill explained that he hated to bother me, but something had come up. "I know this is sudden," he said, and I could hear his hesitation, "but I wonder if you'd mind riding over here tomorrow? And then …" there was another hefty pause. "If you'd consider running over to Montgomery for a day or two? I'm sorry to sound so mysterious," McGill said, "it'd just be easier to explain in person. I know it's a long drive, but if you could fit me in I'd appreciate it. And Jack …?"

"Yes sir?"

"This might be interesting."

I told McGill I'd be there by noon, then laid the phone back in its cradle. Rose stepped into the bedroom. "So what was that all about?" she asked.

I put a hand to my chin, wondering the same thing. "To tell you the truth, I don't know. He wants me to meet him in Atlanta tomorrow and then go to Montgomery; said it'd be easier to explain face-to-face."

"Montgomery?" Rose wondered. "What do you think it is? A basketball game? Maybe some kind of conference or something?"

"I don't know," I said. "If it was something like that I think Bisher would have called." I shrugged. "We'll just have to wait and see."

I went to the closet and dragged my overnight bag off the shelf. "I'll head over there first thing. I'll give you a call as soon as I know something."

Rose Marie moved to the dresser; she started handing me socks and underwear. "I hate that you've just got to drop everything and go," she said. "But I think it's pretty cool, Hall, that Ralph McGill's calling you at home, that he's got a special assignment for you a month before you're supposed to start." She slapped my rear end. "Sounds like this guy likes you."

"Either that or he's going to banish me to the *Montgomery Advertiser*."

Rose shook her head. "No," she insisted, "this is good, Hall." She pecked my cheek. "Who knows, maybe this career of yours is about to go somewhere."

Chapter 3

It was Saturday, about ten minutes before noon. McGill was behind his desk, turned toward the Underwood, eyes narrowed, typing and wrestling with each word of every sentence he fashioned. He wore a blue-striped shirt, open at the collar, and a navy cardigan. A pencil was clenched between his teeth and, at the moment I spied him, nothing in the world mattered more than the words that appeared—one-by-one—on a piece of 20# typing paper.

I rapped on the door frame. McGill leaned over the typewriter, marked the page with the pencil, and began to type again. I watched for a moment—impressed and amused at his concentration—then rapped again, louder this time. He typed ten or twelve more words, finishing his thought, and then turned.

"Jack!" A smile sprang to McGill's lips. He stood, reaching across the desk for my hand. "I appreciate you doing this," he said, motioning me to a chair. "I know this is an awful first impression, and really, I don't make a habit of calling reporters at home and having them rush down here on the spur of the moment...." He hesitated and grinned. "At least not until they actually work here."

McGill settled into his chair, lacing his fingers behind his head. "But I don't need to tell you, the news has got no respect for clocks or calendars. When a story breaks...."

"I understand," I said. "There's no need to apologize."

McGill sat up and pulled his chair close to the desk. "Let me fill you in on what's going on," he said. "There's a situation that's just starting to unfold ..." he started shuffling through a stack of papers. "And I got a hunch it's right up your alley." McGill pulled a notepad from the pile, flipped a few pages. "Couple of days ago," he began, "a Negro woman caused a little ruckus over there." He glanced at his notes. "Rosa Parks, early forties, seamstress, does work with the NAACP, no police record, never caused any trouble before...." McGill tossed the pad back to the desk, "By all accounts a model citizen—until last Thursday."

"And then ...?"

"And then she was riding the bus home from work and wouldn't move back to the colored section. She got arrested and tossed in jail. Yesterday a group of colored women ..." McGill glanced at his notes and rifled through a couple of pages, "Sorry," he said. "I don't have the details on this, but some group of women are calling for a boycott. There are, I'm told, even as we speak, mimeographed leaflets flying all over Montgomery telling Negroes to stay off the buses Monday." McGill paused, the sliest of smiles easing across his lips. "Any of this sound vaguely familiar to you?"

I sighed, a little deeper than I had actually intended. "Yes sir," I said. "It rings a not-too-distant bell."

This kind of thing had happened before, a couple of times that I knew of, once in Baton Rouge, and once in Whitney—where I had been an eyewitness to nearly every detail.

"You know what they did over there, right?" McGill said. "How they pulled it together, how the colored folks cooperated and organized …?"

"Well, yeah," I told him, "I was there. I was in the church when they explained it, rode an empty bus the first day of the boycott.…"

McGill swiveled a quarter turn, clasping his hands behind his head again. "I got a source who tells me they're scrambling to get this thing better organized, that some of the Negro pastors are looking to get involved; maybe turn this into some kind of official organized protest." McGill looked down, brushed lint from his sweater, and then looked up again. "I thought you might look into it," he said.

I knew of course that this was coming. But at the sound of those words—coming from Ralph McGill's lips—two sets of competing emotions suddenly and inexplicably clashed. In my entire life I'd never wanted to write anything other than sports. I had never hankered to do hard news; I had never—not once—coveted a front-page byline. I was wholly committed to the part of life that's supposed to be fun. But at that moment I felt the faintest tug of a new temptation. I felt like a kid at the carnival, about to crawl beneath the tent where I wasn't allowed, to catch a glimpse of some forbidden scene. I felt the distant twinge of a brand-new thrill.

But this was exactly the stuff I had to avoid. At the same instant, a voice screamed in the other ear: "Run! Flee! Get as far as way from this as you possibly can!" I glanced off to the side, struggling to quell the contending voices. Then, turning a palm to the air, I said, "I'm a sportswriter, Mr. McGill; I've never done hard news in my life." I looked at him plaintively. "There've got to be ten guys around here who could do this story."

A reproving smile pulled at McGill's lips. "Tell me something, Jack: How many guys at *The Atlanta Constitution* do you suppose have ever set foot in a Negro church? Or had a serious conversation with a colored pastor?" An old copy of the *Whitney Herald* sat on his desk. He picked it up and scanned a few words I'd written. "You majored in journalism, didn't you?"

I nodded.

"Yeah, well, I think you can figure out how to write it." McGill clasped his hands on top of the desk. "What do you say, Jack; can you look into this for me?"

It never occurred to me to say no to Ralph McGill, but the internal shouting match continued to rage. "You've talked to Bisher about this?" I asked, waffling, still scrambling for time.

McGill returned a thin smile. "Yeah," he said. "He's fine with it."

"And you don't think anybody else'll mind? You're not getting me off on the wrong foot with the news guys?"

He shook his head no. "I need somebody who's got a feel for what these people are thinking," McGill replied, "for what they're feeling, for what they're really trying to do." He drummed a pencil against the desk, waiting.

I rubbed a hand along my chin, feeling now the full weight of Ralph McGill's presence, sensing one more tug of the distant but quickly closing new thrill, and I knew there were no options. "Sure," I told McGill. "I'll be happy to check it out."

"Thanks, Jack, I appreciate it."

We talked for five more minutes, McGill filling me in on what he had, making note of three or four rumors, and listing a few people I'd want to talk to. Then he slid a scrap of paper across the desk. He'd written down a name, address, and phone number. "You might want to start with him," McGill said. "He's been the pastor of a colored church over there for a couple of years. I suspect he can point you in the right direction."

On my way out I called Rose and gave her the news. Yesterday's brightness quickly dimmed. "Oh no," she groaned, "Oh Jack…." She was quiet for a beat, brooding. "What's going on?" she wondered. "Why is this happening—first the football game, now this—and we haven't even moved there yet." There was another frazzled pause. "Why's this thing chasing after us?" she wanted to know. "Why can't we shake loose of it?"

"I don't know, Rose, but what—"

"And why in the world would he send a sportswriter?" she demanded. "That doesn't make any sense, does it?"

"What am I going to do?" I pleaded. "It's not like I'm going to tell him no."

"Of course not," she answered. "But seriously, Jack, why you? These people hired you to cover baseball. This isn't right."

"I seem to possess an unusual background; I guess I'm one of the few reporters in the world who's actually seen a boycott, who's been to a Negro church, who's interviewed a Negro pastor." I rubbed my eyes wearily. "McGill's sure I'll understand it better than anybody else."

"Swell," Rose Marie cracked. "You also understand what it's like to have your home blown to bits."

"Look," I said, "I know this isn't what we hoped for, but—"

"I thought we were getting away from all this, Jack. But we're just getting deeper into it, aren't we?"

"No," I said. "There's a big difference here, Rose. None of this has got anything to do with anybody for hundreds of miles around us. And the story, if there even is one, will be written, filed, and forgotten long before we get here." I glanced at the clock, trying to figure how long it'd take me to drive. "This has got nothing to do with our neighbors, Rose. Or with the kids in Chris's school, or with anybody we have ever known."

"If that were true you wouldn't be going," she replied. "If nobody cared, if it didn't matter to the paper's readers he wouldn't send anybody."

"Well … yeah, but it's not the kind of news that's personal. It's more like Moscow or Berlin. People care, they want to know what's going on, but it's not going to change the way they work or what they do with their kids or how they're going to spend the weekend."

On rare occasions—I've seen it maybe three times in my life—my wife will look at me and wonder why I'm allowed to run loose in the world. She will gawk in disbelief, certain that I need to be locked away in a rubber room, in a place where I can't harm myself or others. And I knew, from the length of the pause and the weight of the sigh, that this was one of those times. I could imagine her: head down, eyes closed, pinching at the bridge of her nose. "Jack," she said, "this is about all of those things. I know it's in another town and another state. But if white people have to sit beside colored people in Montgomery, they're going to have to do it in Atlanta—and in Jackson and Birmingham and Charlotte—and Jack …" the words hung there, suspended in the air between us.

"Yes," I groaned.

"If there's one thing you and I know, if there's anything we can say for sure, it's that bad things happen when colored people and white people get too close."

"All right," I said, accepting the rebuke. "But still, I'm going to be invisible on this one. There won't be a byline or photo. And nobody in Atlanta's ever heard of me. Nobody'll ever know I was there, I promise."

Another pause, followed by another reflexive sigh. Through the silence I could sense the fear welling up inside her. "Be careful about what you promise," Rose said. "And Jack, you be real careful about what you write."

I headed west with Rose's lament still nagging.

This thing with race had sniffed us out and tracked us down. And no matter where we went, we couldn't hide. We weren't alone. The unrest was in pursuit of us all, and closing fast. Questions were being raised. Changes were coming quickly. Our minds were like small funnels, too narrow for the torrent, and the real question, I thought, was this: Who would control the flow? Who was to regulate this conversation? Dictate its tone? Determine the means by which changes are made—and guide people through them?

There was a roar overhead. A four-engine passenger plane instantly filled my field of vision, swooping low into Atlanta Municipal Airport. At the same moment a twin-engine Eastern Air Liner rose gracefully, up and away, passing in the opposite direction. At least ten more planes waited on the runway, engines revving for takeoff.

Bisher had been right. This place was booming. Atlanta, more so than Whitney or Montgomery, was charging forward, occupied with more pressing matters ... at least for now, and as far as I could see. Maybe here there's some exalted, more compelling purpose. Maybe here, somebody will find a way to cope with the change and do what's best for the city.

I pulled in front of a red brick church building at the corner of Dexter Avenue and North Decatur. I checked the address against the one McGill had given me, stuffed his notes into a file, and reached for the door handle.

The building was bigger than I'd expected, and better kept. It was snuggled among government buildings, just a stone's throw from the state capitol, and shaded beneath the cover of its nearby neighbor, the Alabama State Police Department. Freshly painted white stairs ran up from the left and right; they met at a center, gothic-arched doorway that led to a spacious and semielegant sanctuary. Inside, ceiling fans, at rest in the mild December weather, hovered above wooden pews that glimmered in the dim light. A raised and regal-looking pulpit stood at the end of the center aisle, where—on the wall just behind it—a spare wooden cross surely drew the eye of everyone who entered.

I had expected the place to be busy. I thought there'd be minions scurrying in and out, rushing to execute last-minute orders. But there was no one in sight, or so much as a creak to be heard.

"You must be Mr. Hall," a voice pealed from left of the pulpit.

A young Negro man stepped into the sanctuary. He wore a black suit that could have passed for tailor-made, a stiff white shirt, thin black tie, and glistening, spit-shined shoes.

"Reverend King?" I asked.

"Yes," he replied, enunciating the word crisply. "I'm Martin King."

We walked toward each other, both extending our right hands. King's grip was firm. He searched my eyes, sizing me up, I think, and judging from my grip, my countenance, and posture—whatever he could about me. "I just got off the phone with an old friend of yours," he said. "Phil Edwards tells me you're a decent man and fair reporter. He sends his regards."

I forced a smile, my mind racing back to the past year of my life, to the bleakest days I'd ever known, and to the part Phil Edwards, a Negro pastor in Whitney, had played. "Thanks," I said to King. "I haven't talked to Phil in a while; I hope he's all right."

"Progress is slow," King replied, "but he perseveres."

"Yeah," I said, chuckling, "I guess we all do." I pulled my pad and pen out of my pocket. "I guess that's a good segue into our conversation. What about you, Reverend, with the boycott here, are you willing to persevere?"

We slid into the nearest pew, both of us quarter turned to face one another. King's eyes, I noticed, were moist and mournful-looking. He looked weighed down and I couldn't help but to think that nobody so young should look so burdened. "I'm not the one to ask," he replied. "There are others—Mr. Nixon, Reverend Abernathy, Reverend Hubbard—they could tell you more about this than I can."

I scribbled down the names. "You've got phone numbers?"

King nodded.

I crossed my legs, pen poised over my pad, "So what's your best guess? Is this going to get organized, turn into some kind of protracted event?"

King laid an arm over the back of the pew. "Well, right now this is just a one-day thing. We'll see how things go tomorrow, and then …"

"And if they go as planned?"

He flicked a hand in the air, "I can't really say, Mr. Hall. There is no plan. This thing is coming together minute-by-minute. There are people over at Holt Street Baptist putting some ideas together right now; I think they might be recruiting taxi companies to help out. We got people who're trying to get leaflets mimeographed and out to the volunteers.… I wish there was more I could tell you; we'll get through tomorrow and then go from there."

I ventured down a different path. "The rumor's going round that Mrs. Parks might be a good test case," I said. "That she could challenge this thing in court. It'd help her, wouldn't it, if the boycott went a little longer?"

King tossed back an amused grin. "You're way ahead of me," he said. "This is Sunday, and all I'm trying to do is get to Monday."

I flipped my notepad closed, sure that I wasn't going to get much more today. "Fair enough," I said. "Maybe we can talk more tomorrow?"

"If I'm not here, I'll be at Holt Street Baptist," King said. "Be happy to talk when I know something more."

At the hotel I picked up a copy of the Sunday paper. I tossed it on the bed, spreading it out flat to scan the headlines, then reached for the phone. I browsed the sports section, waiting for Rose to answer. The phone rang once, and then a second time. Halfway through the third ring, I heard Rose's voice—muffled and distant—as if she'd covered the mouthpiece with her hand. But I could hear every word of the conspiratorial whisper.

"Why don't you get a fire going?" my wife cooed. "I'll get rid of this call and be right there, Sugar."

"Oh, that's very funny," I said.

"Jack? Jack, is that you?"

"You're hilarious, you know that?"

She burst out laughing. "Just thought you could use a little comic relief," she said. Then, stifling the chuckle, "And I'm glad it's funny, Jack. I'd hate it if we couldn't trust each other."

"How'd you know it was me?" I asked. "And what if you'd been wrong?"

"Just took a wild guess," Rose replied. "And let's face it, we don't get too many calls these days."

I rested against the headboard and told Rose about the day and about my first impressions of the young Negro pastor.

"They've slammed this thing together so fast," I told her. "I don't see how they can pull it off. They've got volunteers going door-to-door passing out leaflets—that's it, that's all the communication they've got—there's no way this is going to happen."

"Maybe it'll just blow over," she said. "Maybe there won't be a story after all."

"That'd be nice," I answered, trying to suppress a yawn. "I guess I'll get up early and drive back over to Dexter—"

And then I saw it. The headline was right there; it was on the front page of the *Montgomery Advertiser,* tall and fat in thirty-six-point type, below the fold: "Negro Groups Ready Boycott of City Lines." "Hold everything," I said. I wedged the phone against my shoulder, picked up the paper and scanned the first few lines. "I take it back, Rose. If there was anybody who didn't know about this thing, they do now."

"What're you talking about?" she asked.

"The *Advertiser,*" I told her. "They ran a front-page story. I can't believe King didn't mention this. They gave 'em the details, told 'em the time and place to meet...." I laughed out loud. "The white newspaper just did what the entire colored population couldn't."

"What's it say?" Rose wanted to know.

"Well, here's the lead: 'A "top secret" meeting of Montgomery Negroes who plan a boycott of city buses Monday is scheduled at 7 p.m. at the Holt Street Baptist Church for "further instructions" in an economic reprisal campaign against segregation on city buses....'"

"Oh swell," Rose said. "Why would they publish that?"

"Somebody thought they were breaking a big story," I said.

"What else does it say?"

"Let's see...." My eyes skimmed down the page. "The campaign's modeled along the lines of the White Citizens' Council program— was initiated by unidentified Negro leaders—a Negro woman was arrested Thursday—violating segregation laws...."

"Well," I said, "I guess it's going to get interesting after all."

I was up at five the next morning, and by six I was traveling west on Dexter Avenue, heading toward town.

Even now, before the sun had made its entrance, Negroes streamed down the sidewalks—laborers, maids, and craftsmen—somber looking, with their eyes cast down or fixed straight ahead—all of them too intent to so much as speak to one another.

I parked the car. With pen and pad in hand I joined the procession, absorbing as much of the spectacle as I could, observing the solemnity of it all, and noting the hard-boiled resolve of a thousand nameless Negroes.

A Sunbeam bread truck—bright gold and blue, a blonde all-American girl sparkling from its side—stocked a local diner. A dairy truck clinked past, a contented cow beaming from its back door. Stacks of twine-wrapped newspapers thumped to the pavement, tossed from the back of a passing blue van. The sounds of a waking city surrounded me and yet, at the same time, there was a reverent hush—as if I stood in the back of an open-air church whose congregation didn't dare speak or laugh or call a best friend's name.

It's always still at dawn; always calm before the city stirs. But today, the colored section of this town fell under a spell that I had never seen cast before. This occasion, this particular cause at this precise time, had spawned some mutant form of self-control and a scene that looked eerie.

I came to the corner; a hand-lettered sign was tacked to a phone pole—cheap poster board, the letters scrawled in a streaky black marker: "People, don't ride the bus today. Don't ride it, for freedom."

Across the street a small crowd had clustered at the E. L. Posey parking lot. Bundled in coats and scarves, they heaved clouds of warm breath into the chilled air. They were old and gray-haired, and young, and middle aged. Some, I could see, were thrilled by the adventure; they were alert, exhilarated by the thought of a new crusade. Others looked lost and frightened.

I jogged across the street, propelled as everyone else was by the brisk air and a brash spirit. I approached one of the men, flashed my pad and pen, and said, "Mind if I ask you a couple of questions?"

He jutted his chin into the air, appraising me. He didn't speak, but the gesture, I thought, was an invitation to try him.

"So what's this all about?" I asked.

He looked at me as if I'd just flown in from Pluto, like I was the only guy in town who hadn't seen yesterday's paper. "The boycott," he said. His eyes swept over his companions. "That's why we're all here."

"Yeah, I understand that," I said. "But what difference is this supposed to make? What do you think you're going to accomplish standing out here in the cold?"

Just then a city bus roared around the corner. A giant red and blue Pepsi-Cola bottle cap was stuck to its nose—this cheery, three-dimensional transit ad that now, breaching the solemnity, seemed ill timed . . . like Bozo busting in on a funeral. The bus chugged past, spewing a wake of diesel-scented fumes. A lone white woman peered out the window, bewildered by the empty seats around her, and marveling at the Negro crowds encamped on every third or fourth corner.

"That right there," the man said. "That's got to get their attention; get 'em to see what's going on down here."

"You don't think they already know?" I asked.

He looked at me—half amused, half befuddled. "I don't think they spent two minutes of their whole lives thinking 'bout us."

"So, how long you willing to do this?" I asked.

For the first time the man looked at me straight on. "Long as it takes," he said.

I walked again. Black people were clustered everywhere. They rubbed their arms to stay warm, some paced, others bounced on tiptoes.

Taxicabs rushed past, all of them bulging with dark-skinned passengers. I couldn't help but to think of the comic photos—of college kids cramming themselves into small cars and phone booths—but I was never tempted to laugh.

The sidewalks swarmed now with waves of colored people hurrying to work, brown paper lunch sacks dangling from two-toned fingers, forging ahead silently. The city began to perk—with a steady whoosh of traffic, with lights blinking red, yellow, and green, with the faint smell of exhaust tainting the pre-Christmas air.

I rounded the bend where Dexter turns to Commerce and found myself in step with an older black woman. She was heavyset, and her gait was slow and lopsided. A felt-covered cloche was pulled to her ears and trimmed in fabric that matched her green and gray scarf. A white waist-length coat strained to make its way around her. She was fleshy and thick and in full possession of that kindly, maternal glow that graces so many Negro women.

"You got far to go?" I asked her.

She bolted upright, startled to find a white man so close beside her. She worked her jaw round a few times, chewing over an answer. Then she flicked a hand forward, "Couple of miles," she said. "Maybe a little more."

"That's going to take a while," I replied.

She looked straight ahead and mumbled, "Uh-huh."

"And it looks like you've been walking a while already," I observed.

Her eyes stayed fixed. "Fifteen minutes I guess."

"You're going to be worn out before you get to work, aren't you?"

We came to the corner of Montgomery Street and waited to cross. She looked me up and down—a matriarch sizing up impertinent youth. "I 'spect my body will be tired," she said. "But my spirit ... my spirit will be rested."

After lunch I went in search of hard news, and the best place to find it, I figured, was Holt Street Baptist.

I wandered down the halls following signs to the office, breezing past men and women who stopped and turned, who raised eyebrows, who lifted fingers as I passed, wondering: "What do you think you're doing here?"

McGill had been right. I'd done this before. I'd been here and seen it; I knew my way around, same as a locker room before a big game. I sailed into the wide hallway, past classrooms and meeting areas, all of them empty—except one. A man was seated there, alone in one of the larger rooms, jotting notes on a yellow pad, consumed by the thoughts he recorded. *I know this guy*, I thought. I'd seen his picture; he'd been at the courthouse with the Parks woman.

I poked my head inside. "E. D. Nixon, right?"

He peered up, leery. "And you are ...?"

"Jack Hall," I said, "I'm a reporter from *The Atlanta Constitution*."

"A reporter?" Nixon put his nose to the air, scenting danger … or maybe opportunity.

"That's right."

"All the way from Atlanta, Georgia?"

"Uh-huh."

He stood and reached for my hand. "Have a seat, Mr. Hall, and tell me how I can help you."

E. D. Nixon was a pro. This guy worked the press like a Hollywood agent. It was all second nature—how to pitch a story, how to tease and tempt a prying newsman. Within minutes he had me prowling for the information he wanted to give. And before a half hour had passed, he dangled the bait I couldn't refuse.

"Every Negro leader in town'll be right here in about an hour," he said. He cut his eyes toward the back of the room, to a folding metal chair stuck in the corner. He slowly reeled the lure. "You can sit right there …" he said, a smile easing over him, "… be the only reporter in the world to have a front-row seat while we make some history."

I glanced at my watch, nodded at him, and said, "Yeah, okay. Maybe I'll stop back by."

It was twelve minutes after three when the group gathered. They had come to plot their next moves, to get organized, and to make plans for a mass meeting that was now less than four hours away.

The first few minutes breezed by—everyone agreed to extend the boycott, to form a committee to run it, and to create subcommittees to tend to the details. But then the conversation turned to leadership:

Who'd be in charge? Who'd be the spokesman? Who'd be the man to personify this extemporaneous movement?

From the middle of the room a hand waved in the air. "I don't know," a male voice dallied, "I'm wondering if we want to go public with this."

Nixon's head recoiled like a just-fired rifle. He angled his chin slightly and squinted his left eye, centering the speaker in make-believe crosshairs. "What the hell you talking about?" he scoffed.

"There's a lot at stake," the man shot back. "White folks ain't gonna take it too kindly."

"He's right," another echoed. "There's gonna be a price to pay."

"Uh-huh," three or voices murmured.

"That's true...." the whispers raced around the room.

E. D. Nixon sneered. He stared at both speakers, as stunned as a father who'd seen his own kid cower before the school bully. He stretched across the table—eyeing one man and then the other. "Let me ask you something," he said. "How you gonna have a mass meeting, gonna boycott a city bus line without the white folks knowing about it?" He shook his head, anger welling up in his eyes. "You guys...." Nixon looked away, disgusted. "You went around here and lived off these poor washwomen all your lives and ain't never done nothing for 'em...." He turned back, taking the measure of the first man. He stabbed his finger in the air. "You oughta make up your mind right now that you're going to either admit you are a grown man—or concede the fact that you're a bunch of scared boys."

"We're not scared," the man snapped, "but we've got to—"

"Mr. Nixon." It was King—just now entering the room. "I'm not a coward," he announced, "and I don't want anybody calling me one."

The young pastor quickly surveyed the crowd. "We need to lead on this," he told them. "The people—they need to see us out front."

From the back corner another hand shot up. Its owner gestured toward King. "How about him?" the man shouted. "Let King be in charge."

King spun toward the voice, doubt suddenly eclipsing the brassy show of self-confidence. He opened his mouth, his right hand crept into the air, and he began to speak…. But the din of acclamation washed away any chance for rebuttal. The crowd immediately concurred—they'd found the lamb they were looking for—and no other nominations came forward. Before King could utter one more word, he'd been unanimously elected.

He sat still for a moment, flustered. The room became quiet, the men and women there reflecting on what they'd done. And then, with corporate-like efficiency, they moved on to other business: They elected officers, chose a name—the Montgomery Improvement Association—and then outlined the agenda for that night's meeting.

The twenty-six year-old pastor, a man who'd been in town less than two years, stared at his watch. "We've got thousands of people due here shortly," he said. "I gotta figure out what I'm gonna to tell them." King stood and bolted for the door.

I slipped out behind him. "I need a minute," I called down the hallway.

He stopped and turned. "I can't spare any more than that," he replied.

I whipped out my pad and pen and marched toward him. "There've been boycotts before," I began. "They've lasted five or six days. You see this going longer?"

"I hope not," King replied. He put a hand to his forehead, massaging wearily. "But I don't know, I haven't thought about it. If we need to persevere, if it takes two weeks, or three weeks, or even a month—then I hope we have the strength for it." He peered up, a man whose thoughts were flailing. "I guess my main concern right now is that we come together, that we stay united."

He turned and walked. I stayed with him stride for stride, my pen still poised above my pad. "Why now?" I asked.

He glanced over; his brows arched high, waiting for me to clarify the question.

"It's not like the bus company changed the rules last Thursday," I said.

King's chest heaved, as though one more brick had been piled onto his load. "I don't know," he said with a shrug. "Maybe we've finally grown too tired. Maybe Rosa Parks simply came to a place where she had to say, 'It's been long enough. I can't do it anymore.'"

"Even if the law says she has to?"

King stopped and turned. "What do you think, Mr. Hall? Are we required to obey unjust laws?"

He began to walk again. I trailed a step behind, making note of the question. "Everybody's been obeying this law for as long as there've been buses," I replied. "On December second, third, and fourth everybody acted as if it were perfectly just. On the fifth Mrs. Parks declares that it's not?"

"Rosa Parks doesn't have the authority to declare anything," King said. "She's just a colored seamstress in central Alabama." He rubbed his right hand along his chin and mouth. "But in her own way … maybe she did affirm what others have declared."

"Others?" I said, "Such as …?"

"The Supreme Court, the Constitution …" King quickly appraised the building, lifting his chin toward the cross, the stained glass, and pulpit. "The Bible," he concluded.

I shot back a suspicious glare. A pause hung between us; two, maybe three seconds passed. "You're claiming some formidable allies there, aren't you?" I asked.

"No," King replied; he stretched the word for emphasis. "They're not my allies, Mr. Hall. I'm theirs."

We pushed through a back door, into the parking lot, into the light of the blinding sun. "That puts a lot of people in a precarious spot, don't you think? The bus company, the city, the state … all at odds with you and God?"

King reached for his car keys; he twirled them once around his finger. "Yes," he called over his shoulder. "And they've been at odds for a long time."

By six o'clock Holt Street Baptist Church was packed tighter than an Elvis concert. The crowd spilled onto the church grounds, flowing into the street for three blocks in both directions. And everyone there—every expression on every face—thirsted to be a part of whatever was about to happen.

Police cars eased by, a silent, restraining presence. In reply, ushers made futile attempts to corral the mob. Deacons rushed outside to set up loudspeakers, hoping to encircle the throng that'd never make it into the building. I gawked at the spectacle, confounded not only by the size of the crowd, but also by its spirit. I strolled the periphery, chuckling to myself, thinking: *This looks like the seventh game of a Negro League World Series.*

I flashed my press credentials and inched my way inside. I slithered down the aisle, squirming past those who'd staked out their territory. A television crew was already there, their camera trained on the pulpit. A stray leaflet lay loose on the floor. I picked it up and read: *This is for Monday, Dec. 5, 1955—Another Negro woman has been arrested and thrown into jail because she refused to get up out of her seat on the bus and give it to a white person. Don't ride the buses to work, to town, to school, or anywhere on Monday. If you work, take a cab, or share a ride. Or walk. Come to a mass meeting, Monday at 7:00 PM., at the Holt Street Baptist Church.*

I wedged myself into a tiny clearing between a pillar and the fifth row of pews. From there I studied the congregation. They were tired after a full day's work, and many, I thought, had to be exhausted after a long walk home. I thought back to the woman I'd seen that morning. They were all of the same mind now as she'd been then: Their bodies were drained, but their hearts were at peace.

They sat impatiently, their bodies taut with anticipation, giving and taking their share of the gossip that stormed up and down the pews. Their eyes skimmed the room, searching for Nixon, Abernathy, or Hubbard—their mountainous expectations rising.

At 7:30—a half hour after the announced starting time—a man stepped into the pulpit, one of the pastors I'd seen that afternoon. Music began to swell behind him. He motioned for the weary crowd to stand, told them where to turn in their hymnals, and then, on his cue, thousands of voices, all renewed with stiff determination, proclaimed: "Onward, Christian soldiers, marching as to war, with the cross of Jesus going on before...."

This fatigued crowd thundered as powerful a rendition of the song as I had ever heard, their necks protracted like feeding sparrows, straining in gleeful expectation of what was to come. The words were filled with flesh-and-blood meaning. They spurred the imagination. They raised the specter that here and now, this night, in this obscure corner of God's creation: "Christ, the royal Master leads against the foe...." This lowly crowd had embarked on a crusade. In their faces you could see—and in their voices you could hear—that they felt the presence of God right there in that room. They closed their eyes, and in each one's mind a triumphant procession passed. In each one's imagination the shades of gold and purple were glorious "Forward into battle, see His banners go..." The song came to a close much too soon, and the crowd reluctantly—and not yet drained of the just-sparked fervor—settled into their seats.

Another pastor said a prayer, and then Martin King stepped to the platform. He started nervously, talking of Rosa Parks's courage and "the height of her character." Shouts of "Amen" and "That's right" garnished his words. King surveyed the flock before him. "You know, my friends, there comes a time when people get tired of being trampled over by the iron feet of oppression. There comes a time when people get tired of being plunged across the abyss of humiliation...."

The crowd began to stomp their feet. The noise thundered through the room catching King by surprise. He glanced down at the pulpit, collecting his thoughts. And then, looking up, he began talking about democracy and the right to protest. He echoed his earlier themes—of the Supreme Court, the Constitution, and God Almighty. "We are not wrong in what we are doing," he declared. "If we are wrong, Jesus of Nazareth was merely a utopian dreamer that never came down to earth. If we are wrong, justice is a lie: Love has no meaning." He paused for a breath, to think, to mop his brow with a clean white handkerchief. The crowd had inched to the edge of their pews. The people's faces shone bright. They leaned forward in anticipation.

"We are determined here in Montgomery to work and fight until justice runs down like water and righteousness like a mighty stream."

The crowd gulped down every syllable. They echoed his words with chants of "Yes," "That's right," and "Keep talkin'." Spontaneous outbursts of applause flared—in a spot here, from a corner there. And King—as smooth an orator as I'd ever heard—paused in every appropriate place, letting the words seep into these parched and shriveled sponges.

He talked about oppression and enduring "the long night of captivity." He offered hope, proclaiming that they, the "disinherited of the land," were, at this moment, reaching out for the "daybreak of freedom and justice and equality." No one yawned or coughed or sneezed.

King gazed down from his regal wooden pulpit. "Let us go out with a grim and bold determination that we are going to stick together.... Right here in Montgomery when the history books are written in the future, somebody will have to say, 'There lived a race of people, black people, fleecy locks and black complexions, of people who had the moral courage to stand up for their rights, and thereby they injected a new meaning into the veins of history and of civilization.'"

The crowd roared to its feet, every trace of weariness gone. They stood—outcasts on the fringe of society—overflowing with zeal. They stood—the poor and nameless, in sudden possession of dignity. They stood, with a renewed vision of what was just and right.

And my spine tingled too. There was a magical rhythm in King's voice, an infectious and irresistible cadence that enticed the imagination. The man inspired hope. He painted this grand picture of what the world ought to be. And as I looked at the crowd, at the boy-pastor, at this church poised outside the margin of mainstream Montgomery, I thought: *This can't end well. These people want more than their city can give. And that can only bring misery … or anger.*

It was, I thought, a fine speech … firmly rooted in Martin King's fantasy.

There was a message at the hotel: "Call home ASAP."

I checked my watch, it was already past ten. I dialed the operator and gave her the number; the phone rang three times, then four. On the fifth ring Rose picked up: "Hello?"

"Is everything all right?" I asked.

"Hey," she sounded surprised. "Yeah, everything's fine. Why are you asking?"

"The message," I answered, "you said to call right away; are you okay?"

"What are you talking about?" Rose asked. "What message?"

I held the note up in the air. "The one that said to call you as soon—"

"Jack, I didn't leave any message."

"It was me." I heard Chris's groggy voice in the background.

"You called your dad long distance?" Rose asked.

"I need to talk to him," Chris answered.

My son's voice came on the line. "Dad?"

"Hey, pal, are you all right?"

"Yes sir," he replied. "I wanted to know what's going on over there. Are they going to let the colored people sit where they want to?"

"I don't know, pal; it's too soon to tell."

"Because I was going to go out and raise some money," Chris said. "I thought we could buy bikes for 'em. What do you think? I bet we could raise enough for ten or twelve bikes—so the colored people could get to work."

"That's nice, Chris, but I think this'll all be over pretty soon. Everybody will probably be back on the buses in a day or two."

"Well, then, maybe we could help 'em pay for the taxis. I saw the pictures on television," he explained, "of everybody walking or riding in taxis."

"Chris …" I heard Rose's voice behind him, "you don't need to get involved in this right now; we need to get ready to move."

"But I want to help the colored people," Chris snapped.

"Well, we're busy with other things right now," Rose said gently.

"They're not as important as this."

"Hey, Chris," I called into the phone.

"Yes sir?"

"I'll be home tomorrow or the next day. I'll give you a full report on what's going on, and then we can decide what to do, okay?"

"All right," he said.

"You get back to bed, okay?"

"Yes sir."

Rose was back on the line. "Hang on for a second," she said. After a moment she continued. "He saw this on the news tonight," she said. "He's been talking about selling hot chocolate, or cookies, or doing odd jobs at the neighbors'—"

"Well, his heart's in the right place, I guess."

There was a disturbed sigh from the Whitney end of the line. "I don't know," Rose replied.

•   •   •   •

King had promised me a few minutes the next morning. I met him at the church, at seven thirty, but he was too antsy to sit still. "Why don't we take a walk?" he said. "See how things are holding up."

"Sure," I replied. "I wouldn't mind seeing that for myself."

The sidewalks and street corners bustled, just as they had the day before, and the buses were emptier than a church on Monday morning. King watched an abandoned Bainbridge Street bus pass. "You know," he told me, "that's a miracle right there, an honest-to-goodness, genuine miracle."

I glanced at him, surprised. "You didn't think they'd support the boycott?"

"Not like this," King said. "To tell you the truth, I hoped for 60 percent … thought we'd be lucky to get it too, but this," he gestured toward the deserted bus, toward the marching crowd, "this looks like everybody."

His gaze swept over the scene around us, absorbing the magnitude of it all. "There's no explanation for that," he said. "No other way to describe it."

I reached for my pad. "Why don't you try?" I prodded. "Tell me why you think they're all willing to do this."

King buried his hands in his pockets. "That's been on my mind all night," he said. "Trying to figure out what they're thinking and feeling. I don't really have an answer yet."

"But a few things must have come to mind?" I prodded.

He bowed his head. "Well, we've seen all this anger over the Court's school decision; that's been hard to swallow—been hard to figure, too," King said. He glanced up, his lips pressed tight together. "The White Citizens' Councils, the legislatures all screaming about interposition and nullification...." He shook his head. "I'm telling you, that hurts; to be so openly hated, and for no good reason."

We walked on; King thrust his chin toward a waiting crowd and said, "These people see all that, they hear it and feel it, and they've got to have some kind of outlet, some way to respond." He paused, and we took a few quiet steps.

"All right," I said, wanting to ponder the idea before I pressed him further. "What else?"

"You know ..." King said, "the second thing might be the Negro himself—the way he sees himself, the way he understands his self-worth, his place in society...."

"Sounds deep," I said, perhaps too lightly.

"It is deep," King replied. He cast his gaze across the street, to a small pack of Negroes marching to work. "For a long time, Mr. Hall, these people have believed they're inferior. They've accepted injustice and exploitation as what they're due, as what they've naturally deserved."

A young woman passed us on the sidewalk. She glanced at King, her eyes lingering over him. "Morning, Reverend," she gushed. King tipped his hat in reply.

"Yesterday," he continued, "you asked me about how a thing could exist for a hundred years and then, after all that time, be declared unrighteous."

"I think that's the question a lot of people are asking."

King placed a finger to his lips. "For all that time," he said, "we've been living under this doctrine of 'separate but equal,' but we've got to be honest about it...." He peered over at me—held my eye for a second. "At least you and me, let's be honest with one another, all right?"

"Sure," I agreed with a nod.

"For all this time the 'separate' has been strictly enforced," he said, "but nobody ever had any intention of enforcing the 'equal.' Living like that ... I think these people lost faith in themselves. They believed they were less than human. They became subservient. They meekly accepted the place that had been given to them...." King studied another few of his passing neighbors. "As long as they did that, the system worked just fine."

"And now we need a new system to accommodate a new Negro. Is that what you're telling me?"

He crooked his head, thoughts still forming. "Partially," he replied. "But that's not really it." King raised an open hand to the air—a punctuation mark to add emphasis. "We need a new system because the one we've got is broken. In the final analysis, this isn't about accommodating Negroes—whether they're new or old or somewhere in between—it's about righteousness and justice."

"I don't know," I said. "From where I stand it seems like everything was cruising along just fine. And now, after a hundred years, you're telling me—telling everybody, I guess—that the Negro's got this new idea and we're all supposed to just go along?"

"It was never cruising along fine," King said. "And a lot happens in a hundred years. Negroes have traveled a bit now; they've visited some new cities. In some places they're starting to make decent money. Here and there—in a few places anyway—they're getting a better education...." We turned full face into the low, blinding sun; King tugged at the brim of his hat. "More Negroes are reading," he added. "And all that's got 'em taking a fresh look at themselves. The Negro's beginning to feel like he is somebody, beginning to see that God loves all His children; that the most important thing about a man isn't what's on the outside—it's not the texture of his hair or the color of his skin. It's the quality of his soul...."

We passed a group who waited for a cab. They called King's name, eager for him to recognize them and to know they had joined the cause. He quietly dipped his chin in reply.

"I think a new self-respect is emerging," he told me, "a new sense of dignity."

"And that," I said, "the Negro's self-respect, that's what's got us all in an uproar? That's what's disturbing the peace we've always known?"

King's head jerked up. "The peace we've always known needs disturbing," he said, his voice sterner than it had been before.

"Does that mean we're at war?" I asked.

We passed a diner and were suddenly enveloped by the seductive scents of fresh-brewed coffee and frying bacon. King tilted toward the doorway. "I could use a little something to warm me up," he said.

We ducked inside and grabbed a couple of stools at the counter. King wrapped his hands around the mug, warming them. "We're not at war, Mr. Hall. At least not with white people." He spun around and stared out to the sidewalk. "But those maids and janitors and garbage collectors, I believe they're now engaged in a struggle *against* oppression, and *for* freedom."

"You mincing words on me there, Reverend? Struggle, war … sounds like a distinction without a whole heck of a lot of difference."

"Oh, I think there's a profound difference," King replied.

I slurped through the steam. "Go on," I said.

"War is violent, Mr. Hall, and violence has never solved a social problem. In fact, it always creates new ones—usually worse than what you had before." His eyes traced the procession of a man walking past—a janitor or laborer. "We'll tell these people the same thing Jesus told Peter, to 'Put away your sword!'"

The restaurant owner hovered at King's shoulder. "More coffee?" he asked. King held out his cup, and the man poured for us both. "Bless you, Reverend," he said as he turned away. "Bless you, sir."

"Okay," I said. "You're not going to be violent. But it's still a war, right? It's still you—all these Negroes marching off to work—against them, the bus company, the city commission, the mayor …?"

"No," King replied. "That's not it, that's not it at all." He turned to face me. "We're not against them; we're actually for them."

I turned and stared, eyes rounded, struck dumb by the claim.

"Look," King continued, "we're not out to defeat or humiliate anybody. We're out to win their friendship. But to do that, they need to understand us, they need to know what we've been through, what we've felt." He bent down to sip his coffee. "Boycott's a lousy word for what we're doing; the implications of it are all wrong. We're not out to punish the bus line, we're not trying to get back at anybody...."

"Come on," I said. "You're punishing them economically. If that's not the point, then what is?"

King's eyes came level with mine. He let a full second pass, and then another one, never looking away. And then, in a voice that was just above a whisper he said: "Shame."

He gave the word time to burrow; let the awkwardness of it flounder there in the space between us. He looked back down. "We're protesting in order to awaken a sense of moral shame. The goal of all this isn't chaos or bitterness. The goal is community; it's deeper and broader fellowship. The aftermath of all this," he insisted, "is redemption and reconciliation."

I shook my head. "I don't know about that, Reverend; from what I've seen—here and in other places—this kind of thing turns ugly fast. If you think this is leading to reconciliation ... I wouldn't hold my breath."

"I understand. I know it's going to take time. And those who have the power, the ones who have the upper hand—I know that change comes slowly to them." King checked his watch. "I should be getting back," he told me.

I tossed a few coins on the counter, and we stepped outside. I draped my coat over my arm. "If change comes slowly," I said, "then this ..." I swept my arm across the cityscape, "this is just the beginning; the opening shot in your nonviolent war."

King smiled cagily. "We're not at war," he said. "And you've got to remember, we didn't plan this. It just happened. We're making it up as we go, taking one step at a time."

He was quiet, looking out over the city. "I don't know where any of this is going," he said. "I got no idea how long it'll last, but I'll tell you something: these people have given in to insult and injustice for a long time. And even though there's never been any open conflict, there's never been true peace either...." King took a step forward. "Maybe this time they won't settle for less."

I trailed a half step behind. "You mincing words again?" I teased. "Telling me there's a difference between peace and *true* peace?"

King forced a smile. "I think you'll find that I'm not a man who minces words."

"Then spell it out."

King studied the sidewalk. Then, raising a finger to the air, he said: "True peace—the kind the Bible talks about—has got to be more than the absence of hostility. It's got to be the presence of something good. You can't have peace until you've got justice and goodwill and honest-to-goodness brotherhood."

We rounded a bend, back onto Dexter Avenue. "So you're aiming for brotherhood with the city commissioners, the bus company, the mayor ...?"

"God loves those men and so I do too." He shrugged ambiguously. "Doesn't mean I like them much right this minute, doesn't mean I feel any great affection for them or for their attitudes. But yes, that's the aim. No matter what they think, no matter how they respond, this protest is about a redeeming goodwill for all men."

I glanced at a passing, empty bus. "You're doing that for the good of the bus company?"

He reached up, tightening his hat onto his head. "Let me tell you something, Mr. Hall: I believe the universe is built to be on the side of justice. Our struggle, any struggle for justice, has what I call cosmic companionship." He looked up, wondering if I'd grasped the weight of his implication. "God is omnipresent, and He is just. Evil may have its day, but in the end—even evil's got to work for good. So yes, I want these men to be on the side of justice. That's the only way we're going to get along. It's the only way the world's going to be as God intended.

"The answer is yes, we're doing this for them."

On the drive home a single thought stayed clamped to my mind—tugging at it, like Slugger yanks on a rag in a game of tug-of-war: *The worst possible thing for me—for my marriage, my social life, my career—was to find a Negro friend.* Martin King was thoughtful and provocative. He had more ideas than Thomas Edison. He was, at the same time, disturbing and magnetic—a kid too young for that much swagger, a boy who painted a picture of a world that was, from so many angles, bizarre, but that teased the imagination with possibilities.

He was like McGill, I thought, a guy with purpose, and a man who would—without hesitation or apology—use the tools at hand to make it real. McGill had a big-city paper. King possessed eloquence. Even now, over the drone of wheels on pavement, I could hear the cadence that made him so memorable. "And you know, my friends, there comes a time when people get tired of being pushed out of the glittering sunlight of life's July, and left standing amid the piercing chill of an alpine November."

The images stirred the minds of his downtrodden listeners, transporting them to the Canaan of King's imagination. "Justice is love in calculation," he had said. "Justice is love correcting that which revolts against love."

I envisioned bus drivers and city councilmen. I imagined white cops and city mayors, and even journalists from Atlanta. How does anyone who's ever recited the Ten Commandments remain unmoved? And once you've seen and heard of the plight of flesh-and-blood humans, by what means do you cling to the status quo?

And his closing, where he described a people who had moral courage, who "injected new meaning into the veins of history and civilization...." I could see his audience gazing up, slack-jawed and dreamy. Who, with those words resounding, remains on the sidelines? Who watches that parade pass and says to themselves, "No thanks, I'd rather watch *I Love Lucy?*"

I pictured him in the pulpit, fumbling at first, but then, gradually, wielding the power of rhythm and timbre, piling one phrase on top of the next, he electrified his people. He lifted them out of their humiliation and carried them off—if only for a moment—to a home where bigotry, hatred, and selfish ambition had been banned forever.

Martin King, like a planet on the fringe of the universe, exerted a gravitational pull, drawing followers into his orbit. But it was a tug I'd resist. I'd stay at the periphery safely beyond reach. I'd take a few notes, maybe write a story or two; I'd extract what I needed, and then move on, in search of something better.

From a distance, I'd watch this young man push the world, trying to force it where it wasn't ready to go.

My story ran on page five, trimmed to a tidy three hundred words, stating the who, what, when, and where of one Monday in Montgomery. There was no byline, and no need for Rose Marie to worry.

• • • •

The moving van pulled up to 5248 Fairhope Lane. It was the fourteenth of December, just eleven days before Christmas.

On our first night there we ate pizza off paper plates and gulped Coke from Dixie cups adorned with "Scenes of the Season." Rose Marie weaved her way between the boxes, drifting from the dining room into the kitchen, around the living room, and then back where she'd started. She stood there, ramrod straight, hands on her hips, strands of hair straying from the rubber band that had ceded control. She wore loose jeans and a red sweatshirt she'd owned since high school.

She circled her subject like an artist. "There's potential here," she declared. She studied each room from every angle. "Yeah, this place is going to be perfect." She turned toward the living room, taking a step or two in that direction, and I believe she may have touched a tear away from her eye.

She dished more pizza onto Chris's plate. "Your dad's got a great job," she told him. "And when the kids at your new school ask why we moved here, that's all they need to know. We don't need to say

anything about Percy Jackson, or about what happened back home."
She cupped his chin in her hand. "We need to keep that in the family,
okay?"

"Yes ma'am," our son replied. He cracked a wide-open smile and
cut his eyes in my direction. "Until Percy makes it to the big leagues,
then we're gonna brag more than the New York Yankees."

Rose Marie mussed his hair and forced a laugh. "Let's just see
what happens, okay?"

That night the two of us lay in bed. Rose Marie turned on her
side, her head propped in her hand. Her black silk nightgown italicized every curve and feminine inflection. Her brown hair fell past
her shoulders, grazing the pillowcase—the perfect frame for her dark
complexion, chocolate-colored eyes, and glittering smile. "I miss
home," she said, "but I know we've been given a second chance here.
I love the house and the yard. The neighborhood's beautiful, and I'm
glad we're here." She reached for my hand. "Let's not ruffle feathers,
okay? As soon as all the stuff gets put away, as soon as we get past
Christmas, we'll start having neighbors over for dinner. Chris'll find
new friends—I saw two boys about his age playing in the street this
afternoon. We'll find a church we like…. If we just tend to our own
business and stick close to home, I think we'll do just fine."

Rose Marie Hall is one of the world's most beautiful women.
And when she looks at me that way, when she smiles, when her eyes
gleam—the only thing I want is to make her happy. "Things are going
to be just fine," I told her. I touched her cheek, just brushing her skin
with the tips of my fingers. "The buses and boycotts are all behind
us now, and I'm not going within five hundred miles of the Sugar
Bowl."

She smiled and shook her hair, the bangs falling deliciously over her left eye. "That's good," she said. "And it's just what I wanted to hear." Then with a bewitching smile and with her eyes never veering from mine, she leaned back and extinguished the light.

*If one falls down, his friend can help
him up. But pity the man who falls
and has no one to help him up!*
—Ecclesiastes 4:10

Chapter 4

And so we limped into Atlanta—scarred, but filled with the hope that we might regain what had been lost in the only other place we had ever called home.

The next day we unpacked boxes, organized rooms, arranged and rearranged furniture. Christmas decorations were scattered on the floor, on shelves, on top of furniture and boxes. And all through the house, my wife's voice trilled—first with Christmas carols—and then with tunes from Pat Boone, the Four Aces, and Frank Sinatra.

Rose Marie hung wreathes; she arranged the manger scene along the mantle, found a spot for the Advent calendar on one of the kitchen walls, and even hung our stockings. After lunch Chris and I jumped in the car. We pulled out of the driveway, heading toward Peachtree. I backhanded his shoulder playfully. "We're not stopping till we find the best Christmas tree in Atlanta. You with me, pal?"

"Yes sir," he said, nodding. But I could tell his mind raced in a hundred different directions. His eyes scoped the new neighborhood, taking in the houses and trees, the park and sidewalks … trying to get the lay of this new land. We found a tree lot just a few minutes away, at the corner of Peachtree Battle. Four or five shoppers browsed the eastern white pines, "Joy to the World" blared from small, tinny speakers, and the air was fragrant with the scent of a distant forest. Chris marched up and down the rows, methodically examining one tree and then another. On his third tour he stopped about halfway down the fourth row. "Here it is," he declared. "This is the best tree in Atlanta."

I strolled up beside him, looked his selection up and down a few times, and put a hand to its branches. "Yep," I said. "I believe you're right."

We tied the tree onto the top of the car. We dragged it into the house, inflicting only minor damage, mostly to our hands and arms. And that evening we stacked our favorite Christmas albums onto the record player. We snacked on popcorn and sipped hot cider, and we began decorating the first tree in our brand-new home.

As each ornament came out of the box a memory came with it: our first Christmas together, the Schwinn Black Phantom we'd given Chris four years before; his uncontrollable glee the morning he discovered Slugger, a puppy we'd found at the pound, yelping and struggling to find his way out of the box and into a little boy's arms.

Every sentence that night began with, "Remember when …?" Or "Do you remember the time …?" And it all brought images of Whitney to mind. Rose Marie did her best to stay cheerful, and the three of us labored to enjoy our family's favorite tradition. But with each memory we longed for home. We were lonely in a strange place with no friends, and there wasn't much we could do to hide it.

I had gone to the basement to search for a missing box of tinsel. Bing Crosby crooned "White Christmas" while Chris untangled lights and Rose Marie laced the mantle with garland. I was back at the top

of the basement stairs wiggle-wagging the box through the doorway
when the bell rang. Outside, a chorus erupted, "Joy to the world, the
Lord has come! Let earth receive her King."

Chris's eyes bulged. Rose Marie raced for the door. "Carolers!" she
cried. "Hurry up, Hall!" There must have been twenty people at the
foot of our front steps: kids and parents and grandparents. The three
of us stepped outside, shivering in the cold, but warmed by this gracious surprise. The air was fragrant with smoke from our neighbors'
fireplaces. The carolers were wrapped snug in coats, mufflers, caps,
and gloves. And their eyes shimmered as they plunged into a second
song: "O come, all ye faithful, joyful and triumphant. O come ye, O
come ye, to Bethlehem.…"

Rose and Chris and I joined them on the second verse, "Sing,
choirs of angels, Sing in exultation, O sing, all ye citizens of heav'n
above.…" We clapped at the end of the song, we laughed, and our
spirits brightened. We helped on the next song too, the whole crowd
of us sang from the front steps of our new home: "Hark! The herald
angels sing, 'Glory to the newborn King.…'"

We had come to the third verse, "Born to raise the sons of earth,
born to give them second birth …" when an older man—he must've
been in his midfifties—climbed the steps. A gray overcoat was the
foreground for a red-striped tie and a brilliant green scarf. His blue
eyes glowed and the flesh around them crinkled, offering the guise
of perpetual kindness. As we sang the last lines he removed the glove
from his right hand and reached for mine. And when we finished the
song he said, "I'm Carson Powers. I'm the pastor of the Presbyterian
church up on Peachtree. Me and a few of your neighbors, we just
wanted to welcome y'all to the neighborhood." He made a quarter

turn, swinging his arm back toward the crowd. "Right here in front," he said, "is Alan and Doris Emerson. They're just a couple of doors down and across the street."

On cue, Doris Emerson skipped up the stairs and handed Rose Marie a warm casserole dish wrapped in a bright red towel. "You can heat this up tomorrow," she said. "I wasn't sure how many to cook for. If it's just the three of you, you might get a couple of suppers out of it." Alan Emerson stood behind his wife. He reached around her, extending a hand and said, "I'm Alan, nice to have y'all here." He looked Chris up and down a few times. "You know, we got a boy about your age; he's a pretty good ballplayer. How 'bout you, you like sports?"

A smile glinted from Chris's lips. "Yes sir," he said. "I like just about all of 'em: basketball, baseball, football...."

"Well, our boy's name is Parker. I'll send him up here tomorrow, have him take you round to meet some other boys, if you'd like."

"That'd be very nice," Rose Marie said. "Thank you."

I could see the gratitude in Rose's eyes. And as much as any man's able, I could hear her yearning—for company, for neighbors to talk to, for the warmth of fellow human beings.

Carson Powers spoke again. With a long arching motion he pointed into the left side of the crowd. "Right over there," he said, "is Dale and Patty Parsons. Their house is directly behind yours, right across the creek that runs back there."

Patty hopped up the steps beside her pastor. She handed Chris a pie plate wrapped tight in aluminum foil. "It's pecan," she said. "I hope you like it."

Dale Parsons waved from the bottom step. "Hey there," he mumbled, never quite meeting anyone's eye. "If there's something I can do to help, you just let me know. I'm pretty handy with tools and, like the pastor said, I'm real close."

I smiled and said, "I might just take you up on that."

Patty Parsons reached for Rose Marie's hand. The woman's eyes were an open invitation. "I know you must be awfully busy," she said, "I can't imagine trying to move at Christmastime, but a few of us are getting together for coffee tomorrow—just to talk and catch up." She looked out toward the crowd. "Doris'll be there," she said, "and Betty's coming …" she sorted through the crowd, "and Helen and Anne'll be there."

A hand shot up at the mention of each name. "So if you come, that'll be six of us."

"Oh, I'd love to," Rose snapped up the invitation. And I heard the relief in her voice—at the prospect of friends. And thankfulness that she'd been included in something so soon. "What time?" she asked.

"'Bout ten," Patty said, "over at my house."

"There's a little makeshift bridge across the creek," Dale Parsons said, "… old pine tree came down a few years ago. I leveled it off, and fit it to size. It's down on your left as you walk toward our place. You can just step right on over if you like."

"Thank you, Dale." Rose squeezed Patty's hand and said, "I'll see you at ten."

Carson Powers tipped his hat. "Well, you folks have a good night," he said. "And if you're interested, we got a Christmas Eve service at six; another one at eight. We'd love to have you join us."

I took Powers's hand into both of mine. "Thanks," I said, "this was very nice of you." I looked out to the crowd. "Thank you all,"

I called. Rose and Chris and I waved as they turned to go, grateful for the company and the kindness. And Rose, I noticed, was especially brightened by the unexpected arrival of flesh-and-blood neighbors.

We stepped inside, glad to be back where it was warm. I rubbed my hands together, rubbed my arms up and down to chase away the chill. "I'll get a fire going," I announced. And then to Chris, "And maybe we can dive into that pie?"

"I'll get this put away," Rose said gesturing toward the casserole. "And heat up some cider."

On the record player, a children's choir sang "We Wish You a Merry Christmas." We sat on the couch, the three of us hunched over plates of pecan pie, warming ourselves, comforted by the snaps and hisses of just-lit kindling, and feeling—just faintly—the promise of good things to come.

• • • •

The next day Rose found Dale Parsons's bridge at a crook in the stream, and made her way to our new neighbors'.

I was in the living room hanging a sunburst clock I'd found on sale at Rich's. It was a few minutes past noon when she crept through the back door. "So, how'd it go," I called, "you have a good time?"

She breezed into the living room. "They were all very nice," she said. "Patty and Doris have kids who go to Chris's school; one's in the same grade, the other's a year ahead. Helen and Ann's kids are older. There are four of them altogether, I think. They're up at the high school."

I tapped a picture hook into the wall. "It'll be nice to get to know some new families, won't it?"

"Yeah," Rose said. She strolled around the room, quietly inspecting my work. "These women try to get together every Thursday morning," she said. "They rotate from house to house." She glanced up slyly. "They'll be here on the first Thursday in January—when you'll be at work."

I returned the smile and said, "Thanks."

Rose came beside me. She leaned her head into my shoulder and laced our arms together. "I'm glad they asked me over," she said. "I was lonely last night, I guess it had been building up all day and just kind of hit me all of sudden. I needed the company."

I kissed the top of her head. "I know," I said. "And I'm glad these women found you."

•   •   •   •

Two days later we visited Carson Powers's church. We found a pew behind the Emersons, and as I surveyed our new surroundings I thought: This will take time. It's going to be hard work—to knead ourselves into the dough of church, work, school, and neighborhood—the places where people visit their best friends, where they talk about the things they love, where they're compelled to be kind, but would rather not be torn.

In a building we'd never seen before, sitting among hundreds of perfect strangers, we sang familiar hymns and repeated creeds we knew by heart. And then Carson Powers moved to his pulpit. He read from Ephesians: "The Lord is at hand; do not be anxious about anything."

He read on—about prayer and a peace that passes understanding—and then he began a sermon.

Before he'd reached the end of his fifth sentence I thought to myself: *This guy's good.* An image of Martin King sprang to mind, of the Negro preacher poised behind the Holt Street pulpit, infusing a crowd with hope they'd never known before. I chuckled silently, struck by the stark contrast. King was half Powers's age, but more imposing. King was more self-conscious; he was in possession of this extravagant oratorical flair, while Powers was at ease. The white pastor was formal enough, but folksy, too. He spoke softly and plainly, as one friend to another, and that day he spoke words my family longed for.

It was forty minutes shy of noon. Sunlight poured through stained glass, bathing the congregation in celestial waves of red, blue, and green. At the same time, the rough-hewn wood—the beams, pews, and pulpit—were earthy reminders of the here and now. The sniffling noses, the squirming kids, the couple holding hands two pews in front of me—music that welled something up inside—these gave voice to the flesh-and-blood present, to life that's gritty and sweet, that's filled with more trouble than any of us would ever want, and with more beauty than we could possibly deserve.

I spotted ten of the twenty people who'd visited my home and welcomed my family. Maybe, I thought, in and through them, He really was here. Maybe, with Doris Emerson's casserole and Patty Parsons's pie—through Dale's bridge, and Thursday morning coffee—perhaps, through the most commonplace things, we'd find some form of the peace Powers described.

"No matter what you've been through," Carson Powers said, "and no matter where you've been, it's part of a plan and purpose that's bigger than you are." He paused, his eyes lingering on my family as if he had some inkling of our recent past. He nodded at me—only I could see it—and he said, "And it all works to your good."

He stepped down from the platform and moved close to his people. He picked another face in the crowd and said, "That doesn't mean it's easy." His eyes swept the room, "Everybody here knows that life's hard. And if you don't ..." he smiled sympathetically, "you will soon.

"But even then," he pledged, "even when we don't understand what in the world's going on ..." Rose Marie touched a finger to her eye, dragging a tear to the side. Then she took my hand, reassured, I think, and strengthened—if even slightly—to face what lay ahead.

I listened to Powers and believed we had come to the place where we might belong. We had come by a path I'd have never chosen, but here we were, in a home we loved, surrounded by decent people, in a glorious building, and buttressed for the moment by a message that was meant for us, and us alone.

After lunch, Parker Emerson took Chris to the park where a band of restless boys squared off in a titanic game of touch football. He and Slugger hustled out of the house, the screen door banged shut behind them, and both looked as though they'd spent their whole lives here.

Rose and I watched from the front stoop—this pack of boys tossing a ball back and forth as they faded from view. "I don't think he's missed home for five minutes," Rose said.

I slung an arm around her shoulder. "If you're a boy and you can throw and run and catch ... it doesn't take long to make friends."

She pressed her hands to the wooden rail. "Well then," she said. "All that time I spent playing catch with him has paid off."

I rubbed her back, conveying through the touch my affection for her. "Everything you've ever taught him has paid off," I said.

The phone rang and Rose rushed to get it. I stood a while longer, admiring my magnificent new lawn. She and Chris were off to a good start, I thought. But in the back of my mind a pair of thoughts nagged: Martin King's boycott was into its third week, with neither side showing so much as a hint of weakness. And the Sugar Bowl, where a Negro would soon play football on Southern soil, was now just a few weeks away.

I'd have never admitted it to Rose Marie, but I was nervous.

•   •   •   •

By Christmas Eve, our house was filled with more charm than the spring cotillion. Not a corner or crevice had gone unnoticed, and the evidence of Rose Marie's magic—stockings, garland, wreathes, and candles— was everywhere, and it was all picture-book perfect.

We'd strung lights outside, and wreathes adorned each window, all of them garnished by snow that had been sprayed from a can, as enchanting as anything Mother Nature might have wrought. From the street, as you looked up the rise, our place looked and smelled and even sounded merrier than the North Pole.

The Christmas tree filled one corner of the family room. It glittered with ornaments and icicles. Gifts were scattered underneath, their red, green, and gold paper shimmering beneath lights, casting their own muted glow. We were wrapped in the aroma of a six-foot eastern white pine, with the music of Christmas floating from the living room into every nook of our new home.

I looped one end of my tie over and around the other and stepped into the hall. I called down toward Chris's room, "We need to leave in five minutes, pal."

He peeked out the door. "I'm all ready," he said.

"Yeah, well step out here and let's have a look."

He trudged down the hall, huffing a mild protest. He wore a new black suit, a white shirt as crisply starched as a banker's, and a special red and green tie that Rose had found "adorable."

Reflexively, I brushed at the boy's lapels, and it hit me—how tall he'd gotten. Somehow, beyond my powers of observation, he'd sprouted past the top of my shoulders. I tightened the knot of his tie. He'd gotten thicker too, and his body was hard. I shoved the tie to the right and noticed, for the first time, that hairs had sprung from the bottom of his chin. I slapped his shoulder and smiled, a little sad that his boyhood was passing. "Elvis'd be jealous," I told him.

Rose Marie stood before the full-length mirror. She twisted slightly, left then right, looking over her shoulder, examining the back of her red dress, flattening its errant creases. Her hair flipped at the shoulders, wispy bangs swept over and past her left eye, and I stood still, powerless to do anything but admire the scenery.

"There's nothing you could do to look one bit better'n that," I told her.

She smoothed the dress, twisted, still craning to see behind her. "You know what?" she decided. "This is gonna have to do."

We looked at one another by way of the mirror. My eyes slowly traveled the length of her body. "It'll do just fine," I said.

Ten minutes later we walked down the center aisle of Second Presbyterian Church. Candles flickered from elegant wood-carved sconces. A piano, three violins, and a harp softly trilled "Joy to the World," while fidgety kids, scattered throughout the room, wriggled in an earnest search for anything interesting.

We slid into a pew near the back of the sanctuary. Alan Emerson waved from the other side of the aisle as the ensemble segued into "Hark! The Herald Angels Sing." Behind us, a green-robed choir began to gather, bunching up into the center and side aisles. They shuffled busily, hurrying to their proper place. The room became still. And then, on some prearranged signal, the organ thundered its prelude. The music from a full orchestra climbed to the rafters, it reached its climactic moment—and the choir marched. Green robes streamed down the aisles, the choir joyously proclaiming, "Angels we have on heard high, sweetly singing o'er the plains, and the mountains in reply, echoing their joyous strains. Gloria in excelsis Deo. Gloria in excelsis Deo."

The room, in that instant, was filled with majesty. Four hundred expectant voices beseeched one another to "Come to Bethlehem and see Christ whose birth the angels sing ..." They filled the sanctuary with unbounded joy, trumpeting the thrill of this almost unimaginable occasion, stirring reverence, awe, and at least five other emotions that have not yet been named.

At the song's close there was a pause, a minute to absorb what had just befallen us, and to let it settle.

Carson Powers eased into the pulpit. As he opened his Bible he greeted the crowd and motioned for us to sit. He thumbed a few pages, in search of his passage, and I settled back, waiting to hear the story again—of Caesar Augustus's census, of Mary and Joseph's trek to Bethlehem and finding no room in the inn; of the manger and wise men; of shepherds and the heavenly hosts singing….

But Carson Powers pulled a fast one. He stood in the pulpit, his Bible spread flat on his palm, still paging forward. "You remember when Jesus first started preaching?" he began, "when He was in Nazareth, the first time He taught in the synagogue?"

This wasn't starting out like any Christmas message I'd ever heard.

Powers flipped one more page, found the spot he was looking for, and began to read—about preaching good news to the poor and proclaiming freedom for prisoners. He read about restoring sight to the blind, releasing the oppressed, and proclaiming the year of the Lord's favor.

Well, I thought, *I've got to give the man credit for originality: He didn't read the first word about babies or farm animals or frankincense and myrrh.* Powers edged away from the lectern. He tucked the Bible under his arm and said: "We hear a lot of talk these days about the true meaning of Christmas. We gripe about commercialization and materialism—and we got more'n enough reason." He scanned the congregation. "Tonight, in this place, we focus on the true meaning of Christmas. And this right here is it." He tapped at his Bible. "The words I just read are the reason we celebrate."

Powers put a hand to his chin. "That day in the synagogue Jesus was letting folks know that He came to make everything different, He came to make it all new, to put everything that had gone wrong right.

He came on Christmas to overhaul every last speck of the universe, to make it, as it says a few pages over, 'the home of righteousness.'

"And that means you and me got work to do. If what I just read is true—and we all believe it is—then the reason we're here is to help out." He walked slowly, stabbing the Bible with his finger again. "If this is true," he said, "then it's our job to make every last thing the way it's supposed to be." He cracked the Book open, rereading the words silently. "And you know what? Christmas morning'd be the perfect time to start—with our wives and husbands, with our kids, our friends, and neighbors. Everywhere we go, with everything we do—we ought to make it brand-spanking-new—as free from greed and jealousy and resentment as we've got the power to make it." Powers stopped and faced the congregation. "Whatever little patch of ground we got, it ought to become the home of righteousness and justice." His eyes traveled the width of the room, filled, I think, with the hope that what he'd said made sense—and that it might make a difference.

And then he concluded: "That, friends, is the true meaning of Christmas. Let's go home and think about it."

On that cue ushers moved into the aisles, passing candles down the rows. The lights dimmed, and we sang "Silent Night," each person lighting his neighbor's candle, progressively flooding the room with a gentle glow.

And then the service was over.

As the crowd moved and mingled together, Alan Emerson hurried up beside me. "Hey, Jack," he said, "I know this is last minute, but why don't y'all swing by our place on the way home? We've got some eggnog and cookies. Doris'll put some hot chocolate on. What do you say, you guys up for it?"

"Oh, we'd love to stop by," Rose pounced on the offer.

"Great," Alan said, "I'll check with a few others; see if they can join us."

Dale Parsons, Ivy Davis, and I sat in the living room while Alan stacked logs onto the andirons. Chris and Parker retreated to the back of the house to play electric football, while our wives invaded Doris Emerson's kitchen.

Alan poured drinks and passed them round. He moved to his favorite chair, raised his glass, and said, "Merry Christmas, gentlemen."

We replied and sipped from our glasses. Then Alan turned to me. "So, tell us what you'll be working on, Jack."

"Baseball mostly," I told them. "The Crackers and the Southern Association. In the off-season I'll float around and help out where I'm needed; probably cover some local basketball, fill in on football—stuff like that."

"What's up first?" Ivy asked. "Any idea?"

"I'll get to know my way around a little, I guess. Bisher said something about the Tech-Kentucky game. It's early next month, the seventh or eighth maybe?"

Alan winced, as if he'd just been stung. "Drew the short straw on that one, didn't you?" he laughed.

"At least you'll get to see Kentucky," Ivy said. "That'll be worthwhile."

"Poor Tech…." Alan shook his head. "No consistency, no bench—that game'll be over in the first ten minutes."

He got up and poked at the fire, and with much more enthusiasm he said, "But football—now that's a different story."

Our wives paraded into the room. They carried trays piled high with snacks and desserts. They arranged it all on the coffee table and then found their seats beside us.

"Tech had a heck of a year," Dale continued. "And I got to tell you, back in September, I'd have never guessed those guys would win nine games."

"And have a shot at ten." Alan exclaimed. He savored his drink and the thought of a bowl victory.

The reporter in me couldn't resist, and I nudged the conversation in Bobby Grier's direction. "Pitt's an interesting team," I said.

"They're hard to figure, aren't they?" Ivy agreed.

"You know, I think the long layoff might hurt a team like that," Dale thought. "They seem to run hot and cold, don't they?"

"That has been their pattern," I said. I waved my hand over the crowd. "You guys seem like Tech fans. What do you make of this thing with Griffin and the regents?"

"Actually, I'm the only Tech fan in this bunch," Alan replied. "Ivy over there ..." Alan rolled his eyes, "he went to Georgia. Dale's a Tennessee man."

"All right, what do you think?" I asked Alan.

He grinned and tipped his glass. "We won nine games, that's what I think. And we're going to the Sugar Bowl; I don't care if Pitt brings communists and Martians."

"The colored kid doesn't bother you?" Rose asked, her tone flat and perfectly neutral.

Alan shrugged. "Not as long as he plays for Pitt."

A sly smile crept across Ivy's face. "You see what happened in Athens the other day?" he asked.

"I saw it," Doris cried. "And I think you ought to be ashamed."

Ivy laughed, "Probably," he said. "But you got to admit, that was funny."

"What?" Rose asked. "I missed this."

"Bunch of boys over there got a little miffed at the governor," Ivy explained. "So they decided to show a little righteous indignation and—"

"They launched a panty raid," Doris scoffed, a blush tinting her cheeks. "I'm not sure I understand how that's a political protest, but...."

"Come on, the Bulldogs are supporting your team," Ivy exclaimed. "It ain't likely we'll ever see that again."

Rose leaned forward. "The kids at Georgia protested *against* the governor? They want Tech to play?"

"Yeah," Ivy said, "that, or they were looking for a reason to root around in the girls' underwear."

"Might get 'em expelled," Doris said. "At least that's what I read."

Rose surveyed the room. "And y'all don't mind if this colored boy plays down here?" she asked.

Alan drained his glass, "Don't get me wrong," he said. "I don't want anybody trying to integrate our schools; that'd be a whole different story. But Pitt, Notre Dame ... I think we all got better things to do than worry about them."

"And besides," Ivy added, "it'll give that old boy a chance to see what Southeastern Conference football's all about."

"You hope it does," Doris cautioned.

I glanced at Rose, silently assuring her: *You see, this is going to be all right.*

Anne Davis started a plate of cookies around the room. She looked at Rose with a scheming smile and whispered, "So what's Chris getting for Christmas?"

Before Rose could answer Alan Emerson tilted his empty class toward the crowd. "I'm going to freshen this up," he said. "Can I get anything for anybody else?"

"I'll come with you," I replied, and tagged along into the kitchen.

Alan grabbed a couple of ice trays out of the freezer.

"Rose tells me you work for Delta Air Lines," I said, "in the accounting department?"

He nodded. "Work on new projects mostly; logistics, financial analysis, budget projections..." he smiled thinly. "Thrilling stuff like that."

"Company's growing," I said, "at least it seems that way."

"Like a weed in June," he replied. He handed me one of the trays.

"So what are you working on now?" I cracked the ice into the empty bucket.

"For the past few months I've been working on this thing called the hub-and-spoke." He cocked his head a little. "It's a little different way of thinking about how we do business."

"How's that?"

Alan was at the sink, refilling ice trays. "Right now we fly 'point-to-point,'" he explained. "If you're in Richmond and you want to go Charlotte, you take a plane to Charlotte. But the fact is, there's not a whole heck of a lot of demand for a Richmond to Charlotte route, which means the plane's half empty most of the time, which means we lose our butts on that particular flight. The new system'll create a hub ..." he formed a circle, touching the thumbs and fore-fingers of both hands together. "That'll be in Atlanta," he said. "All our flights will originate here. We'll fly from Atlanta to Richmond, then turn the plane around and come right back here. Then we'll fly you from Atlanta to Charlotte." He carried a pair of trays back to the freezer. "If I'm right, we'll cut operating costs, make travel cheaper for passengers ..." he glanced back, smiling, "and make a ton of money."

"Sounds like a pretty big deal," I said.

"Could be ... if it works."

I leaned against the counter, "And you're the guy who's respon-sible for this? You're putting the whole thing together?"

"Well, I'm not alone; we got plenty of guys working on it. But yeah, I guess so."

"Heck of a job," I said.

"I guess," he replied.

"You don't sound too thrilled."

"Oh, it's a great project and I mean to get it off the ground." He grinned, "Pun intended. But, I don't know. I've been thinking that one of these days I might like to have my own thing—you know—start a business from scratch, grow it into something substantial...."

I handed him another of the refilled trays. "Like what?"

Alan chuckled, "I don't have the faintest idea. But I keep my eyes open, you know, to see if something grabs me.

"I don't know why I'm carrying on about this," he glanced up, embarrassed. "No need to mention it to anybody else, okay?"

"Won't leave the room," I promised.

He angled his head toward the living room, asking if I was ready to rejoin the others. For the next hour, Rose and I spent time with new friends, and we felt as though one day we might really belong.

It was nearly ten when we started for home. Outside, the air was crisp, a half-moon dazzled in a glittering sky, and a frisky breeze scattered the season's last deposit of unraked leaves. You couldn't help but be restless for Christmas morning.

As we strolled toward home Rose draped a hand over Chris's shoulder. "We need to get you to bed," she told him.

He yawned and offered no argument. We took a few steps more. Chris pulled his jacket tight against the cold; he glanced up, stuck both hands into his back pockets, and then looked back down. And then, from straight out of the blue, he said, "I'm thinking we should go to the game."

Through a yawn I mumbled, "What game's that, pal?"

"The Sugar Bowl." His voice was fatigued but thoughtful. This wasn't out of the blue; it was something he'd thought about, a deduction he'd carefully come to. "We ought to be there," he said.

His mother's eyes flashed to mine.

"Why?" I said with a chuckle. "You don't care about either of those teams."

"No," he said, "but I think we should sit on the Pitt side." He looked to his mother and then me. "We ought to be rooting for the colored guy."

We'd reached our driveway. Rose's eyes darted up to mine again, and with as much calm as she could summon she said, "You've got to get ready for school; your father's got to be here for work…. And besides," she said with a smile, "a writer for *The Atlanta Constitution* can't go around rooting for Pitt."

"But we need to help this guy," Chris said. "We shouldn't let 'em run him out of town the way they did Percy, not if we can help it."

I put a hand on the boy's shoulder as we headed up the front steps. "He's been playing all season, Chris, and nothing's happened to him. This boy's doing just fine. Really."

I slid into bed that night at peace. But sometimes, even when things are right with the world, the mind swirls with meddlesome thoughts. And on Christmas Eve, my imagination ran wild with thoughts of Martin King.

As I drifted into sleep, I heard the words he'd spoken from the pulpit and to me as we'd walked the colored section of his central Alabama town. I could hear him as plainly as I'd heard Rose ten minutes before. I could have touched him too. I was there, transported back to Holt Street and to Dexter Avenue and to the coffee shop on Washington.

And then, as if someone had flipped the channel, the scene changed. My mind was tuned to Carson Powers and to his peculiar take on the true meaning of Christmas.

The channel changed again. King and Powers sat side by side, gathered together in the middle of my dream for a little late-night conversation.

King said he was tired of being "trampled by oppression."

Powers understood. He agreed with the Negro pastor that the time had come to release the oppressed.

Colored people, King argued, had suffered through "a long night of captivity."

And white people, Powers replied, were obliged to proclaim freedom for prisoners.

According to King, the powers and authorities had strayed from righteousness.

It was up to all of us, Powers insisted, to make "our patch of ground the home of righteousness."

King, when he looked out over his people, saw the "disinherited of the land."

Powers, in his church, saw people who possessed good news for the poor.

King believed Negroes should inject new meaning into the veins of history.

Powers implored a white congregation to "make all things new."

In my dream that night, King insisted that works of justice have cosmic companionship, and that God is eternally on the side of righteousness.

Powers believed in wholesale redemption, and that men were put here to make the world better.

In the light of day, I don't suppose that either man would have called the other his ally. But that night—Christmas Eve 1955—I was trapped in this imaginary conversation where two preachers possessed interlocking pieces of an illusory puzzle.

January 2, 1956

Chapter 5

We had the television tuned to the right channel. The sofa and chairs were in position. And plenty of snacks had been strategically placed around the living room, dining room, and family room.

In thirty minutes our guests would arrive. And in an hour, we'd watch the kickoff of the 1956 Sugar Bowl: Georgia Tech versus Pitt.

"I'm nervous," Rose confessed. "I'd hate for something to go wrong...." She chewed on the tip of her thumbnail, "I just don't want to get into all this integration business with a houseful of new neighbors."

"I think all that's died down," I said. "Seems like everybody's had time to get used to the idea."

Rose eyed the local section of the newspaper. "They've still got extra security at the governor's mansion," she reminded me.

"Yeah, but that's because people *want* Grier to play. The others have stayed pretty quiet."

"Today would be the day to change that," Rose pointed out.

Chris moseyed in and filched a chip from one of the bowls. "I know I'll be rooting for Grier," he said.

"Not on your life," I snapped. "At least not out loud."

"Why?" he complained. "We should all be pulling for him."

"Because Mr. Emerson's a big-time Tech fan," I told him. "Because your new buddy Parker is too. If you're over there rooting for Pitt it's going to annoy the daylights out of them."

"You need to be hospitable," his mother scolded. She stared at Chris, her jaw tight, eyes wary. "The last thing we need is you starting up some big discussion about mixing races. Do you understand me?" She turned for the kitchen.

His eyes tracked her into the next room. "Yeah," he muttered, a trace of anger flaring. "I understand perfectly."

I flinched at the tone—at the tension I hadn't expected. "All right," I said, clapping my hands together, "what else can we do to help get ready?"

The Emersons arrived first, Alan and Parker both sporting bright gold Georgia Tech jerseys. Five minutes later the Davises followed, trailed by the Parsons, and then the Powerses.

For a half hour we ate and drank and traded small talk about the Rose Bowl, Orange Bowl, and Cotton Bowl. And then, five minutes before kickoff, we gathered in front of the set. Alan Emerson was hunched forward, nervous and antsy for the game to begin. My palms were damp too, and Rose's eyes brimmed with worry. Chris sat crossed-legged on the floor, eyeing his mother disdainfully, and keeping an eye open for Bobby Grier. His buddy Parker was beside him, as tense as his old man.

The camera cut to the referee. He blew his whistle and dropped his hand—the game was on.

We'd put Alan in a front-and-center seat, and the man gave each play every ounce of his concentration. His muscles tensed as Tech broke the huddle. He followed every move their halfbacks and fullbacks made. He watched the Pitt linebackers fill gaps; he followed the stunts of their defensive line—taut as a banjo string the whole time.

After their first three downs Tech punted, and it came time for the first set of commercials.

Alan fell back into his chair, expelling a breath he'd held for the full first series. "That's all right," he said, "just testing their line, feeling 'em out a little."

"Their defensive front is huge," Ivy observed.

"And they ain't exactly slow," Dale added.

"But they'll wear down," Alan assured his neighbors, "Trust me, by the fourth quarter those guys'll be sucking air."

The game faded up from the last commercial. The announcer reset the scene: It was Pitt's ball, first-and-ten on their own thirty-five; still early in the first quarter, there was no score.

On their first play from scrimmage Pitt quarterback Pete Neft fumbled the snap. The ball dribbled along the ground—loose—three feet behind the line of scrimmage. Neft dove for it. A mad scramble followed—players frantically diving into a pile. Three referees rushed to the scene. They blew whistles and waved their hands. One by one, they unpeeled giant players from the still wriggling, squirming mass. At the bottom, they found Allen Ecker, a Tech lineman, cradling the ball like it was a sack full of diamonds.

Alan Emerson leaped out his chair. "Yes!" he declared. "Now there's some defense for you."

Tech had great field position at the Pitt thirty-two. Wade Mitchell took the snap. He faked to the fullback off left tackle; he faked again, to the halfback sprinting around left end. Mitchell tucked the ball to his hip and followed them to the left side. He suddenly stopped. He turned and took off toward the right sideline. He took the ball off his hip—spotted Don Ellis crossing into the end zone—and threw.

A Pitt defender stayed with Ellis stride-for-stride. Both players went up for the ball, there was contact, both men fell, sprawled on the ground, as Mitchell's pass sailed overhead, incomplete.

Alan Emerson jabbed his finger at the set. "Interference!" he screamed. "You gotta call that!"

I didn't say it, but I thought to myself: *Looked like good defense to me.*

The back judge, who couldn't have been more than five yards behind Ellis, saw things Alan's way. He reached into his back pocket, and he tossed a flag.

And then, at the same moment, we all noticed: The penalty had been called on Bobby Grier.

The crowd erupted in boos. The camera panned scores of outraged faces, Pitt fans pawing the air in anger and disbelief. "Oh no," Rose whispered. "They're going to come after the colored boy, aren't they?"

The referee stepped off the penalty, placing the ball on the two-yard line. The boos swarmed, louder and angrier. Chris peered into the set. "Does anybody see the cops?" he asked.

Ivy Davis chuckled easily. "They're not booing the colored guy," he said. "They're booing the ref. Those are Pitt fans down there."

Alan glanced over. "That kid was all over him," he said, smiling sheepishly. "The ref was standing right there...."

I'm not sure now how much of it was real and how much was imagined, but right then, sitting in front of the set, hearing the crowd, watching their faces—it seemed as though unchecked rage swirled round the south end of the Sugar Bowl.

On the next play Mitchell was stopped on the quarterback sneak, but Pitt was offsides; the ball was placed on the one. Next play, another sneak. This time Mitchell plunged in for the score.

Tech's glee blended with Pitt's fury. As Mitchell kicked the extra point, a mixed chorus of boos and cheers engulfed the stadium. And with nine and a half minutes left in the first quarter, Tech took the 7-0 lead.

A Gillette razor commercial eased Alan's mood. He stood to stretch, relieved that his team had a seven-point cushion. "We got this thing in the bag," he joked with Carson Powers.

"It's still the first quarter," his friend replied. "And you caught a couple of very serious breaks right there—on the fumble and the penalty."

"Oh, come on, it was a good call." Alan tossed a few chips onto a paper plate. "Tell him, Jack—that kid was mauling our guy."

Chris poured more Coke into his cup. "Looked clean to me," he murmured, casting a glare in his mother's direction.

"I don't know," I groaned. "Honestly, I thought Grier made a nice play."

The game was back on, and Alan hurried to his chair. As he rushed through the living room he said, "Remind me to make you guys an appointment with the eye doctor."

The rest of the game was a defensive struggle, with neither team able to muster much offense—or, I thought, a lot of imagination.

As the game wore on, Tech clung to the seven-point lead. But Alan had been wrong: It was the bigger team who'd worn down Tech's smaller line, and with just over a minute to go Pitt mounted a furious drive. They moved the ball methodically down the field—to the fifty, to Tech's thirty, down to the twenty-yard line. There were thirty seconds to go. The clock stopped to move the chains. The Panthers moved to the fifteen, then across the ten—twelve seconds to play. They pushed the ball to the five—six seconds to go. Pitt raced to the line of scrimmage—three seconds left, two, one—the buzzer sounded an instant before the snap of the ball.

Alan Emerson sprang from his chair, hands in the air—signaling victory and unbridled joy.

Pitt had out-rushed and out-passed the Yellow Jackets, but Mitchell's touchdown was all they needed. Tech won their tenth game of the year—and their fifth consecutive bowl, 7-0.

My new neighbors relaxed. They stood and stretched and began to mingle. They headed for the bathrooms and the kitchen. They filled their plates with post-game desserts, and their cups with just perked coffee.

I sat for a few minutes more. Bobby Dodd was on—beaming— talking about how his kids had overcome adversity, how they'd showed courage and stuck together. In the background Tech's band played "I'm a Ramblin' Wreck from Georgia Tech and a hell of a engineer...." Players hugged their parents and girlfriends. Behind them, young fans mugged for the camera.

These guys had won on a suspicious call against their opponent's only Negro player ... and in Louisiana. There had been thunderous boos, and even through the television you sensed the crowd's anger. But Ivy had been right; the hostility had never been aimed at Grier.

•   •   •   •

There'd been strife before the game. There had been furious objections to Bobby Grier's presence. Our governor had made references to Armageddon and the end of the life we'd always known. Legislators feared the destruction of our most treasured traditions. My wife had worried about smoldering mobs.

But on the morning of January 3, after a Negro had played against white boys on the Deep South's own soil, the sun had come up in the east—as brightly as it had the day before.

I found Rose at the breakfast table, the sports section open before her. Pages two and three were dominated by sequential photos of the game's key play—of Wade Mitchell plunging in from the one. Arrows pointed to the critical block, to Mitchell bulldozing into the end zone, and to the ball breaking the plane of the goal line.

Rose glanced up, smiling. "Today's the big day, Hall. You ready?"

I poured a cup of coffee, looked to the floor taking careful inventory. "Let's see: shoes, socks, underwear … yeah," I said. "I think I got everything."

She grinned. "It's a new chapter, Hall. Today, you're playing in the big leagues."

I slid into the seat beside her. I looked out to the hollies and pines and gnarled, leafless maples. "I hope we've done the right thing," I said.

"Too late now," she said, smiling. Then Rose grabbed my hand. "I'm excited for you, Hall. Big city, big paper—this is right where you belong."

"We'll see."

I glanced at the paper. "What's it say about the call in the end zone?"

"Not much," Rose replied. "Ellis says Grier pushed him. Grier claims it was the other way round."

"Now there's a shock for you."

Rose laughed. "Yeah, threw me for a loop too," she said.

"Anything else? Anything happen after the game?"

Rose shook her head. "Nothing. In fact, Grier says he had a good time, says everybody was nice to him ..." she peeked up. "Except the back judge."

I rubbed her neck and shoulders. "See there," I said, "nothing to worry about."

"Doesn't look like it," Rose sighed. "But I'm still nervous."

I leaned over and kissed her. "You know what?" I said, "the world needs more good football games."

She cocked an eyebrow. "What's that got to do with anything?"

"That game was so good—everybody was so wrapped up in it— they didn't have time to worry about the colored kid."

"Yeah, well, when the colored kids start showing up at schools," Rose Marie said, "I don't think they're going to be so intent on history and math."

"You never know," I said. "Maybe they'll be studying Wolfe or Rawlings that day; nobody'll ever notice."

I took my cup to the kitchen sink. "Listen," I said, "I'm going to head in early; see if I can find my way around the place, get settled in…. You'll tell Chris I said good-bye?"

"Sure," she replied. She set her cup down on the saucer. "You know we're going to have to talk with him, Jack. He can't be cheering for every colored athlete in the world … especially with our new neighbors."

I took a peek at my watch. "He starts school pretty soon," I said. "He'll make friends, start getting involved in clubs and classes—I'll think he'll find plenty of new distractions." I stacked my cup in the rack. "But he and I will have a little chat about the way he talks to you. That bothers me a lot more than cheering for Bobby Grier."

I bent down to kiss her head. "I'm looking for the right time to do that, okay?"

Rose patted the top of my hand. "Yeah," she said, "thanks." Then she lifted her cup and said, "Do good, Hall. I'm proud of you."

•   •   •   •

My first few days were lonely and awkward. I felt like a Class-C player pretending to be a major-league talent, and it must've been ten times a day that I wondered: *What in the world am I doing here?*

On Tuesday I edited a few wire service stories. Wednesday I rode over to Athens to do a five-hundred-word profile of a high school kid—a quarterback named Francis Tarkington—who was headed to Georgia next fall.

"I gotta tell you," I grumbled to Rose that night, "interviewing a seventeen-year-old named Francis—that is not why I moved to a major market."

Thursday I wrote about high school basketball, covering the two games nobody else wanted.

But then, on Friday the sixth, Bisher tossed me a bone. And that morning I was off to Mobile to cover the seventh annual Senior Bowl. Finally, I thought, I had something—a morsel, a crumb—this little appetizer that I could actually get my teeth into.

In the first quarter Joe Childress, an Auburn fullback, plowed into the end zone from the two, capping a sixty-six-yard drive. In the fourth quarter he did it again—on the same play—to score the game's only two touchdowns. Like the Sugar Bowl, this had been all about defense, and Don Goss, the monstrous, 265-pound tackle from SMU, had been the game's undisputed star.

Sunday morning I peeked out the living room window, watching for the paperboy. I tossed sections A, B, and C aside; I came to sports, turned to page three—and savored the half-page piece I'd written. I reread the lead three times. I read the play-by-play recap of the first scoring drive—the spectacular run by Auburn's Fob James, another good gain by SMU's Don McIlhenny—then I read it a second time. I loved the description of Hardy's fourth down pass to Schnellberger. And I'd worked in some nice quotes from Paul Brown, who'd coached the Southern squad that year.

It was a game of little consequence, but there had been a record crowd of nearly thirty-two thousand. There'd been drama; there'd been pain and conflict and mystery for sixty full minutes. And that meant I'd had the chance to exercise a few writing muscles that were starting to get flabby.

Maybe that's what Bisher had in mind.

Late Monday morning he tossed a Teletype page on my desk. "Southern Association just named last year's all-star team," he said. "Grand total of one Cracker made it. How 'bout grabbing a few quotes from him and getting me a hundred words by the end of the day."

"No problem," I said as he raced away.

I was scanning a bio of Earl Hersh, the Atlanta outfielder who'd made the all-star team, when a man approached my desk. He might have been six-one, maybe a hundred and sixty-five pounds—a high school quarterback in his playing days, I suspected. He had light wavy hair, a little too Tab Hunterish for me. He wore a pinstriped shirt, red tie, and a navy suit that must have set him back eighty bucks. He stood before my desk thumping a rolled-up paper against his thigh; he motioned toward the nameplate. "You Jack Hall?" he asked.

My eyes flashed to the nameplate, then back to my visitor. "Yeah," I said.

He dropped into the chair beside the desk and reached for my hand. "Dalton Dorsey," he announced, "I'm a reporter over in state and local."

"Yeah, I know your name," I replied, my mind thumbing through mental files trying to place him.

"I did a piece on Martin Luther King's old man," Dorsey said. "Ran alongside that thing you did on Montgomery."

"That's right," I recalled. "Nice piece."

"Yeah, thanks," Dorsey replied. Then he flattened the scrolled paper on top of my desk. "But let me tell you something, this right here," he tapped his finger on my coverage of the Senior Bowl. "This is first-rate. I'm telling you, this is gripping stuff you got here—especially for a 12-2 game that doesn't matter much to anybody."

"Thanks," I said, not entirely sure I'd received a compliment.

"And I like what you did on that Grady High School game the other night; you got a nice little style going there, Hall."

And then, just as quickly as he'd come, Dalton Dorsey got up to go. "I like it," he mumbled down the hall, "like it a lot."

I chuckled as I watched him hurry away, wondering to myself: *Who is this guy? And what's he want with me?*

Then I picked up the phone to call Earl Hersh.

• • • •

Tuesday morning I made my first official visit to Ponce de León Park, to meet Clyde King, the Crackers' manager. King had been hired in midseason the year before—in the midst of a disastrous campaign. He was eager to set the world right, and with Frank Di Prima, Bob Montag, and Jim Frey he felt like he had a team that'd get back to the top of the standings.

When I got back to the office Dalton Dorsey was waiting, feet propped on my desk, studying the latest issue of *Life* magazine. Anita Ekberg graced the front cover, and the way Dalton held the magazine it looked as if her head had been propped on his shoulders. I chuckled at the image. "Can I get you a cup of coffee, Miss Ekberg, maybe a doughnut?"

He lowered the magazine. "Nooo," he said. "I'm fine." And then, tossing the magazine onto the desk, he said, "Just wondering if you were up for lunch?"

I glanced at my watch, as if in the middle of January I could possibly be too busy. "Sure. Where'd you have in mind?"

"There's a little sandwich shop down on Poplar. Food's mediocre, owner's cranky most of the time...." Dorsey flashed his movie-star grin and slapped the desk. "But hey, since you're the new guy, I'm buying."

We pushed our way into the cramped restaurant. Hungry businessmen were still marveling over Tech's win and Bobby Dodd's incomparable genius. Lawyers had wandered over from the courthouse, and at the back two tables, a flock of secretaries pecked at tuna salad sandwiches.

Dorsey grabbed a spot in the middle of the room. We ordered, our young waitress growing nervous, wondering how she'd keep pace with the swelling crowd. The place hummed with conversation and business and friendship. Dalton scooted his chair up close to the table. "So, how do you like *The Atlanta Constitution*?" he began.

"I'm warming up to it. It's a little slow right now—being new, and this being the off-season for me. But I did the North-South game; that was a decent assignment. And the Crackers put Hersh on the all-star team—gave me a chance to talk a little baseball." I folded my arms on top of the table and said, "I'm not complaining."

"What about that thing you did last month in Montgomery?" Dorsey asked.

I looked at him, puzzled. "What about it?"

"Little different for a sportswriter," Dorsey said. "You like that kind of work?"

"It was a nice change of pace, I guess." I shrugged the subject away. "It was something McGill asked me do—what was I going to tell him?"

Our food arrived. Dalton reached for the ketchup. "You know, I had a look at that piece before they trimmed it. Too bad it couldn't have run the way you wrote it," he said. "That was solid journalism; you had this nice little narrative flair." He looked up, the perpetual smile in perfect position. "You ought to think about fiction," he teased.

I rolled my eyes. "I don't think so," I said. "I got no time, and no inclination, either."

Dorsey aimed a forkful of french fries right between my eyes. "We all got the inclination," he said. "There's half a manuscript in every desk drawer in the building."

"Not mine," I assured him.

"Not yet," he smirked.

The harried waitress refilled our tea, and Dalton reached for the sugar. "What do you think about things over there? In Montgomery, I mean?"

I glanced at Dalton as I chewed a fresh bite of a roast beef sandwich, wondering how, with all the things in the world there were to talk about, we'd landed on this.

I swallowed and said, "That's a tough question."

"Really? Why's that?"

I lowered my fork. "I don't know," I told him. "There's something going on over there ... something ... I don't know. I can't quite put my finger on it."

I stared into the iced tea for a second. "They've kept that thing going for over a month now. People are walking two, three miles a day—some a lot more than that. They've organized car pools, they've got a communications systems in place—and none of it was planned ahead of time." I smiled, imagining the old woman I'd talked to back in early December. "Maids and janitors over there—I'm telling you—they're more disciplined than the dad-gum Russian army. And they're paying a price for it too." I glanced outside, at all the busy people rushing back to work. "You know, it wouldn't have surprised me if it'd gone on for a week—even two. But a month?" I shook my head and said, "There's something to this I don't understand."

Dalton shoved his plate to the side. "What do you make of King?"

"I haven't figured him out either. The guy's painfully young; he's naive as a kitten. But he's smart, and you got to hand it to him: He's the one who's holding it together."

"Probably got some outside help, don't you think?"

"Wouldn't surprise me," I said. "But still, he's the guy they're following."

"You like him?"

I hesitated. But then, as casually I could sound, I said, "I guess so. Like I said, he's bright, pretty intense … the guy's a heck of a preacher." I folded my arms across the table. "And you know, at the end of the day, he's trying to do what's right. Whether or not it is … I don't know." I leaned back, angling my chin at Dalton. "Why are you so interested in this?"

He brushed the question aside. "His old man—Daddy King—he's an interesting guy." Dalton poised a french fry in the air. "From the little I know, I think he might see things differently than the kid."

"Uh-huh. So you're wanting to study the King family's dynamics?" I asked.

Dorsey popped a fry into his mouth. "Actually, I am," he said. "But here's where I'm really going with this...." He sat back in his chair. "Months ago, after the *Brown vs. Board* debacle, I did a couple of pieces looking at the local angle. I interviewed teachers, principals, a handful of politicians. In doing all that I crossed paths with a couple of reporters from up North." Dorsey shook his head with sad bemusement. "Jack, we're an absolute mystery to those guys. The papers up there, the TV networks, the magazines, they're walking around in the thickest dad-gum fog you can imagine. When they look at this whole race thing—when they see everybody all bent out of shape, when they hear the politicians shouting and hollering—it's like they woke up on Pluto."

"Yeah," I replied softly, "I've seen some of that too."

Our conversation rested there. Quietly, Dalton reached for his knife; he seesawed it back and forth between his thumb and forefinger, thinking and organizing his next few thoughts. The knife came still and Dalton said this: "So I was thinking, maybe you and I might do a little something on the side. Maybe we do a feature on the Martin Kings—senior and junior. We weave their story into this boycott thing. We look at both sides, give people a Southern view of what's going on—one that's calm and sensible." Dalton inched forward. The two of us sat there in the middle of this dumpy sandwich shop, practically nose to nose. "I got to believe that *Look* or *Life* would lap that stuff right up. And the fact is, they don't have anybody who can do it."

Dalton sat back, waiting for my reaction.

I backed away too, wondering how I'd gotten here. "I don't know,"
I began. "I like the idea, like the angle. From a story standpoint it
sounds pretty solid...."

"I hear a 'but' in there," Dorsey interjected.

"Might be a little far-fetched, don't you think, *Life* magazine?"

"No," Dalton shook his head. "It's not as crazy as you think, trust
me."

"Well, even if it's not, your neighbors may not appreciate that
kind of thing as much as I do." I ran a hand along my chin. "I'm
betting your friends aren't big Martin Luther King fans," I told him.
"And your coworkers over in state and local—I'm guessing they're not
cheering this boycott on. So even if we come up with a good story,
there might be a price for it you don't really want to pay."

Dorsey bobbed his head sympathetically. "I know where you're
going with that," he said, "I really do. But you know what? I think just
the opposite is true. We're talking about objective journalism here.
We're just laying out the cold, hard facts, laying out different points
of view. We'll put something out there that's well-conceived and well-
organized—and you and me—we'll make this thing a work of art."
Dorsey made a quarter turn; he crossed one leg over the other. "If we
write the article I got in mind, our neighbors'll thank us for it."

"I don't know, Dalton, this is touchy stuff."

"That's the point," he declared. "That's exactly why we need to
do it. Jack, there are people all over the country who think everybody
south of Baltimore's a drooling, tobacco-spitting moron. Somebody's
got to do something about that. Somebody's got to get the Southern
view out there." He tilted his tea glass in my direction. "Who else is
going to do it?" Then his gaze turned playful. "And let me tell you

something else: A byline in *Life* magazine ... that wouldn't hurt a man's career."

I tossed back a frown, as if to say, *Yeah, but what are the odds?* Then I leaned back, my mind taking its first turn around the concept. "It'd be perfect for a magazine," I thought out loud. "They'd give us four or five thousand words to tell the story; there'd be plenty of room for photography—and you know what's going on over there, it's a photographer's dream."

"Those big photos that *Life* and *Look* run ..." Dalton's tone tantalized. "Gripping stuff right there, Hall. I know a guy. We can pitch this to him, and I promise you, he'll listen."

"I don't know," I said to Dalton. "You think this is for real? You think your guy might honest to goodness go for it?"

"Yeah," Dorsey said. "I know for a fact that he's looking for writers who speak Southern."

I swirled the ice in the bottom of my glass, taking the measure of my new friend. "Why are you talking to me about this? I mean, we hardly know each other. If you need a partner, there've got to be ten guys you could go to."

"You did that piece on Montgomery," Dalton said. "And I've read everything you've written since you've been here. You got that nice narrative style...."

I rolled my eyes again.

"Look," he said, "I was curious about why McGill'd send a rookie sportswriter to cover a bus boycott. I asked around, did a little digging. Let's just say I think you'll bring some perspective to this that nobody else can, okay?"

I picked up a cold french fry, dragged it across my plate,

weighing these improbable circumstances. "Maybe I'll jot a couple of ideas down," I said. "We can compare notes in a day or two, see if we think there's anything there."

Dalton tossed a couple of bills on the table. "It's a date," he said.

•   •   •   •

The seasons had conspired against me. We were still weeks away from spring training, and more than a month from opening day. My brain had been fried by Atlanta's worst basketball, and my mind, like radar stationed on the Russian border, perpetually searched for a worthy target.

And in the winter months, there wasn't but one blip on the screen: Montgomery.

From the moment we left the restaurant a thousand thoughts swarmed my mind. There was a cast of complex characters. There was intrigue and conspiracy. There were secret meetings in smoke-filled rooms. There was danger, and the ever present threat of violence. Ideas, images, and story angles jumbled together—one thought led to the next, which led to another, which led to still one more—ideas feeding on themselves, yet multiplying in the process. I jotted them down as fast as they came, moving every thought from mind to paper, hurrying to make room for the next new thing.

That night I called Dorsey at home. "You know," I told him, "we could do a sidebar about accidental allies—about the white women who drive their maids to work. They don't know it—or maybe they do and they just don't care—but they're aiding and abetting the enemy. They're against the boycott—they hate everything about it—but they're making sure it works. You gotta love the irony, don't you?"

The next morning I found a note on my desk. I unfolded the scrap of paper that read: "Colored church over there's got a white pastor. Could be a nice twist???" It was signed DD.

I wandered over to the newsroom, found Dorsey, and held his note in the air. "This might be good," I said. "But that guy's from up North. He may not understand this any better than the *New York Times*."

Dorsey slumped in his chair. "True," he figured. He swiveled back and forth, his hand over his mouth. "What about white pastors versus colored pastors? Or white churches versus colored churches?" He tapped a finger to his chin. "I don't know," he said, "just a thought."

My mind raced back to Christmas Eve, to my vision of Powers and King bantering back and forth. "I like that," I said. "You might be on to something." I stuffed the paper into my pocket. "I don't know what, but let's keep thinking." I turned to go. "We'll compare notes tomorrow."

But neither of us could wait. That day, four more messages passed between his desk and mine: ideas, characters, possible sidebars, photos and captions.... Dorsey had thrown meat to my malnourished mind, and the juices flowed. He and I, together, with this one article, would reveal a whole new world to millions of *Life* readers.

• • • •

Rose balked at the idea. She pinched her furrowed brow, wondering what in the world I was thinking. "Have you lost your mind?" she asked. "Have you forgotten everything we've been through? Every-thing we talked about for the last year?"

I assured her that I hadn't. I promised, "We're going to give our side of the story; we're going to provide the perspective nobody's given; that nobody north of Richmond's ever heard. The whole idea," I explained, "is to give these people a few ideas they've never considered."

Rose reached over; she pressed her fingers into my scalp, moving her hand right to left and back and forth. "Somebody hit you on the head," she declared. "You have got to have temporary amnesia."

"No, Sally, nobody hit me in the head."

"Jack, please," she groaned, "stick to baseball, will you?"

I gave her time to simmer, and then ventured down a different path. "Let me ask you something," I said. "Where was I working a year ago?

"At the *Whitney Herald,*" she huffed.

"Circulation of about a hundred and two copies," I teased. "And where am I now?"

"*The Atlanta Constitution,*" Rose replied dutifully.

"Circulation considerably higher," I informed her. "And if we pull this off, if this article gets written and accepted, where will my byline be then?"

"*Life* magazine," she conceded, "circulation of about three billion."

"You're not that far off," I told her.

"I like the sound of it," she confessed, "but still ..."

"This is our side of the story, Rose. We're going to balance what the Northern press's been saying."

Rose twirled a lock of her hair, thinking. "And your friend's right, I suppose. You'll bring something to this that nobody else can." She pulled her knees to her chest, imagining my name in the world's most famous magazine. "Nobody could write this story the way you could, Hall; there's nobody who understands this better." She reached for her glass, "*Life* magazine …"

"Let's not get carried away," I warned. "This is just an idea, and it's a long shot at best."

"I know. But maybe you should do it, Jack. And if it doesn't work out this time, I don't know, maybe you should try again. This race mess … it's going to be around awhile."

For the next three nights Rose was waiting at the door, wanting to know if Dorsey and I had talked, if we'd reached his friend at *Life,* if we'd gotten our pitch letter put together.

And every night I tried to calm her. "We're working on it," I said. "Dalton's talked to the guy and he knows it's coming." I'd pour a couple of drinks. "We just need a little more time."

Rose Marie squeezed my hand, hoping, I think, to transfer her resolve into my body. "You need to get it there soon," she said. "They need to see that you're serious."

I met Dalton for breakfast Saturday morning. We finalized the outline, put the finishing touches on a cover letter, and picked two samples of our best work. The package was ready.

Monday morning he wandered over to my desk. He brushed his hands back and forth in triumph. "It's in the mail," he announced. "And I called my buddy up there—he's on the lookout."

I tossed a pencil onto the desk and sat back in my chair. I felt stupid—like some drip who thought he could date the homecoming queen. "All right," I sighed, "I guess now we wait."

Dalton raised his right hand, fingers crossed: "I'll let you know when I hear something." He turned to go.

"Hey, Dalton."

He stopped and looked back.

"What are we going to do if they say yes?"

He flashed his signature grin, raised both hands in the air, and said, "Heck if I know."

• • • •

The next day McGill wanted to see me.

I rapped at his door and stepped inside.

He looked weary. Slowly, he removed his glasses and slumped into his chair. "I thought you'd want to know. Last night Martin Luther King's home was bombed."

I heard the man clearly. He had pronounced every word perfectly, but they didn't register. I took two more steps into the office.

"You all right?" McGill asked.

"They bombed his house?"

"Nobody's hurt," he assured me. "There doesn't seem to be anything more than some property damage …" he said as he pitched his glasses on top of the desk. "But somebody's sent him a pretty strong message."

"Yeah." I peered up at McGill. "We sending anybody over there?"

He shook his head. "Wire service stuff'll do for now. But we're keeping an eye on it."

I nodded. "Thanks for letting me know." I held his eye. "You'll tell me if you hear anything more?"

He pressed his lips tight. "I will."

I rushed to see Dalton. He was on his feet, pacing a tight circle, phone pressed to his ear. He hung up the instant he saw me.

"You heard about King?" I asked.

"Two seconds ago," he replied. "I was just trying to call you."

Dalton fell into his chair. He rapped a pencil against the desk, thoughts weaving back and forth like pulled taffy. "You think you could talk to him?" he asked. "Would King give you an interview?"

I knew exactly where he was going. "I think so." I checked my watch. "I'll call him—call the church anyway—to see if I can run him down."

"I'll call my buddy at *Life*," Dalton said. "I'm going to tell him that we got the inside track on this, that we can get the story nobody else can."

"Get his deadlines," I called over my shoulder. "I got to do a basketball game Friday night, but I could be in Montgomery first thing Saturday—if I can get the meeting."

Dorsey reached for the phone. "Get the meeting," he yelled.

I left King a message, and then phoned Rose Marie.

"Jack, that's awful," she groaned. "How bad is it? Do they have any idea who's responsible?"

"I don't know anything," I explained. And then I told her that I had a call in to King, and that I hoped to go to Montgomery over the weekend.

"I'd like to go with you," Rose said. There was no pause or hesitation to think. "I'll have to check Chris's schedule to see what he's got going on, but if I can, I'd like to talk to his wife—you know ... since we went through this too."

I was quiet for a second, surprised by Rose's reaction. But I simply said, "That'd be nice. I'll mention it when I talk to him."

I had King on the phone five minutes later. He quickly recited the facts: He had been at church addressing a meeting, while his wife was at home with their infant daughter—a friend was there with them. A neighbor had seen a light-colored car pull up to the house; a man got out and tossed a bomb onto the front porch. "That's about all I know right now," King told me.

"Listen, I need to talk to you about this face-to-face," I replied. "And I need to do it Saturday morning; might need an hour, maybe a little more."

"I don't know," King said evasively. "I've got a sermon that needs polishing and...." An awkward silence hung between us. I let it lie there. Finally, he said, "I guess if you're willing to drive all that way— and if you're willing to give us a fair hearing—well, I'd be willing to talk."

"I may want to talk to a couple of others," I said. "Maybe Nixon and Abernathy?"

"I'll let them know," King offered. "And if you're going to talk with them, you might as well get with Fields and Hubbard too."

"And you'll set that up?" I asked.

"Yes," King said, but I sensed his uncertainty. "You're going to do this right? I'm not going to regret this, am I?"

"We're going to do it right," I told him. "I'm not promising you're going to like every word. I'm not even promising you'll like the story. But I promise we'll be fair."

"Can you get here by lunchtime?" King asked.

"Yeah," I said. I told him that Rose wanted to ride along. "We'll get an early start. I'll aim to be there before noon."

"Come to the house," King replied. "We'll start with a tour."

Dorsey had reached King's father. He'd found a handful of other Negro leaders too—the editor of the colored newspaper, a college president, a businessman. "They're all telling King to get his fanny back home," he told me, "to get his family out of Montgomery to someplace safe."

"That ain't gonna happen," I promised Dorsey. "The guy's too attached to those people; he identifies with them—and I'll tell you something else: He's got some strong opinions about leadership. He ain't going nowhere."

The Dorsey grin flared. "You gotta love it," he said. "Son versus father, leadership versus safety, the good of the cause versus the good of the family…. We got us a story here, Jack."

"And that ain't the half of it," I said. "We've got to talk to the mayor and the city council. We got to find somebody at the bus company…."

"And they've got some kind of committee trying to work this out," Dorsey added. "We'll need to talk to a few of them." He started scribbling out a list. He stopped and drummed his pen against the paper, "And you know who else?—the White Citizens' Council."

"Yeah, and a couple of cops, too—not the muckety-mucks—the guys who're actually on the streets."

Dorsey scribbled it all down. "We need to know if they've got any leads or suspects; what they're doing to investigate...."

I folded my arms and leaned into the wall. "Are we spinning our wheels here, Dalton? Has this thing got a prayer of finding its way into *Life* magazine?"

Dalton stopped writing. He looked up and said, "This story's got legs, Jack. It's going in a hundred different directions. It's been in *Time*, it's been on national television. And you, my friend, are a white reporter who's a personal friend of Martin Luther King." He gave the thought a little time to settle, then concluded: "I'd say that's a prayer."

I wandered back to my desk and scanned an AP story about the Sugar Ray Robinson–Bobo Olson fight; there was a story about an American figure skater who'd actually won a medal in the winter Olympics. I looked over the high school basketball assignments. I was bored with crummy basketball.

In Montgomery there was drama. There was more suspense on Holt Street than in Alfred Hitchcock's weirdest nightmare: The underdog protagonist, Martin King, challenging W. A. Gayle, the mayor of Montgomery. Colored maids dueled the big bus company. Janitors taunted the white business community. And King—the boy-pastor—shook a fist at history—a modern-day Don Quixote ... dreaming the absurd.

• • • •

I was perched on the top row of the Druid Hills High School bleachers. It was halftime, North Fulton was up by six, and looked to be pulling away. I scratched out an outline of what I'd write about the first half, racking my brain in search of an angle that'd make this interesting. I felt a hand on my shoulder, heard a familiar voice, and then saw Dalton Dorsey sliding down beside me.

"Geez, it took me ten minutes to find you," he complained. "There's got to be five hundred kids in here."

I glanced around the gym, laughing. "You're hard up on a Friday night," I said. "Surely you've got something better to do than this."

"Sadly," Dalton said, "I don't." He found room for his feet on the bench in front of him. "But no matter what happens here tonight, I do not plan to read a single word you write about it. Not even you could make me interested in this."

"You might want to keep it down," I said. "To everybody here, this is like the seventh game of the NBA finals."

"And if it was my kid," Dalton said, "I'd feel the same way."

Dalton put a hand on my shoulder; he squeezed it firmly and said, "But I didn't come here to talk about basketball."

I cocked my head, meeting his stare. "You heard something?" I said.

"Got a call about an hour ago."

I took a deep breath. Basketballs thumped on the hardwood floor. The hum of the crowd filled the white space around us. The scoreboard's red and green lights glowed.

"And …?" I stretched the word from the baseline to the foul line.

Dorsey's grin flared. "We're in," he said. He squeezed harder. "They want ten thousand words—and they want a draft in two weeks."

Glee and panic surged through a trillion pores. "Are you serious?" I stared at Dalton, my mouth gaped wide. "I thought there was a chance but ... I didn't really think this'd come through."

"It's a wacky world," Dalton answered. "They're sending a photographer; we'll have to work out a few details with him. But you can tell your buddy Martin King that unless we mess this up, his story'll be in *Life*, and it'll be there soon."

I sat there, suddenly deaf to the commotion around me. Dampness welled in my eyes and I laughed nervously. "I can't believe this," I told Dalton. "I can't believe this honest to goodness came through."

Dalton stood. "You better believe it," he said. Then, smiling, he added: "And you better not screw it up, you hear?"

I fired back a flippant glare: "It ain't me I'm worried about."

"No," Dalton smirked, "me neither." He extended his hand and said, "Congratulations, Jack."

"Yeah, you too." Our grip lingered, both of us gradually tightening our grasp. "We'll talk Sunday, okay?"

Dalton bobbed his head and started down the stairs.

• • • •

Rose and Chris and I piled into the car. With the Ford's heater straining to catch up to the cold, we sipped coffee and hot chocolate, and in the last hours of a chilly Saturday morning, the three of us headed west toward Alabama.

Rose Marie read out loud from Friday's paper, mostly to pass the time and to spark some conversation, but by the time we'd reached Newnan we'd exhausted yesterday's news and rode quietly for a while.

Then, for no more reason than to break the silence, I said, "I'm surprised you want to do this."

"Why's that?" Rose wondered.

"You're not exactly a big fan of colored protests," I said.

Rose brushed a strand of hair from her eye. "Yeah, but this …" she angled her face into the sun, "this is different. Nobody should be attacked in their own home. They've got that little girl there.…" Rose glanced at the passing scenery. "I wish they'd stop this boycotting business—it's all nonsense, if you ask me—but I don't know," Rose said. "I just feel like I'm the only one who knows what she's feeling right now, like I'm the only woman in the world who possibly could." She reached to her hair again, twirled it around a finger. "I can't stand a single thing these people are doing," she said with a sad chuckle. "But I feel like I owe her something … you know what I mean?"

"Yeah," I said, "I do."

Rose looked outside again. "I'm going to ask her if there's anything she wants the world to know—if there's anything she wants to see in this article. Is that all right?"

I stared at her, mouth sprung wide, my wife piling one surprise on top of the other. "You turning into a reporter?"

"No," Rose shook her head, "I'm just going to talk to her, mom-to-mom. I'm going to ask her plainly if there's anything she wants people to know—as a mother."

"Uh-huh," I said, my gaze lingering. "I love the idea, Rose, but—" my puzzled stare persisted.

"What?" she asked.

"You realize that whatever she says—if we use it—it's going to cause people to feel sorry for her. And once they do that, they're going to cozy up to her cause."

Rose turned and crumpled her brow. "I don't intend to utter one word about her cause," she said.

My stare persisted.

"Look, Jack, everybody knows these people are troublemakers, but that doesn't give anybody the right to attack a baby girl."

We pulled to the curb at 309 South Jackson Street. It was 11:50.

New windows had replaced the shattered glass, but soot scarred the front of this family's home, and I believed—for just a second or two—that I'd sniffed the lingering traces of gunpowder. A paint-splattered tarp covered the south end of the front porch; there were half-full buckets of eggshell white stacked against the wall, and a stepladder leaned into the porch railing.

Rose Marie stood before the house, frozen for a moment, squirming under thoughts of our own past. We moved up the nicked and charred concrete steps. A baby fussed in the distance and music—gospel, I think—seeped outside. I looked at Rose and then at Chris; I took a deep breath, then rapped on the door. A second later the music went silent, footsteps clambered toward us, and the door swung open.

King wore dark slacks, a long-sleeve shirt—white and pressed razor sharp. His greeting was cordial, but I wouldn't have called it hearty. He and I reached for one another's hand, I introduced him to my family, and we stepped inside.

His wife stood in the center of the room waiting, her baby

daughter resting quietly now against her shoulder. The house was neat and nicely furnished, not much different from mine.

Coretta King, with a gracious but guarded smile, motioned us to the nearest chairs. We sat and our time began with small talk: Martin and Coretta King and their infant daughter, Yolanda—with Jack, Rose Marie, and Chris Hall—two families, one black and one white—bound together by the same violence.

After a few minutes, King took us outside. He showed us the spot where the bomb exploded; splintered wood and broken glass were piled nearby. Coretta King told us that she and a friend had been in the front room. "I heard a thud on the porch," she explained. "We were afraid it might be something dangerous, so we hurried toward the back of the house, to where the baby was." Her eyes dampened as she struggled to describe the sound—the suddenness of it, the shock of the blast, the instant when her heart was strangled still by panic.

Rose put a hand to Coretta King's back. She rubbed a gentle, small circle. "I know, I know," she said. "I once heard the very same sound."

Coretta King held her child tighter. She swayed back and forth, rocking the baby to sleep, and she told us about the sick sensation that had bubbled up inside her—the burst of queasiness, the buckling of her knees, the surge of terror....

"Yes ..." Rose stretched the word with a soothing tone.

King's wife described a flood of despair, and as I listened I thought: She needs this—to tell another woman, a mom—how she'd grabbed the child and clutched her close, frantic to protect her helpless infant daughter.

We stepped to the end of the front porch. Chris stood next to King, and I noticed he was nearly the same height as the Negro pastor. He crouched down to pick up a stray shard of broken glass. "I wish I'd been here to help you," he said. He rolled the glass in his fingers, calling back to mind the worst night of his own short life. Then, with an edge to his voice that I hadn't heard before, he added: "I wish I could help you find whoever did this."

Martin King laid a finger to his chin. "You know," he said, "I appreciate that. I'm sorry about what happened to you, too, but people like us—people who've been the victims of violence—we got to find a way to make friends out of enemies." King looped an arm over my son's shoulder. "If we're really going to change anything, we got to win hearts, not just battles. Violence," he told my son, "… just gets us more violence."

Chris met King's eyes. I don't think he was too sure about what the pastor had said, but then—probably to be polite—he nodded his agreement.

We stepped back inside. King and I retreated to his study where sandwiches and tea were waiting. We eased into our conversation, catching up on things since we'd last been together. I learned about negotiations with the city and the bus company. He told me more about the bombing, about the reaction of the police, the mayor, and the colored community. I busily jotted it all down.

I told him that Dalton Dorsey had been talking to his father. King threw his head back and groaned. "Your friend will get an earful, I'm afraid."

I chuckled at the reaction. "Why's that?"

"My father … let's just say he's concerned," King explained. "He'd like us to come back to Atlanta, at least for a while, and he's never been stingy with his opinion."

We talked for an hour more, and then King glanced at his watch. "I've got to spend some time with tomorrow's sermon," he explained, "and you're due at Abernathy's in ten minutes."

I flipped my pad closed. "I appreciate the time," I told him.

King hunched forward. He clasped his hands between his knees and said, "You're going to handle this right, aren't you?"

"I told you I would," I said.

"I know," King replied. He gnawed his lip and rubbed his hands back and forth nervously.

"Look," I told him, "when we first met we agreed to be honest with one another. So I'm going to be up front with you: One of the reasons I'm writing a story for *Life* is because I know you, because I can pick up the phone and get in to see you on a Saturday morning. The last thing I need right now is to screw up my relationship with you." King put a hand to the back of his neck, considering for the first time, I think, that his friendship might be an asset. "At the same time," I continued, "*you're* getting a story in *Life* too, and that's because you know me. If we're smart, this can work out for both of us. Through me, you get access to millions of people—mostly white—who don't have a clue about what you're doing. Through you, I get the inside track on a story that's starting to get interesting." I let this simmer for a while: "If we trust each other, we've both got plenty to gain. If we don't, there's a whole bunch we could lose."

We stood and moved toward the door, King's arms now folded across his chest, head down, mind pondering the stakes before us. He reached for my hand. "We ought to try to build that trust."

We headed to First Baptist Church, where I met with Ralph Abernathy, E. D. Nixon, and Uriah Fields. Chris and Rose waited in the sanctuary with homework and magazines. Ninety minutes later, the three of us were back on the road and headed for home.

"You get what you were looking for?" Rose asked.

"I got plenty to start," I said. "If I need anything else, I think I can get it by phone."

"But you're coming back, aren't you?"

"I don't think there's time," I told her.

Rose twisted round, swinging her left knee onto the seat. "This is going to be hard to write, isn't it?"

I shrugged casually. "I don't know; it's going to be longer than most of the stuff I do, and it might take more time to organize."

"Yeah, but that's not what I mean."

I looked at her, brows peaked.

"These people don't fit the mold," she said. "They're smart, they speak well, they're neat and clean…. They're not what most people have in mind when they think about colored people."

"True," I replied. "But how's that complicate the story?"

She laid her arm over the back of the seat, thinking back on her time with Coretta King. "You're going to have to decide who to write about," Rose answered. "Is the article going to be about the handful of pastors who went to college? About the one colored woman on the face of the planet who went to some conservatory and plays the violin? Or about the maids and sweaty janitors who actually ride city buses, the ones who'll be rubbing up against white people after a full day's work …? The ones who—"

"Nobody's wanting to rub against white people," I interrupted.

"They just want to sit in an empty seat on an empty row—if it happens to be available."

"Yeah," Rose said, "for now."

"It's not going to kill anybody," Chris chimed in from the backseat.

"Oh Chris, not now," Rose groaned.

"I'm just saying …"

"You need to say a little less," she snapped, "at least on this subject."

"At least to you," Chris muttered.

•　•　•　•

Dorsey visited with King's father. He interviewed C. A. Scott, the editor of Atlanta's Negro newspaper; he tracked down Rufus Clement, president of Atlanta University, and Benjamin Mays, Clement's counterpart at Morehouse. He also spoke to T. M. Alexander, a Negro businessman. These were friends and confidants of Daddy King's, and men who'd know what was on the pastor's mind.

At the same time, I got hold of W. A. Gayle, the mayor of Montgomery. Later, I spent two hours grilling Clyde Sellers, the police commissioner and a member of the committee Gayle had assembled. And then, just before dinner, I got in an hour with Luther Ingalls, head of the White Citizens' Council.

Dalton and I revised the outline and decided who was going to write which sections. We agreed to hand off our work to one another, that each of us could change anything, and that we both had to be satisfied with every word and comma. For the next three days we swapped drafts. Over lunch and late at night, we scribbled notes in the margins. We fought each other to save the good stuff, and—sometimes reluctantly—agreed to toss the bad.

Lying in bed Thursday night, reading the fourth draft, I smiled for the first time in days: I was starting to like the article that was coming together.

On Friday, Dalton used a vacation day and drove to Montgomery. He met a photographer there who, over a grueling weekend, captured the heart of King's fledgling movement—and of those who opposed it. We met at the office late Sunday afternoon. We made one more round of changes; we typed our sixth draft; we each proofed it three times. And then, with high hopes, and with feet that felt colder than a glacier, we deposited it in a nine-by-twelve manila envelope. We hurried across Marietta Street to the post office and released our creation to a copy editor neither of us had ever seen before—at *Life* magazine.

●　　●　　●　　●

Two weeks later, on Thursday evening, February 17, Rose brewed fresh coffee; she set desserts out on the dining room table and positioned three borrowed ice buckets in each corner to chill champagne that was, for a lowly sportswriter, way too pricey. Sinatra sang in the background, followed by Dean Martin and Perry Como. Later, when the mood had grown more festive, we'd moved on to Elvis Presley and the Platters.

At 6:45 Dalton Dorsey arrived with his wife, Natalie, and their fourteen-year-old daughter, Ansley. Under his arm he carried a box, in the box was an oversized envelope, and in that envelope were twenty advance copies of *Life* magazine. They had arrived that afternoon, sent from New York, airmail and special delivery to Dorsey's home. We gathered in the living room—his family and mine. We surrounded the coffee table—the adults perched on the edge of the sofa and chairs, the kids kneeling—all of us too nervous to breathe.

Dalton handed the box to me. "Go ahead," he said. "You do the honors."

I shook my head, "I'm too nervous. You do it."

Dalton ran a key over the packing tape. He pried the box open and peered inside. Slowly, he withdrew the envelope. He ran his thumb under the flap, cracked it open, and peeked inside. He glanced around the room, his hands trembling, and then withdrew the magazines. Claire Bloom adorned the cover. She gazed straight ahead, her left hand held over her heart—in costume as Lady Anne in the new film *Richard III*.

Dorsey handled the magazines as if each one was an original masterpiece. He laid them on the table. Gently, he opened the top copy to the table of contents, ran his finger down the lines, and then—without wrinkling a single page—turned to page thirty-two. King's image burst off the left-hand page. He stood, ascended in the pulpit of the Holt Street Church, his hand stretched out over the congregation, as if bestowing his blessing on them.

Mayor Gayle faced him from the right-hand page. He leaned across his desk, stone-faced and defiant—a man who wasn't about to concede an inch of anything.

The headline, set in forty-eight-point Gotham, blared: "Nothing Is Black and White in Montgomery." A subhead ran underneath, talking about the length of the boycott and the hardening resolve on both sides.

Dalton hovered over the table, a man rejoicing in his possession of just-acquired art. "Well, there you have it," he murmured.

"Heck of a spread." I reached for a magazine. Slowly, I turned the pages, scanning photos, captions, and subheads. I read a sentence here and there, recalling the familiar words, and enjoying them as much now as I had when I wrote them. And for five full seconds, my eyes would not budge from the byline.

The doorbell rang. Rose hurried to greet Alan and Doris Emerson. Dale and Patty Parsons rushed up the driveway right behind them. Carson and Betty Powers trailed a minute later. And then two more couples—friends of the Dorseys—followed.

That night we drank champagne, we feasted on fancy cheese and tiny crustless sandwiches, we laughed for three solid hours, and Dalton Dorsey and I bathed in the adoration of our friends. Around eight o'clock Carson Powers stood before the fireplace. He tapped his glass and waited for the room to come still. "I'd like to propose a toast," he said. He raised his glass: "To Jack Hall and Dalton Dorsey, on their extraordinary accomplishment ..." Powers scanned the crowd, his pastor's smile the perfect punctuation. "To our friends who've used their talents brilliantly, and for the good of their neighbors."

A chorus of "hear-hear" rang through the room. Glasses clinked, and kind-hearted people reveled in this moment of good fortune. After the toast, Powers continued. "With your indulgence," he said to the small gathering, "I'd like to invite the authors to tell us a little about what they've done, and to read their composition."

"We insist," Alan Emerson cried. The others egged us on with decorous applause.

I waved them off. "No, no, no, it's way too long."

"And besides ..." Dalton cautioned, "there's a lot in there that'd put a damper on just about any party."

"Why don't you each read a favorite part?" Rose Marie called from the dining room, "Just a couple of paragraphs."

I looked at Dalton—who craves the limelight more than a movie star—and the two of us stepped to the mantle. I told my friends that I'd met Martin Luther King on two occasions; that he was young and still unseasoned. "But he's smart," I told them. "And when this guy makes a speech, I promise you: There's nobody yawning."

"Wish I could make the same claim," Powers teased.

I read a passage where King described his hope for justice and his thoughts on the meaning of the "beloved community."

Dalton read an excerpt about how, in Gayle's opinion, the Negroes' demands were not only illogical but—the mayor pointedly explained—illegal. And there was nothing he could do.

As I read, and as I listened to Dalton, I liked what I heard. The story was tough, but the words, like the champagne, went down with a warm, soothing sensation. This, I thought, was good. It weaves two stories together. King and the Negroes' resentment was almost audible. You could feel it in King's tone and in the fire of Abernathy's arguments. At the same time, Gayle's anger radiated off the page. The councilmen, the cops, and the bus company managers—as Dalton read the words, you sensed their fear—like wounded animals backed in a corner. With no warning, these men had been forced to defend a hundred years of history. The world suddenly looked to them to explain the status quo and to champion the only way of life the South had ever known.

Somehow, both sides made sense. You couldn't help but sympathize with King. And yet, Gayle's anger seemed so well founded. Readers—at least those with the capacity to hold two thoughts at one time—might see the world from another's perspective, I thought.

Later, as our friends mingled, I said to Dalton, "It's good, isn't it?"

He stared into his glass for a second. Then he said, "It is." He put a hand on my shoulder. "I'll never know how we pulled this off, but it is, undeniably, one fine piece of work."

I sipped the bubbling champagne and gazed out toward our friends. "Tomorrow night I'm covering the Avondale High School basketball game. From *Life* magazine to one of the worst sporting events any human has ever seen—in less than twenty-four hours."

Dalton's grin blazed. "Life's grand, ain't it?"

I raised my glass over the assembly—our neighbors talking together, laughing—gathered in my home to pay us homage. "You know what?" I said. "It's getting there."

I wandered over to Alan Emerson. He sat in my favorite chair, feet propped on the footstool, reading the magazine. "You know, you can take that home," I told him.

He looked up and closed the magazine. "Jack, this is good. I had no idea you could do this."

I laughed reflexively. "That's funny coming from the guy who's restructuring Delta Air Lines' entire business."

"I'm serious," Alan insisted. He reopened the magazine, eyes skimming the pages. "This is as good as anything I've ever read." A smile cracked his lips. "I live across the street from dad-gum Herman Wouk."

"Well … that might be a stretch."

Alan read a few more lines, shaking his head, as if trying to comprehend Einstein-level math. "I've never known anybody who wrote for *Life* magazine. I got to tell you, I'm impressed."

I rolled my eyes, uncomfortable with the praise. "Just sentences and paragraphs," I said, "along with some darn nice photos."

Dalton walked up beside us, a half-empty bottle dangling from his left hand. "Pour you boys a refill?" We both declined, and then Dalton folded himself onto Alan's footstool. "This is nice," he said. "I can't help but think there ought to be more parties in my honor."

"At least once a month," I deadpanned. "It'd only be right."

Alan held the magazine on his lap. "So you're the brains behind this?" he said to Dalton.

"No," Dalton laughed. "The instigator, maybe, but not the brains. Jack did most of the heavy lifting."

Alan thumbed his way through the magazine. "How many people get this thing?" he asked. "Any idea?"

"It's a bunch," Dalton answered. "I'd put it in the neighborhood of five million—maybe more."

Alan froze. He looked at me, his eyes bulging. "Five million! Good grief. This article—these words and sentences you just strung together—they're going to be read by five million people?"

"Actually it'll be a lot more'n that," Dalton said.

Alan turned.

"You got to factor in the pass-along rate," he explained. "They figure that maybe six to eight people read each magazine. You go to the doctor's office, they've got a copy in the waiting room; there might be twenty or thirty people who pick it up. One in Jack's house is going to be read by at least two, but they have lots of company so it's probably more like three or four." Dalton tapped at the magazine, "That issue right there, by this time next week more than forty million humans will have seen it." Dalton tipped his glass Alan's way. "If you stopped to think about it, it'd scare the daylights out of you."

Alan stared at Claire Bloom's photo. He looked up—at me and then at Dalton. "Forty million people … that, gentlemen, is some honest-to-goodness power."

The last of our guests had gone. The dishes had been cleaned and stacked. And my wife and I—after one of the best nights we'd ever had—were due for a contented rest.

We looked in on Chris, who had fallen asleep, fully clothed and breathing deep, on top of the twin bed in his darkened room. Rose slipped inside. She rubbed his back gently, "Come on, sweetie," she said. "Let's get you ready for bed."

Chris groaned, perfectly content to stay right where he was. I put a hand to his shoulder. "Come on, pal, don't you want to get into your PJ's; slip under the covers?"

He sat up, rubbing his eyes. "All right," he mumbled. He hesitated and then stumbled to his dresser, opened the top drawer, and rummaged round for his pajamas. Then, standing there, slowly coming alert, he said, "You think the Negroes ought to be able to sit wherever they want?"

"Sure," I said, "they pay their fare just like everybody else; if there's a seat I think they ought to be able to take it. But let's talk about it later; it's time for bed now."

"What do you think?" he asked his mother.

Rose stumbled into a reply. "Well, I-I-I think your dad's right," she said. "There's no reason why they can't adjust the colored section if there's room." She smiled impatiently and gestured down the hall. "You need to brush your teeth."

Chris plopped down on the bed, pajamas slung over his shoulder. "What do you think is going to happen if you sit beside a colored person?" he asked Rose. "I mean, you act like you're going to catch rabies or something. I just don't get it."

Rose Marie expelled a long and withered breath. "Come on," she said. "It's late."

Chris stood and raised both hands into the air. "What do you have against colored people?"

"That's not fair," Rose snapped. "You know good and well I don't have anything—"

"As long as they sit in the back of the bus, as long as they go to their own schools, as long as they play on their own baseball teams...." He was wide-awake now, and the words were sharp, meant to tear with a jagged edge.

Rose buried her face in her hands. "Come on, Chris, we've got to get ready for bed."

The boy stormed past his mother, racing for the bathroom. "We ought to be helping 'em sit wherever they want to," he said seething. "We ought to be on the right side for once."

"Chris ..." Rose groaned after him.

The bathroom door slammed—and my wife's shoulders sagged.

She reached up, kneading her forehead, tears pooling in her eyes. "I just don't.… This kid is a broken record," she whined. "This just goes on and on and on.….."

"He's looking for somewhere to vent," I guessed. "And you'd be the safest place."

"Yeah, well, I hate it," she moaned. "Whenever this comes up he turns on me; he makes me the bad guy, he acts like everything's all my fault." Rose pulled a couple of tissues from a box and blotted the tears. "He's moving further and further away from me, Jack. He's going to be gone soon."

"He's just feeling his own way. It's hard to be fourteen—especially these days—and especially when you've been through all he has." I moved to Rose and wrapped my arms around her. "But that's no excuse for talking to you that way." I pressed her tight against me. "You go on to bed. I'll wait here and have a talk with him."

"Don't make it worse, okay?"

"I'm not going to make it worse. We're just going to have a little chat, man to man."

Rose fisted both hands and gently drove them into my shoulders. "I don't want him moving further away, Jack. I want my little boy back where he belongs."

•   •   •   •

For two weeks the praise poured in.

Our editor at *Life* had seen "a ton of mail," and it was, he told Dalton, the perfect blend. Plenty of people hated it, and we'd stirred up more than our fair share of cancelled subscriptions. But overall, the response had been warm, and almost everybody—on both sides of the issue—was grateful for a peek behind the curtain. "I love it when that happens," he told Dalton. "It means we handled the story just right."

McGill was impressed too. And the guys in Sports jabbed with a nice mix of sarcasm and admiration.

Chapter 6

Spring training had finally started, and the Crackers were itching to redeem themselves. I had my feet propped on the corner of the desk, scratching out notes for a story: "Outlook for the '56 Season." My tie was pulled to the second button, shirt cuffs were two turns toward the elbow, and a bottle of Coke was within easy reach.

"Looks like a tough way to make a living," a familiar voice observed.

Alan Emerson stood before my desk. His suit was pressed to creases that could have sliced cheese; he had the top two buttons of his suit fastened, tie knot centered perfectly, overcoat slung over his arm—you'd have sworn he stepped straight out of *Esquire*.

I glanced back to my notes, as if his presence were as common as a typewriter's. "This is a picture of hard labor," I replied. "If you're Herman Wouk."

"Uh-huh," he muttered quietly.

I peered up, my smile sprawling. "What in the world are you doing here?"

"Had an appointment downtown," Alan replied. "Thought I'd take a chance, see if you had time for lunch."

I glanced at my watch, then back to the outline. And then, grateful that my friend had made the effort, I tossed the pad aside. "You bet," I told him, "that'd be nice."

"What about your buddy Dalton, think he'd like to tag along?" Alan asked.

"Might," I said, a little surprised, "Let's swing by his desk and see."

The three of us talked baseball for ten minutes, and politics for five more before our food arrived. Alan unfurled his silverware and laid the napkin across his lap. "You working on anything interesting?" he asked Dalton.

"It's all interesting," Dalton replied with a flourish. He tilted his chin impishly. "That's the job ... to make life interesting."

Alan pulled a french fry through a puddle of ketchup. "So what are you making interesting right now?"

Dalton rapped three packets of sugar against the table. "When you wake up tomorrow—you, my friend—will be enthralled by the story of E. E. Rogers, a thirty-seven-year-old teacher who set fire to a school building up in Hall county." He dumped the sugar into his tea, his smile widening with thoughts of the story. "This loony bird wants to run for school superintendent; this was his way of campaigning for new buildings up there."

Alan laughed, not quite sure he knew what to make of Dalton Dorsey. "That'd be the first thing I'd turn to," he said. Then Alan turned to me. "What about you?"

"Ah!" I replied, "We are counting down the days to opening day and to the only season that truly matters." That swung the discussion back to baseball—to the Crackers, Cardinals, and Braves—to our hopes for the coming season. And then, for a few minutes, food supplanted conversation.

Alan gripped his hamburger with both hands. I noticed his eyes cutting back and forth between Dalton and me. He looked restless. He dabbed at his mouth with the napkin, then set it back down. And then, after about three minutes of that, he said: "Listen, I had an idea I wanted to run past you guys … just to see what you think."

Dalton and I swapped glances.

"Sure," Dalton said, "what's on your mind?"

Alan reached under his seat; he opened his briefcase and pulled out a copy of *Life* magazine. He paged to our article and said, "I keep thinking about this. I can't get over the fact that forty million people might read your article."

"I told you not to dwell on that," Dalton teased.

Alan smiled and leafed through a page or two. "I asked the guys in our ad department what a full page ad in this thing costs. I checked newsstand sales and double-checked the circulation figures." He looked at me and then at Dalton. "This thing's got to be a money machine."

"The owners aren't worried about next month's rent," Dalton said, "I'm pretty sure about that."

Alan flipped back to our article. "I'm obviously not an expert," he said, "but it seems to me like you guys are pretty good at this." He looked at Dalton, grinning, "… like you know how to make life interesting."

Dalton shrugged and said, "We're okay. We haven't been fired yet." He tossed me a prankish glance, "… at least I haven't."

"It's not just words and paragraphs," Alan said. "It's ... I don't know, it's more engaging than that. This thing draws people in, makes 'em want to read more—to see what happens next."

"Look, you're nice to say that," I replied, "but you got to understand something." I poked at the magazine. "That actually is a good story. I mean, it's got all the elements: heroes, villains, conflict.... There's more tension in Montgomery right now than in a midnight visit to Red Square. I tossed my friend an impish smile. "It didn't take Herman Wouk to throw that one together."

"You guys are selling yourselves short," Alan argued. "Both of you have—"

"Whoa, whoa, whoa ..." Dalton waved a hand in the air. "You were going to run an idea by us?"

"Yeah," Alan nodded. He laid the magazine flat on the table, leaned forward, and said, "I know this is crazy, and I know it's coming straight out of the blue, but what would you guys think about starting a magazine?"

His head swiveled from me to Dalton and then back again. "You guys'd take care of all the content. I'd take care of the business."

Dalton and I looked at one another. We stared down at our plates, then off into the distance—but neither of us found an answer.

"It might be ridiculous," Alan said. "But the timing for something like this ... I don't know. With everything that's going on right now, it seems like the South could use a first-rate magazine. We need a voice—a calm, articulate, intelligent voice." His eyes traveled from me to Dalton, down to the magazine, then up again: "Why not you guys?"

We sat quietly for a few seconds, then Alan added: "Neither of you knows me very well, but I'll let you in on something: I'm as good at business as you are at writing. I don't mean to sound like a jerk; I just want you know: I can put this thing together."

Dalton and I stayed mute as rocks, forcing Alan to fill the void. "Like I said, we don't really know each other, and a thing like this, we'd be morons to just jump into it...." He closed the magazine and tossed it back into the briefcase. "So why don't you guys think about it? If it sounds interesting—even a little bit—why don't we get together ... I don't know ... maybe once a month, do a little brainstorming, talk about the kind of magazine we'd like to see.... That'd give us a chance to see if we get along, to see if we want to do the same things. You know, date a little bit before anybody gets married."

I grabbed the pepper shaker; I rolled it back and forth between my hands, tapped it gently on the table, trying to gather up some kind of reply. I had been a newspaperman since my junior year in college. I had never thought about anything else, had never aspired to be anything more. And yet, for some impulsive and seemingly capricious reason I said, "I don't suppose it'd hurt to talk."

Dalton dragged his fork through a remnant of runny coleslaw. "I honestly don't see myself ever leaving the paper," he said. "But it'd be fun to get together with you guys." He glanced up, flipped a palm to the air and said, "I wouldn't mind doing a little brainstorming."

Alan handed our waitress the check and enough cash to cover it. "You know, you're right," he said to Dalton. "If nothing else, it'd just be fun."

●　●　●　●

We chose a little diner on the west side of Fourteenth Street. We'd meet on the second Saturday of the month; we'd begin at seven and finish no later than eight-thirty. And we promised that we would, without fail, bring ten ideas. Good or bad, it didn't matter; we wanted quantity. We wanted raw material, we wanted this massive lump of clay to shape and mold, and then, much later if ever, we'd chip away what didn't belong.

In the months that followed we'd bring other magazines and pick them apart—page-by-every-blessed-page—ripping out things we liked, listing ideas we wanted to steal and polish, and making note of the ugly, stupid, or hackneyed things we were desperate to avoid.

We listed advertisers who'd drool over this thing we imagined. And we listed investors too—corporations and businessmen—whose prosperity was tied to the eleven states of the old Confederacy. We talked about readers and demographics. But mostly we talked about the South—the things we loved most about the place where we lived—and the things we wished others loved too.

Alan picked me up at six fifty on Saturday, March 10. I remember how cold it was, that winter had bared its teeth one last time the way it always does when you least expect it. Alan tapped his horn lightly and I'd rushed to his car. It was, mercifully, a short drive. The two of us hurried from the freezing-cold car into the warm restaurant. Bells on the door jangled behind us as we shucked coats and hats and hung them on a rack near the counter.

Dalton was already there, waiting in the third booth down the left-side aisle. Alan and I still shivered as a pretty waitress poured coffee that'd provide the cure. I cradled the mug to thaw my fingers. I looked around, taking careful inventory of the customers, waitresses, and cashier. We couldn't have picked a better spot. This place was wide-awake. We were surrounded by the people we wanted to talk to. We were engulfed by smells that spark the imagination: coffee, bacon, and fresh-baked biscuits. And the ambient sounds—the clinks and clatters of a busy diner—these are the things that kindle the best conversations.

Right here—this was a slice of the life we loved.

That first morning, Alan Emerson leaped into the discussion. There was barely a word of small talk—I hadn't even stirred the cream into my coffee when he said, "Gentlemen, if I were going to create the perfect Southern magazine, I'd have a section in every issue about how darn beautiful the place is: the mountains and beaches—and the pine forests that stretch to eternity...." I still remember his eyes—they cut from me to Dalton—alive, and with a tiniest touch of moisture. "If we did it right," Alan said, "we'd bring people to tears with that stuff."

"That's a nice start," Dalton replied. "And you know something, we ought to lobby Congress ... we ought to get those old boys to pass a law that says you cannot die till you've spent three days in Asheville, North Carolina."

I chuckled. "I know you're kidding," I said. "But wouldn't that be a great publicity stunt—if we got thousands of people to write their congressmen asking for something like that? We'd have newspapers and TV stations all over it."

"Maybe even a few from up North," Alan said.

"We could get a little campaign going," Dalton said, picking up steam. "Get every human in western Carolina to write their representative; see how many letters they'd send."

"And we could get a little competition cooking," I said. "Different towns, different regions—see if they can outdo whoever came before them; see who believes their spot's the most beautiful."

"Geez, we'd create a name for ourselves right off the bat," Alan replied.

"And we'd have a bunch of folks calling in for a free trial issue," Dalton answered.

A gleam sparked in Alan Emerson's eye, and he jotted it all down in his gold spiral notebook.

"Maybe we call that section 'Places to See Before You Die,'" I suggested. "And we begin by telling people that they'll die poor if they never visit the Smokey Mountains, if they never see the French Broad River, or a town square that's quainter than a gingerbread house."

"And you know what? They *will* die poor," Dalton went on, "if they never breathe air that's so pure and clean…" a grin squirmed from between his lips, "…that not even you could describe it. I'm telling you—and this is God's honest truth—in October, if you stand outdoors in Asheville, North Carolina, you trip the circuits on the five human senses." He swirled his coffee slowly, images of fog-shrouded mountains lazing their way through his imagination. His tone had become nostalgic, revealing a sentimental side I'd never seen before. "No creature that perceives color or that has any conception of beauty can fully bear that sight," he told us.

Dalton hitched his shoulders and leaned forward. "I swear it makes you want to cry—because when you stand there, when these enormous hills surround you and they're all blazing in three thousand shades of red and orange and yellow—when you see a fifty-foot waterfall tumble down to a spring-fed river, when you hear the water rushing over rocks and boulders, when you stand two thousand feet above the earth and see the lazy bends in the French Broad...." Dalton had to pause. "I'm telling you," he finally said, "it all wells up inside and it has got to find a place to spill over."

We sat quietly for a while, feeling clumsy and surprised that this had become so honest so soon. But we were not disappointed.

"If we were going to put a magazine together," Dalton continued, "we'd need to take people down the Cumberland Trail, bring 'em face-to-face with a few Smokey Mountain black bears, then set 'em on top of Grandfather Mountain. And we would dare them to breathe."

One more moment passed, then Alan said, "Maybe then we'd take 'em down the Tennessee River; let them glide past Chattanooga— Signal Mountain on one side, Lookout Mountain on the other."

"Could give them a little history lesson along the way," I suggested.

"Oh, that's nice," Alan said, his head bobbing, scribbling in his notebook. "Gives a whole other dimension to this."

"But you want to keep that separate," Dalton jumped in. "You want these things to stay focused—to be about history or beauty or quirkiness.... One idea per story."

Alan's nods picked up speed. "Yeah, yeah," he agreed. "I know what you're saying."

I shifted the conversation further south. "You know, I was in Florida last year and I felt the same thing you did. We were tucked away in the northeast corner, up in that sliver that pokes into Georgia." I raised my cup to my lips, remembering. "I was up early every morning and I took the dog down to the water; we walked across this warped and rickety old boardwalk—thing was weather-beaten and bleached gray by the sun. And it creaked and groaned as we passed through the dunes. That place wasn't like anything I'd seen before. It wasn't like Daytona or Pensacola. The dunes down there, they weave and roll, one on top of the other. There's some kind of vine that snakes its way over and between the slopes, and the sea oats … they've got to be four or five feet tall, and they just sway in the breeze…. The air down there's nothing like it is in the mountains. It's always warm, but in the morning it's soft and sweet-tempered. And the funny thing is: there's nothing pure about it. It's gotta be a half-dozen scents all jumbled together: salt and fish and seaweed … but it's just as nourishing as anything in Carolina, and I'm telling you, the lungs won't hold what the heart wants to inhale."

I closed my eyes for a second, imagining the splendor of Amelia Island. My gaze wandered to Alan. "Pelicans skim the top of the water," I told him. "They fly in perfect formation, like a squadron on a predawn mission under the radar, swooping up and down, wings tipping into the foam. Behind them, just before the sun rises, it rims the clouds in these florescent shades of yellow and red. You see these colossal shafts of white light blasting up from beneath the surface— and then, if you wait five more minutes—the sun peeks over the horizon. It's orange and bright, and from the first moment it roils…." I looked up at my friends. "Down there, I'm telling you, the sun makes a grander entrance than the queen of England."

I raised my cup halfway to my mouth, picturing what I'd seen— and also listening to the sounds I'd heard. "I know we can't do it in a magazine," I said, "but I'd love for people to hear the place. All the sights down there, the things I just told you about—it's all been set to a soundtrack that's perfectly scored—and it would, I swear, bring tears to Toscanini's eyes. The waves slap the shore in this steady, soothing rhythm. The breeze whistles, the cries of the seabirds swirl together. It's a symphony that's not like anything you've ever heard before." I glanced at Dalton again. "It's just like you said. Nobody—no matter where they have ever been—can stand where I stood, and not think they'd caught a glimpse of heaven."

We talked about the mansions that line the streets of Madison, Georgia. Alan marveled at the majesty of Charleston and Savannah. Dalton brightened again as he imagined the small towns that dot the South's highways: Hickory, Dahlonega, Oxford, and Asheboro.

And then Alan shoved his plate aside. "Listen," he said, "I hate to break this up, but it's eight thirty-five. If we're going to keep our wives onboard with this, we got to get out of here."

We paid the cashier, bundled back up, and stepped outside. "Won't be hard to come up with ten ideas for next month," Dalton said.

Alan jangled his keys and said, "I didn't think it would be. We'll do this again," he said, "same time, same place, on April 11."

For ninety-five minutes we had devoured eggs, bacon, and grits. We had drained three pots of coffee. We laughed. We picked one another's brains. We jotted down notes as one thought gave shape to the next. We had, in our first meeting together, learned how much we loved home. And of all people, it was Dalton Dorsey who had given the conversation a reverent tone.

By the following Tuesday we discovered that none of us could wait another thirty days. There were too many thoughts that wouldn't keep. Calls flew back and forth. Notes came in the mail—just words scribbled on scraps of paper: some new idea, a raw concept, the germ of a story. Nothing was organized or outlined; it was brainstorming by long distance—random thoughts that needed ventilation—that had to be shared in order to become real.

Springtime smothers Atlanta beneath a blanket of indescribable glory.

In April, with the dogwoods and azaleas bursting like bottle rockets, with the city suddenly teeming in red and pink, with Bradford pear trees erupting everywhere in flashes of blinding white, we—along with the rest of creation—yearned for the season that lay ahead.

It was, by God's indescribable good grace, time to play baseball.

The Atlanta Crackers had been Southern Association champs in 1954. They'd won ninety-four games two seasons ago, and drawn more than three hundred thousand fans. But they'd taken a stupendous fall in '55. They'd finished seventh, winning a measly seventy games. Clyde King was determined to restore the world to its natural order. But whether he did or not, I was relieved that every face on the opening-day roster was as white as a new bride's gown. Which meant that even if we finished dead last, there was no reason we wouldn't play in peace.

Even so, we never get more than a few hours' rest in this world, and the first shock of the new season came fast—and from a source I'd have never expected. It was a Saturday morning in early April. We had the paper spread out on the table between us. Chris and I had already talked about the Braves and Cardinals, and then, as was becoming our new custom, we moved on to the Crackers.

"Fox is pitching tonight," I told Chris. "He looked a little shaky in spring training, didn't he?"

Chris, sitting no more than two feet away, did not hear the question. He glanced up, but his mind had wandered off somewhere between Mars and Saturn. He stirred his cereal, weighed down, it seemed, by thoughts too hefty for a boy to carry. And then, with no comment on the question I'd asked, he said: "Can I bring a friend tonight?"

"Sure," I told him. "I can get a couple of passes if you want. You can bring Parker and Kenny both. You guys can sit up to the press box with me—it'll be fun, all the guys up there together."

Chris silently toyed with his Sugar Crisps. His eyes did not—for even the slightest fragment of a single second—meet mine. "I was thinking of somebody else," he muttered.

"You can bring anybody you want," I assured him. "Who you got in mind?"

I saw an eyelid quiver—just barely—and then he said, "Ansley Dorsey."

Rose Marie fumbled her cup. It clanged against the saucer. She bobbled it, coffee sloshing onto the floor. Her eyes rounded with terror. "Th-th-that'd be real sweet," she sputtered. Rose gawked at me, pleading and scrambling to muster a smile. "They live close by don't they, Jack?"

"Right up by the school," I said, desperate to restore calm.

"Have you already asked her?" I said to Chris.

He returned the faintest nod a human can give. "I said something to her yesterday at school. She was going to ask her parents." He lifted his eyes and I could see that boyish blend of embarrassment and fear. "I told her I'd call her today."

Rose stepped behind him. She reached around and hugged his neck; she laid her cheek against his. "It'll be fun," she said. "And it'll be nice for me to have another girl along."

"Okay," Chris said. "I'll call her later." He scooted his chair back, called to Slugger, and rushed outside.

The door banged shut, and Rose slumped across the table. "Oh Jack, I did not see this coming. My little boy wants to be with a girl!" She plunged her face into her hands. "I am not ready for this."

I laughed nervously, as stunned as Rose, and feeling like I'd missed something more obvious than a triple play. "He's fourteen," I said. "How did this get by me?"

Rose stood and moved to the bay window. She stared at her son roughhousing with his dog. "Look at them." She clasped her hands, resting her chin on steepled fingers. "He needs to stay just like that. He needs to stay right there, out by the creek playing with his dog … a little boy."

"He's taller than you are," I replied, "and on the phone—most people can't tell if it's him or me." I walked up beside her and massaged her shoulders. "Another new chapter," I said.

"The new chapters are coming too fast," Rose replied, her eyes still fixed on our boy and his dog. "I'm losing my grip on him."

I kept my eye on Chris that night. He and Ansley were like the positive poles on a pair of bar magnets—one repelling the other as soon as they moved within three inches of one another. For nine full innings he looked clumsy and afraid, like a kid who'd been forced to go to a cotillion. But I knew, and his mother did too, that there'd be no retreat. Along with the gawkiness I caught the wistful glimpses of a boy who'd been smitten. I saw the up-and-down sighs of a male who'd been ensnared by long blonde hair, soft skin, and deep, dark eyes. I saw the telltale signs of an addict who'd had his first taste of the drug that'd never let him go.

First thing Monday morning, I thought, *I've got to buy a copy of* For Boys Only: The Doctor Discusses the Mysteries of Manhood, *and I'm going to have to have one more talk I can no longer avoid.*

• • • •

I was in Birmingham to cover three games against the second-place Barons. On Tuesday afternoon June 5, I was scheduled to interview Phil Page, the Barons' manager. I waited in his office, browsing book spines, furtively skimming papers on top of his desk, checking out family photos, and one of him   from his rookie season in 1928—when he pitched for the Detroit Tigers. I settled into a couch that was so old the fabric glistened. I sorted through five loose sections of the *Birmingham News* and there, on the front page, the headline hit me: "Montgomery Bus Segregation Doomed by Federal Court." I bolted upright, flattened the page on the coffee table, and studied the lead: "A three-judge federal court panel ruled city bus segregation laws in Alabama unconstitutional but delayed issuing a formal order to carry out the decision...." In a two-to-one opinion, the paper reported, the court had ruled that state and city laws violated the Fourteenth Amendment of the U.S. Constitution.

Good grief, I thought as I skimmed the story, *King won.* The boycott was now six months old, and he'd done it: The guy had pulled off the impossible. I marched to Phil Page's desk, dialed the operator, asked her to place a call to Dexter Avenue Baptist and to transfer the charges. Twenty seconds later a receptionist connected me to King.

"I just saw the news," I said, trying my best to sound pleased.

"This is a good development," King replied. There was restraint in his voice, but I could hear his deep sense of satisfaction—the same sort of hope you hear in the dugout when your team's up by three runs in the bottom of ninth. "Things are looking up," he said cautiously, "we're all hopeful."

"Look," I said, "I'm in Birmingham and I'm late for a meeting now. I was thinking—if you can spare an hour—I'd drive down there tomorrow on my way home. You got time for a cup of coffee?"

"For *Life* magazine's best writer?" King was clearly feeling his oats. "I think I can fit you in."

An hour later, after I'd finished with Page, I phoned Rose. "Did you see the news?" I asked her, "about Montgomery?"

"Are you kidding!" she scoffed. "Chris had cut the article out of the paper before I finished making breakfast. When I picked up the front page I was staring at a hole." I heard her grieved sigh. "He's got it tacked to his bulletin board," she said. "So, yeah, I've seen it."

I told her I planned to swing by Montgomery on my way home—to see if I could find a backstory that was worth telling. "That means I'll probably have to drive straight from there to the ballpark," I explained.

"Straying a little far from sports there, aren't you, Hall?"

"Yeah," I confessed, "but there might be something there." I couldn't help but picture Dalton and Alan, to imagine the conversations we'd had about our make-believe magazine, and the pipe dreams we'd shared. "Who knows," I said wistfully, "it might be good to stay close to this guy."

"Fine," she mumbled, "if that's what you want to do. But look, there's no reason to bring this up with Chris, okay? Unless he asks, let's keep your little detour between us."

"All right," I said. "I'll see you tomorrow night after the game."

•   •   •   •

King and I bellied up to the same counter where we'd been six months before. "So what's this all about?" I asked. "This is a pretty sudden turn of events."

King hiked his left brow, eyeing me the way bewildered wives gape at their doltish husbands. "It's been six months," he reminded me. "I think we've moved past sudden."

"Well, maybe you're right," I said.

King stirred cream into his coffee. "Four women filed the suit," he began. "We challenged the state laws this time, hoping to get into federal court; thought we might have a chance there." He shrugged both shoulders. "This time things went our way." The young pastor couldn't contain a contented sigh. He spun around to face the street, to watch his people parade past the small diner. "It's not over," he said, "and nobody's counting any chickens that haven't hatched, but maybe ..." he pressed his lips tight and then continued, "maybe the world just edged closer to the side of justice."

"Were you surprised?" I asked. "Was there anything that tipped you off, that made you think this was coming?"

King tugged at his right ear, recalling scenes from the courtroom. "We've been disappointed so many times," he said. "You never take anything for granted. But there was a point—when Judge Rives questioned one of their attorneys—that I thought they were leaning our way."

"Yeah," I said, "go on."

King tapped at his lip. "It was funny," he said, "they—I'm talking about their attorneys—they kept talking about violence and bloodshed. They were telling the court that if they stopped segregation the city'd be in chaos." King gave his head a tilt to the side, recalling, I think, what he'd heard just two days before. "The judge asked him straight out if one man ought to be denied his constitutional rights in order to prevent another man from committing a crime." King twisted toward me. "When I heard that I leaned over and whispered to Fred Gray—I told him that was a good sign."

"So what now?" I asked. "I'm guessing they'll appeal?"

"They've got ten days to decide. In the meantime everything's status quo."

"Which means you're staying off the buses?"

King returned a determined nod. "As long as they're segregated, we're staying off the buses."

•　　•　　•　　•

Dalton and Alan and I missed our June meeting—I was on the road again. We missed July, when Dalton was on vacation; then met in

August, September, and October. And then decided to pick things back up after the holidays.

But every month we spent more time together. Our families gathered for dinner. The six of us played bridge and went to the movies. And Alan, Dalton, and I learned that we were kindred spirits. We discovered that we loved the same things. We consumed each others' energy; we realized that the company of the others made us better than we were alone.

A man loves his wife. He wants to protect her and care for her and provide for her; a man wants to be as close to her as he is to his own skin. But over those months there was—in this wholly different sense—a way in which the three of us found his lifelong partners.

● ● ● ●

For Rose Marie, Chris, and me—1956 had been a year to savor.

We healed. We made new friends and forged new paths.

Work was good that year. The Crackers bounced back, and through that summer and into the fall I covered the dazzling play of Meeks, Di Prima, and Daniels.

And for months I'd basked in the glory of a byline in the world's best magazine.

Rose Marie collected a neighborhood full of friends. She climbed the ladder at the PTA, wormed her way onto church committees, and dabbled at the fringe of the neighborhood Welcome Wagon.

By the time fall arrived Chris had grown past my shoulders and came nearly nose high. His body was hard as a cinderblock, and the muscles in his arms, legs, and chest looked like the work of a Renaissance sculptor. That summer he hit ten home runs, pitched two no-hitters, and became feared on baseball diamonds all over Atlanta.

More alarmingly, he grew into full-fledged love with Ansley Dorsey. He held her hand in public. When he sat beside her they were closer than the "A" and "B" volumes of the *World Book* encyclopedia. He called her every night, and the two of them lingered on the phone for hours—their larynxes physically incapable of forming the words "good-bye," their minds persuaded that hanging up was an act of unspeakable betrayal.

Rose and I and Dalton and Natalie kept our eyes peeled and our fingers crossed. And I begged Dalton to tell me the minute he saw anything that made him nervous.

That Christmas, I suspect, was one that Martin Luther King relished. On December 20, 1956—six full months after the District Court's ruling—the Supreme Court's order finally arrived. Alabama's segregation laws were—officially and forever—declared unconstitutional.

Dalton and I traveled to Montgomery again—this time to take a historic ride.

On December 21, at about six a.m., King and Ralph Abernathy boarded the South Jackson Street bus, officially ending the world-famous Montgomery bus boycott. Photographers, reporters, and TV crews had gathered early. Bulbs flashed and cameras whirled as the bus angled into the curb. The door swung open, and King—smiling, yet determined—started up the steps. The driver, peering down from his seat asked, "Is this the reverend?"

"That's right," King replied. He deposited a dime and a nickel, turned into the aisle, and then took the third seat from the front. He sat hip-to-hip and thigh-to-thigh with Glenn Smiley, a white pastor from Texas. Abernathy, all smiles, and with the look of a ballplayer who'd just won a league championship, sat in the second row, just in front of him.

Dalton and I drifted farther back, out of the way, but where we could witness the culmination of King's improbable and inexplicable crusade. We rode quietly through town; there was only one other passenger at first, a Negro woman, maybe fifty, who sat toward the back, where she was accustomed. A few others boarded along the way. And then, twenty uneventful minutes later, the ride was over. King and Abernathy stepped off at Court Square, where more cameras and reporters waited.

As Abernathy stepped down to the curb, he turned to King and said, "That was a mighty good ride."

King, beaming at the end of this 381-day ordeal, replied, "It was a great ride."

I rapped on the door frame. "So how'd you do it?" I asked.

It was later now, at Dexter Street Baptist, at our ten o'clock meeting.

King reached over his desk to shake my hand. "I don't know," he said, his voice weary but shaded with triumph. "I really don't." He fell back in his chair, his mind sorting through the events of the past year. "The only thing I can tell you for sure is this: It wasn't me."

"I didn't see the photographers taking anybody else's picture," I cracked.

"And that's a shame," King replied. "So many people did so much." He laid a finger to his chin, reflecting. "But it wasn't them either; this wasn't man's effort; something else was at work here."

I opened my hands, a tacit, open-ended question.

The young pastor reached for a pen and drummed it against his desk. "I told you before," he said, "the world was created to be on the side of justice. This thing began supernaturally, and that's how it held together. There's no other explanation."

I thought about it for a second—not sure, given the evidence, that I could refute the claim. "If that's true," I said, "then where's it go from here?" I squared up directly in front of him. "You're telling me that God Himself acted in the town of Montgomery, Alabama, and that as a direct result Negroes in this one town—in this tiny pinprick of all creation—can sit in the front of a city bus ...?" I held my open hands in the air, mystified by the improbability of such a modest miracle.

"I didn't tell you I understood it," King said. He glanced away, and a couple of seconds swept past before his eyes came even with mine. "You know, when I think back on this, when I explain it all to my children and to their children, I'm going to point to November 13. That," he said nostalgically, "is the day we should remember."

The date didn't ring a bell with me. I shrugged and flipped a palm to the air.

"We were in court," King explained. "The mayor was trying to shut down our carpools. The city claimed that we were a public nuisance; they said we were operating 'without license, fee, or franchise.' And they were suing us for fifteen thousand dollars—their cut of the lost revenue." King rested his head on the back of his chair; he closed his eyes, calling the memories forward. "I had to appear at a mass meeting the night before, and I had to tell everybody—all these people who had sacrificed so much for so long—I had to explain that we were going to lose the only transportation system we had." He glanced up, tight lipped and somber: "That would have been the straw that broke us. And that night I told them—I said, 'This might be the darkest hour before the dawn.' I stood in that pulpit and reminded them that we'd acted in 'daring faith,' that we'd believed God was with us, that we'd seen our faith vindicated time after time...." Once more, King lifted his eyes to mine. "I told them that we had to keep that faith, that we had to keep going, that we had to believe that 'a way would be made out of no way.'" His gaze lingered, conveying a new depth of honesty between us. "That's what I said, but I'm not sure I believed it. I looked over the crowd that night—I looked in their eyes—and I could see the doubt. I could see the hope draining out of them. And for the first time in ten months I thought it might all come to nothing; I thought that after all that time, after all these poor people had been through—that we were going to fail."

"But the court ruled in your favor?" I guessed.

"No," King said, a slender smile now creasing his lips. "We lost the case." He swiveled in his chair, looking more comfortable and relaxed. "I was in court the next day—on the thirteenth. I was at the defendant's table; it was about noon and the judge had just called a recess. I was gathering my notes together when I heard a commotion in the back of the courtroom. The mayor was back there huddled up with a couple of lawyers. Three or four reporters rushed inside—they're all anxious-looking and whispering back and forth. I turned to Fred Gray, and I was about to tell him that something was wrong, but before I could finish the first sentence Rex Thomas—one of the reporters from the AP—hands me a piece of paper. He holds it out to me and he says—I'll never forget it—he says: 'Here's the decision you've been waiting for.'"

King chuckled lightly, remembering, I suspect, the expression on Thomas's face or, more likely, on mayor Gayle's. "I reached for the paper; I was trying to keep my hand from shaking, and I skimmed the first few lines. That's when I learned that the Supreme Court had ruled in our favor. They had—in that very hour—affirmed that the segregation laws were unconstitutional." King leaned back, the smile brightening. "Our hour of defeat had turned to triumph. I'd just seen God make a way out of no way."

I gnawed on the tip of my pen, impressed by King's story and even amazed by the serendipitous turns it had taken. But there was that piece of it that just wouldn't jibe. I pressed him a second time. "So God intervened, and this is the sum total of all He had in mind? The God of the entire solar system miraculously made a way for fifty thousand Negroes in Montgomery, Alabama?"

King leaned forward and said, "No, He made a way for righteousness, which means He made a way for everybody."

An awkward couple of seconds filled the space between us.

"Look," he said, "I don't know where this goes. I don't know how it gets there. But I do know this: Big things almost always begin small; they almost always begin with lowly people." He put a hand to his chin, thinking back. "Rosa Parks," he said, "she didn't have any of this in mind. Jo Ann Robinson—the schoolteacher who passed around all those leaflets—not in her wildest dreams."

King swiveled easily, picturing the faces of all those who'd been involved. "Think about all the contingent factors," he mused. "The people who were in the right place at the right time: Nixon, Hubbard, Fields, Abernathy, Fred Gray—even me. There was the front-page story in the newspaper, and even the things that seemed so evil at the time: the city council's stubbornness, the mayor's refusal to talk, the attack on my home.... One thing led to another which led to the next—and it all came to a climax at six o'clock this morning, on the South Jackson Street bus." He picked up the pen, rapped on the desk again, savoring the victory. "What's next? I don't have any idea. But I got a feeling ..." he looked away, ideas stirring, and said, "I got this notion that it's just getting started."

I rolled my eyes and sighed fretfully. "Yeah," I murmured, "you're probably right."

King's chair creaked with the tiny twists he made. "I don't know what's in store for me," he said. "I don't know if my part's over or just getting started...." He peeked up, smiling thinly. "But I'll tell you what, if there's more I'll give you a call."

I peered up from my notes and chuckled. "Thanks," I told him. "But if I'm not there, I'll be in the press box at Ponce de León, okay?"

King's head bobbed sympathetically. "All right. I understand." Then his smile took a sly turn; he leaned back and tossed a hand in the air. "Let me ask you something," he said. "Why do you suppose God uses humble people to do big things?"

"That's your theory, not mine," I said grinning.

"My guess," King said, "is that He wants to make sure we don't mistake our power for His, so He uses people who don't have any: a colored seamstress like Rosa Parks; a railroad conductor like E. D.

Nixon; a teacher at a colored college like Jo Ann Robinson...."

"Uh-huh," I muttered, waiting.

He leaned in and hunched over the desk. "If God's going to do something here, if He's bringing us to the place where we live up to the meaning of our creed, where we see that all men are truly created equal ... I don't see Him doing that through Eisenhower or Nixon or Sam Rayburn." He stroked his chin, a pastor brimming with thoughts of the things God might do. "But it'd be just like Him, wouldn't it, to use maids and garbage collectors and day laborers." He snared my eye again. "Be a shame for a good, young reporter to miss something like that."

"Yeah," I said, my smile lingering. "But you know what: The Atlanta Crackers had a great season, and it looks like next year might even be better. It'd be a shame to miss that too." But then, as my smile faded, I said, "But who knows? Let's just see what happens."

"All right," King said. "But do me one favor, will you?"

"What's that?" I asked.

"In the off-season, keep your eyes on this country's colored people; when you're not watching baseball, take note of the difference between us and our opponents. You think you can do that?"

"And what will I see, Reverend?"

He rested his chin on a fisted hand. "More of what you saw here," he said. "When the Negroes of this city protested, nobody got hurt. Nobody got dragged out of his house and strung up on some back-country road. Nobody burned a cross at a Montgomery bus stop. Nobody saw anything that resembled the Ku Klux Klan or the White Citizens' Council." He looked at me, harder than he had before. "This wasn't a victory for fifty thousand black people. It was a victory for all of us; it was a victory for justice. We have a different agenda; we've got different goals and a higher purpose ... they demand different methods, and the world ought to take notice."

The next day's *Montgomery Advertiser* noted, "The calm but cautious acceptance of this significant change in Montgomery's way of life came without any major disturbance." But the town's peace wouldn't last. In coming days a young Negro girl was beaten. Random shots were fired at passing buses—a pregnant colored woman was hit in the leg. King's reasons for optimism faded, and the worst was yet to come.

Chapter 7

Nineteen fifty-seven opened ominously.

It was just nine days into the new year when King had come to Atlanta. He came with Abernathy to meet with a corps of Negro leaders, to see where events, and Providence, would lead them.

I caught up with him at Ebenezer Baptist early one morning, before his meetings began. "So, you taken any bus rides lately?" I began.

King allowed a thin smile to slip through. "Yes," he said. "And they've gone smoothly."

"So things have died down?" I asked.

"Hard to say for sure," King replied. "But I think so."

We spent a half hour talking about his need for a rest, his optimism—despite the setbacks—that things would get better, and the likelihood that a more pervasive movement was beginning to stir.

"Well, I'll keep my eye on things," I told him.

King chuckled, "Like basketball, baseball, football ...?"

"Yeah," I said, "for now. But I got two eyes, you know."

He smiled. "You were fair to us," he said. "You and your boss have both been fair. If something worthwhile comes up, I'm going to let you know. You can decide what you want to do with it."

I nodded appreciatively. "Fair enough," I said.

We could not have known that his first call would come less than twenty-four hours later, at three o'clock the following morning—when the phone's ring never signals good news.

"Hello," I muttered hesitantly.

"There've been some bombings."

There was no mistaking King's voice. "Where?" I asked. "Where are you?"

"I'm still here," King said, "in Atlanta. The bombs have gone off in Montgomery. I don't know how many yet, but I know they hit Abernathy."

"Anybody hurt?" I asked. I closed my eyes, dreading his answer.

"No," King replied. "He's here with me; he's talked to Juanita a couple of times; his family's safe." King paused. I heard him take a deep breath. "She thinks they got Bob Graetz's house too, and that they may have hit the churches."

I sat up on the bed picturing Graetz, the white pastor of a Negro church. I groped for some kind of appropriate reply, and then, frustrated that human language is inadequate for times like these, "I'm sorry," was the best I could manage. I fumbled around for a few more seconds, and then finally said, "You've talked to Coretta? Your house is okay?"

"Yes," King said, "they're fine." A cumbersome moment hovered between us. "Well," he said, "I told you I'd let you know if anything happened … I got to get with the airline now, to see how fast we can get home."

"Sure," I told him, "I'll catch up with you later."

I rushed downstairs to call Dorsey and McGill. We met four hours later and discovered that things were worse than King knew. He'd been right: Abernathy's home and church had been badly damaged, and Robert Graetz had been attacked too. But three other Negro churches were in ruins: Bell Street Baptist, Hutchinson, and Mount Olive. One look at the first photos and you could see: This wasn't a hint. This wasn't a prank to make a few Negroes nervous. This was fire and brimstone; it was a prophetic message—a warning to every Negro alive—to change their ways … or face the consequences.

And the message got through. Before noon the same day, pamphlets popped up in Negro neighborhoods blaming King for the violence and urging the colored community to rebel. One said: "We got shot at while he rides. He's getting us in more trouble every day. Wake up. Run him out of town." Another claimed: "We been doing OK in Montgomery before outside preachers were born! Ask Reverend King's papa and mama if they like his doings—ask them if they're going to help in Atlanta. Better quit him before it's too late."

• • • •

Dalton pitched a copy of the *New York Times* onto the table. He slid into the booth beside Alan and flattened the front page, showcasing a photo of the rubble that was once Mount Olive Church.

"If I were going to create a Southern magazine," he announced,

"I'd have a section called 'Southern Genius.' I'd run ten pages a month that talked about Southerners who are making the entire planet smarter and richer and prettier...." He lifted a corner of the paper, studied the photo—a scowl marring his usually jovial face. "Because this, gentlemen, is what our Northern neighbors think of us."

"Oh no," Alan corrected him. "That right there, that's what the entire world thinks."

I tossed the breakfast menu aside. "We could use a little distraction, couldn't we?" I said.

"I don't think the Second Coming could chase that off the front page," Dalton whined. *The Times, The Globe,* and *The Inquirer*—they're having too much fun with this."

"You know, you're probably right," Alan replied. He crossed his arms over the table. "Think about the conversations we've had here— the places, the people, all the things there are to see and do ..." he said as he picked up the newspaper. "And today, this is all anybody knows."

Alan cradled his coffee mug, his eyes shifting back and forth between me and Dalton. "Nobody's telling a different story," he said. "There's no point of comparison, no rebuttal. This is the only story that's out there."

We fell quiet. And for a moment, nobody was sure where the conversation should go, or how far we were willing to take it.

Dalton spun the paper around and scanned a few words. "You know," he said, "I was hoping we could talk about music this morning—about country and bluegrass and rock and roll—about all the great music we've given the world."

I slurped at a cup of refilled coffee, images of Elvis Presley, Buddy

Holly, and Johnny Cash springing to mind. "That'd be a long con-versation," I said, "and a good one. I came with an agenda too," I confessed. "I'd wanted to talk about writers: Faulkner and Styron and Wolfe and Warren." I tossed my friends a sly smile. "Wouldn't it be something to do a whole feature on women: Welty, McCullers, Rawlings, Margaret Mitchell; this new gal who's right up the road here—O'Connor—have you read her stuff?"

I grinned at Dalton, "That'd raise a few eyebrows, wouldn't it?"

"Ah, now that's bold," he said, a hint of the old grin reemerging. "Geez," he said, "we'd need a half day just to think through the list. But a literary tone, a little sophistication ... that might be nice right now."

Alan stretched across the table. "But nobody's doing it," he said. "When people think about the South they're not thinking about Faulkner or the Smokey Mountains or Elvis Presley." He tapped on the newspaper. "They're thinking about this."

I picked up the paper and studied the image for the third time. "This is not who we are," I said. "This is not what we're about." I observed the broken stained glass, the smoldering pews, a scorched wooden cross. "We're the people who've got what the whole world envies, the things that make life good and fun. We've got—"

"You're right," Dalton broke in. "But nobody north of Richmond believes it. Right now, we're the weight that's bringing the country down."

"And that's going to cost us," Alan said. "In every way imaginable—economically, socially, educationally—that's going to cost us all."

We glanced at one another—suspecting that the same thought was on everybody's mind—but that no one was willing to say it.

• • • •

In those days the world refused to stay dull.

In July, Percy Jackson, the colored ballplayer we'd befriended in Whitney, was traded to the Milwaukee Braves and immediately summoned to County Stadium. Which meant it wouldn't be long before he made his first appearance on a big-league diamond.

Chris checked the box scores every morning to see if Percy had played. On Sundays he checked the TV listings, hoping that the Braves had been scheduled, and that we'd see him playing alongside, and against, the game's biggest stars. In late July his wish came true.

"I want to have Ansley over to watch the game," Chris told us.

His mother stood at the kitchen sink; I watched as she looked to the ceiling, eyes closed, counting to ten. "Well, you know," she said, trying to sound calm, "if we invite her over, we're going to have to tell everybody the whole story."

Chris stared into his cereal bowl. "I know," he replied.

"And that could make things a little complicated," his mother continued.

"I *know*," Chris repeated.

Rose reached for a dish towel and dried her hands. She shifted her weight from left to right and then back again. "I'm not sure about this," she sighed. "I don't want you to be dishonest, but sweetie, I don't want you getting into a big mess if you don't have to." Her hands stayed busy with the towel, "You're still young, and we don't really know where things are going with Ansley; I don't think it'd hurt to wait a while before you get into all this."

Chris expelled a long and audible breath. "Mom, I want to

watch the game," he said. "And I want to watch it with Ansley." He appealed to me. "You want to watch it with your friends, don't you? Wouldn't that make it more fun?"

"Yeah," I said, "it sure would. But I want you to think about what Mom's saying, Chris. This is risky. Your friends—and ours, too—they may not be too thrilled that we're all chummy with some colored guy." I narrowed my gaze, reminding him of our not-too-distant past.

His chest filled with air, then emptied. "I've never told anybody about Percy," he said, "but I know Ansley won't mind. We've talked about colored people a hundred times.…" He turned to me again. "We read your article, we've talked about the boycott, we've talked about what we'd do if colored kids came to our school.…" Chris's eyes traveled from me to his mother. "This isn't going to bother her."

"It might upset her mom and dad," I said.

Chris shrugged. "Maybe, but I don't think so."

"They might think you're a bad influence," I went on, "… might not want you hanging around their daughter anymore."

"I read what Mr. Dorsey wrote in *Life*. He's not going to think that."

"Yeah, well, the article in *Life* was about Montgomery," I told Chris. "That's pretty far away. It was about people we don't know— things that don't really affect us. But now … well, now we're talking about the man's daughter."

"I don't think he's going to mind," Chris said. "But if he does, I guess I'd rather know now than later."

Rose Marie rushed to a screaming teapot and lifted it off the stove.

I watched her, worried about where this might go, and if the strain would further the distance between them. "What are you thinking?" I asked her.

She wrapped a teabag around her spoon. "I'm just not sure it's the right time," she said. She fumbled with the cup and saucer, hiked her shoulders and cast a glance toward the table. "I don't want him keeping secrets. I don't want him to be dishonest...." She set the teabag onto the saucer and looked away.

"Listen," I said to Chris, "her father already knows about this— I'm not sure how much really—and honestly, I don't think he's going throw some big fit—but I don't know." I looked at Rose, "Let's have them all over a few minutes early; we'll tell them why we're eager to see Percy—we'll just lay it out there and see what happens."

"Well," Rose groaned, "if we're going to tell the Dorseys we might as well tell the Emersons; fess up to everybody at the same time."

I looked to Chris. "What do you think, pal, should we tell Parker and his folks too?"

"Fine with me," Chris said. "But when we're done, I want to talk to Ansley alone."

"All right," I said, "what if we do this: What if we have everybody over a half hour before the game. We'll cover the basics all together, and then..." I put a hand on Chris's shoulder, "if you want to talk with Ansley a little more, the two of you can go for a walk later. How's that?"

Chris nodded. And with that settled, his mind shifted gears. He looked up, grinned, and said, "Percy's going to be on national television."

———————

At the end of our story Dalton Dorsey rose from his chair; he moved to the couch, to the spot beside Rose, and put a hand on her shoulder. "Did you really think this would be a problem?" he asked. He looked at Alan and Doris, then to me: "We knew this, Jack; maybe not all the details, but it's is hardly a revelation." He reached across Rose and slapped at my knee. "You did the right thing; that's why I came looking for you." He stood and went back to his chair, the Dorsey grin flashing. "So, this Jackson kid, from what I've read it sounds like he's going to be around for a while."

Quietly, and in a grateful tone, I assured Dalton: "This kid's for real."

Doris Emerson moved to the empty space beside Rose. "You know," she said, "I don't think the Negroes playing ball is any problem at all. I mean, when it's all boys, when it's just sports ... I can't see the harm in that." She turned to Natalie Dorsey, her brows arched high, beseeching further confirmation: "It's not like coloreds and whites going to the same dance or sitting beside one another every day in the same class, is it?"

Natalie fluffed her daughter's hair over her shoulders. "No," she said, "and we really should be doing more for the Negro." Natalie held Rose's eye, "I think ya'll did a nice thing for this boy's family. He seems to be off to such a good start playing professional baseball." She admired her girl's long blonde hair. "We should all be trying to help those who have less than we do."

I winked at Chris, my signal to him that this couldn't have gone better.

We settled in for the CBS Game of the Week, and in the seventh inning Percy Jackson entered his first major league game. Chris saw him instantly; he saw him trot out of the dugout and onto the field. The boy scrambled up close to the set and angled a finger into the screen. "There he is," Chris exclaimed. "See him?" He crept to within inches of the television, gazing intently, as if under some kindly spell.

We watched Percy field a warm-up grounder and toss the ball back to Frank Torre. Dizzy Dean, the announcer, casually noted the change along with a pair of others. But for us, this was one of life's culminating moments. Much of our unpleasant past had been leading to this: to the time when a shy colored kid—a boy we'd known in another lifetime—would take the field for the Milwaukee Braves.

Percy went 0 for 1 that day; he flew out to center in the eighth inning, but he'd hit the ball hard. And in the ninth he fielded a sharply hit grounder for the first out of the game's final inning. Chris beamed for sixteen consecutive minutes.

As the Braves trotted off the field, the camera swept across our friend's sweaty black face. Ansley stretched her arms over her head; she yawned and said, "Do you think you'll ever see him again?"

"Oh yeah," Chris said, "I don't know when, but I'm sure we will."

"I've never met a real baseball player before," she said. Her eyes lingered on the set as Dizzy Dean recapped the hits, runs, and errors. Then she turned to Chris. "And I've never known anybody who's been through all that you have."

Chris held the girl's gaze; he motioned to her—a slight gesture that passed between the two of them, alone. Then he stood and reached for her hand. "We're going to walk around the block," he announced. "We'll be back soon."

They returned an hour later. Ansley's eyes were puffed and red, and her cheeks were streaked wet with tears. But the tears, I was sure, had not come from anger or indignation. They were the product of this girl's maternal instinct, and there was—behind the sadness and behind the youth and beyond the fledgling emotions that swirl with young love—a kind of resolve. I saw it in the firmer grasps of their hands, in the lingering stares, the resolute nods.... I saw in him, and in her too, youth's ever-present need to right the world's wrongs, to fight injustice, to stand with the poor and powerless. I felt a queasy twinge, watching new emotions pass between them. These two, I saw, had crossed a threshold. In that hour their relationship had changed, had gone deeper. I made a mental note to keep watch, to see where they'd lead one another.

*Of all treasons against humanity, there
is no one worse than his who employs
great intellectual force to keep down the
intellect of his less favored brother.*
—William Ellery Channing

Chapter 8

On September 4, 1957, Hazel Bryan, a teenage girl I'd never seen before, changed my life forever.

It's not likely you know the name, but you know her face. And you, along with every human who was alive at the time—and every human who has lived since—have been changed by it.

The story began two weeks before, late on a Thursday afternoon. I was tossing pencils and pads into my briefcase, looking forward to that night's game, when Dalton strolled in. Casually, as if he lived in a world with no deadlines, he asked, "So, how's your calendar look for the next week or two?"

I glanced up. "I don't know," I mumbled, "the usual stuff I guess. Rose's been bugging me about Labor Day. She thinks we ought to have you guys over after the game." I tossed my scorebook into the case. "But I don't know."

He looped his eyes, "Why, we'd love to come," he said. "Thanks so much for asking." Then Dalton shifted his weight; he laid a finger against his lip and said: "Any chance you could take off a few days, maybe the tail end of next week, a day or two after Labor Day?"

I made a quick mental scroll through my calendar. "I'd have to get Moore or Carter to cover a couple of games," I said. "But I could probably pull it off. Why?"

A grin slithered across Dalton's face. He rocked back and forth, heel to toe, the smile gleaming brighter. "I just heard from our guy at *Life*," he said. "They're doing this big feature on the first day of school, sending reporters to five or six cities that are integrating for the first time. He wants to know if we'll cover Little Rock."

"Little Rock?" I said. "I haven't heard about anything going on over there."

I heard the slow hiss of Dalton's impatience. He leaned over my desk, planted both hands on top of it, and said, "You might've missed the point there, hotshot; let me try this another way: An editor at *Life* called and said, 'Do you and your idiot partner want another byline in the world's most famous magazine?' Does that put this in better perspective for you?"

My mouth loosened to a smile. "Well, when you put it like that...." But then, still curious, my mind taking its first lap around the possible new assignment, I said, "I thought Nashville was the big trouble spot."

"It is," Dalton declared, "and that's exactly why they want two guys in Little Rock."

I glared at him.

"We'll contribute a couple hundred words to the main story," Dalton said. He rested his foot on the wooden side chair, "Then you and I will do a companion piece—five thousand words about how Little Rock planned and prepared; you know, an in-depth look at how one Southern city stayed calm in the midst of change. This thing's tailor-made for us, Jack."

And that was true, but still ... the whole idea seemed so preposterous—that two no-name reporters were suddenly writing features for *Life*, traveling the South, documenting the key events in our region. "Yeah, that sounds good," I said, my mind still drifting. "It just seems weird that they—"

Dalton threw his hands into the air; he turned and stormed away. "I'm calling him back right now," he hollered over his shoulder. "I'm telling him that we're thrilled, delighted, ecstatic ... that Hall thinks Little Rock's the story of the century."

There wasn't much time to prepare, but there wasn't a lot of need.

Since the infamous Brown decision of 1954, Little Rock had been a model city of the New South. They'd integrated the bus system without a whimper. They'd formed an Industrial Development Commission to lure business. Arkansas had elected a progressive governor, Orval Faubus, who'd promised to improve life for the poor—white and colored both—and he had, through every month in office, proved true to his word.

Schools throughout the state—in Van Buren, Fort Smith, and Ozark—moved forward with plans to integrate, and no one, so far as we knew, had ruffled more than a few feathers. In Little Rock, Virgil Blossom, the superintendent of schools, had spent two years visiting every civic group that had an address, promoting a carefully constructed plan to mix schools so gradually, "that hardly anybody'd even notice," and there'd been no more than token resistance.

"This is the story we've been looking for," Dalton assured me. "A Southern town that's just going with the flow, doing what's got to be done, slow and easy." He turned and grinned. "We just got to find a way to make it interesting."

"There've got to be a few colorful characters in this," I replied. "I mean, you can't go through life with a name like Orval Faubus and not have or quirk or two."

"Or Virgil Blossom," Dalton noted.

"Small-town politics, race, the South … there's an angle in there," I told my friend. "I don't think it'll be hard to find."

•　•　•　•

Friday, August 31

It was the last day before a long weekend. Harry Ashmore, the editor of the *Arkansas Gazette* wore white slacks and a short-sleeve shirt open at the collar. His black hair was slicked straight back, brown loafers sheathed his sockless feet, and I swear, I have never seen a man more completely swathed in cheerful self-confidence.

Ashmore, like McGill, was famous. The man had literally written the book on the subject at hand: *The Negro and the Schools.* He was charming and bright and nearly as funny as Steve Allen. To some, he was the embodiment of the New South. To others, he was a demon who wouldn't rest until he'd destroyed the things they treasured. Through his paper and the power of the written word, he was a force no Arkansan could ignore. Governors, mayors, and city councilmen trembled before him. But he was a friend of Orval Faubus. And he was the first man we wanted to talk to.

Dalton and I wandered into the *Gazette* newsroom, immediately warmed by the chaotic sounds of typewriters and phones, by the palpable air of urgency, and by frantic reporters scrambling to stay on schedule.

Ashmore sat perched on a desk, four reporters—out of town-ers, I guessed—gathered round him. He tracked us as we snaked through the maze, and when we'd come to within three desks he cried out, "You gotta be Hall and Dorsey." He pushed off his roost and tossed an arm over Dalton's shoulder. "I was just telling these boys about that piece you did on Montgomery. I still got it around it here somewhere—damn thing hacked me off so bad."

My head snapped up. "Why?"

Ashmore tightened his grip on Dalton's shoulder. "It always sort of frosts me when I see something I wish I'd done," he said. The grin now glowed with admiration. "That was top-notch, and I keep a file of the good stuff."

At the sound of Ashmore's words a chill raced through me—of wonder and appreciation—trying to imagine how I, a sportswriter from just south of nowhere, had arrived here, accepting compli-ments from Harry Ashmore, about an article I'd written for *Life* magazine.

Reporters from around the country had begun to gather. We'd come to cover the same story, to pay homage to the great Ashmore, and to take our ten-minute turn in his presence. "Come on in," he said, guiding Dalton and me into his office. He motioned to a pair of empty chairs: "So, you guys are doing a little background on this, right?"

"Yeah," I said, "and we were hoping you could point us in the right direction."

Ashmore rocked back, tapping his fingers together. "Well, there are three or four people you need to talk to. You'll want to start with

Blossom, of course; he's responsible for the plan..." Ashmore couldn't conceal the disdainful smile. "I gotta tell you, the man's a full-blooded Rotarian, but … he's done a decent job. The plan makes sense, and I got to hand it to him, he's worked like hell to sell it." He hesitated a second, the grin refusing to fade, "There's nothing ol' Virgil'd like more than to see his name in *Life* magazine."

Ashmore swiveled, the back-and-forth movement propelling his thoughts. "You'll need a half hour with Faubus," he continued. "That'll be background—on Arkansas, on how this fits into the big picture—that kind of thing." He reached for a pad and pen. "I can set that up for you.

"If you want the Negro perspective, talk to Daisy Bates. She's a writer," he said. "She and her husband put out the local colored paper; do a helluva job too. She also runs the local NAACP office …" a twinkle lit Ashmore's eyes as he said, "and she is a constant pain in Virgil Blossom's butt. That alone makes her worth talking to."

I jotted down the name and flipped the page. "As smooth as all this's gone," I said, "there's got to be a loser. Somebody, somewhere around here has got to be pretty ticked about all this."

"Oh, there's more'n a few," Ashmore assured us. "If you got the time and stomach for it, you ought to spend a few minutes with Jim Johnson; he's a legislator. And there's Amis Guthridge, head of the Citizens' Council. Both of 'em love to make Faubus squirm," he cut his eyes from me to Dalton, "… and they're pretty good at it."

"Good enough to mess things up?" Dalton asked.

"No," Ashmore shook his head. "It's too late for that now."

I looked to Dalton. "How 'bout I take Blossom and Guthridge?" I said. "You take Faubus and Johnson."

"Fair enough," he replied.

I turned back to Ashmore. "Anybody else?" I prodded.

"You might try the Mothers' League," he said, "they're a bunch of women whose kids go to Central High. They've been trying to postpone this thing...." He scribbled down a few names and slid them across the desk. "I think they've filed suit in every court we got. These three ought to be good for a quote or two."

That afternoon, after a three-hour interview with the president of the Capital Citizens' Council, I rushed back to find Dalton—knowing, as he surely did—that we'd stumbled into something unexpected, something that might rock the quiet town we'd come to cover.

It was, I remember this distinctly, twenty-three past four. Dalton was in the hotel dining room. He'd commandeered a pair of two-top tables, had sheets from a yellow legal pad strewn across them, a portable typewriter cocked at a forty-five-degree angle, and a pencil protruding from behind his right ear.

I fell into the chair beside him. He stopped his work and leaned back, looking me up and down, stroking his chin as if making an appraisal. Clanks, thuds, and the murmur of muffled voices leaked through the kitchen door. The aroma of frying onions and fresh-baked bread swirled, and we both sat silently, slavering at the prospect of what we'd found.

Dalton reached for his pencil; he tapped it a few times, then tossed it onto the pad. "Let me ask you something," he began drolly. "Do you know how to spell *Pulitzer*?"

I threw my legs over the seat of the empty chair between us.

"Yeah," I said, aping his tone. "I've been practicing for when I have to congratulate McGill."

Dalton propped a foot on a fourth chair, smiling. "I'm serious," he said. "I believe we might've wandered into a drama that'd make Shakespeare drool. And if we're half the writers I think we are...."

"You come across something tasty out there, Dalton?"

He looked right and left, like a spy ready to spill ten top secrets. "This is gonna make 'Hamlet' look like a nursery rhyme," he said. His gaze strayed to a phantom spot in the distance. "If we dig about six inches deeper, Jack, we're going to hit Southern politics at its down-and-dirtiest. If you got half of what I think you did, and if we don't screw this up...." He cocked his head again. "P-u-l-i—"

"You might be getting a little ahead of yourself," I told him. But then, with a smile as wicked as his, I said: "But there's something here, and it's under everybody's radar."

"Except ours," Dalton beamed.

He dropped his foot to the floor and pulled up close to the table. "Jim Johnson's as nice a guy as you'd ever want to meet," he told me. "Good looking, friendly; he's got that appeal—you've seen it before—that kind of charm that puts a crowd in the palm of your hand." Dalton rapped the pencil up and down—a cylinder powering his mind as it milled a fresh batch of new ideas—"I don't know, Jack, school starts in ... what, a couple of days? This guy hasn't given up. In his mind, Virgil Blossom's plan is not a done deal."

I couldn't resist the role of devil's advocate. "But the courts have all ruled. He's out of options."

Dalton's laugh brimmed with contempt. "Jack, this guy stopped caring about the courts three years ago. He's taking his case straight to the people, who, he thinks, will go straight to the governor. Who, he thinks—when he can't stand the pressure any longer—will interpose state laws."

"Oh, come on," I scoffed, "Nobody thinks Faubus'll disobey a federal court order."

"Johnson does," Dalton said. He leaned in closer. "I'm telling you, Jack, this guy cannot bear the thought of colored kids in white schools. It makes him sick to think about it; it keeps him up at night; he's not about to—"

"Yeah, but we know a thousand guys like that," I said. "That doesn't mean—"

"No, no, no," Dalton shook his head emphatically and continued. "I promise you, we do not know anybody like this. This guy's not simply protesting, Jack. He's declared war; he's out to ..."

"Raise an army?"

"Yeah," he said, "that's a good way to put it." Dalton scribbled the words on his pad. "Jim Johnson's out rousing the masses. He's telling them—right now, today—that they hold the power, that they're the final authority, that they can overturn this thing. And let me tell you something—that old boy does not know the word *retreat*."

I thought about the stories I'd heard from Amis Guthridge. I gave Dalton a sideways glance, the pieces of the story now starting to come together. "This all goes back to Hoxie, doesn't it?"

Dalton let the pencil fall to the pad. "Yep, where he and Guthridge first shared their hopes and dreams for a better world. You can just picture it, can't you? Hoxie, Arkansas: rolling green hills, silver silos against a pale blue sky. There's gotta be a feed store in the center of town—old guys in overalls sitting out front—chewing and playing checkers."

I picked up the brush and continued painting on Dalton's palette. "The white families and colored families get along just fine. They live in their own neighborhoods; keep a proper distance, but shoot, with all the talk that's going around the school board figures there's no sense busing black kids twenty-five miles to school...." I rounded my eyes at the simplicity of their conclusion. "They'll just send everybody to the same school—and nobody hears more than a grumble or two."

"Until ..." Dalton proclaimed, "Jim Johnson came to town."

We each retold the stories we'd just heard; about how Johnson and Guthridge whipped up a small town where nobody knew they were supposed to be mad. They'd gone door-to-door passing out pamphlets. They traveled dirt roads in a rusty, pockmarked Plymouth, a loudspeaker strapped to the top, rousing crowds and calling them to the courthouse square. Two men inflamed a county full of once-contented people. Where there had been tranquility, they sowed bitterness. Where there'd been trust, there was now Jim Johnson's own brand of unrighteous anger. And within weeks, the Hoxie school board canceled summer session.

"Johnson's beat the system once," Dalton said. "He doesn't see any reason why he can't do it again. In his mind, Hoxie was the dress rehearsal; Little Rock's the show."

My partner reached for his pencil again, images of some tiny farm town traipsing through his mind. "You know, the FBI came to shut him down," Dalton said, "and Johnson took 'em on."

I bit my lower lip and nodded, "So I've heard."

"Can you imagine that? Honest-to-goodness G-men going door-to-door in Hoxie, Arkansas? Guys in gray suits pounding at the door, flashing badges...." He sat back, smiling sadly. "Some old farmer answers the door; poor slob probably can't spell FBI, has never been out of Lawrence County, Arkansas." Dalton paused and looked up, "Nice, huh?

"But the biggest mistake they made ..." my friend continued: "They ticked off Jim Johnson. They picked a fight with the meanest son of a gun in Arkansas and just made him more determined."

I rubbed a hand along my chin, struggling to make sense of what we'd learned. "You know," I told Dalton, "I'm not crazy about this integration business. I mean, we're all nervous about where this is going, what it all means. But I don't understand these guys—I don't understand why anybody sets out to rile people who seem to be getting along." I planted an elbow and propped my head in the palm of my hand. "I sat across from Amis Guthridge, sat in his living room sipping tea; he was just as friendly as Alan Emerson is.... The man looks me straight in the eye—he's talking about Hoxie—and he says: 'I told those people what's really going on. I told 'em the truth—that this ain't about schools or education or equality. I told 'em this is about one thing: Niggers marrying whites.' He leans over, the man's as serious as Jonas Salk fightin' polio, and he tells me: 'Niggers don't care one bit about going to our schools, they want in our bedrooms—period.'"

Dalton stretched halfway across the table, pencil now poised in midair. "And let me tell you something, Jack, the man believes it with his whole heart. Johnson does too."

"That sharecroppers and dirt farmers in Hoxie, Arkansas, have given ten seconds of thought to marrying white girls? Come on."

"The thought of it, Jack—the mental image they got rolling around in their heads—it haunts these guys every minute. I don't know about Guthridge, but Johnson's too scared to stop fighting. He swears that Central High's staying white as a cotton ball. The man looked me in the eye and said, 'I guaran-damn-tee it.'"

A couple of beats passed, and then Dalton Dorsey beamed like a kid with a brand-new puppy. "Blossom and the school board think they're about to be heroes," he said. "They think Tuesday's Little Rock's time to shine, but Johnson's got something up his sleeve, and I don't believe I'd bet against him."

"No," I groaned, "I don't guess I would either."

Others drifted into the restaurant now. Waitresses and busboys suddenly appeared; they folded napkins, set tables, prepared for the night's crowd. Dalton glanced at his watch. "You hungry?" he asked.

"Yeah," I said, "I guess I am." I checked my watch too. "I think I'll splash a little water on my face and call Rose. You want to meet back here in a half hour?"

Dalton started to gather his things. "Sounds like a plan," he said.

Dalton sipped from a glass of something that was gold and shimmered in the soft light. He scribbled notes onto his pad, as fully absorbed by Jim Johnson's story as he'd been thirty minutes before and still oozing with glee that it was all ours.

I settled into the waiting chair, mildly refreshed and ready for round two. Dalton dipped his chin at a second glass. "Have a drink," he said.

I lifted the tumbler chin high, nodded to my partner respectfully, and said: "To a good first day."

Dalton echoed the words, and we both sipped, expelling a satisfied, "Ahh."

He pitched his pen on top of the table. "All right," he said, "we already know that I've uncovered a Pulitzer-worthy story. So how'd you spend your day?"

"Glad you asked," I told him. I studied my drink, quickly rummaging through two hundred minutes of conversation. "This group Guthridge runs," I began. "If what he says is half true, they've got more power than the utility company. And it's interesting; they're nothing like the Montgomery group. To hear Guthridge tell it, there's not a banker, lawyer, or businessman who's ever set foot in the place. They're all farmers and housepainters and car mechanics—guys who don't do much of the moving and shaking around here."

"But you just said they were powerful," Dalton interrupted.

"It's a blue collar town," I countered, "and the group is huge."

Dalton tightened his lips and nodded.

"According to Guthridge," I continued, "Blossom's been selling the plan, but not to them. He's been talking to the Rotary and garden clubs; he's been out to the country club, but from what I hear, he doesn't know a single farmer by name. Central High School's in a working-class neighborhood, and he hasn't bothered to say *boo* to the plumbers and electricians who live there."

Dalton rolled his free hand open. "So, what's going on?" he said. "I wouldn't think this guy's stupid."

"It's about priorities," I replied. "Guthridge says that Blossom's a climber. He wants to run with the big mules, get cozy with the rich and powerful. From what I'm told—and I've only got the one source—Blossom's not doing any of this to help the little guy; he's out to impress the big ones."

"Which leaves Guthridge and Johnson free to rabble-rouse their brains out." Dalton put a hand to his chin, wondering: "Has anybody at the school board got a clue about this?"

"Well ... I believe they're starting to notice. The Citizens' Council's been out working the bars and barbershops and bowling alleys. They're out there every day, passing out newsletters and pamphlets, and Guthridge swears the rumbling's starting to get loud." I paused, waiting for Dalton to glance up. "And I'm told that Blossom's feet are starting to get very, very cold."

Dalton held the glass to his lips, eyebrows hiked in anticipation.

"We got two days to go and Guthridge wants to pour it on. He wants to get the mothers more involved—it's Guthridge who's been pulling their strings all along—and they're not done with this."

"What've they got in mind?" Dalton asked.

"I don't know," I replied. "I don't think they do either. But I do know they're organized; I know there are more than a hundred and fifty of them; I know they come out of ..." I flipped through my notes, "they're out of the Broadmore Baptist Church. And I know they are not happy."

I pitched my notebook aside. "Talk about subtle power," I told Dalton. "It's easy to pick a fight with Johnson or Guthridge; they're both mean as snakes. But how do you beat up on a cafeteria full of weeping mothers?"

Dalton look heavenward, "P-u-l—"

"They've lost their court cases," I said to Dalton. "But they're nowhere near surrender."

We sat quietly for a few seconds. I tried to imagine what we'd hear from the other side, and how it'd mesh with what we already knew. I pictured Guthridge, bent forward, elbows on his knees, roiling with zeal—an underdog who'd scrap to the final bell. "I'll tell you something," I told Dalton, "right now, while you and I sit here sipping mediocre bourbon, there's more going on behind the scenes than at every theater on Broadway."

"Yep," Dalton agreed, "and these two guys—they might not have gone to Vanderbilt—but I bet they can sniff wounded prey from a hundred miles. And I bet they know when to strike for the kill."

"Guys like this," I said to Dalton, "they're crawling out of the woodwork now. It's guys like this who bombed those churches, who threatened King and Abernathy—who are making us all look so stupid."

"They're scared," Dalton said, "and that makes them dangerous."

Our waitress sauntered up and asked if we were ready to order. I sighted a plate two tables over, angled my head in that direction, and said, "I'll have a steak, as big and rare as that one." I tilted my empty glass toward her. "And one more of these."

Dalton slapped his menu closed. "Make it two," he said.

•　•　•　•

Virgil Blossom was bigger than a tackle for the Green Bay Packers. His head would've been a nice fit on Goliath's body, and he wore thick, black horn-rimmed glasses that only accentuated its size. His hair was dark and slick. His eyes were black as fresh-poured tar. And the first time I saw him he looked like a man who was one straw from breaking.

He'd holed up in a room at the Sam Peck Hotel, two floors above mine. At ten past one on Sunday afternoon I rapped on his door.

"There's really not a lot I can tell you," he began.

"Well, that's perfect," I replied easily. "I probably don't need much."

He motioned toward a chair.

"So, I guess everything's all set for Tuesday?"

He took a deep pull from his Lucky Strike, then expelled smoke into the air. "Sure," he said, "we've been working on this a long time. Why wouldn't it be?"

He paced his hotel room, dragging from the cigarette with barely a pause between puffs.

"No reason," I said. "The Thomason woman's lawsuit, that's all settled, I guess?"

He nodded and grunted, "Uh-huh."

"And the colored kids, they know where to go and what to do?"

Blossom crushed the cigarette into an ashtray. He rubbed the back of his neck, paced to the end of the room, turned and glanced at me, and then quickly glanced away. "Yeah," he finally said, "I'm sure they do."

I flipped my pad and reached for a pen. "You know, I'm not from the newspaper," I said, hoping that might calm him. "Whatever we talk about, it's not going to be in print for two or three weeks, not till long after the first day of school."

Blossom lit a fresh smoke, took a long drag, and blew a cloud into the space between us.

"You might think of me—of the article I'm doing—as a chance to let the world in on the big picture, to tell 'em what you hope to accomplish over the long haul."

Blossom seemed to mull the information over, the cigarette now dangling at his side, held loosely between two fingers.

"If something were to go south on you, or if the plan hit some kind of snag—I might help explain it," I said. "I got the time and plenty of space to give a little background, provide some history. The newspaper guys, they pretty much need to know *what* happened. I'm more interested in *why.*"

Blossom sucked the cigarette to a blazing red glow. "You're not publishing anything till the end of the month?" he confirmed.

"That'd be the earliest," I promised. I reached for the Gideon's Bible, placed my left hand on top: "I swear," I told him.

A room service cart squealed in the hall outside. Muffled sounds from a television seeped through the east wall. An air conditioner droned in the background. "There might be a glitch or two," he said, his voice so soft I could barely hear him.

I sat back in the chair trying to look calm, like a psychiatrist ready to tap an emotional vein. "A glitch?"

Blossom gazed out the back door. "Yeah," he said, his voice wavering. He turned; his eyes were red as cherries, and when he pulled the cigarette from his lips his hand trembled. "We got to keep the colored kids away from that school."

I poised the pen over the pad. "Why?" I said. "After all that work? After all the planning?"

Blossom teetered on the brink of tears. He looked down, brushed an errant ash from his shirt. "We had everybody onboard, we picked some good kids...." He pulled on the cigarette again. "This should've been easy."

I sat quietly, waiting for him to fill the silence.

He moved a hand to his mouth and rubbed along his neck and jaw. "Seventeen kids," he moaned. "In this entire city, we're talking about seventeen Negro children."

"And that's seventeen too many for some people?"

He flicked ashes onto the carpet. "Hell, you ask some people around here—they'll tell you we're this far from doomsday."

"But that can't be a surprise," I said. "You know that Johnson and Guthridge have been beating the bushes all summer."

Blossom collapsed into a chair, sweat gathering at his lip and forehead. "Those two ..." his jaw clenched, then he continued, "they're leading the charge straight back to the past." His foot bounced in the air; his eyes danced. "That's their business I s'pose, but this time ..." the sentence evaporated into the air.

"This time, what?" I asked.

"They're stirring up trouble," Blossom snarled. "And I don't mean political trouble. This time they're getting downright dangerous."

"Dangerous how?" I prodded.

Blossom propped his elbow on the arm of the chair, resting his chin on a clenched fist, smoke curling up around him. "Riots," he whispered.

I waited quietly again.

"People are on their way right now," Blossom said. "Caravans are streaming toward Little Rock; boys coming in here to take matters into their own hands." Virgil Blossom's lip quivered. "If those colored kids try to enroll at Central...."

I watched him, thought about the position he was in, the consequences that loomed, and the weight of responsibility. "So what are you going to do?"

Blossom shook his head. "I don't know," he said. He crushed the cigarette into the tray beside him. "I've been pleading with Bill Smith to bring a lawsuit for days. Me and Faubus, we've both been begging the court to step in, to stop this thing before somebody gets hurt."

I stopped scribbling in midsentence, "Smith?"

"A lawyer," Blossom said, "he works for Faubus."

"So the governor's now working to *stop* the integration of Central High School?" I asked. "He's doing this now, with two days before school?"

Blossom glanced up and then right back down. "We're wanting the courts to rule on our segregation laws," he said. "We got four of 'em; they'll never stand up," Blossom said, "but that'd give us three or four more days and...."

"And give you political cover," I said. "If there's trouble, you want the courts to take the blame."

Blossom sat quietly, foot twitching, as restless as a father outside the maternity ward.

I thought back to Guthridge and Johnson, to Dalton's conclusion that they were scared and therefore dangerous. And I wondered how far they'd be willing to go. "Do you really think these caravans are coming?" I asked Blossom. "Has anybody seen them? Does anybody actually know somebody who's involved?"

"My own daughter's getting some ugly calls," Blossom replied. He stabbed out his fifth cigarette. "We got to stop this," he said. "We got to protect our own people. If we don't ..." Blossom stood and walked to the sliding glass door. "This is such a pretty town," he said. "We had so much going for us; the future looked so bright. But now...." The big man's voice trembled. "Things are gonna get ugly."

•   •   •   •

I found Dalton right where I'd left him the day before, a tall glass of half-drunk tea resting beside him, the remnant smells of Sunday fried chicken lingering in the restaurant air.

An older couple sat toward the back of the dining room. They were white-haired, still dressed in church clothes, holding hands across the table. Through the glass panes of the kitchen door I spotted a colored busboy and a white waiter, their backs pressed against shiny silver appliances, talking about baseball or high school football or the weather or the cranky customers who'd been sitting at table seven. They laughed and then frowned and their eyes flashed with shared stories and the coziness of everyday conversation. These were people at peace—content where they were and with what they had—who saw no need for life to make a sudden turn.

I pitched my pad on the table, dropped into a chair, and said, "So, how's life treating the Arkansas governor?"

I had expected the blinding flash of Dorsey's smile, but instead, he plopped his chin into an open palm, as forlorn as a kid who'd just busted a favorite toy. "I'll tell you something, Jack; politics in this town ... it ain't for girls."

"It is a contact sport," I agreed.

Dalton reached for the pencil stuck behind his ear. "It's hard to figure," he said. "I just spent ninety minutes with the governor of Arkansas. This guy's the chief executive, the top of the dad-gum food chain—and everybody for a hundred miles around has either lied to him or deserted him or more than likely both."

"Well, how nice," I said. "You spend an afternoon at the governor's mansion and what do you find? Conspiracy and betrayal." I shook my head, chuckling. "Can you imagine my surprise?" Then I smiled dimly, trying to look sympathetic. "So who's turned on him?"

Dalton cocked his head, staring at me as if I'd just spoken to him in Russian.

I flipped an imploring palm. "Who's betrayed him?" I asked.

Dalton's stare lagged two beats longer. "Blossom," he finally said.

"What are you talking about?" I asked. "These guys are in cahoots, they're working hand in glove, both of 'em trying to get the plan delayed."

"I don't think so," Dalton said.

I stared back, eyes narrowed.

"Blossom's working," Dalton said, "but it ain't with Faubus."

"I don't understand," I said. "They want the same thing."

Dalton folded his arms across the table. "We've heard about this court case," he said. "The Thomason woman trying to postpone integration...."

"Yeah," I said, "and all the appeals ..."

"Well, as it turns out, the governor testifies in federal court. He's out there in public telling the judge that the situation is dangerous, that lives are at stake, that innocent people are going to get hurt—"

"Which is exactly what I heard from Blossom," I said.

"Which is no big surprise," Dalton replied. "Blossom's been feeding him this stuff for days." Dalton inched closer. "But in court, when it's Blossom's turn to testify, he swears he hasn't heard a thing. As far as he knows, there's not a lick of danger; he can't think of one good reason why integration can't go on according to his perfect plan." Dalton sat back, sadly bemused. "Blossom didn't tell you any of this?"

"No," I said, "he somehow failed to mention it. But this doesn't add up. Blossom's scared to death. He's upstairs right now, and I'm telling you, he'd rather be sailing on the *Titanic*. The man's desperate."

"And Orval Faubus is his only hope," Dalton said. "But in court, when Blossom took the stand, he pulled a Benedict Arnold; he left Faubus all alone and looking real stupid."

"Why would he do that?" I wondered.

"Well, think about it," Dalton said. "If he forces Faubus to do the dirty work—if Faubus is the one who kills the plan—Blossom's still a hero; he goes to the country club with his head held high."

I nodded slowly, "And nobody'll ever know if the danger was real." I twirled a teaspoon, imagining the new scenario: With the threat of violence looming, Virgil Blossom dares the governor to just sit still. "So now Faubus is surrounded," I surmised. "Johnson and Guthridge are closing in from one side, Blossom and the school board are coming from the other."

Dalton downed his last gulp of iced tea. "Southern politics at its down-and-dirtiest."

I cracked a sly smile. "You know, you actually look like you feel sorry for this guy."

"I don't know," Dalton smirked. "I mean, here he is the governor of the state; he's done some good things, kept a few promises, helped the poor. And now, when it gets a little dicey, his best pals double-cross him."

I clicked my pen and began to write. Slowly and deliberately I enunciated the words: "Dorsey-feels-sorry-for-politician." Then, smiling, I said, "Just making note of it."

"Look," Dalton explained, "Faubus has done more than his share of stupid things; there's no getting around that. And he's done them because he's a slimy politician, because he'd rather get elected than breathe. But I don't know, he just seems to be the least slimy of this particular bunch."

My partner doodled a few stray lines on his pad. "I could be wrong," he said, "but I don't see the mean streak in this guy—not like we've seen in Griffin and Gayle—and nothing like Guthridge and Johnson."

"So," I clamped my arms across my chest, "you're thinking he's the angle: that this is a story about a governor who's been betrayed, lied to, abandoned, manipulated by friend and foe alike …?"

Dalton shrugged. "Maybe," he said. He reached for the tea again. "It's going to be fun to watch, I can tell you that much. The phone over there's ringing off the hook—everybody passing the buck, trying to make him the scapegoat." Dalton rocked the glass back and forth. "The pressure's building. He keeps hearing that gun sales are up, that the coloreds are buying knives and pistols, that people are streaming into town, that they're armed to the teeth and bent on keeping those kids from setting one foot inside a white school." Dalton paused; he raised his eyes level with mine. "He told me more than once, he knows there's going to be bloodshed."

"Which does make this his problem," I said.

"Yeah ... if it's true."

"You think it is?" I asked.

Dalton tapped the pencil a few times and shrugged. "I think some desperate people have run out of options. To them, this is a fight for the 'Southern way of life.' If it turns out that all the talk about violence is a hoax—some last-ditch effort to save Southern society ..." he turned his hand open, "let's just say I wouldn't be stunned."

I sat back, recalling my conversation with Blossom. "You know, it does seem weird that we haven't noticed anything. I mean, we've been riding around town for two days and haven't seen the first sign of a caravan—and we're pretty perceptive guys."

"Does make you wonder," Dalton said.

"And he's getting all this from Blossom?"

"Blossom's one source," Dalton replied. "The state police chief's another." He leaned back, lacing his fingers behind his head. "I guess the important thing is, Faubus believes it. And I'm telling you, Jack, it's tearing him up inside. Right now, this guy's strung tighter'n Elvis Presley's guitar."

"Uh-huh," I said. I pinched at my lip, wondering. "You know maybe...." I stopped, my mind straining to carry each morsel of information to its most-distant conclusion.

"What?" Dalton asked.

A cautious smile plucked at my lips. "Maybe he's playing you," I said. "Maybe it's Faubus who's playing everybody."

Dalton's brow crested with curiosity.

"What if he's the source? The police chief works for him, right? What if Faubus is manufacturing all this?"

"No," Dalton exclaimed, "I don't see how …" But then he paused. A gleam lit the corner of my partner's right eye. "Because he's a slimy politician…."

"Yeah," I replied, "and because he'd rather get reelected than breathe." I scooted in closer, "Johnson's outflanked him. The farmers and housepainters and electricians—that's who put Faubus in office."

"And Johnson's been quietly sliding 'em into his corner; he's been using this to paint Faubus as the radical integrationist."

"Johnson's run for governor once," I said.

"And he does not like to lose." Dalton looked away, pondering the possibility. "Geez," he said. "This little town'd make Machiavelli tremble."

"Southern politics …" I concluded. Then, with a shrug, I said, "So what's he going to do? If he's got all this evidence of guns and mobs, what's the plan?"

A moment passed, and then Dalton's pain gave way to the more familiar wag. "Oh, didn't I tell you?" he said mischievously. He leaned forward, eyes darting right and left—the spy again, ready to divulge the secret code. "He's put the National Guard on alert, Jack. He's ordered them to get their gear together and to wait for his call."

"Holy—" I threw my napkin at him. "Geez, Dalton, don't you ever hold out on me like that again."

Dalton smiled. But then his countenance turned grim. "If he calls 'em out, Jack, this story takes on a dimension we never dreamed of. If he calls out armed troops, this thing's bigger than Montgomery."

"You think he will?"

Dalton turned loose of a weary sigh. "Hard to say. He's scared. He doesn't want innocent blood on his hands. The political pressure's got to be killing him." He tapped the pencil three more times. "Yeah," he said, "I think he's leaning that way."

After dinner I called home. My wife always shares the excitement of a good story, but the retelling of this one made her sad and frightened.

Her fear had nothing to do with any threat to my safety. It was, instead, for every mother, kid, and community that faced this change. Rose Marie—like so many of the women of Little Rock, like me, like any white person willing to be honest—could barely conceive so drastic a change. She'd seen the earlier experiments fail; she'd seen firsthand, and on more than one occasion, how the blending of black and white produced a compound that was too volatile to manage, and that almost always burst into flames. She'd watched the anger burn. She'd witnessed grief in the aftermath. She knew this was a bad idea for both races. And whenever the subject came up, there was the inevitable clash with her only son.

But tonight, the subject quickly turned and brightened. Chris had come home thrilled by a piece of great news: Next Thursday night he'd play his first junior varsity football game, and he'd be the starting defensive end.

"You need to talk to him," Rose said. "He can't wait to tell you."

My son came on the line. "Hello," he said, the tone as wooden as a block.

"Mom tells me you got some news."

"Yeah," he said. I sensed his excitement percolating beneath the stiffness.

"You gonna start next Thursday?" I asked.

"Yes sir," he said, a chuckle just beginning to surface.

"Nice!" I exclaimed. "I'm going to make sure we cover that game. And who knows, if you play good enough you might get your name in the paper."

Chris laughed. "Yeah, you never know."

"So what'd the coach say when he told you?" I asked.

"He just said that I'd looked good in practice, that he liked my toughness." Chris sniggered again, embarrassed.

I pictured him in his pads and helmet, thinking about much he'd grown, about how strong he'd gotten, how much faster he'd become in the last year. And now, I'd learned, he was "tough."

"I'm proud of you," I told my son. "And I'm going do everything I can to be at every game you ever play, you hear? And Chris ..."

"Yes sir?"

"I bet you're going to be the toughest kid who ever played in Fulton County, Georgia."

There was a pause. I suspected he was mulling the possibility over. "Yeah," he finally said, "maybe so."

•   •   •   •

Monday morning Dalton and I rushed to the *Arkansas Gazette*. Reporters from around the country had assembled, all of them there to chronicle Central High's first day of school, but not a one of them expected a story worth his byline. These guys had drawn the short straw, and every one of them wished he were in Nashville.

I introduced myself to men from St. Louis, Baltimore, Memphis, and Detroit. There was an older guy there, frumpy looking, bald, wearing a wrinkled gray suit and a crooked bowtie. He looked more like a college professor than a reporter. He reached for my hand: "Benjamin Fine," he said, "from the *New York Times*."

"The *Times*?" I cocked my head, surprised. The *New York Times* was one of the few big papers that had a Southern bureau. It was in Chattanooga, staffed by John Popham, a debonair Virginian who I'd bumped into three or four times before. "So where's Popham?" I asked.

Fine shrugged. "I'd guess Nashville." He jammed his hands into his pockets and explained, "I'm the education reporter—we're thinking this is probably more up my alley."

"Yeah," I half chuckled, "probably so." Then I slapped the old guy's shoulder and said, "But you better stay on your toes."

Reporters wandered around the newsroom wondering how to kill a holiday in a town they didn't know. They checked the movies. They wondered if there was a ballgame in town, or if there was somebody who might take them fishing. They propped their feet on empty desks and read old magazines.

Dalton and I huddled in a corner, away from the crowd, and began to weave our story together. We needed Ashmore to fill in a few gaps, and Dalton wanted to dig a little deeper, to see if we could learn more about Faubus's motives.

Ashmore was swapping stories with a handful of old friends. Dalton and I attached ourselves to the crowd, listening, laughing at the punch lines, and waiting for a lull. At the first opportunity I said, "I wonder if we could run a couple of things by you?" I shot my eyes toward the editor's office.

"Yeah," Ashmore replied with a nod, "sure thing." He slapped one of his pals on the back. "I'll catch up with you boys a little later," he said. Then showed Dalton and me inside.

"I need your take on Faubus," Dalton said, closing the door behind him. "It seems like this guy's in a heck of a spot and—"

Ashmore laughed. "Bet your ass he is," he said, "and it's his own fault. Orval's been playing both sides of this fence all along; been saying whatever he thinks'll keep both sides happy, and tomorrow morning, it all catches up to him."

"Yeah," Dalton said, "but how …?"

Ashmore's phone rang. He picked it up, signaling Dalton to hold his thought. Gradually, he slumped deeper and deeper into his chair, his frown setting hard—a man in sudden and mounting pain. He put a hand to his forehead and rubbed anxiously. "What time?" he asked, as if expecting the arrival of pestilence. He checked his watch and snarled. "All right," he told the caller, and then, slowly, he placed the phone back in its cradle.

Dalton and I stared silently, wondering and waiting for an explanation.

"Faubus just asked for TV time," Ashmore murmured, his thoughts now distant and churning. "He's going on sometime around ten o'clock." The man's chair groaned as he turned. He closed his eyes. "I know what that idiot is going to do," he said. "I just know it." He stood and raced for the door. "Sorry," he said, "I've got to go."

Word spread like an airborne virus, and the sleepy newsroom stirred. Dalton and I raced back to the desks we'd claimed. "I need a phone," Dalton exclaimed, "someplace where nobody'll hear me." We scanned the room, scurried down a hallway, and spotted a vacant office. Dalton slammed the door; he thumbed through his notebook, found a number, and dialed.

I heard the faint ring tone—a second time and then a third. And then a hollow-sounding voice answered.

"Is he doing it?" Dalton's tone was low and urgent. "Is he calling out the Guard?"

I couldn't make out the mumbled reply.

"I won't tell a soul," Dalton promised. "I'll never use your name; I'll never reveal you as the source."

He dropped into the chair, scribbled notes furiously, uttered an occasional "uh-huh," and then hung up the phone. He gazed up; eyes glossed with wonder. "He's done it," Dalton declared. "Faubus has called out the National Guard. They're going to surround the school at nine o'clock tonight; Faubus'll be on the air at ten fifteen. And right now ..." Dalton paused, making sure he'd reeled in every bit of my attention. "Right this minute, you and I are the only reporters who know it."

"We've got to call McGill. We got to get something to him ..." I checked my watch. "They're an hour behind us; we'll have to have something there in the next hour." I picked up the phone, my index finger hovering above the 0. "We can scoop the entire world on this," I told Dalton.

We spent the next fifty-five minutes typing and revising the story that nobody else had. We'd kept every confidence we promised—and on Labor Day 1957, Dalton Dorsey and I broke the biggest story of the year. And, as things would unfold, one of the biggest in history.

That evening, while everyone else scrambled for clues about what Faubus might say, Dalton and I slipped out to have a look at the action.

Little Rock Central High School was once named the most beautiful school in America, and nobody who's ever seen it wonders why. There's a reflecting pond, tranquil and calming as a lullaby, centered at the base of the building. From either side, a pair of grand stairways—wide and elegant—sweep up and away in graceful curves to three arched entrances. Above them, etched in the same stone, the statues of four Greek goddesses bestow the blessings of Ambition, Personality, Opportunity, and Preparation.

Standing at the edge of the pond, craning your neck upward, you're humbled by its majesty. Standing before this building, enfolded by the stairways, arches, and statuary, it dawns on you that the acts of education—teaching and learning—are noble endeavors. And that they are, when rightly perceived, worthy of a building this beautiful.

And yet, by nine o'clock that night—September 2, 1957—the beauty and nobility both would be forever scarred. That night, under the cover of darkness, a scene would unfold that neither you, nor I, nor any U.S. citizen could have ever envisioned.

Canvas-topped trucks—army green and camouflaged—rumbled through the narrow streets of this quiet, middle-class neighborhood.

Military jeeps had jumped the curbs. Soldiers, wearing crisply pressed uniforms, spit-shined shoes, and helmets that gleamed in the moonlight lined the sidewalks. Rifles, with bayonets attached, were slung across their shoulders.

Little Rock police scurried to set up barricades at each entrance; they examined diagrams, studied plans, and discussed what kind of credentials would be needed to pass.

Dalton and I stood at a distance and watched the spectacle—shocked, but also enthralled.

"Is this Berlin?" I whispered.

Dalton, with grief saturating the single syllable, simply said, "No."

I reached into my pocket and fumbled for two dimes, three nickels, and a couple of quarters. "You got any change?" I asked Dalton.

"Yeah," he said, reaching into his pocket. "I think so."

I handed him my coins. "You need to call *Life*," I told him. "They'll know a photographer somewhere close by—somebody who's not already working for the local papers—somebody who can have his butt down here before dawn." I waved my hand toward Ponder's drugstore. "There's a phone right there."

We hurried back to the *Gazette* to watch Orval Faubus. The television's gray light flickered through the room, over the dejected faces of Harry Ashmore, Hugh Patterson, the *Gazette's* publisher, and J. N. Heiskell, its owner.

Reporters from ten or twelve cities stood behind them, quiet with anticipation, pens and pads at the ready, wondering how, at this point, they could possibly scoop the guy beside them. Dalton and I stood in the back of the room, as interested in their reaction as we were in Faubus's speech.

The Arkansas state seal faded up on the screen. An off-camera announcer informed us that we were watching a special presentation of KARK news, and the words "Message from the Governor" flashed across the screen in bold, italicized letters. And then, the drawn, fatigued image of Orval Faubus appeared.

The governor talked about how, since he had taken office, the life of Negro citizens had improved. This was evidence, he said— hard and irrefutable—"that the citizens of Arkansas have not been unmindful of their problems as they relate to the good relations of the races and that the citizenship as a whole have met their responsibilities."

Moving to the subject at hand, he explained that the federal court had ruled and that the integration of Central High must proceed. He turned to his right, to face a second camera; his expression shifted from grief to determination. "There is," he said, "evidence of disorder and threats of disorder which could have but one inevitable result, and that is violence which can lead to injury and the doing of harm to persons and property."

He went on to explain that Virgil Blossom had been threatened; that a telephone campaign "of massive proportions" was underway calling on the mothers of white children to assemble at the school Tuesday morning; that there were caravans descending on Little Rock, men from all over the state coming to convene at the Central High campus.

Now looking grave and paternal, he turned back to camera one.

There were police reports, he said, that an unusually large number of weapons had been sold in the Little Rock area, "mostly to Negro youths," and revolvers had been confiscated from high school students, colored and white, both.

Faubus stared down at his desk. There was a pause—just the slightest hint of hesitation —then he explained that litigation was still in process.

The reporters in the room hadn't drawn a breath in the last thirty seconds.

Faubus claimed that the courts had not ruled on Arkansas's segregation laws. There were, then, legal matters yet to be resolved. The camera pushed in closer. The governor peered directly into its lens and said: "I feel strongly that time should be given to litigate these measures to final conclusion in order that we may see clearly and unmistakably what is the law of the land—either state or federal...."

From the front of the room, Ashmore groaned.

Faubus explained that he had, after much prayer, decided to place units of the National Guard and the state police at Central High School. Their mission, he assured his audience, was "to maintain or restore the peace and good order of this community." The militia, he said, were not there as segregationists or integrationists; they were there to protect lives and property.

The governor made one more turn to camera two. The soldiers, he explained, could not complete this mission "if forcible integration is carried out tomorrow in the schools of this community...."

"Then they're segregationists!" Ashmore bellowed.

"Shh!" Patterson urged him.

"The schools in Pulaski County," Faubus concluded, "must be operated on the same basis as they have been operated in the past."

On my third attempt I got Virgil Blossom on the phone. "So what now?" I asked.

"I got no idea," the man groaned. "The whole school board's over here scratching their heads, wondering what in the world the man just said." I pictured Blossom, stubbing out one cigarette after another, not quite sure if he should be frightened or relieved. "We got people hammering out some kind of statement," he said. "Are you at the *Gazette* office?"

"Yeah," I replied.

"It'll be there as soon as we get it worked out."

"Give me a hint," I prodded. "What's the bottom line?"

I sensed uncertainty at the other end of the line. And then, haltingly, Blossom said, "We're telling the colored kids to stay home. We'll get with Judge Davies first thing in the morning and go from there."

Thirty minutes later the board released its statement. It read: "Although the federal court has ordered integration to proceed, Governor Faubus has said that schools should continue as they have in the past and has stationed troops at Central High School to maintain order. In view of this situation, we ask that no Negro students attempt to attend Central or any white high school until this dilemma is legally resolved."

•   •   •   •

We crammed in a few hours of restless sleep. And then, a half hour before dawn, we grabbed coffee and biscuits; I yanked a copy of the *Arkansas Gazette* from a bundle that was still baled in brown twine, and we sped toward Central High School.

My first glimpse of the campus stirred an audible groan. What had seemed like a dream the night before was now a harsh and eerie reality: Armed soldiers lined the streets of this quaint Southern town. Their helmets glistened; gun barrels and bayonets flashed in the gentle light of the new day. And my heart, weighed down by the truth of what was right before my eyes, dropped like a paratrooper. I shuddered at the sight, my thoughts flailing—wondering how, wondering by what series of events, a thing like this could have possibly happened.

This, of all mornings, should have been full of promise: Bright-faced kids sported new clothes; they carried clean and sturdy notebooks, and a fistful of never-sharpened pencils. They'd soon meet new teachers and reunite with friends. They'd explore new subjects and discover parts of the world that would fire their imaginations.

Billowed white clouds tarried across the blue background. The air was summery, but tinged by a fresh breeze. And even the birds, it seemed, sang excitedly—darting from wire to limb to roof—curious, I thought, about the throng that had gathered beneath them.

But for parents and students, every trace of goodness had been blurred, and only one thing was in perfect focus: five hundred militiamen.

Adults and kids streamed up and down narrow side streets toward Central High. Small crowds began to cluster. People stood on front porches, some still in bathrobes, sipping from cups of steaming coffee—rattled and wondering what ill had befallen their drowsy Southern town.

"Big crowd," Dalton observed.

"And it's not even seven," I replied. "What do you think, four, maybe five hundred?"

"I guess," Dalton replied. "I've never been too good at that kind of thing."

From my throat, into my heart, down my chest, and into the belly this sight burrowed to a new depth of sorrow. Ordinary moms and dads had gathered along the quiet streets of a middle-class neighborhood. Troubled parents crowded sidewalks; they blocked driveways, gawking at the wreckage around them. Kids climbed the maples, pines, and magnolias—eager as race fans for a clear view of the collision we all knew was coming.

Dalton spotted Tom Davis, a reporter from the *Gazette*. We walked up beside him. "So, who are all these people?" I asked.

He nodded a silent good morning. "A bunch of 'em are from the Citizens' Council," he said. He raised his chin toward a flock of jittery women. "They're from the Mothers' League, and the rest—I think they're just folks wondering what the heck's going on."

Down the block, a small crowd stirred. A woman marched to the end of a driveway, then five feet farther into the street. She raised a Confederate flag into the air. She waved it, struggling slightly beneath its weight, but with visible and palpable devotion. And then—we could just barely hear—she began to sing. Her voice was, at once, reverent and sad and filled with gumption: "I wish I was in the land of cotton, old times there are not forgotten …" A somber chorus swelled around her, twenty, maybe thirty feminine voices—steeled and tenacious—joining the refrain: "Look away, look away, look away, Dixie land."

Davis tossed a hand in their general direction, "I'm sure you recognize Mary Thomason," he said.

"Who doesn't appear to be giving in," I observed.

Davis shook his head no. "And the woman who's moving through the crowd there," he pointed again and continued, "the one passing out some kind of paper, that's Margaret Jackson."

"Who looks to have some fight left as well," Dalton noticed.

"Yeah," Davis affirmed, "fight would be the one quality neither of those gals lacks."

An hour later, with no sign of the Negro students, the crowd dwindled away. Dalton hurried off for a chat with Margaret Jackson. I rushed to federal court, to catch up with Virgil Blossom.

That afternoon I pushed through the revolving doors at the Sam Peck Hotel and raced for the dining room. "Tomorrow!" I exclaimed to Dalton, "it's gonna be tomorrow!'

His face twisted to a puzzle. "Geez," he said. "That didn't take long."

"There's no evidence of outside agitators," I gasped. "And Davies—the judge—he says he can't find one good reason to suspect violence. He ordered the school board to integrate Central High first thing in the morning."

"What about Faubus's evidence?" Dalton asked. "What about the police chief? The caravans? The gun sales …?"

I shrugged and said, "The federal judge ain't buying it."

When I called home that night Rose Marie turned grim at the news. "Jack," she told me, "I know something terrible's gonna happen over there; I can just feel it."

I couldn't come up with one true claim to calm her.

"Bad stuff always happens," she insisted, her voice quaking. "I'm glad I'm not there. I don't know what'd I do, Jack. I might be right there with those women. I might be in court. I might be on the streets ..." her voice faded. "I don't know what I'd do...."

"These gals might be a little extreme for you," I tried to sound casual.

"Jack, when there are soldiers surrounding the school, when they're putting white children and colored children in the same locker rooms, when they're going to eat side by side in the same cafeteria—what, exactly, would be too extreme?"

• • • •

Wednesday morning Dalton snatched a newspaper that hadn't been off the press for more than a couple of hours. He scanned the front page while I drove to Central High School.

"So ..." I tried to rush him along, "what's it say?"

"Well ..." he drawled, "I don't think Ashmore's conversations with Faubus have gone too well."

"Meaning ...?"

"He's got a front-page editorial," Dalton told me. "The title's *The Crisis Mr. Faubus Made*." He skipped down the page. "Ashmore's saying that nobody's verified any threat of violence; that Faubus has got to decide whether he intends to pose a constitutional question; the effect of his action is to interpose his state office between the local school district and the Unites States Court...." Dalton shook the creases out of the paper and then read directly from Ashmore's editorial: "... the issue is no longer segregation vs. integration. The question has now become the supremacy of the government of the United States in all matters of law." He skimmed down a few lines further. "... it is time for him to call a halt to the resistance ... before his own actions become the cause of the violence he professes to fear.

"So," Dalton said, "there you have it."

I knew the Southerner in him hated this story—that he was grieved that any of this had ever occurred—but the reporter was giddier than a prom queen. "I can't believe we're here," he said. "This is the biggest story since VJ Day."

By this time, eight of the original seventeen Negro students had decided to stick with their old schools. The remaining nine would meet that morning at Daisy Bates's home. We'd been told that they'd travel together, that Bates and several Negro pastors would walk alongside, providing the kids with moral and spiritual cover. We knew they'd arrive late, after the white kids had settled into their first class, and that they'd enter through a side or back entrance, hoping to avoid hostile crowds and nosy reporters.

Dalton and I, along with a growing horde of other journalists, scurried for crumbs of information, gleaning what we could from parents, teachers, and the kids who passed us by. But mostly we kept watch, waiting.

Guthridge had roused a better-than-decent crowd. Protesters

lined the streets, five and six deep in places. Parents swarmed at the intersections, and you could feel the delirium in the air. You could sense a kind of frenzy—the presence of some unknown element that slowly, working outside our consciousness, mangles gentle people into an angry mob.

Confederate flags fluttered in the breeze. Protest signs punched into the air. "I don't know …" I muttered to Dalton, "Faubus might've been right about this."

Police and National Guardsmen stood at attention—stern and dead-cold silent. They held their rifles across their chests, slanted from shoulder to hip at a forty-five-degree angle—local boys, mostly, here on business they could have never fathomed.

Dalton and I rushed along Twelfth Street, keeping our eyes open, making mental notes along the way. We crossed Park Avenue and came to a one-bench bus stop that occupied the corner. "Hang on a second," Dalton said. "I want to get this down before I forget it." We sat on the bench, scribbling on notepads, trying to capture the scene before us: Three Confederate flags—bright red, with deep blue stripes, waved across a patch of cloudless sky. The crowd stirred like livestock before a thunderstorm, and so many, we noticed, were women. My gaze fell on a brunette; she was my age, maybe a year or two older. Her hair had been curled, combed, and sprayed—every strand in perfect position. She wore a sleeveless yellow dress, belted at the waist, with matching, open-toed shoes. She held a toddler by the hand who, it seemed to me, was charmed by all the sights, sounds, and colors.

I watched her closely. Her eyes darted back and forth across the crowd—to the soldiers, to the passing cars and buses. She stared at the school—eyes wide and vacant looking—as if she'd stumbled onto the scene of some terrible crash. With her free hand she reached to the corner of her left eye, to blot the tears she couldn't quite hold.

Across the street, on the opposite sidewalk, I came to an older woman. She wore a dark dress with lace at the neck and shoulders, three white buttons fastened from neckline to waistline. She wore sensible black shoes. Her cheeks and neck and chin sagged with the fleshiness that comes with age. Her eyes, I noticed, were narrowed to slits, and her mouth drooped at the corners into a permanent, dejected scowl.

These were not wild-eyed activists. They were hardly radicals or rabble-rousers. They could not have possibly been outside agitators. They were a mother and a grandmother. They were wives and PTA members and church volunteers—not much different than Rose Marie.

Others in the crowd had moved from sadness to anger, and the anger was quickly mutating into open defiance. We read the words on every sign: 'See you later integrator,' 'Back to the jungle,' and the less imaginative: 'Go home niggers.' We heard shouts and corresponding chants from each pocket of protest.

A bus pulled in front of us blocking the view. "Come on," Dalton complained. He waved a hand, shooing the bus forward. "I'm working here," he snarled.

"It is a bus stop," I reminded him.

A middle-aged maid climbed down the bus steps. A salesgirl followed, then a teacher—who was trailed by a teenage colored girl. She wore sunglasses and clutched a blue spiral notebook; the kind the kids all carry to school. The black girl turned toward Central High; she surveyed the area—her chest swelled with a deep breath—and then, with her head raised high, with this posture of great resolve, she started forward.

I elbowed Dalton hard to the ribs. "That's one of the kids!" I gasped, "I've seen her picture. She's one of the nine." I checked my watch. "She's early."

"Yeah," Dalton whispered, "and alone."

The bus pulled away, leaving us in a cloud of gray, foul-smelling exhaust. I backhanded Dalton's knee. "Let's go. It's time to follow the story."

We eased off the bench and trailed at a safe distance.

"I thought they were all coming together," Dalton said.

I shrugged. "That's what I heard."

This girl's name, we'd later learn, was Elizabeth Eckford. Her family did not own a telephone, and she'd never gotten word of Daisy Bates's plan. She looked like any kid on the first day of school—neatly dressed in a white shirtwaist with a deep gingham hem, white buck loafers, and bobby socks. And I was struck that day by her poise—by how this girl held her shoulders back, her head up, and kept her eyes forward.

As she neared Central High, the white crowd stirred, and a murmur rippled its way around the campus. Eckford neared Fourteenth Street, where hundreds of National Guardsmen flashed into view. She stopped for a moment and sighed; her shoulders turning loose of the tension, relieved by the sight of such ample protection. Her pace quickened.

In the distance a pack of white students began to move in a wide circle, like hungry wolves closing in on a stray lamb. Closer, the taunts began to fly.

Eckford marched forward, her head now bowed and her lips clamped tight with determination. She hurried for the sidewalk, to the line of soldiers, racing to put them between her and the swelling mob. She was twelve yards away when she broke into a jog, rushing to slip behind their protective shield. She had closed to within ten feet when an armed guardsman threw out his right hand, fingers splayed wide. He slid his left foot to the side, blocking the girl's path. "No colored allowed," he snapped. "You need to go on home."

She froze, dazed by the unexpected blow.

"What do you mean, not allowed?" I shouted. "The court—"

"Order of the governor," the soldier barked. Then, more quietly, "Just now came."

"Faubus ordered you to block these kids? Today?"

The soldier stood straight as a flagpole and just as silent.

The Negro girl hurried past the traffic barrier, twenty yards farther to a spot where white kids passed freely. Behind her, the mob grew with every step; they'd begun to surround her, racing up beside her, angry, and now emboldened by the Guard's indifference. "Go back to the damn jungle!" someone screamed. "Yeah, go back where you came from, nigger."

From her left flank a pair of white girls rushed up beside her. They swaggered alongside, swaying their hips brashly. One of them looked Eckford up and down, inspecting her hair, face, and clothes.... Without stopping she turned to her friend: "Would you look at those shoes," she cooed haughtily, to the giggling delight of those around her.

Eckford stared straight ahead, clasping the notebook tighter.

Behind her, just to the right of the two girls, a young man flailed his arms in the air. "Lynch her!" he screamed, touching off a new barrage of taunts and jeers.

There were five hundred guardsmen there. There must have been a hundred state police officers watching the scene unfold. Not one of them budged. Not one of them made the first attempt to calm the crowd, to protect the colored kid, or to preserve any semblance of order.

Photographers now skirted the crowd. The colored girl came to the second entrance. She turned toward the school, but two guardsmen closed ranks, blocking her path for a second time.

The sassy white girl crept up close behind her. She thrust a hip to the side and sneered with more contempt than McCarthy has for communists. She hurried forward, to within inches of the colored girl's ear. Her lips curled to a snarl ...

At that moment, a photographer's bulb flashed.

"Nigger!" the white girl sneered, her face mauled by rage.

Elizabeth Eckford hurried to the next block. She turned again, and for the third time was denied what the courts had granted.

Reporters watched the spectacle. Television and radio crews followed close beside her, recording every move, word, and gesture.

Eckford marched frantically now—aimless and searching for refuge. She spotted Ponder's drugstore and cut to her left, rushing for safety.

The crowd closed in, shouting and swarming around her like a cloud of frenzied bees. She reached the store, barreled up the steps, and lunged forward, grasping the door handle, when—at the last possible second—the lock twisted closed, leaving this girl's fate to the will of a frothing mob.

She turned and stood with her back to the door, cornered. The shouts grew louder. Her chest heaved up and down—wounded prey facing down a predator. Then she lowered her head and plowed through the mob. Insults and slurs poured down, pelting her as she passed. She trudged forward, to the Sixteenth Street bus stop; she dropped onto the bench, her shoulders hunched, head bowed, coiling into a tight, protective shell, trying to block the screaming mob from her mind.

A teenaged boy—a fellow student at Elizabeth Eckford's new school—stood behind her, no more than two feet away. "Just sit on the bench, tar baby. That's what you are." The lines on his forehead creased in a deep-set "V"; his face flushed with rage. "Nigger," he seethed. "Nigger! Nigger! Nigger!"

The colored girl coiled tighter, her head nearly to her knees. She touched a hand to her brow. Tears now appeared, flowing over her cheeks, across her nose, trickling down her neck—inflaming the crowd further.

From the right side of the mob a white man pushed his way through the crowd. He made his way to the bench and sat beside Elizabeth Eckford. "Look," I said to Dalton. "That's Fine, the guy from the *New York Times.*"

Benjamin Fine put his arm around the colored girl's shoulder.

"What the ... what's he doing?" Dalton asked.

"Something he's gonna regret," I replied.

Fine spoke to her, too softly to hear above the din. The girl nodded, just faintly. He then placed his hand under her chin, lifted it, bringing her eyes level with his.

"Nigger lover!" someone screamed.

"Yankee Jew," another cried.

This time I could read Fine's lips. "Don't let them see you cry," he told her. "Do not let these people see you cry."

The girl shuddered, straining to regain her composure. Fine lowered his hand, as spite and resentment washed over the Arkansas Negro and the New York Jew.

A white woman—older, gray-haired, and plump—burst onto the scene. "Leave her alone," she shouted at the crowd. She looked one boy square in the eye. With hands jammed onto her hips she hollered: "Can't you see she's scared?"

"We don't want her here," the kid growled.

The woman stared daggers right between his eyes. "You'll be embarrassed by this six months from now," she sneered, prompting more angry screams. She stood at Eckford's side, a hand resting on the girl's shoulder. "It's going to be all right," she said. "Just hold on."

A bus finally arrived; it seemed as though hours had passed. The woman grabbed Eckford's hand; she pulled the girl up, put her arm around her waist. "Come on," she said, "I'll go with you."

"Take your nigger and get out of here," a scream shot from the crowd. "Don't come back," someone shouted. "Take the bus to Africa …" the jeers poured on until the bus had faded from view.

The mob lingered a few moments, savoring the kill, and then began to drift away, believing, I think, "One down, eight more to go."

"I wonder if we can find her?" I said to Dalton. "It'd be nice to get a quote or two—after she's had a chance to settle down."

"We got all their names," Dalton replied. "It can't be hard to…."

A National Guardsman stormed past Dalton, brushing his shoulder as he charged Benjamin Fine. He spun the reporter around by the shoulder, pushed him backward, and jammed his finger into the old man's chest: "Try that again," the soldier hissed, "and you'll get a firsthand look at a Little Rock jail."

Fine stared back, bewildered.

"You're inciting a crowd," the soldier barked. "You're making this whole thing worse than it already is."

And it was true. Every journalist there would have agreed that Fine insinuated himself into the story. His presence had altered the course of events, and he had, there was no getting around it, further provoked an angry mob. And if all that weren't enough, he was a Northerner and a Jew—which had given the mob a flesh-and-blood reason to point and scream: "Outside agitator!"

Benjamin Fine had violated a cardinal rule of journalism. But I knew, and I suspect others did too, that of all the people there—soldiers, journalists, photographers, parents, teachers, and neighbors—only one man showed the first sign of compassion; only one guy treated that girl as I'd want someone to treat my child. Only one guy had the guts—and the heart—to do the right thing.

I walked away from the tiny bus stop, head down and ashamed that with all I knew, with everything I'd been through, it hadn't even occurred to me to break a few rules for the sake of simple kindness.

On the second ring, Rose snatched the phone from its cradle. "When are you coming home?"

There was no "Hello," no "How was your day?" no "What's new over there?" Only this hard, cold question.

"What's wrong?" I asked.

"Your son," she snapped. With her tone came a distinct and perfectly formed image: I could see her pacing past the kitchen sink to the refrigerator, then yanked back by the phone's elastic cord, her pretty face mangled by grief and exasperation.

I sat on the bed, folded in half, bracing for bad news. "What happened, Rose?"

Over the next few minutes I learned that Chris and Ansley Dorsey had been suspended from school. Rose explained how they'd circulated a petition demanding that their school integrate and that the principal, teachers, and school board comply—"without hesitation"—with the Supreme Court's ruling.

This can't be happening, I groaned to myself. *This kid's a teacher's pet; he's always been everybody's favorite.*

"They've been going kid-to-kid trying to gather signatures," my wife continued. "They're telling anybody who'll stand still long enough to listen that their own school's in defiance of the law, that if they don't ..."

My thoughts plunged from one level of despair to the next— trying, but failing, to imagine the scenes Rose described. As I listened, it struck me—that Chris was the same age as the kids I'd seen earlier. I pictured the throng that had swarmed Elizabeth Eckford, who'd heaped malice on this girl the same way Chris had seen others batter Percy Jackson. I saw their young, contorted faces. *Some of those kids*, I kept thinking, *were the same age as my own son.*

I closed my eyes, feeling a headache begin its merciless charge.

"I guess he got all worked up about what's going on over here?" I said.

"Oh yeah," Rose replied, "both of 'em have been reading every word their daddies write. And I'll tell you something, Jack: she's as bad as he is."

My lips thinned to a blade. I pictured them together, holding hands, walking side by side, reading and studying together. It wasn't hard to imagine how one would stoke the rebellious fire in the other. "Well, in a way that's good," I said, "at least we can work together on this, with the Dorseys, I mean." I sat up, stretched my arms, legs, and torso, twisting into shape like a doll. I prayed silently that this thing would magically pass, but then, faced with its inescapable presence, I said, "I'll call Dalton as soon as we hang up."

"The principal's having a fit," Rose continued, "and the other parents...." There came a rueful sigh from the Atlanta end of the line, "I don't think they're going to be too pleased with our son—or his parents."

"No, I don't suppose they will." I moved my free hand to my forehead, trying to slow the pain's advance. "So, when's he go back to school?" I asked.

"The minute he promises to stop," Rose answered

A ray of brightness flashed. "Well that's good," I chimed. "At least we can get that taken care of."

"Except he won't do it," Rose said flatly.

And the light vanished as quickly as it had appeared.

"He's got a right to free speech," Rose said. "The school can't stop him—it's his right."

The ache was now speeding from irritation to full blown, throbbing pain. "Is he there?" I asked.

"He's in his room, sulking."

"Why don't you put him on?" I said. "I'll take a swing at this."

I instructed Chris to stop the petition drive, to go back to school, and to obey his teachers.

"But why?" he demanded to know. "Why should I obey them when they're wrong?"

For the next few minutes my adolescent son and I discussed authority, civility, and just plain good manners. We talked about the importance of rules and respect for other people.

"Fine," he declared. "But what about the law? What about justice? And what about my rights?"

I pulled the phone away from my ear, gawking at the handset, certain that some alien creature had taken possession of Chris Hall's body. I was frustrated, in pain, and too tired for this. But, reluctantly, I branched down a new trail, talking about ethics and morals. We'd gotten about one minute into the exchange when it dawned on me that this was the first of a new kind of conversation. These were deeper questions, and they required complex answers. This was not a paternal lecture disguised as a discussion; it was a dialog between a father and a son who was molting the skin of his childhood.

"You've got rights," I assured him, "and you should be free to exercise them, but not while you're at school."

"When then?" he insisted on knowing.

"On your own time," I said, "after school, or even before school. But Chris?"

He was silent, waiting for the "but" that loomed.

"Can you wait until we talk about this? Until Mr. Dorsey and I get home and we can spend some time together? How 'bout it, pal?"

"I'm not going to change my mind," he assured me.

"I'm not asking you to change your mind," I promised. "I just want to help you think through a few things, that's all."

He huffed into the phone but didn't speak.

"I'll just be another day," I told him. "Let's talk, and if you still want to do this, I won't stop you, I promise."

There was hesitation, followed by a second sigh, and then a begrudging, "All right." Then, without saying good-bye, he handed the phone to his mother.

"I stuck a patch on this," I told Rose. "But it ain't gonna hold."

"Jack, we can't have this boy going around—"

"I know, I know," I told her. "I'll talk with Dalton, and then you and I—we'll get this figured out as soon as I get home."

I heard the trembling breath. I imagined her pacing, looping the phone cord around her fingers. "I know you're busy," she said. "I know you've got a lot on your mind. I'm sorry about this."

"Hey, it comes with the territory," I replied, "… this whole teen-ager business."

"Yeah," Rose said softly, "I guess it's just more than I imagined."

"I don't know if anybody's ever ready for this kind of stuff." I tried to sound comforting.

"Jack …" her voice quivered.

"Yeah?" I said.

There was no reply.

"What is it, Rose?"

"He'll barely talk to me," she said. "He glares at me like I'm evil, like this is all my fault. He tells me I don't understand. He says …" her voice got lost in a tangle of sniffs and muffled sobs.

"I'll be home soon, Rose. We'll talk to him and get this sorted out."

"He's never talked to me like this," Rose said.

"I'm sorry," I told her, "I'll be home soon." I pictured her, leaning against the oak-paneled pantry, her head down, wiping away the tears. "I love you, Rose; I'll be there just as soon as I can."

"Yeah," she whimpered, "okay."

I pressed the switch hook, then dialed Dalton's room.

"So you heard?" he said.

I sprawled across the bed. "Geez, Dalton, what are we going to do?"

"Look," he said, chuckling, "Natalie's frantic about this, and I know Rose is too, but Jack, think about it: they're kids, they're growing up, they're flexing a few new muscles...."

"Couldn't they break curfew, maybe skip school, sneak a beer out of the fridge ...?" I pinched at the bridge of my nose. "I'm telling you, Dalton, if Rose gets so much as one call from an angry mom ..."

"I know, I know," Dalton replied. "Look, I told Natalie that you and me and the kids will get together and talk this thing through."

"Yeah, that square's with what I told Rose," I replied. "But, Dalton—we're going to have to come up with something good. I'm telling you, Chris has got his heels dug in on this, and it sounds like Ansley does too."

"Yeah, I know," Dalton said, "but let me ask you something: You ever do something stupid when you were a kid?"

"Sure," I told him, "plenty."

"And you turned out all right—I mean, you're a hack, but still...." Then, after the pause, he said, "They're good kids, Jack, and they're both sharp as a scalpel. How bad can this be?"

"I don't know, but I guess we're gonna find out." I sat up on the bed. "Look, we've got a lot of work to do here. Let's sleep on it, and then come up with a plan on the flight home."

"All right," Dalton replied. "And Jack, try to relax. Right now, our kids are the least of our problems."

•   •   •   •

It was with Chris and Ansley still on my mind that the photo greeted me.

I could still hear echoes of Rose's sobs when I saw it—three columns wide and ten inches deep, splayed across the front page of the *Arkansas Gazette*—the image that changed my life forever.

First thing that morning I, along with three quarters of the civilized world, stared straight into the face of the snarling white girl; the one who'd crept up close to Elizabeth Eckford, who had mocked her, who had, at the moment the camera shutter closed, spat the word "Nigger!"

By the end of the day the photo was famous, and everyone, in some way, had been affected by this image of young Hazel Bryan.

I scanned the *Gazette's* story—I didn't think it was as good ours—but at the end of each paragraph my eyes strayed back to the photo. This girl—just a teenager, a kid who couldn't possibly know the full meaning of the day's events—was, as of this moment, the incarnation of unrestrained anger. In the photo her eyes are narrowed to slashes. Her mouth is open, teeth bared—an alpha dog defending every last inch of her territory. Her cheeks are pocked with lines of fury. She is possessed, a young woman consumed by the threat that stands two feet in front of her.

From the first moment I knew what it meant. I could instantly read the minds of doctors, lawyers, and journalists in New York and Philadelphia—and in London, Paris, and Washington. I tossed the paper across the table to Dalton. I tapped my finger against the photo and, echoing a now familiar theme, I said, "That right there is the image of the New South. As far as the world's concerned, that girl is the personification of the place you call home."

He picked up the paper and inspected the photo. "Ain't pretty, is it?"

"It is a lot of things," I replied. "Pretty isn't one of 'em."

We sat for a moment, both of us pondering the photo, and both of us, I think, were wondering what was on the other's mind. I sipped my coffee; I couldn't help but think back to other break-fasts we'd had. "You remember what we were saying the first time the three of us met at the diner," I said, "about how beautiful the South is, about all the places that would've made Eve forget about Eden?"

He nodded and said, "Sure. And I remember what we were say-ing the last time, too—about music and books."

"Yeah, well," I told him, "beginning today, when people think about the South they ain't gonna be thinking about Faulkner." I tapped at the photo again. "I hate this," I grumbled. "I've said it before, and I'll say it now: This is not who we are. This is not what we're about." I inched across the table. "We can't let this stand, Dalton. We can't let the whole world think this is the sum total of what we've got to offer, we can't...."

"Whoa, whoa, whoa," Dalton threw up a stop sign. He leaned forward, eyeing me suspiciously: "Are you thinking what I think you're thinking?" Dalton stared into his coffee: "Are you thinking the same thing I am …?"

I leaned back, turning loose of one very reluctant sigh. I was, all of a sudden, weighted down with a new burden—like a cartoon character who's just been handed a two-ton anvil—and it occurred to me, almost comically, that this was an affliction baseball writers rarely suffer. "I don't think we've got a choice," I told my partner. "Somebody's got to fix this; somebody's got to flip this coin to the other side. I don't know, Dalton; I just got this feeling—a hunch, I guess—that we're the ones to do it."

Dalton's head bobbed—with affirmation or understanding or maybe it was begrudging acceptance. He turned a palm and said, "I don't see anybody else who can. Ashmore, McGill, Hodding Carter—they're tied to newspapers, they've got owners to answer to, and they're never going to write more than a thousand words."

"And half the world thinks they're communists," I said. "They're decent guys, and everyone of 'em writes like a dad-gum poet, but they carry a ton of baggage. We need a fresh voice, something new, a voice nobody's ever heard before, some perspective nobody's given." I studied the photo again, anger and sadness welling up inside. "When we get home, let's get with Alan first thing."

"I'm with you," Dalton said, "and we might want to get with our wives second."

• • • •

The Little Rock story was a long way from over, but it was time for us to head home. We tossed our suitcases into the trunk of our rented car. Silently, we traded wary glances, knowing it was time to tackle the ticklish subject of our rebellious children.

As I pulled into the flow of traffic I cut my eyes at Dalton. "You know," I began, "I am sometimes amazed at my own genius."

"Well," he said, "that'd make a grand total of one of us."

"Seriously," I told him, "I've got the perfect plan. I know how to rein those kids in; I know how to get 'em to do exactly what we want."

His eyebrows remained poised in doubt. "I'm all ears," he said.

On the plane ride home I divulged my two-pronged plan: To inspire and divert them. We'd invite them to become partners in our new venture; we'd ask for their help, we'd lure them into a higher calling—and keep them close beside us. "We treat 'em like they're forty-two years old," I explained to Dalton. I pulled yesterday's *Gazette* out of my briefcase. "We tell 'em, 'Look, if you want to change the way people like this act, you've got to change the way they think.' We talk about what happens when people are forced to do things against their will, before anybody's laid the groundwork."

Dalton rapped his hand against the photo. "And they conclude that this is what's going to happen at their school—if they keep their little campaign going."

"Bingo. We say, 'Look, they crammed integration down their throats—just like you're wanting to do—and this is what happened.'"

"But we've got a better way," Dalton ran with the hypothetical argument. "We're looking at the big picture, wanting to change a whole society not just one little high school, blah, blah, blah.…"

"We bring them into our conversations about music, books, sports.… We sit 'em down beside us when we talk about how, before there's going to be any real change, people need a new perspective, they need to see things in a different light—including themselves."

I'm nodding my head as I say this, convincing myself as I explain it to Dalton. "In some roundabout way we tell them: You can force people to change—which they'll hate. Or you can inspire them to change—which'll make 'em love you forever."

Dalton slouched back in his seat. "You know what?" he said. "I like it. In fact, for these two kids, it's perfect. They'll haggle a little bit, just to make a good show, but they'll come around, and they'll love it."

A bell dinged through the cabin. The "fasten seatbelt–no smoking" light flashed on. And the pilot informed us we'd be landing in twenty minutes.

Providence is, by its essence and nature, mysterious. It works beyond the boundaries of our finite minds, and sometimes the results, literally, tickle us to tears.

When we got to the airport we rushed to the nearest pay phone. Dalton plunked a dime into the depository. He asked for Alan and waited. He tapped his foot—on hold for ten, fifteen, twenty seconds. Then, when Alan came on the line, he twisted round to face me. He told Alan that we'd just gotten in, that something had come up and we needed to talk—now, if he could slip away.

I watched as Dalton nodded. He clamped his teeth over his lower lip. "Yeah, sure," he muttered. He glanced at his watch, "All right," he said. "Yeah, we can be there." He shifted his weight, frowning at

Alan's half of the conversation. "Okay, that's fine," he replied. "We'll see you in half an hour."

He hung up and stepped outside, looking like a man who'd just stumbled across trouble.

"So …?" I asked.

"Something fishy's going on," Dalton said.

"Like what?"

"I don't know," Dalton replied. "He just didn't sound right. He sounded worried—like something might've gone wrong." He shrugged and flipped his palms, "He wants to meet at the diner in a half hour."

We piled into our usual booth. Dalton and I had come with our agenda; Alan had apparently arrived with his, and it felt like a field of land mines lay between us. We started with small talk: "How was the trip?" "Did you get some good stuff?" "Sounds like Ike's gonna get involved.…"

Alan stared into his cup, twisting it back and forth, no more than an eighth of an inch in either direction. "Listen," he said, "I know this is your meeting, but there's something I need to tell you guys."

Dalton and I squirmed. With a faint dip of the chin I prodded him on.

Alan took a nervous slurp of coffee. "I-I-I should have told you about this sooner," he said. "I should have kept you in the loop, but honest to goodness, I just didn't think anything'd happen so soon."

"Just spit it out," I said. My tone was friendly, trying to ease my friend's pain and melt the chill.

He cut his eyes from me to Dalton. "All right," he said, "I've talked to a few people about the magazine idea; I just sorta laid out the concept, told 'em why we think it's a good idea, why the time's right ..."

Dalton leaned across the table, smiling. "You know what 'spit it out' means, don't you?"

Alan raised his hand, a plea for patience. "All right, all right," he said. "Bottom line: I got the money."

I cocked my head—like a dog who'd gotten wind of a shrill whistle.

"I explained the concept," he said timidly. "I roughed out the financials; showed a few people what kind of return we might expect, showed 'em a payout schedule...." He stared down again, shaking his head. "I literally scratched this stuff out on a napkin and they bought it. They want to give us a bunch of money. Right now!"

Dalton exploded in laughter.

And through tears of inexpressible relief I said, "Then take it."

By God's good grace our wives and kids leaped onboard.

"Jack, you'll be perfect for this," Rose gushed. She smiled at me as lovingly as she did the day we got married. "And it's time you stepped out from McGill's shadow." She hugged me and held on for ninety affection-filled seconds. "This is good," she purred. "This is where we belong. This is the reason we came to Atlanta."

She kissed me. She smiled. And at that precise moment, she began her own transformation—from reporter's wife to first lady of the South's smartest magazine.

Chris and Ansley did not haggle or debate. At the idea's first mention, they began brainstorming, and we weren't three minutes into the conversation before they swore they'd take writing and photography classes. They vowed to go to work for the school newspaper, to learn to do research, and to see if maybe, through the power of words and images, they could effect some lasting change at their own school.

Years later I'd tell Dalton that they were part of a new generation, that they had instinctively grasped the magazine's power; that they knew, more intuitively than we did, how to use the media to effect change.

We had, as the saying goes, our ducks in a row. But there was one more person I needed to talk to. Before I did something so drastic, I wanted to hear from Carson Powers. The pastor, I thought, was smart, he loved my family, he was objective, and he'd tell me the bare and unvarnished truth. And so, I laid it all out for him, too.

Powers listened to every word. He nodded his head thoughtfully. He mumbled "uh-huh" in the appropriate pauses. His eyes brightened at our best ideas, and at the end of my monologue, when I asked for a reaction, he looked at me, puzzled. And then he said: "Well, heck yeah, you ought to do it."

Powers leaned over his desk, "What you just described, Jack— that's the job of being human."

I stared back, eyes glazed as a football player's in biology class.

"That's why God put us here," Powers explained, "to create new things, to think new thoughts, to bring abstract ideas into tangible, real-live being."

He leaned back, folding his hands behind his head. "Let me ask you something," he said. "When God finished creating the world, when it was all said and done, all proclaimed to be real good, how many books did Adam and Eve have to read?"

I did not have the foggiest notion of where this was going. "None," I said—though, by the way he'd posed the question, I wasn't too sure.

"All right," he replied. "And exactly how many songs you suppose He gave them to hum while they were out there working the garden?"

I shrugged and ventured, "None," for a second time.

"Uh-huh," Powers mumbled. His chair squealed as he swiveled. "And how many magazines did He get printed up for them to read before they went to bed at night?"

I laughed and repeated, "None."

Powers opened his hands. "Don't you see? That's the job. That's why He put us here—to take what He gave us and keep going, to make the place better, smarter, safer, healthier...." He paused, and then, holding my eye, he said, "So let me ask you: If you guys pull this off, are people going to be any smarter than they are now?"

"That's the idea," I said.

"Are they going to be better entertained—I mean, in a good way—with something that's bright and smart and dignified?"

"Yes, I hope so."

"If you do this, will anybody understand things better? You plan on giving 'em something that helps them make sense of the world—that gives them what they need to make better decisions?"

I nodded and said, "Yeah, we do."

He settled back into the chair. "You got the money?" Powers asked. "Has Alan raised enough to get this thing off the ground without you guys having to risk your houses?"

I hitched my shoulders and said, "We figured what we'd need, and then raised twenty-five percent more."

"All right, last question," Powers replied: "What's Rose Marie think? Is she good with this?"

I chuckled and said, "I think she's more excited than I am."

Carson Powers slapped his desk. "That's all you need to know. If this is what you think you ought to be doing, if your wife's with you, and if you've honest to goodness counted the costs—then it's time to get off your butt."

I laughed. But then, peering up cautiously, I said, "There's one more thing I want to run by you."

"Shoot," he replied.

I looked down; my voice was hushed and a little shaky. "Well, like I told you, we're doing this to showcase the South. We want to highlight everything that's good. And right along with what you were just saying, we're hoping to make it better; we want to make the people better; we want the South to be the best place where anybody could ever live...."

Powers smiled and said, "That's on the money, Jack."

"Yeah, well ..." I rubbed my hands together and continued, "we've talked this over; shoot, we've probably batted it around a thousand times, and the three of us are pretty sure that racial integration's coming."

"Uh-huh," Powers mumbled cautiously.

"Seems like things have been running along just fine the way they've always been. But the fact is—whether we like or not—it's coming. The question's not if, but when. And I guess the most important question of all is how."

"And that's behind what you're wanting to do?" he asked.

"It's a part of it," I answered. "We're thinking maybe we can help manage it—just real subtly—maybe get people used to the idea a little bit at a time. Don't get me wrong; we're not pushing the idea. That'd be suicide. We just want to deal with what's bound to happen, to see if we can't help folks cope."

I could not read one thought in Carson Powers's mind.

"It's a lot easier to integrate a magazine than a school," I continued, chuckling. "But, when the time comes, one might make the other a little easier." I peered up at him. "You got any thoughts about that?"

A couple of seconds passed in silence. Then Powers said, "You need to be real careful there, Jack."

I looked at him, brows peaked, demanding elaboration.

"The thing is," he continued, "we're all trying to sort this out, and I'm not sure anybody has. Until then, until we've been ..."

"Including you?" I interrupted, "You're still sorting this out, too?"

He held my eye for a second. "Yeah," he replied, "including me. Look, if you wanted to persuade people to make things better for the Negro, I'd be cheering from the cotton-picking rafters. We need to build better schools for those people; we ought to be making sure their facilities are every bit as nice as ours. Shoot, that's just the Christian thing to do. But outright integration ..." Powers turned his head, clearly wrestling with the images that sprang to his mind. "I don't know, Jack; that's the kind of thing that sounds real nice, but ..." he stopped and chewed at his lower lip. "It's just that when you get right down to it: It's going to take you to some places you really don't want to go."

"But that's the whole point," I said. "That's all the more reason to manage it, to try to shape how it happens, to try to draw some boundaries while we can."

"Yeah," Powers said, "I can see that, and I'm not saying it doesn't make sense. But if a thing's wrong, if it's going to end up being bad for everybody ... I don't think we want to be a party to that, do we?"

I rubbed at my eyes, suddenly weary. "You know," I said, "I remember the first time I heard you preach. It was Christmas Eve; we'd just moved here, and I remember thinking: *This is the weirdest dad-gum Christmas sermon I've ever heard.* You talked about making things new, and I remember the exact phrase—it stuck with me—that we ought to make whatever patch of ground we got the home of justice."

"Yeah," Powers said, "I remember that one."

"Look," I said, "you know I'm not an integrationist, I'm not some outside agitator, I'm not a communist trying to screw up the good things we've got here. I'm just a no-name reporter playing the cards we've been dealt." I squared my eyes with Powers's. "But I got to tell you something: There are times when I think about what's going on right now—with the schools and buses and with baseball teams and football teams—there are times when those words prick, and I can't help but to wonder if we've got this right."

Powers fell back into the chair. He traced a finger across his lip and said, "Yeah ... I know what you mean."

•   •   •   •

In late September our story appeared in *Life*. We had, the editor told us, "taken a complex story and made it simple." Another commentator called it "the best-informed piece that had yet been written on the subject." It was, many said, "objective and accurate, but not unkind to any constituency."

I heard one reporter refer to it as "gritty." And my old journalism professor told me it was "entertaining and meaty."

We didn't win a Pulitzer; that would go to Harry Ashmore. We weren't even nominated, but we did earn respect. We had, within our small fraternity, gained visibility, and for the moment, we were "in." We were a pair of up-and-comers—the two guys to keep your eye on. And Alan Emerson spun our stardom into gold. He peddled us to every investor who had a thousand bucks to spare, assuring them that Pulitzers were on the way, and that Hall and Dorsey—a pair of Southern boys who had a way with words—were the fastest rising stars on journalism's horizon.

Alan could charm a buck out of Jack Benny, and the money poured in. The rich lined up, hoping to bask in the glory of so glamorous an enterprise. But they, like us, had a vested interest in a peaceful and prosperous South.

The drama of Little Rock played out over the next eighteen months. Shortly after we left, the president of the United States federalized the Arkansas National Guard. Days later he ordered units of 101st Airborne into a city of his own country, ordering them to enforce the nation's laws and to protect its citizens—regardless of their color.

At the end of the school year, the people of Little Rock, who had once envisioned their city as the enlightened model of the New South, voted to close their four public high schools. Nine colored kids were too much for the city to bear, and the specter of Negro students—the mental picture of colored kids sitting in the same classes, reading the same books, listening to same lectures … showering in the same stalls—was too much for the mothers of Little Rock to imagine.

The people of this idyllic Southern town declared—loud and plain enough for the world to hear—that no schools were better than mixed ones—and that a segregated society was worth the costs that had to be paid.

Five days in Little Rock changed my life. A fifteen-year-old girl, pictured on the front page of the *Arkansas Gazette,* propelled my life in a new direction. The power of that one picture converted me. And that morning, at a breakfast table in the Sam Peck Hotel, Dalton Dorsey and I joined the ranks of men who would move the world.

• • • •

Thoughts of a new business consumed us. We met during lunch hours, at night, and on weekends. The three of us became obsessed with our new mission, but the work made us tired, anxious, and sometimes, even irritable. The burden, after just a few weeks, was heavier than we had imagined, which meant that October arrived just in time. Because in October, the whole country casts its cares aside. Together we sit back, relax, and savor the World Series.

On Sunday, October 6, my friends gathered together hoping, for the second time that season, to watch Percy Jackson play baseball. This time the mood was more festive, and we witnessed an old friend make a bizarre play at the game's most pivotal turn.

The Yankees led the series two games to one, but that day Warren Spahn was cruising. In the top of the ninth the Braves were ahead four to one—just three outs away from pulling even. Spahn retired the first two batters easily—we were already talking about game five, about who'd pitch the next three games, and whether or not the Braves could win one in Yankee Stadium—when Yogi Berra, the Yankees' catcher, rapped a cheap single. The next batter, Gil McDougald, sent a sharp ground ball between short and third. Suddenly there were runners on first and second, and the tying run stood at the plate.

"They got to take him out," Chris said. "He's out of gas; I can see it from here."

"Nobody's in the bullpen," Dalton replied. "Looks like this is his to lose."

Elston Howard, the first Negro to wear a Yankees uniform, came to the plate. Howard was young, but that afternoon he worked Spahn like a veteran. Patiently and methodically—fouling off a couple of pitches that were too close to take—he worked the count full.

"He's going to blow this," Chris muttered.

Howard stepped out of the batter's box, tapped his cleats clean, then stepped back in. He leaned over the plate, bat twitching above his head, waiting.

Spahn went into his stretch, checked the signal, checked both runners, and then delivered a fastball—belt high, smack-dab on the outside corner.

In the split second it takes a Warren Spahn fastball to travel sixty feet, six inches, Elston Howard must've wondered why Christmas had come so early. He swung ferociously, launching a lousy pitch into the fourth row of the left-field bleachers. And just that fast, the game was tied.

Chris buried his face in both hands. "I knew it," he groaned; "I told you this was gonna happen."

In the bottom of the ninth Adcock, Pafko, and Crandall went down in order, and it was on to extra innings. In the top of the tenth

Tony Kubec scored on a Hank Bauer triple; the Yankees took a five-to-four lead, and a sense of doom flooded County Stadium.

The game faded up from the last commercial. NBC's Mel Allen was resetting the scene when Chris screamed, "I knew it!" He raised his chin toward the screen. "I knew it," he said again; "Percy's going to pinch-hit for Spahn."

The pitcher was due to lead off the inning, and sure enough Fred Haney, the Braves' manager, had called on Percy Jackson.

Tommy Byrne's first pitch was a fastball, low and inside. Percy skipped out of the way and nearly fell facedown as the ball skidded past Berra, all the way to the screen. Percy regained his balance and began trotting toward first. But Augie Donatelli, the home plate ump, called him back.

Percy turned in disbelief. With his bat still in hand he pointed the barrel at his right shoe.

"He's saying it hit him," Chris said.

Donatelli removed his mask. He planted both hands on his hips and shook his head no.

Jackson lifted his foot in the air, insisting that he'd been hit, but umpires are rarely moved by a player's passion. Donatelli turned and walked away, but Jackson wouldn't surrender. He raced past the ump; he sped past Berra—marching all the way to the wall behind home plate. He picked up the ball and twirled it round, as if inspecting merchandise at a fruit stand. He stomped back toward home, handing the ball to Donatelli, and pleading his case one last time. The ump examined the ball; he looked at Percy's foot, and then back to the ball. And then, to the surprise of millions watching, he pointed to first. He awarded the base to Percy. It is, to this day, the only time I've ever seen an ump change a call. And he did it in the bottom of the tenth, of game four, of the 1957 World Series.

Byrne rushed toward the plate, furious. Casey Stengel, the Yankees' manager, charged from the dugout—beet red, his hands and arms flailing. And the home field crowd roared its approval. The next day we learned that the ball had grazed Jackson's foot, and that he'd found a smudge of black shoe polish to prove it. Donatelli, persuaded by the physical evidence, had made the right decision.

A few minutes later, Percy Jackson scored on a Johnny Logan double to tie the game. Five minutes after that, Eddie Matthews lashed a two-run homer for the 7-5 win, and Chris was delirious. Our old friend had played the starring role in the weirdest play we'd ever seen. He'd kept the Braves' hopes alive and given Eddie Matthews the chance his team needed.

Two days later, on Tuesday, October 8, I did something I'd never done before. I told Chris he could skip school. The three of us: Chris, Rose Marie, and I huddled around the television. We watched the Braves win the world championship. And we now had a friend—a shy kid from our own hometown—who had won an honest-to-goodness World Series.

Part 2

Chapter 9

I still think back on the early days, when we talked at breakfast and dreamed; when we gathered in our first office, swearing to one another that whatever we did we would, by golly, be remembered; that every writer, editor, and publisher at *Life, Look,* and *Time* would thumb through our magazine and marvel; that they would see the sheer audacity, and wish they had half our courage.

Five times a day we promised one another that we'd never run scared, and that no one, ever, would accuse us of being too cautious. If we failed, well, at least we'd make a splash they'd hear in New York, Chicago, and Los Angeles. We would, we used to say, make a difference, even if we never made it to our third issue.

In the fall of 1958, after months of planning, after we'd interviewed writers, editors, proofers, and designers, after we'd stolen an ad guy from the *Saturday Evening Post*—after we'd haggled over departments, features, and sections—we finally crammed ourselves into a small office on Broad Street, just a five-minute walk from *The Atlanta Constitution.* And there, halfway between Marietta and Peachtree, we gave birth to *Down South* magazine.

We gathered in a conference room that felt crowded with three people. We stuck a flip chart at the head of the table and scribbled down every quarter-baked idea that crossed our racing minds. We drank lousy coffee, came in early, and left too late. We worked on prototypes and sample pages. We sweated microscopic details. We drove designers nuts, nit-picking every font and photo. We argued about everything—all of us insisting that we create "this thing" that had never been done before.

"This has got to be right," I must have insisted a thousand times. "We don't get but one first chance."

When the time came to choose our first cover story I thought we'd need armor. "It's got to be Elvis," Dalton insisted. "He's the biggest thing in the world, and the boy is Southern to the bone."

"Oh please!" I groaned, "Talk about predictable."

Alan suggested a story about the new Atlanta airport. The City Commission had just approved ten million dollars to build it. "And it's going to change everything," he said. "I'm not just talking about Atlanta. This is going to change the South; it's an honest-to-goodness new beginning."

Dalton rolled his eyes. "Gee, I don't know," he said, "but maybe, if we set our minds to it, we might come up with something sexier than an airport."

"I'm telling you," Alan replied, "when that thing opens, business begins to boom."

"We could do a sports guy," I suggested. "Billy Cannon's shredding every defense in the conference; he's gotta be a contender for the Heisman."

"That's nice," Dalton said, "and LSU looks unstoppable, but the timing's bad. We're going to have to shoot this thing before the bowl games."

I wrote Cannon's name on the flip chart. "Maybe he's good for February?" I said.

"You got a few business guys," Alan suggested. "Changes going on at Coke and Delta...."

I started pacing my side of the room. "We gotta have somebody who's recognizable," I said. "Somebody who's got some star power." I laced my fingers on top of my head. "Who's big?" I asked. "Who's the biggest name in the South?"

Dalton squeezed off a single shot: "Could that be ... Elvis!" he screamed.

I ignored him and leaned into the giant window frame. "We could get kind of toney, maybe ride over to Oxford and interview Faulkner."

Dalton cocked an eyebrow, intrigued. "Faulkner looks so cool," he said. "The moustache, that whole Southern gentleman thing ... the guy's a classic."

"But what do you tie it to?" Alan wondered. "I like the idea, and I agree, Faulkner's cool, but it's not like he's got a new book hitting the stores in January; at least not that I know of."

Dalton was now pacing the opposite side of the room. "Come on," he grumbled. "Who's done something nobody'll ever forget?"

"There's King," I said. "He fits the bill."

"Excuse me," Dalton replied, "I meant to say: who's changed the world, and could actually help us sell magazines."

"Along with a page or two of advertising," Alan added.

The three of us racked our stretched-past-their-limits brains, scratching out ideas, crumpling paper, and tossing it into the trash. We threw out fifty more names—of politicians, athletes, musicians.

And then, meekly, Alan said, "Here's one for you...." He looked at me and explained, "He's not recognizable; he could walk down the middle of Peachtree and nobody'd know him, but maybe we turn that to our advantage; let it add a little mystery."

I stared at Alan, as puzzled as a girl at a football game. "So who is it?" I asked. "Let's hear the big idea."

Alan's throat bobbed. "Sam Phillips," he said.

I turned toward the window, pinching at the bridge of my nose, more confused now than I'd been two seconds before, wondering furiously, *Who's Sam Phillips?*

I watched as Dalton sorted through his mental files in search of a face that went with the name. "Okay, okay," he stumbled, "it's on the tip of my tongue...."

"Memphis?" Alan whined. He looked down, shaking his head. "For crying out loud, I can't believe you don't know this guy."

"It's coming to me," Dalton claimed, "give me a second."

Alan turned to me. "He's not Elvis," he said. "But he's sure enough the guy who discovered Elvis. He runs a company called Sun Records."

"That's right!" Dalton exclaimed. "Now I remember. And he's turned out a bunch of these guys, right? Johnny Cash ... somebody else?"

"Yeah," Alan replied, "and he's developed this reputation as the guy who can spot talent, who knows how to develop it, bring it along ... that kind of thing."

"Yeah, yeah, yeah," I said, "I've heard of him. Who else is he working with?"

"I'd have to check," Alan answered. "Carl Perkins, maybe? I'm not sure."

I paced two more lengths of the room, running my mind around two or three angles. "This might be genius," I said. I turned to Dalton: "It could give you a back door to Presley; maybe give us a slant that hasn't been done before."

"And you know what I like," Dalton said. "If we do this, we create the star. We're not piggybacking on anything; we're not jumping on somebody else's bandwagon. From day one, we're the guys who bestow stardom." Dalton began to laugh. "We do this thing right and, I don't know, maybe we dub this guy: the man who invented rock and roll."

"You know what?" I said. "We might just do that." I glanced at the clock and said, "We still got some time; why don't we see what we can dig up on him?" I tossed a cup into the trash and headed for the door. "We'll have people thinking that this guy's done more for music than anybody since Beethoven."

I called Sun Records, and in twenty minutes I knew Sam Phillips was the perfect choice. He was to the music business what we hoped to be to journalism. He was doing with records exactly what we hoped to do with a magazine. And he and his company were a decent reflection of us and ours.

Sam Phillips had indeed discovered Elvis Presley and Johnny Cash. But the hidden jewel in Phillips's story—the thing nobody knew—was this: He'd recorded more Negro artists than any record label in history. And his hope, from the very first day, had been to bridge the gap between the races—to show one that the other had something to offer.

"You ought to do this story," I told Dalton that night. "You can finally get this Elvis thing out of your system."

"Yeah, probably," Dalton said with a chuckle. "Unless it's really a race story, then you ought to do it."

"It's got to be about the music," I told him. "We'll find a way to work the race angle in there, but let's get the music story right." I checked my watch, knowing it was past time for all of us to head home. "Tell you what, you start on it; if you need some backup you know where to find me."

"Or …" Dalton said, "we could do a second story—on Memphis, on the music, the food, Beale Street—we could both go, take an extra day and polish off a pair of stories."

"Two birds with one stone," Alan said. "Might even save us a few bucks."

"And it'd add some nice continuity," I said. "I like it."

•   •   •   •

"I came here for the first time when I was sixteen," Sam Phillips began. "It was back in thirty-nine, a bunch of us drove over in my buddy's old Dodge. We cruised through town, right down Beale, and I'm telling you, there wasn't a one of us who could believe our eyes. There were people everywhere; they were out in the street—colored and white— all of 'em dancing and singing and swaying to the music…. And the music—good grief—it was everywhere; it poured out from every door and window; it blared out of the rib shacks and bars and dance clubs...." Phillips gazed up, hearing the music from a distance of nearly two decades. "That's when I knew this was where I belonged.

"I wanted to record the guys who improvised," he told us, "who did music a different way—and who, because they didn't fit any existing mold—had nowhere else to go. They deserved to be heard. I'm talking about these colored guys who could sing and play the blues ..." he closed his eyes, listening to the memory of it. "You'd hear these boys and you would swear: The world was gonna end right then and there.

"And the white guys...." Phillips gave his head this little tilt to the side. "I'm telling you, they're crawling all over the place, and they've got that country-and-rhythm thing going...." You could practically see the images float across the man's mind. "That music'd make a six-foot bouncer bawl like a little girl."

He reached back for the old studio logs, checking the names of his earliest acts. He scanned down the page, tapped at one of them and smiled, and then at another. "You guys ought to stick around till Sunday," he told us. "Make the rounds to some of our better churches. You'd hear a few of these folks, and you would swear the rapture was going full tilt without you."

He tossed the papers back on the pile. "Nobody was getting this stuff down," he said. "Nobody was even paying attention. Can you believe that? There wasn't one label who'd risk a lousy reel of tape on these guys...." Then he sat up and a grin began to blossom. You could see that look—kind of childlike and mischievous—a boy creeping up close to the cookie jar. "But I knew white people were listening to this stuff. They'd never admit it, but late at night, when nobody's looking—there's a bunch of white folks digging the blues … and I had a hunch there could be a whole bunch more."

"And why's that?" Dalton asked. "What's got all these white people secretly hooked on the blues?"

Phillips took a deep breath, gathering a handful of thoughts together. "The blues tells the truth," he said. "It's life—unvarnished and laid bare—just the way it is out there where people live—especially the poor—the ones who've been down so long they can't see any way up…. I think that's what pulls on us, that's what draws us to the light." He settled deep into his chair. "I knew this stuff had to appeal to somebody besides a few blacks in west Tennessee. I knew … I just knew we could get this into bigger markets."

Dalton settled back, his pencil pressed to his lip. "So why you?" he asked. "You did this thing nobody else was doing. What do you know that they don't?"

"The music," Phillips replied flatly. "The guys who're running the other labels, they all grew up listening to the same thing, and now they're making more of it. It's what they know; what they like."

"But you grew up with the blues?" Dalton sounded surprised.

"I was lucky," Phillips said. "When I was a kid in Alabama there was this colored church just down the road from ours. Their service must've lasted half the day, so I'd kinda mosey down there, find a spot near an open window, and listen till it was time to go home. And I gotta tell you: the joyful noise those folks made … it was different from ours."

He leaned forward again, elbows back on his knees, resuming the position he took for more serious comments. "Somehow I got hooked. I don't know why really; it just stirred up something inside, gave me this—I don't know—this kind of yearning, this sense that no matter how much you'd heard, you needed to hear just a little bit more.... You know what I mean?"

A dewy smile swept over him. "In our little town there were two kinds of poor people: black field hands and white sharecroppers. If you lived there, you lived with the music. You couldn't help but hear it—these songs that lifted them up, that carried them away from the drudgery: the blues, country, gospel.... You heard it in the fields. You heard the black women sing while they did the washing and ironing and sweeping. You'd heard it on Friday nights, on street corners down in colored town."

He rocked back savoring the remembered sounds. "That music provided relief," he said, "but not escape. That's what makes it different; that's the thing that tugs on you."

"So you came to it through a side door," Dalton said. "You were standing in the wings, listening in?"

Phillips shook his head. "No," he said, another pensive grin rising. "We had this old colored man who worked for my father, Silas Payne. Uncle Silas and I used to sit on the front porch and he'd spin the wildest stories any kid ever heard. He'd tell me about the sausage and butter-cake trees that grew tall in Africa. He told me stories about the Molasses River...." A sparkle wriggled into Phillips's eye. "And he was the first man to utter the magic words: Beale Street."

"And I'm guessing he was a musician," Dalton said.

"His guitar was always within reach," Phillips replied, "and every story came with a soundtrack; he'd make it up right there on the spot. I'd close my eyes, and let that music wash over me; let it work its way beneath the skin...." He looked back to Dalton. "That's where

I learned music—not notes or reading or anything like that—Silas taught me a kind of music that flowed out of who you are, out of what a hard life teaches."

"And he taught you to play?" Dalton asked.

Phillips chuckled, "You know, I just wasn't wired that way; it never really occurred to me to sing or play. But those days with Silas, growing up listening to the field hands and servants, that's when I fell in love with the music."

Phillips swiveled in a tight arc. He inventoried the things around him: the recorders, editing equipment, microphones.… "When I got into the radio business it all kind of bubbled back to the surface," he said. "That's when it dawned on me: what I'd be able to do with the music."

"So you're mostly a businessman," Dalton said, "who just happens to have this creative flair?"

Phillips laughed. "Maybe," he replied. "I don't know. I really think of myself as a conductor more than anything else; as a guy who's got an eye for talent, who's got a knack for drawing it out, matching up the right song with the right artist—that sort of thing."

Dorsey perked. He'd just heard his cue to shift where he'd been dying to go.

"And Elvis is a prime example?" he asked.

Phillips shook his head slowly. "No, not really," he said. "Just the most famous."

"But when you heard him, you must've known right away," he said. "The talent had to be obvious."

Sam Phillips burst out laughing. "Not even close," he replied.

Phillips settled back and began the story. "Elvis was just a kid when he stumbled in here; boy didn't have the confidence God gave a newborn kitten, and when you talked to him he'd stare at his shoes; barely able to muster more than a 'yes sir' or 'no sir.'

"So he stops in here one day," Phillips went on. "I wasn't around, but Marion, my assistant, she thought he was a nice kid so we scheduled a little time. I matched him up with Scotty Moore, a guitarist who'd been around for a while, and Bill Black, a bass player who'd been with the Starlite Wranglers. I asked them to work up a little something; I guess they were in the studio four or five different times, and I remember Bill saying that he didn't see much in Elvis."

"But you let him play anyway," Dalton probed.

"Well," Phillips shrugged again, "the studio wasn't booked, and the whole thing was real casual—nobody had made any promises." Phillips stood and moved to the window, where he could see into the studio. "You know," he said, "in those few sessions he just hadn't found his own voice. He was trying to imitate Dean Martin and Bing Crosby; every so often he'd try to throw in a little Hank Williams twang, but it was coming out all whiney. It just wasn't Elvis."

He gazed back into the studio. "I was watching from the control room; he was still doing this nasally crooning thing, singing a song called 'I Love You Because.' It's a sweet song, and you never know when lightning'll strike, so I hit the record button—you know, just in case. But right then, it couldn't have been two seconds later, they decide to take a break. Scotty's down there mumbling something about taking ten and then trying again."

A sparkle crept back into Phillips's eyes. "So Elvis starts singing by himself. He's in there all alone, just horsing around, jumping up and down, acting all crazy. Well, Bill picks up his bass and joins the act;

he starts acting liking an idiot—so now they're both hopping around in there. Next thing you know, Scotty wanders in and starts up doing the same thing." Phillips shook his head, laughing. "I'm still in the control booth while all this is going on—editing some tape, I guess, I don't know—but I had the door open and I could hear all this ruckus going on, so I stuck my head out and yelled, 'What're you guys doing down there?'

"Scotty gave me this little shrug and said, 'We don't know.' And I remember, I told them to back up; I told them to find a spot to start, and to do it again. They all looked at each other, mumbled back and forth a few times, then Scotty counted down, and they began to play.

"The song that Elvis, Scotty, and Bill Black played that day—it was July 7, 1954—was 'That's All Right.' It was a song that Big Boy Crudup, a Negro blues singer, had recorded seven or eight years before, and it was—every note of it—as raw as meat in a butcher shop.

"Presley's version was no more refined.

"They were just in there having a good time," Phillips remembered. "But the thing is: They held it together. These three white guys, right down there in that studio—they took a blues song and made it their own." Phillips leaned into the window. He folded his arms and said, "This time, Elvis wasn't imitating anybody; he wasn't trying to impersonate Crudup—this was all Elvis—and I'm telling you, that was the first time anybody had ever heard *him*." He dipped his chin, imagining the scene for what must have been the ten millionth time. "He showed all that looseness, that same kind of swing and swagger that we've seen thousands of times since … but that nobody had ever seen before."

Phillips ambled back to the desk, hands thrust deep in his pockets. "I'd said it I-don't-know-how-many times," he chuckled. "If I could find a white guy who sounded black—we'd make a million bucks."

Dalton turned his head, surprised. "That wouldn't be hard to find," he said. "There are plenty of white...."

Phillips threw up a hand, shaking his head no. "You don't understand," he said, "I wasn't looking for a guy who could imitate a colored singer; people have been doing that since Al Jolson. I wanted a white singer who *was* colored—who had the same sensibilities, who had the same feel for the music, who had the same sound inside him as Crudup and Ike Turner and the Prisonaires.

"If we could find that, then we'd have something to sell. And we would, by golly, have given the world a gift they'd be grateful for."

"And Elvis had it?" Dalton said. "This sensibility you were looking for?"

"Yeah," Phillips said quietly. He looked up. "You ever met him?"

Dalton shook his head no.

"He grew up dirt-poor. He dressed funny, his hair looked weird, his old man once did three years at Parchman. Elvis Presley spent his whole life feeling self-conscious, knowing he didn't quite measure up, that he didn't really belong with the 'better people'...." Phillips peered up, "And let me tell you something: He still feels that way."

"And that's where this temperament comes from?" Dalton asked.

"Presley's got more in common with the black field hands I knew in Alabama than with you or me," Phillips said. "He'd be more comfortable hanging out with them, singing with Uncle Silas, than he would with Pat Boone or Tab Hunter."

"And so that afternoon," Dalton said, "when Presley let his hair down, when he just so happened to sing 'That's All Right'—that's when this dirt-poor weirdo became the king of rock and roll? Is that what you're telling me?"

"Yeah," Phillips said, "that's where it started."

Years later, someone would discover tapes of the recording session Phillips had described. They wouldn't know what it was, or recognize the voices, but they'd play it for a man named Jim Dickson, a studio musician who'd been around at the time. Dickson would hear the tapes; he'd recall the people, the day, the precise moment.... "That," he would say, "is what it sounded like ... ten minutes before rock and roll was born."

Dalton pushed further into Phillips's tale. "So that's what kicked off this whole music revolution, Presley fooling around with an old blues song?"

"That's what people say," Phillips replied. "And I guess it's true. But I don't think you can ever pick just one thing." He peered into the studio again, another memory taking shape in his mind. "Whenever I hear that, I always think about my old buddy Willie Kizart; I wonder what he'd say."

Dalton replied with the blank stare. "I don't know him," he confessed.

"Willie was driving over here from Clarksdale with Ike Turner," Phillips began. "This was back in fifty-one; they had all their stuff strapped onto the top of the car and somehow—somewhere between here and there—Willie's amp wriggled loose. The thing flies off the roof, bounces off the trunk, and must've tumbled fifteen, twenty yards down the highway. Well, they're sick about it of course; there's no way it could've survived. But they go back and get it and tie it back on. They get here and we can see it's busted up pretty good. The speaker cone was a mess; had a crack running all the way down the side of it." Phillips rubbed along his jaw and chin. "Well, there's no way to fix it, and heaven knows, none of us could afford to replace the dang thing, so we just started messing around, trying to see what we could do."

Phillips was bent forward, eyes flashing, hands flailing all over the place. "So I stuffed this wad of paper in there, just trying to press the stupid thing together, to see if I could get it to work. Well, I couldn't," he said. "None of us could get it to sound the way it was supposed to, but—" he waited until Dalton and I leaned closer— "the thing sounded good. It wasn't perfect. Shoot, it wasn't anything like the way it was supposed to be, but it sounded good. So instead of pretending like it wasn't there, I over-amped it—I took the distortion and blew it wide open, and I'm telling you—and I know it sounds crazy—but it sounded like we'd added a saxophone. And old Willie—he did not miss a beat; he went right along, playing this great little boogie riff ... Ike was on piano, Raymond Hill blew the daylights out of an honest-to-goodness real saxophone. And Jackie Brenston—I'm telling you, he sang like a man three times his size that day...." Phillips turned back to the studio, where the apparition was as real as my chair. "That was one of the first songs we did," Phillips said, "and it's still one of the best."

His gaze lingered a few seconds more.

"So what was it?" Dalton finally asked, "The song?"

I put my hand in the air, like a kid in the third grade. "I think I know."

Phillips lifted his chin in my direction.

"Didn't Jackie Brenston sing 'Rocket 88'?"

"Bingo," Phillips replied. "And that, gentlemen, just might have been the first rock-and-roll record ever made."

"That was a terrific song," I said.

"That's the record that really kicked things off for us," Phillips replied. "You may have heard of jalopies, you heard the noise they make, let me introduce you to my Rocket 88...." He looked up, smiling. "Sounds like rock and roll to me."

• • • •

Friday morning, while I was with a photographer at the Peabody Hotel, Dalton was back with Phillips, hearing about how he'd stumbled across Carl Perkins, Jerry Lee Lewis, Roy Orbison, and Johnny Cash.

While I was snapping shots of lobby chandeliers, Dalton was listening to the first recording of "Great Balls of Fire." While I was in a blazing kitchen learning the fine points of "wet barbeque," Dalton was playing and replaying the first ten takes of "Blue Suede Shoes." While I was listing Beale Street's ten best restaurants, Dalton heard the first recording of Johnny Cash singing: "I keep a close watch on this heart of mine ... I keep the ends out for the tie that binds / Because you're mine, I walk the line...." As I sat at the hotel bar slurping coffee, I wondered why I'd let him get the best story either of us had ever worked on.

And then, as I hummed "Blue Suede Shoes," I suddenly flashed back to Montgomery's bombed-out churches. I was, for three seconds, back at the Sam Peck Hotel with Virgil Blossom, and then face-to-face with the snarling Hazel Bryan … and I had to pause—overcome by some strange emotion—overwhelmed by the goodness of what was around me, the richness of it all, the sheer delight of it, and the creativity. My heart pumped pure gratitude—beyond its known capacity—for Sam Phillips, for the best barbeque in the world, for the blues and rock and roll and gospel, for Beale Street and the Mississippi River—for the South, and all the things it had to give.

• • • •

We were back in the conference room, combing over Dalton's first draft. It was rough, but the style was just right, and the tone—he'd captured our personality perfectly: a little sassy, more casual than *Look* and *Life*, with just the tiniest trace of irreverence.

The piece was fun; it was filled with Sam Phillips's behind-the-scenes anecdotes and the stories he'd told of the serendipitous accidents that had led to so many of the songs we knew by heart. Dalton had given readers this delicious peek behind the curtain, but it wasn't gossipy; the story wasn't littered with tidbits to tantalize teenage girls—it was serious and informative, yet charm oozed from every word. This was about men and music, and the wizard who stood behind the curtain pulling it all together—not in New York or Los Angeles, but in, of all places, Memphis, Tennessee.

Dalton had done this wonderful job of blending narrative with interview—a kind of hybrid article that, I swear, he must've invented over the weekend—and it was masterful.

I was up and pacing the room, scanning the story for the third time. "I hate your guts," I told Dalton. "This is just flat-out good."

"Awww," he stretched the word to ten syllables, drenching every one of them in false humility. "I had a look at that piece you're doing on the best barbeque in Memphis," he replied. "Now that ... that's a thing to behold."

"You're a riot," I shot back. "And you know what? I dare you to find a better barbeque story, anywhere."

Dalton tapped at the paper in front of him. "Seriously," he said, "I know this needs work, but there's a heck of a story in here."

I was propped against the window frame, making a few marks here and there in the margins. "I'd like to find a way to get the race music in here," I said. "I wonder if we can slip in a little something about the blues; show people how it's worked its way into the world, through Presley and Lewis and Perkins...."

"Yeah," Dalton said, "I was thinking we might do a sidebar about Big Boy Crudup, talk about his version of 'That's All Right,' give a little history. Maybe we could do a couple more—on Willie Kizart and Ike Turner, the Prisonaires ... get 'em sprinkled in where we can."

I read for a few seconds more, churning on Dalton's thought, and thinking there was probably a better way. "I wonder if we can find some kind of correlation?" I said. I pushed off the wall and paced. "We got the umbrella piece about Phillips and Sun Records. We run all this good stuff you've got about Presley, about how they stumbled into one another, and then, right there with it, we do the Crudup sidebar. We make the transition to Jerry Lee Lewis, talk about 'Whole Lot of Shaking Going On,' then—on the same page—we do a hundred and fifty words on somebody who corresponds to him the same way Crudup does to Elvis—a colored guy he's emulating, or who he likes...." I looked up to see if Dalton was following: "Instead of just randomly dropping in a few sidebars, we match up each white guy with a black guy who's influenced him.

"Shouldn't be that hard," I said. "I mean—you know Roy Orbison's been listening to black music. Carl Perkins, Warren Smith—you can hear it, can't you?"

Dalton leaned back, his lip curled, mentally trying to make the matches. "I like it," he said, "... if we can get it to work."

For the cover we envisioned a glamour shot of Phillips striding straight down the middle of Beale—late at night, haloed by a million watts of neon—and looking like he'd been the mayor for the past twenty years.

We were toying with headline ideas, but I liked Alan's original thought, even if he had been kidding, something along the lines of: "The Man Who Made Rock and Roll," or "The Father of Rock," or "The Maestro of Memphis," or ... I don't know, we'd try a hundred different ideas before we settled on one.

Dalton's piece was getting close to its final form. It looked like we'd do a page on Carl Perkins and "Blue Suede Shoes." We'd do five or six hundred words on Roy Orbison and Carl Mann, the same for Jerry Lee Lewis—and we'd devote three full pages to the discovery of Elvis Presley, and the first rock-and-roll song that any human had ever heard.

But the backstory was still weak. We'd thrown in a few boxes on Crudup, Kizart, and Brenston. We'd done a little longer piece—it'd made Alan laugh out loud—called "The Making of 'Rocket 88'"—talking about a cracked amp stuffed full of wadded paper; we'd even found some great art—a sporty illustration of the famous Oldsmobile that'd make the perfect visual. But that part of the story just wouldn't go where we tried to steer.

"I don't know," Alan said. "The colored guys are interesting, and I understand why we want 'em in here …" he said as he peered over the top of his glasses. "But it just seems like they're a distraction to me."

I sat at the head of the table—reading, listening, and scratching out a few thoughts of my own. "Remember," I chided him, "we said we'd be bold. We said we'd never run scared."

"But that's not the problem," Dalton replied. "This isn't working organizationally; I think that's what's bothering Alan. The sidebars are good, but they're not matching up the way we hoped they would. It's feeling like they're just stuck on—like a hood ornament on your car." Dalton tossed his pen aside. "We're just not there yet."

I flipped through the pages, reading the sidebars for the sixth time. "The Presley-Crudup thing's good," I said. "But I guess it's kind of forced after that." I pitched the pages onto the table. "So what are we going to do? There's gotta be a tie-in, some natural connection, some way to open a few side doors into the main article.…" I slumped back, massaging my forehead. "What's the angle here?"

Jeff Rogers, an art director who'd been working on the masthead and interior design swiveled back and forth impatiently—lips bunched and jaw clenched—a man giving birth to a plan. He popped up from his chair and marched to the flip chart; he sketched a rectangle across the page. "Let's say this is a two-page spread," he began. He drew a line three-quarters of the way down. "You run your main story up here, across the top. You talk about Phillips and Presley and Jerry Lee Lewis—all the white guys go up here. Then," he paused as he tapped the marker in the space beneath the line, "along the bottom, you run a whole different narrative. Forget the one-to-one correlation, forget the sidebars and side doors; just put your colored guys down here." He drew three or four squiggly, horizontal lines. "You run your copy here," he said. Then he sketched a couple of smaller boxes, one along the gutter, another at the outside margin, "and you stick your photos here … of the colored guys."

He turned to face us. "You keep 'em small. The layout tells people that this isn't the important part; that it's just an interesting aside. But you get the point across." He tossed the marker into the tray and headed back to his chair. "You don't have to tie the two together. Let design fix that problem for you."

I beamed at Jeff Rogers and said, "The boy's a genius."

"And you know what?" Alan added. "That'll look so darn good … we can sell it for the cool factor alone—nobody'll care if it's about a couple of colored guys."

Dalton ambled up to the flip chart. He waved his hand over the drawing. "Maybe the top half's in color," he said, "and we do the bottom in black-and-white?"

Jeff rocked back, hands locked behind his head. "Maybe … or …" he eased out of his chair. "What if we do it the other way around?" He grabbed the marker. "Maybe we do the bottom in five-color, we add a layer of black down here," he said as he began drawing over the lines he'd already made. "We pull every bit of it out of the faces and skin tones—get that rich black feel." He turned to Alan and me. "That'd give us a little unexpected elegance down there."

"Nice ..." Dalton chimed. "I like where this is going."

"*Life* or *Look* would never dream of doing something like that," Alan said.

I rested my chin on a fisted hand. "It's going to be a trick—to rework what we've got into a whole other story...." I turned to Alan. "And we're going to get some push back; you need to know that. But it'll be worth it." My gaze traveled from Alan to Dalton to Jeff Rogers. "This is exactly the kind of stuff we said we'd do."

Dalton, still standing at the flip chart, zeroed in on me. He rapped his hand against the bottom of the page. "You want to take a shot at this; rework those sidebars and come up with something for this bottom section—you know—the part that's just an aside?"

I met his stare head on. "You know what, I'm gonna do that." I stacked the pages into a neat deck; I smiled at my partner and said: "I just hope that after I'm done, somebody—a few readers anyway— might remember to go back and read the main article."

Fifteen hours later I was on the road to Memphis, alone this time, and vowing to do "an aside" that'd make music lovers drool. Phillips said he was looking forward to the visit, and he promised to run down a couple of his earliest acts—a pair of blues artists who might be just what the story needed.

"This," Phillips told me, "is my greatest discovery." He slapped the big black man's shoulder and let his hand linger there, gripping him with more affection than most men have for blood brothers. "This man is better than Elvis; he's better than Johnny Cash and Roy Orbison. This right here," Phillips announced, "is the Howlin' Wolf himself— Chester Burnett."

The Howlin' Wolf—all six feet five inches of him—stood to shake my hand.

"Chester spends most of his time in Chicago now," Phillips said.

"But I'm back here all the time," Burnett explained, "checking on the farm and my family."

"Well, I'm glad you're here today," I replied, "… and willing to spend some time with me."

"Happy to help Sam out any way I can."

"So, how'd it get started," I said, "between the two of you, I mean?"

Phillips's grin warmed the room. "This old boy moseyed in here one day wearing his field overalls," he said. "He carried a straw hat down at his side … looked like he'd come to pick cotton."

"And I had these great big shoes on," Burnett chuckled. "I had to cut holes in the sides of 'em—to make room for these big old corns on the side of my feet."

Burnett wore a thin moustache and an irrepressible smile. And every physical feature, despite his enormous size, invited you to come closer and to make yourself at home.

"I'd been farming over in Mississippi," he told me, "and that's where I learned the blues—over in Ruleville. But after the army, I ended up in West Memphis and settled there."

"Tell the man where you used to play," Phillips insisted.

Burnett glanced away, embarrassed by the now hazy past. "We all got to put food on the table," he said. He gave a quick hitch of his shoulders. "I kept pretty steady playing the whorehouses over this way, but I played some other places too—the Negro ballparks, a few clubs...."

"A deejay over in West Memphis put me onto him," Phillips said. "And from the first note I heard, I knew he was different." Phillips tilted his head back, summoning the past. "When I first heard him play, I could hear—just off in the distance, this real basic Mississippi Delta blues—and that would have been plenty right there—I mean, we'd have cut some records if that had been all there was ..." he leaned in toward me. "But I'll tell you something: Somewhere between here and the Delta, he learned to set the music free. I mean, he learned to let it run wild, and the second I heard him I said, 'That's exactly what I'm looking for.' I turned to the bartender, 'That right there,' I told him, 'that's where the soul never dies.'"

"So," I said to Phillips, "you talked to him, got him to come over here and record; what was that like, the two of you working together?"

Phillips studied the big man beside him. "Like nothing I'd ever seen or heard before." Phillips laughed; he placed a hand on Burnett's shoulder. "The guy comes in here in his overalls; he's ten feet tall, he's got these feet that're bigger than the Jolly Green Giant's—I used to call him Big Foot Chester.... But the music ... the music he played that day—I can hear it as clearly right now as I could then."

Five seconds must have passed while Phillips reveled in the imaginary music. "When this guy plays," Phillips continued, "his whole face lights the room. When he's going full speed, I'm telling you, you better have some shades handy." Phillips closed his eyes and settled into the memory—of the day in 1951—when Howlin' Wolf played in his studio for the first time. "He sat right there," Phillips said, "probably on that very stool. He had those Goliath feet planted this far apart, he was blowing a hurricane through this old beat-to-death French harp; I didn't think the veins in his neck were gonna hold ten more seconds—and I'll tell you the truth: There is nothing I'd rather see right now than that very same sight." He squeezed Burnett's shoulder. "When this man sings," he told me, "he is nowhere but deep down into that song."

"Willie Johnson played guitar that day," Burnett remembered. "And that old boy could do his own share of damage."

"Ah, he was good," Phillips agreed. "You guys could flat play."

"What'd you sing?" I asked Chester.

He looked at Phillips, the two of them sharing the memory. "I believe it was 'How Many More Years?' wasn't it?"

"That's right," Phillips said. "And we did 'Baby Ride with Me' too."

Phillips rolled his chair to a bank of equipment. He tossed a playful grin in Burnett's direction. "I got a little surprise for you," he said, his hand poised over the play button. "You ready?" He stabbed at the reel-to-reel player, the spools began to whirl, static crackled through the speakers, there were muffled, indistinguishable voices in the background, then Phillips clearly saying: "Whenever you're ready."

There was a three-beat pause, then a second voice: "Three, two, one ..." And then came the siren sound of Howlin' Wolf—Chester Burnett—singing: "Well ride with me baby, ride with me all night long / well ride with baby, ride with me all night long / ride with me baby, then I'll take you home...."

Phillips let the song play to the end; the tape slithered through the machine and flapped around in the take-up reel. Hesitantly, he reached up and hit the *stop* button, swiveled back to me and said, "Now, you've heard what I did."

He pitched a smile to Burnett, his affection seeping through every pore. "We've done all right here," he said to me. "We've produced our fair share of hit songs. But you need to know: I have never found anyone who was anywhere close to this man's equal."

He draped his arm over the giant black man's shoulder. "This man right here," he said, "is my greatest discovery."

I went back to the hotel to freshen up before dinner. The image of Howlin' Wolf wouldn't budge from my mind. I heard the music over and over again—and savored every note: "Well ride with me baby, ride with me all night long...." And the wonder of the story—of how he and Phillips had found one another—just kept welling up inside me, like one wave after another, each one bigger and more profound and more—it's hard to explain—more of this thing I couldn't keep inside.

I envisioned Chester Burnett in his overalls and straw hat. I imagined Phillips with his hand on the Negro's shoulder—the fondness bubbling up in both men—and I knew that I'd been chosen to tell their story. I knew now, in a way I hadn't known so fully before, why we'd created the magazine. And I could not, without the restraint of another's presence, contain the emotion. I reached for a tissue and blotted tears that wouldn't hold.

———————

After supper that night we crossed the bridge to West Memphis, Arkansas. The two of us rode into town, through the colored section of the city, and up to the Sixteenth Street Grill, a hole-in-the-wall juke joint off the main drag.

"I recorded this guy before we started Sun," Phillips explained. "He wasn't as far along as Burnett—still isn't, to tell you the truth—but I like him, and I know he's got a ton of talent." He cut me a quick glance. "He's recording out west now—that's a long story—I just hope they can pull it out of him, because this guy might really be good."

Riley King sat at the bar sipping a glass of a pale brown liquid. He was tall and spindly looking. His hair was swept back in a steep wave, and he beheld the world through a pair of dark, almost sullen eyes.

The three of us moved to a table, ordered drinks and a few things to snack on. The place was packed tight and filled with the din of a hundred conversations. A jukebox thrummed with the sound of a black voice singing, "… take my seat and ride way back / and watch this train move down the track …" Then came the reverberating whine of a harmonica, the metrical scratch of a washboard, and in the background, a rhythm guitar held it together, "Baby, baby / I'm going to bring it on home to you."

We sat in a low-hanging fog, the byproduct of Camels and the hand-rolled smokes of working-class men. Glasses clinked around us, dishes clanked, hands and fingers beat on the bar keeping time to the music. I sipped from a longneck beer and asked Riley King about his connection to Phillips.

"Well, I'd been singing gospel," he began timidly, "and I'd always sung alone; had never been in anything like a professional band before." He looked up, just briefly. "I played on street corners back in Mississippi; I'd go out whenever the bills came due, just hoping to make enough to keep the lights on. But I'd heard Sonny Boy Williamson on the radio, and I'd heard that he'd come here, to West Memphis. I wanted to play the blues like he did, so I just came looking for him."

King sipped from the drink and savored the soothing tingle. "I didn't know any better," he said. "And one day I just walked in the front door at KWEM—that's where Sonny Boy played—and I asked 'em if they'd let me sing on the radio." He tipped his glass, grinning. "And they said yes.

"That's how I met Sonny Boy, and that's when I got serious about the blues."

He looked to Phillips, who nodded for him to go on. "Well, one thing led to another; I ended up doing my own show over on WDIA. We used to—"

"And that's where I heard him," Phillips interrupted. He flung a hand toward King, "We got together on a couple of songs after that."

King's head bobbed, a song running through his mind. "'She's Dynamite,' that was a great song." He eyed Phillips again, and then looked to me. "That's as much his song as it is mine."

"How's that?" I said.

"We might've done a little experimenting with that one," Phillips admitted. "It's a little—oh, I don't know—let's just say it might be a little more energetic than Tampa Red's version; got a little boogie feel...."

"You done anything else I might know?" I asked.

"He's done plenty," Phillips answered, "'Three O'clock Blues'— that's the song that kicked things off for him. He did 'You Know I Love You' and 'Woke Up This Morning.'"

"'Three O'clock Blues,' I said, "I know that song." I turned my head, trying to bring it to mind. In a stilted half-talking-half-singing voice I mumbled the words, "My baby's gone, gone away from me / My baby's gone, I'm in misery ..." I glanced up at King, "That's it, right?"

He dipped his chin and smiled, "You got it," he said.

"But that's by ..." I rubbed a hand along my chin, struggling to come up with a name.

Phillips laughed and slapped his friend on the back. "This right here," he said, "is the Beale Street Blues Boy, B. B. King."

"Okay ... I know you." I cut my eyes back and forth between them: "So you two started out together?"

"Yeah," Phillips replied. "We did some stuff early on."

Riley—B. B. King—folded his arms across the table. "The Bihari brothers recorded 'Three O'clock Blues,' he said. "They're the ones who kinda kicked things off for me. But if hadn't been for Sam, for the work we did together, they'd have never known my name—and neither would anybody else."

And nobody—ever—would have heard "Three O'Clock Blues," "You Don't Know Me," "Please Love Me," and whatever else this young guitarist might have to offer.

•   •   •   •

Late that night I drifted out of the Peabody and found myself wandering the Memphis bank of the South's most-storied river. I sat and watched it ripple past, my mind circling a thousand thoughts—not just on this article—on the stuff that was, as Dalton and Jeff Rogers had so aptly put it, "just an aside," but on the bigger picture: of our business, and what we might really do.

I was just beginning to see the magnitude of what Phillips had accomplished. I was, after hearing Burnett and King, after listening to the music these men had made together, getting a truer picture of Sam Phillips's vision. From 706 Union Street, a tiny storefront two hundred yards off Beale, he'd set out to mingle black and white culture, to bring us all the best of what each had to offer, and to blend it into something new, something better than any of us would have ever known living secluded lives.

In Sam Phillips, I saw qualities I envied: a quirky, creative flair, a compulsion to create and cultivate, an inborn need to bring out the best in others—to ring out every last drop of whatever God had put in—and to spread it indiscriminately around the world.

And in an odd way, I thought—if you looked at it from a certain kind of weird angle, Phillips was a bit like Martin King. He gave the Negro a place to sit, side by side with his white neighbors, where he was free to use his gifts fully.

Music, records, the radio business, and his own nearly boundless imagination were the tools Phillips used. With them, he freed what was inside; he released what was bound up in the hearts of the poor, and he turned up the volume for us all to hear. It was, though Phillips would have never used the phrase, his own version of King's "beloved community." He mixed the races in a way nobody ever had before, and his purpose was to elevate us all.

I pitched a stone toward the river, thinking about the contingent factors in my own life—the step-by-step path that led me here—to this spot, on this night, at this exact bend in the Mississippi River.

The silhouette of a long, flat barge rounded the river's north bend. A cool gust kicked past, sending fall leaves pattering by. It was after midnight and my mind ricocheted off one thought and on to another. I was the editor in chief of America's newest magazine. And I, like Phillips, had to deal with the life and the gifts I'd been given.

Uninvited—from a distance and through time—Carson Powers began to nag: *If a thing is wrong, do we really want to be a part of it?* he'd once asked. *Do we want to start down a path that leads where we do not want to go?*

The barge eased south, past one beguiling city—rich with the blues and home-cooked barbeque—on its way to another, resounding with jazz and the Cajun spice of jambalaya.

I gazed up at the glittering sky and thought to myself: I'm friends with Percy and Walter Jackson. I drink coffee with Martin Luther King. I've met Daisy Bates and Elizabeth Eckford. And I'd just spent an evening with B. B. King. I knew people that Carson Powers didn't. And I now knew that they possessed gifts that would sweeten our lives—and that our gifts might add spice to theirs.

I watched the Mississippi pass, wondering what would matter in a thousand years. And who, when my great-grandchildren ran the business, would have had the more profound effect on the world: W. A. Gayle, the mayor of Montgomery, or Sam Phillips, the founder of Sun Records? Who, fifty years from now, would have had the greater impact: Marvin Griffin, the governor of Georgia—a man who had power, influence, and more friends than a movie star,

or Martin Luther King, a Negro pastor who couldn't get a seat in
most of Atlanta's restaurants?

B. B. King once played on street corners to pay his power bill.
Howlin' Wolf Burnett had played in overalls and cut-up shoes. I'd
listened to Willie Kizart make a miracle through a cracked amplifier
he couldn't afford to fix. And I wondered, there on the east bank of
the Mississippi, who'd done more to make the world better: them,
or the Arkansas state legislator Jim Johnson?

•　•　•　•

Today, when I gaze at the plaques, awards, and photos that grace my
office wall, I linger on the framed and signed photo of Chester Burnett, the Howlin' Wolf. He'd sent it in response to a package I'd sent
him—a handful of magazines along with a letter that thanked him
for his time, his music, and a story that couldn't help but to inspire
our readers.

Burnett had expressed gratitude to me, for caring about his music,
for making it known to a wider audience, and most importantly he
said, for "doing what you can for Negro musicians."

Others were also grateful. More than six hundred readers wrote
in reply to that first issue, nearly all of them praising the effort we'd
made. *Down South* had touched a tender nerve. There were, we discovered, others like us—Southerners who longed to feel good about
where they lived and what they'd done—who were thirsty for respect
and a little appreciation.

Subscription cards flooded the office, all in the company of a
check for a one-, two-, or three-year subscription. Our phone nearly

wore out its ringer, with advertisers requesting rate cards and wanting their Southern clients to be seen in the company of such "fair and positive content."

We had, it seemed, made the right kind of noise. And we would survive to see a second and third issue.

• • • •

In those early days we'd been lucky. After Little Rock, there had been a lull in the South's unrest, and we were sure that it was a gift to us, that it was time specifically given to me and my partners to figure out who we were and to lay a foundation for the work to come.

It was also time for my son to ponder. For him, this was a time for ideals to take root, when he'd fertilize and prune the convictions that sprout in a young man's mind. And King was always there, overshadowing everything. King was this streaking comet that dazzled before him—this man he'd met and touched and talked to—who, since Montgomery, had been on the cover of *Time*, had been a guest on *Meet the Press*, had visited with Eisenhower and Nixon and with a handful of leaders from foreign nations.

Chris gulped every word, he clipped pictures and articles, and, if there was any chance that King had made headlines, he camped in front of the television five minutes before the nightly news.

We saw King often. He, along with Abernathy and several others, had formed the Southern Christian Leadership Conference, a civil rights group headquartered four miles from my office. He shuttled back and forth between Montgomery and Atlanta, and whenever he was in town, if our schedules shared a half-hour hole, we'd grab some time together. Chris begged to come along—to ask questions, to get the insider's news, and to bask in the presence of his hero.

As the weeks went on, we watched King wear down. He was, in those days, a man who served two masters, and each was jealous for his time. His father badgered him to return to the pulpit and to tend to the flock on Dexter Avenue. But any semiobjective observer could see that King heard a different call. It was equally obvious that he couldn't resist the fame. For King, it was light to a moth. He basked in the glory, and it fit him as comfortably as the tailored suits he now wore.

In this interval—this rest that we'd been granted—King grew restless. He itched to perform on a bigger stage, and I knew that one church in a small Alabama town couldn't hold him. Even now the road beckoned. He traveled to Negro colleges, promoting nonviolent protests; he visited with every black pastor who'd talk to him, championing the importance of the Negro church and the crucial role of its pastors. He courted disciples like an itinerant salesman, instilling in them his vision for the "beloved community," persuading them that nonviolent, direct action was the means by which they all, working together, could bring the concept into corporal, visible being.

In this interval that we'd been given, King longed for another success, for another Montgomery, for one more event to spur the movement forward. He kicked off 1958 with a massive voter registration drive. On February 12, Lincoln's birthday, he'd organized mass meetings in twenty-one Southern cities. At one of them he proclaimed, "America must begin the struggle for democracy at home." He condemned the hypocrisy of advocating free elections in Europe when, in the Southern United States, they remained a gauzy illusion.

"To Negro Americans it is ironic," he argued, "to be governed, to be taxed, to be given orders, but to have no representation in a nation that would defend the right to vote abroad.…"

That day King informed every Southern leader, every national office holder, and every journalist who was willing to listen: "We must and we will be free. We want freedom now," King declared. "We want the right to vote now. We do not want freedom fed to us in teaspoons over another hundred and fifty years by Southern senators … who are not elected in a … legal manner. We Southerners," he said, "Negro and white, must no longer permit our heritage to be dishonored.…"

I had not heard the speech, but in my mind, when I'd read it later, I could feel the rhythm. I could hear that now-famous King cadence, and even I was moved.

But Chris … the speech ignited something new in the boy's imagination. The concepts, the reality of what was around us—in our own city and in the region where we lived—the truth and irrefutable logic of the case King made … it all inflamed his blossoming sense of moral justice. And launched him on yet another righteous crusade.

After school, he and Ansley plotted new ways to register Negro voters. They dreamed out loud about going door-to-door in colored communities, teaching residents how to fill in the forms, of holding classes in Negro churches, setting up tables on the courthouse lawn, gathering signatures on petitions, and writing letters to elected officials demanding an end to the unfair rules that barred Negroes from casting legal ballots.

"And there's no reason to stop here," Ansley waxed on. "We'll go to Macon, and then Columbus, and then we'll move on to Birmingham and Montgomery. And from there, to Jackson, Hattiesburg, and Biloxi."

Rose seethed in silence. She bit her lip and rolled her eyes. And when the talk became too much to bear, she'd slip outside and count to five hundred. "Jack," she whispered late one night, "that boy is not getting a driver's license until this kind of talk dies down." Her jaw stiffened, and captious lines creased her brow as she envisioned the places he might go. "Can you imagine," she said, the terrible picture taking shape in her mind, "what would happen if he dragged that girl into the colored neighborhoods …?"

King's "Citizenship Crusade" made another small mess of my life, but the Negro masses failed to rally. This time, there was no joining forces, no willingness to pay the price to end injustice, no surging desire to band together, hand in hand, to confront so evident an evil. And, if you listened closely, you could hear the rumblings of discontent—especially among the young. They grumbled that King had cozied up to elite white leaders. They'd grown wary—because he dressed like them and sounded like them and hobnobbed endlessly in their company. And it was obvious that they—the whites who possessed power—admired and embraced him.

Suspicion festered and corroded the bonds of Negro unity. But there was rhyme to King's reasoning. He needed support from white Northern liberals, which meant he had no choice but to curry favor. So, he worked through the church, an age-old institution they admired. He advanced the principles of Christianity and nonviolence, creeds that posed no threat and promised no harm. He appealed to the Bible and the Constitution, the two documents that almost every-one revered. And he painted this all-encompassing picture. He spoke of God's kingdom, not his. He spoke of freedom and justice for all, not merely those of a single color. He never advanced some startling new doctrine. He preached the things we all hold dear, and only asked that those gifts be fully shared.

Chris and I caught him after a tough day late that winter. He was exhausted and anxious about his future, and I was nervous about mine. "You know," I told him, "maybe it's time to change tactics ... get behind the NAACP for a little while. They got more money than Peru—and more lawyers than the Justice Department. You thought about working this from a little different angle?"

I saw the pain flash across King's face. There'd been rumors that he and Roy Wilkins, the NAACP leader, were a pair of alpha males contending for the same pack. And I guess, if I'd bothered to think it through, the philosophical rifts were plain: Wilkins worked the courts. He sued and appealed, and then appealed again, working a system that might take ten years to bear fruit. King didn't have that kind of time. He favored direct, nonviolent action—demonstra-tions that were visible, that confronted white America right where it lived, that demanded a quick response, and that unfolded before cameras.

In a voice tinged with regret King said, "There's a tendency to think our movement's an outside job. You listen to the governors and mayors and they all sing the same song: The Negroes were happy, life was good, everybody was doing just fine—and then the outside agitators came to town."

"The NAACP's from the outside?" I joked.

King laughed cynically. "New York's just a stone's throw from Moscow," he said. He leaned across the small table we shared. "Look, we need the NAACP. Our movement, our organization, it's nothing more than a supplement to theirs. And you're right, they're big, we're small. But this has got to be a Southern movement. We need to let those mayors and governors know that everything is not all right. They've got to see that we—Southern Negroes—are not content, that we won't settle for the status quo any longer." The colored pastor stared at some phantom spot in the distance. "Negroes in Georgia and Alabama and Mississippi—they've got to be the ones to deliver that message."

I liked Martin King. I found it hard to wish him anything but well, but I couldn't escape the irony that day. Here he was, plotting to tell the world what was wrong with our region. In an hour I'd meet with Dalton and Alan, where we'd plan to show them what was right.

"Don't be looking at me like that," King joked. "We want the same things. We might come at it from a different direction; might see things from a slightly different angle, but we both want a place where people thrive, where they're free, where everybody loves his neighbor."

I angled my head, wondering if that's what I truly wanted. But then, smiling, I said, "Yeah, I guess so."

"But nobody loves their neighbor," Chris piped up, "not the way you mean. And I don't see how you're going to change that."

King turned and took stock of the boy. He nodded slowly, as if weighing the reply. "You're right," he said. "They don't. And that's what we're out to change." He rested his chin on clasped hands.

"That's why we protest," King explained. "A mass demonstration shows the injustice. It's a picture of the inequality—a giant image of the hypocrisy.

"And sooner or later," King continued, "it's got to sink in. Sooner or later it's got to soften even the hardest heart."

We sat silently for a few seconds. King stared past me, out toward Auburn Avenue, to a passing barber, a city bus, a young mother loaded down with a single sack of groceries and a four-year-old son. "If we're peaceful," he told Chris, "if we root the protests in honest Christian love, then I believe it will come sooner." His gaze lingered outside, on an old man staggering by—a pint of something wrapped in a brown paper bag dangling from his hand. "If we can change men's hearts, the laws will follow."

"Good luck," I replied. Then, afraid the words had cut too deep, I doubled back. "What I mean is it's going to take just as long to change hearts as to change the laws, especially when most of the Negroes just want to be left alone. Ultimately, I think you're going to get a lot of what you want. But I'm not seeing anything that looks like another Montgomery, at least not right now."

"No," King said, "I'm not either." He raised his chin, wondering, I suspect, about where things might go. "You remember what I told you a long time ago—that this wasn't about rights for the Negro, that it was about justice, that our goal was righteousness for all people? ... If we achieve anything less than that, we've failed." A bewildered frown pulled at his lips, "But we need that galvanizing issue, something that inspires, that sparks—"

"I don't see the difference," Chris blurted out. "White people can ride the buses, they can vote, they can sit anywhere they want at the movie theater.… It's the colored people who don't have the rights. They're the ones who—"

"*Nooo,*" King stretched the word, reeling the boy back toward him, "we don't want to be thinking about groups; we don't want to be compartmentalizing whites and blacks, or one neighborhood versus another."

"But this is about Negroes," Chris said. "It's about freedom and equality for them. They're the only ones who need it."

"Yes," King granted, "but we've got to be thinking bigger than that." King paused. Then, as I'd seen him do from three different pulpits, he raised his right hand into the air. "This isn't about the fact that your father can vote and a black man can't. It's about the whole of society." King held tight to the boy's eye. "You and me, we live in the same country—in the same house, so to speak. If it's unjust for one, it's unjust—period. If we're members of one society, of this one single household—and in God's eyes we are—then injustice to me is necessarily injustice for everyone."

"I don't know …" Chris mumbled. He looked to me, his face twisted to a giant question.

"Well," I said, "in the abstract I guess I can see that …"

"This is absolutely concrete," King broke in. "The end of all our efforts—mine and yours, in whatever we do—has got to be redemption. It must be the creation of a community in which all men, of every color, live together in love and justice." King bent forward, resting both arms across the table. "I'm talking about the truest expression of Christianity here—the clearest possible picture of the church."

My mind, as if by reflex, raced back to Carson Powers, to the time he'd told me that outright integration could only lead where we couldn't go. "I know plenty of good Christians who aren't willing to go that far," I said.

"And that's why I'm working on them," King replied, "and not the courts. Montgomery and voting and the Brown versus Board decision—the purpose isn't to end segregation." He turned to Chris and paused, waiting to corral his full attention. "Let me tell you something: I wouldn't spend five minutes working for desegregation." He tapped his forefinger hard against the table. "We must work for *integration*, and that is a vastly different thing. This is not about rights or laws; it's not about winning legal battles or public relations wars …" His eyes lingered on my still malleable, young son. "It's about community. It's about justice for all, based on mutual love."

King let the words hang, hovering in the air around us. Then he swung his hand in a wide loop, as if circling the table the three of us shared. "If we live in brotherhood," he said, "if we live in one beloved community, then, if my rights are violated, the community's rights have been violated. If you're cheated, then I—because we comprise this one community—I've been cheated too." He leaned still closer, his head just inches from Chris's. "We do not only exist as individuals," King whispered. "We exist as a community, and its bonds cannot be broken."

Chris was first to look away, struggling to reckon King's calculations. "Nobody lives like that," he said flatly.

"But one day," King replied, "if the Bible's true, that'll change. And that means we need to begin now."

Chris's puzzled look—and I suspect mine, too—persisted.

"It all comes to that," King explained. "You've read it: the Holy City, the New Jerusalem, the dwelling of God with men—that's where history is headed."

Chris plunged his face into both hands, the poor boy's mind flooded past capacity and still groping for more. "But what's that got to do with anything?" he groaned. He stared at King between the slits of four fingers. "I know about heaven; I've heard all that a hundred times. What's that got to do with voting?"

King's grin burst wide. "Can you imagine—when God's kingdom comes—that some people will be able to vote and others can't? That some people will be forced to the back of the bus? That some people can eat in restaurants and others—who are also made in the very image of God—cannot? The laws have got to change," he told Chris, "and the courts, they've got to legislate moral behavior, but they can't dictate love. The courts can't force upon men a desire to redeem the relationships that God intended ..." King said as he raised a finger. Slowly, he pointed at Chris. "It's our job, yours and mine, to move in that direction—to give this world a glimpse of the one to come." His tone shifted into a parody of his own oratorical style: "Thy kingdom come, thy will be done—*on earth....*" King smiled paternally. "That, young man, is the connection. It's all about the coming kingdom, the creation of the beloved community, the place where God dwells among His people...."

Slowly, Chris lowered his hands. He returned King's stare, his eyes round in wonder, and his mind swirling with the cosmic purpose that King had proposed.

• • • •

Later that year, in September 1958, King had nearly been killed. He had written a book, *Stride Toward Freedom,* his personal account of

Montgomery. At a book signing in Harlem, at Blumstein's department store, a woman rushed to the front of the line. She demanded to know: "Are you Martin Luther King?" Given the affirmation she needed, she plunged a letter opener into the left side of his rib cage. The weapon lay against his aorta, and if he had so much as sneezed, the doctor later reported, even that small movement would have killed him.

Chris, who normally eats like a ravenous dog, went three days with barely a nibble. For as long as King was in peril, he stayed within arm's reach of a radio. He checked the newspaper every morning and Chet Huntley every night—moving his lips in silent prayer that King would pull through. "I don't understand why anybody would do this," he grumbled. I explained that the woman wasn't well, and that this wasn't the premeditated attack of an outraged enemy.

"Yeah," Chris said, "but still...." He looked up, his eyes damp and frightened. "We need to pay attention to him," he said, "to learn all we can, to listen to what he says ..." he turned back toward the television. "Because you never know...."

Since Little Rock, the South had been still. But I knew the calm couldn't last. We all knew that somewhere, outside our field of vision, King's movement was gathering strength for its next assault on the only way any of us had ever lived.

Dalton and Alan and I would become middlemen in this delicate transaction, and I hoped that somehow we could make the South a shining light, that we'd find a thousand innovators and visionaries—sons of the South who were moving the world in a better direction. And the next guy on my list was six hours south, in Daytona, Florida.

•   •   •   •

Bill France was the mastermind behind NASCAR. And he was, in his own way, as artistic as Sam Phillips. His fertile mind had just given birth to a new race, the Daytona 500, and to a track that'd make test pilots drool.

I'd gone down there early for a press-only tour, to interview France, to watch a few preliminary races, and to rub shoulders with stock-car racing's biggest stars.

I strolled down pit road with thirty reporters, listening to France explain that the track was a tri-oval, that the front stretch was banked at eighteen degrees, the backstretch was nearly flat, but the turns, he said—he pointed down the track into the vertex of turn one—"Those turns,"—we were all gaping like kids at the freak show—"they're steeper than a Swiss ski slope." He dropped his hand, turned, and faced the reporters. "On this track," he explained, "the drivers're gonna run full throttle—all the way around."

From the infield I gazed into the turn, certain that I'd wandered onto the set of a science fiction movie; the corner was so sheer you'd fall from the top of it. My thoughts drowned out France's next few sentences. Nobody, I said to myself, who's got an IQ over eighty-five would drive a car into those turns. Nobody—not with a double dose of King Kong's testosterone—would drive that fast, bumper-to-bumper, and stay in the groove of a thirty-one-degree banked speedway. It is simply not what rational men do.

But that Sunday, when the green flag fell, my heart bolted. It raced its way around my rib cage, desperate for cover. And I will promise you this: You have never heard thunder roar so loud as fifty-eight race cars accelerating to full throttle, all at the same moment. You have never seen reds and greens and blues and yellows flash by in such a blur. You've never felt so much wind spawned by the speed of automobiles. The sweat has never flowed from your palms quite like this, anxious over the fate of fifty-eight daredevils. You have never—ever—watched men drive machines so fast and so close together that you forgot to breathe.

At the first Daytona 500, Lee Petty and Johnny Beauchamp raced the last thirty laps bumper-to-bumper. They ran so fast for so long that every once in a while they'd let the other pass, content to ride in the slipstream, both men hoping to rest their overtired engines. But on lap 199, Beauchamp had run out of real estate, and it was time to make a move. As the two cars roared into turn one for the last time, his Thunderbird tapped at the back of Lee Petty's Olds. They charged down the backstretch, Beauchamp's grill to Petty's bumper; not so much as a flare of sunlight flickering between them.

As they hurtled out of turn four, the T-bird dipped low. It moved side by side with the Olds, and then nosed ahead. Petty pulled even. Then the Oldsmobile roared a foot in front. Then the Thunderbird. Then the Olds. Then—

The checkered flag fell; forty-seven thousand fans were on their feet, delirious and confused—looking back and forth to one another, wondering, guessing, wishing—but not one human knowing for sure who'd won.

"Petty!" I screamed.

The reporter next to me was on his feet. He pointed down to the track, aiming at the finish line. "No, no, no," he said, "Beauchamp nipped him; he got right there at the finish line."

"Nooo," I said, scowling. "Petty had him by three feet."

All around us, reporters argued. Throughout the grandstand, fans were locked in mortal debate. The two cars had been clocked in the exact same time, and after five hundred of the fastest miles anybody had ever seen—nobody knew who'd won.

We watched the scoreboard and waited. Minutes ticked by. Reporters sat, fingers poised above their typewriters. Others waited at the phones while friendly debates raged everywhere: It was Petty. No, it was Beauchamp.

Finally, number 73 appeared on the scoreboard: Beauchamp was the winner.

"Oh no," I cried out loud, "that's impossible!" I pawed at the air, disgusted. "That's just wrong," I whined.

"I told you," my neighbor declared.

Half the crowd erupted in cheers, the other half groaned as Johnny Beauchamp wheeled his way down victory lane.

The newspaper guys rushed to file their first reports, and we all hustled to the press trailer, eager to hear from both combatants.

"I had him by two feet," Lee Petty told us. He shouldered the grime from his face. "There's no use protesting; I'm sure the decision will stand … but in my own mind, I know I won."

Outside, through the trailer's tiny window, a flash of color caught my eye—something in the infield, up high in the air. I edged closer for a better look, glanced up, and was suddenly bewildered by the sight of five fans climbing the tower. There must've been fifty more standing below, cheering them on. I watched as the climbers reached the platform; the ringleader hurried forward and lifted Lee Petty's number off the scoreboard. The whole crowd of them shuffled to the left and did the same with Beauchamp's. Then, in an act of triumph, the leader hoisted Petty's number 42 high in the air; he turned, pausing at every point of the compass, showboating for the crowd. Then, slowly, and to the delight of the crowd below, he posted 42 in the first-place position, declaring Petty the champion.

I scribbled a few notes, chuckling, and wondering how many fans in how many sports cared enough to risk that kind of a climb to make themselves heard.

A few minutes later Beauchamp was telling reporters, "Petty's a real good driver, and a fair one. I got on the inside at the finish and didn't think I'd make it because there was a slow car in my lane. But I squeezed through," he said as a sly, gap-toothed grin eased over him. "Might've accidentally bumped him as we went across the line."

I had the quotes I needed. I rushed back to the press box—an impossible deadline lashing me forward. We'd been holding the March issue, waiting for this story. Every other page had been written, laid out, typeset, and proofed. All but these six pages were ready. I had to write the story; I wanted a sidebar on Beauchamp's pit crew; I still had to get with the photographer to pick the four best shots—I prayed that he'd gotten one of the two cars side by side at the finish line.

I hustled upstairs, back to my typewriter. But I stopped just long enough to put in a long-distance call to Alan. "You will not believe what I just saw," I told him. "There were fifty thousand people here; we watched cars circle a track for five hours, and at the end, every one of us was gasping for air."

•　•　•　•

Monday morning the three of us sipped coffee at the conference table. "We got to get behind this thing," I told my partners. "This whole car racing thing—especially Daytona—this is one of the gems we've been looking for."

"Not too lowbrow for us?" Alan wondered.

"No," I said, "not if we do it right." I plopped my arms across the table. "This thing was incredible," I told them, "and it is Southern right down to the tread of Lee Petty's tires. I'm telling you, it was fun, it was exciting, it had this festive air—as spine-tingling as any Ole Miss football game you've ever been to. There were moms and dads and kids …" I let the sentence drift into two or three seconds of silence. Then I looked each of my partners in the eye. I reached into an oversized envelope. Slowly, I withdrew an old copy of the *Montgomery Advertiser* and slid it to the center of the table—photos of bombed out churches splayed across the front page. I let it sit for a while with no comment. Then I reached in again, this time for the *Arkansas Gazette*. I pushed it forward, the photo of Hazel Bryan staring up at us all. I sat at the head of the table, perfectly silent for five full seconds, forcing Alan and Dalton to think back on the stories that'd gotten us started. And then, with a more playful smile, I held up our cover shot—of a grimy, gap-toothed, and grinning Johnny Beauchamp. I pitched it on top of the two newspapers. "When people think of the South, " I asked them, "which image do we want them to see?"

Alan reached for the *Gazette*. "You know what," he said, "we need to keep this old gal right where we can see her." He smoothed the paper against the table and then stood. He snapped off two pieces of Scotch tape and fixed the newspaper to the conference room wall. "This right here," he said, "is the reason we're in business."

I grabbed the Beauchamp photo. "If we get behind this, if we cast it in just the right light, this could be good for us, good for the region. Shoot, this could mean a lot to the whole country."

"And I don't imagine *Life* or *Look* was there?" Alan asked.

"You know ..." I replied, smiling, "I don't remember seeing them." I tossed out a fourth photo—of the two cars racing side by side. "This thing was fast and loud," I said to Dalton. "They drove five hundred miles, bumper-to-bumper; they averaged over a hundred and thirty-five miles per hour, and the first- and second-place cars finished about a half inch apart." I spun back toward Alan. "This is a sport for everybody," I explained. "The drivers, they're just guys, not a whole heck of a lot different from you and me. And the cars, they look just like ours...." I scooted my chair forward. "And tell me something," I said: "Who doesn't dream of driving a hundred and fifty miles an hour? It's about cars," I blabbered on. "Every red-blooded man in America loves cars. And we—the South—we're going to give 'em cars like they never dreamed of."

I stood and taped Beauchamp right beside Bryan. The three of us looked at one another, content for the moment, believing that Bill France, the Daytona 500, and really fast cars were weapons in our battle to redeem the South's good name.

And so, on our third cover, for the March 1959 issue, we featured the grease-streaked face and gap-toothed smile of Johnny Beauchamp, the winner of the very first Daytona 500.

It was as big a blunder as any magazine has ever made. And one of the best things we ever did.

Wednesday, just as a hundred thousand copies rolled off the press, the call came from Daytona: The officials had reversed themselves. After looking at every image that every photographer had taken from every angle, they declared Lee Petty the winner.

Dalton was a picture of undiluted agony. "What are we going to do?" he groaned. He shook his head, grief stricken. "It's just our third magazine, our third magazine and it is a complete disaster."

"Maybe not," I told him. "In fact, this whole fiasco, in and of itself, is a pretty cool story. I bet we can take advantage of it; maybe even have some fun." I put a hand on my mourning friend's shoulder. "Why don't you get started on a piece for the May issue that wonders out loud about how many games are so close, so exciting, so excruciating to watch—that it takes three days to declare the winner?" I slapped his back and said, "You know any sport up North that's this much fun: Lacrosse? Badminton? Hockey? This is great," I told him. "When people think of the South they're going to think: *Those old boys have got one wild sport to offer.*"

●   ●   ●   ●

Dalton sunk all thirty-two teeth into the challenge. He began by interviewing three officials at the Daytona 500, and he explained, step-by-meticulous-step, how they decided that Petty had won. We printed the same photos they reviewed. Along the bottom of pages thirty-two, thirty-three, thirty-four, and thirty-five we showed clips of the newsreel footage—frame-by-frame. We enlarged images from eight different angles, taking readers behind the scenes, giving them every scrap and shred of information the judges had, inviting them to make the call.

Dalton recapped two more stock-car races, recreating the drama that had once unfolded at Darlington and Martinsville, and sprinkling in the death-defying tales of Fireball Roberts, Buck Baker, and Junior Johnson.

From there, he moved to the South's best-loved game: college football. He interviewed a handful of our best-known coaches: Wally Butts at Georgia, General Robert Neyland from Tennessee, Johnny Vaught at Ole Miss, and Paul Dietzel, who'd been at LSU for the past four seasons. Each man described the most suspenseful game he'd ever coached. It was as if readers marched the sidelines—as if they were there, in the midst of the chaos, with the clock ticking down, with no time-outs, with assistants and players all in a frenzy—listening in to bold calls of pure genius. And reliving—through the memories of the game's great coaches—young players' acts of courage. Each man, refined through Dalton Dorsey's craft, reminded us all of why we love college football.

The February blunder became a platform to extol Southern sports. It gave us a reason to feature skilled athletes, daring tacticians, and stirring contests. And because of the mistake we made two months before, we thrilled readers with memories of breathless competition.

Dalton's story would run beside one of mine—about Southern ballplayers who'd made good. I'd scheduled a trip to Milwaukee over a weekend when Chris could get away from school, sure that there wasn't much he'd enjoy more than meeting Eddie Matthews, Lew Burdette, and Wes Covington. I knew he'd jump at the chance to talk to Hank Aaron, the Negro all-star from Mobile, Alabama. And of course he'd treasure every moment with Percy Jackson.

When the two boys spotted one another they reacted like life-long friends. They laughed together and joked, and there was, you could see it plain as the fifty-foot scoreboard, this connection between them—this inexplicable bond—like you see between soldiers who've fought side by side in the same fierce battle. I watched them, thinking that each one would still come to the other's aid, and that each of these boys would, if called, defend the other's cause.

Jackson was now a full-fledged star. For the past couple of seasons his batting average had bounced around in the .305–.315 range. With Eddie Matthews at third, the Braves had tried him in the outfield. And they, along with every baseball fan in America, watched him run down fly balls like a lion after wildebeests. His arm was more powerful than an antiaircraft gun, and he believed—I mean, he knew better than he knew his own birthday—that he could mow down any runner, at any base, from anywhere within 250 feet. This kid dove for balls. He splayed his body across the field. He stole bases. He slid. He rolled in the dirt. While he was between the foul lines he never moved at anything less than full speed, and fans loved him.

Two years before, after breaking Wally Butts's heart, Chris had decided to play football for Alabama's new coach, Bear Bryant. He was heading into his sophomore season and looked like a good bet to start at defensive end. Percy couldn't help but marvel at the sight of him. "Good night," he howled. "What've they been feeding you?"

Chris held out his arms in this grand, fraternal gesture. "Nothing but nuts and berries," he said. He reached into his knapsack and pulled out an Alabama baseball cap. He handed it to Percy and said, "I thought you'd look good in this."

Percy reached for it and punched at the inside, billowing the cap open. He held it up for inspection. "That's nice," he said. He pulled the brim down to his eyebrows. "You know, I always wanted to play college football; I'd have kicked your tiny butt all over the field."

"Uh-huh," Chris replied. Then he glanced out toward the diamond, at the giant scoreboard, out at the stands behind home plate. "I'm thinking you might want to stick with what you're doing," he said.

The three of us eased into a conversation about what life was like for Percy. "It's good," he assured us. He'd strung together three good seasons. He'd made friends; he traveled with his team on the same planes and buses. He ate in the same restaurants. "For the most part," he told Chris, "I do what everybody else does." He peered up slyly and said, "I don't live in the same neighborhood as Matthews or Burdette, but I can't complain." He tossed a ball into the air and caught it. "It's not like it used to be. Things are good here."

There was a moment's lull, which gave Chris an opening he'd been waiting for—a chance to ask the question that'd been nagging for two years.

"Hey, I've been dying to ask you something," he said.

Percy looked up, eyes rounded with anticipation.

"In the fifty-seven series, in game four: Did that ball really hit you?"

Percy's grin spread like a grease spot. "You saw me take first base, didn't you?" he replied.

Chris cocked his head suspiciously, silently demanding a more definitive answer.

Percy's smile brightened, but he sat there—silent—content to let the doubt linger.

"Well, did it?" Chris insisted.

"Yeah …" Percy fessed up. "Not hard—but it got me where I needed to be."

Later, the two boys slipped into the inevitable conversation, reliving the most terrible time in both their lives, talking about how far they'd come and recognizing that there was still a good distance to travel. As I watched and listened I understood that their lives had taken the same turn at the same time; that at the moment of a bomb's explosion their attitudes had been irreversibly altered—and their relationship forever sealed.

I had an appointment with Fred Haney, the Braves' manager. "I need to run," I told Chris. "You gonna wait here?"

"Yeah," he said. He picked up a stray glove and looked at Percy, "You want to toss the ball around?"

"Do you know how to throw a baseball?" Percy asked. "It's round, you know?"

Chris cocked an eyebrow. "You better hope Matthews doesn't wander by," he said. "Because once he sees me, he'll think you throw like a girl."

I stood at the edge of the tunnel, watching. Chris basked in Percy's company. He liked him; he liked that he'd made good—that this quiet colored kid from our hometown played on national television and had won a real live World Series. He liked that Percy Jackson palled around with Warren Spahn and Dell Crandall and Ernie Johnson. And the thing I think he liked most was that he—this white kid from Whitney—had a famous Negro friend. For him, it wasn't something to hide. It wasn't one of those things you weren't supposed to mention. For Chris, a Negro friend was a badge of honor, a sign of changing times, the mark of a new generation, and a judgment on the status quo.

• • • •

At dinner the next Sunday Chris told his mother, "It was pretty cool to be in the Braves' locker room. And you wouldn't believe County Stadium. I can't imagine what it'd be like to step up to the plate in a place like that, to stand in the batter's box with all those people watching...."

Rose smiled at him and, looking forward to his sophomore season, said, "You'll know what it's like next year when you're playing in front of a packed house at Denny Stadium."

"It was just like when I was a kid," Chris prattled on. "I was out there playing catch with Eddie Matthews and Frank Torre and...."

"We thought you'd have a good time," Rose said.

"Yeah," he replied, his tone turning pensive. "And it was really good to be with Percy again."

Rose returned a dim smile. She raised a glass to her lips and said, "I'm sure it was."

Chris set his fork down. He planted his elbows on the table and folded his hands. "I was thinking that maybe he and I could spend a few days together, maybe over Christmas break. I'll have a few days off; it'll be the off-season for him ..." he said as he cut his eyes to me. "I thought we might even ride over to Tuscaloosa; Percy said he'd love to see what a big-time college football program looks like."

Rose made a smooth shift into a defensive gear. She smiled and said, "You know what, maybe he could come see one of your games instead. Chances are he'll have some time in the fall, and I suspect he'll be down this way." Rose spun in my direction. "Maybe his parents could come too," she said. Then, turning back to Chris she said, "You could show everybody around—your teammates would probably love to meet a big-league baseball star—and then, after the game we could all find a place to visit for a while, maybe somewhere on campus."

I felt the first tremors of a distant quake. I knew this wasn't going to be that easy, and I tensed, dreading where my wife and son were likely to go.

"Great idea," I said and looked at Chris. "… don't you think?"

"Yeah," Chris replied, "but I was thinking it'd be nice to spend some serious time with him. I'd like to get to know him again; find out what things have been like for him."

Rose sat back—that puzzled, just faintly annoyed frown taking over. "Well, how would that work? I mean, where would he stay? Where would the two of you meet …?" She opened her hands, wondering and said, "Where exactly would you spend this time together?"

Chris looked away, shaking his head. "Why do you do this?" he groaned. He stared at his mother as if she'd just declared her undying allegiance to Auburn. "Why can't you ever just do things the easy way?"

"All right …" I cautioned.

"She's always doing this," Chris protested. He glared at Rose, stoking his own fury. "He'd stay right here. We'd spend time together here, in this room, in the living room, out on the deck. He'd sleep here, in the guest room nobody ever uses." His glare burned hotter. He leaned across the table: "And you know what? We'd walk down the sidewalk right in front of the house. We'd walk past the Emersons' and the Parsonses' and they'd all see the colored boy, right here in their own neighborhood, and they'd all know you've got a nigger in your house."

"Stop it!" Rose snapped.

"Stop what?" Chris fired back. "That's what you think. If he wasn't some lowly nigger you wouldn't hesitate to have him. You'd be—"

"Hey, hey, hey," I interjected. "That'll do." I forced Chris back with a glare. "You know what? I don't really think Percy'd feel too comfortable here. In fact, I think it'd be pretty awkward for him. So why don't you invite him to town, and for his sake, I'll put him up in a hotel." Then I laughed, hoping to ease the tension. "I guess he can afford his own hotel, can't he?"

I looked at Rose. "Maybe he could come here for dinner one night; we could all spend some time together then?"

Rose radiated more heat than a furnace. "Chris, you need to get real about this. You know good and well he can't spend the night here," she said.

Chris met the unflinching stare. "No," he said, "I really don't know that. It's your house; you can do whatever you want. You can invite anybody you want in here—who's going to stop you?"

Rose pressed her lips thin as a razor. She looked at me, and then, mocking his tone, flinging a carefree hand to the air, she said, "He's always doing this …"

Chris grabbed the edge of the table with both hands. "You might enjoy a visit to the twentieth century," he cracked. "It doesn't matter what color he is; this guy's my friend. I can't believe you're telling me that he's not allowed in my own house."

"Chris!" I snapped, "You need to dial it back."

With some mixture of resignation and grief and anger Rose said, "Would you just stop it? You're on the honor roll for crying out loud; you're smarter than this. You put on this big show like you're some righteous friend of the Negro…. I got to tell you, Chris, the act's getting old."

She sat and seethed, appraising her son. She leaned toward him, her eyes searching his. She tapped her finger against the table. "You really think a twenty-two-year-old black man can come into this house, sleep in our guest room, eat in our dining room, shower and shave in our bathroom…." She stopped, her head swiveling right to left: "You honest to goodness believe that?"

Chris smoldered silently.

"Look," I said, "why don't we—"

"You know better than that," Rose scoffed. "So can we just drop this?"

"Okay," I interceded, "I think we probably—"

Chris threw his napkin into his plate. "Yeah," he said. "You bet we can." He stood and jammed both hands against his hips. "You know what … maybe I'll go to his house. Maybe I'll spend the night there. Maybe I'll eat at their table. And you know what else, maybe his folks are actually capable of entertaining a new thought."

He turned and stomped away. The front door slammed, rattling the pictures, windows, and mirror.

Rose fired her water glass into the wall. "Damn it!" she screamed. "Damn it! Damn it! Damn it!" She buried her head in her hands, sobbing. "He's got to stop this," she cried, "or so help me…."

"He'll be back soon," I said, trying to soothe her. "He'll calm down."

She shot up from her seat, snatched her plate up from the table, reached for mine, and then grabbed Chris's. She marched into the kitchen, still sniffling, still seething. "I don't care if he does or not," she muttered.

• • • •

In Atlanta, in the month of May, the air is filled with nothing but promise. Despite our March blunder, despite my ugly problems at home, every sign pointed forward. Every comment about *Down South* urged us on, and almost every letter congratulated us for the good work we were doing.

My favorite had come from McGill. It was hand delivered early one Thursday morning, and I relished the words, my old boss's boss rambling on about how much he liked the Phillips piece, about how good the magazine looked, about how *Down South* would soon be the "sophisticated voice of the New South." It was a gracious gesture that had made my day, and I knew it'd do the same for Dalton's.

I strolled into his office; the six-foot window stood half open, and the breath of a spring breeze relaxed inside. He was on the phone, this kid-at-the-candy-store grin plastered across his face, head bobbing—a man whose world—because of who or what was on the other end of that line—was in perfect order. "All right," he said, his hand in the air signaling me to wait. "That sounds good. I'll have him get in touch with you later today. Okay, bye now."

He hung up the phone. "She's gonna to do it," he sang. "All of it; she's going to do everything we asked."

My mind was on McGill, except for a few stray thoughts that had wandered around a profile I'd been writing of Adolph Rupp, the Kentucky basketball coach. My aging brain wouldn't stretch further, and all I could muster was a dumb, blank stare.

"O'Connor!" Dalton exclaimed. "She's going to write a couple of essays for us and at least two book reviews—so long as she gets to pick the books."

I took a cautious step inside. "Really? I hope you told her she can review comic books if she wants to."

Dalton swiveled back and forth, his chin resting on tented fore-fingers, the smile a snapshot of eager anticipation. "I don't really think she needs me to tell her," he said. "She ain't exactly shy."

I fell into a chair, my mind wrapping itself around the news. "Do you know how good this is?" I put a hand to my mouth, wonder-ing where this might go. "I didn't really think she'd do it. I thought she'd...."

"But why wouldn't she?" Dalton argued. "We're already better than most of those little rags she writes for."

"Yeah, but still...." I looked at Dalton soberly, like a man coming to grips with a surprise inheritance. "She puts us in the big leagues," I told him. "She gives us the literary pop we've been looking for."

"That she does," Dalton agreed. "And by the way, Faulkner hasn't said no. He may be up for something in a month or two; said he was thinking about doing a sports piece for somebody...." Dalton hitched a shoulder. "Might as well be us."

"Let's have him do a piece on Ole Miss football," I said, snickering. "He could walk to the stadium."

I settled into the chair, feeling like a twenty-point underdog who'd just won the big game. "So what's the next step?" I asked.

I was talking to Dalton, but this was the angst that came with every feature. We were in a constant battle against Hazel Bryan. We'd put her picture in every office, to remind us that we raced against inevitable bad news. She hovered over every move—snarling, pressing us to move fast before the whole world looked south again, to be grieved by front-page images of black and white mobs; before somebody burned a cross; before some governor—Patterson, Coleman, or Vandiver—found a new reason to call out the National Guard.

How, I wondered furiously, could I flaunt one of the country's best writers? I traced a finger along my lip. "She's got to do something on Southern writing," I mumbled, half to myself and half to Dalton. "We need her to mention Faulkner and Williams and Welty.... She can even talk about Carson McCullers." I peered up at Dalton, a fingertip pressed to my lip. "You think she's up for something like that?"

"Don't know why not," Dalton said. "I told her we'd have a couple of ideas; my guess is she's got one or two of her own." He handed me a slip of paper. It had a date, time, and address scrawled across it. "I told her you'd drive up there this weekend to talk it over. She's expecting you for lunch on Saturday."

I took the paper. "Thanks," I said. Then I tossed McGill's note across the desk. "And I brought this for you."

I got up to go. At the door I turned and stared at my watch. "You know what?" I said, "This might be it, Thursday at ten forty-two a.m., this might be as good as life gets."

"Nah," he replied. "We're just getting started."

Dalton was right; these were the first of the days we'd always remember. The next night we'd been invited to cocktails at the Capital City Club. I spotted McGill; he was chatting with Elmo Ellis from WSB who, with courage and grit, was to radio what McGill was to newspapering. Governor Vandiver held court with a flock of gray-suited sycophants. Mayor Hartsfield was ten yards to his left, explaining himself to Jack Tarver, who was now the president of the *Constitution* and *Journal* both—the competitors forced to pool resources to save money.

I strolled the perimeter, holding tight to Rose Marie's hand. She'd taken to this life like Musial took to hitting. When she dressed for a party, and when she decided to unleash her full ordnance of charm, she could beguile a room like this faster than I typed the last paragraph.

We came to the bar, both of us holding an empty glass. The bartender had wandered off, to get ice I suppose, or to restock a dwindling supply of Johnny Walker. I strolled around back and found what we needed; I uncorked the bottle and reached for Rose's glass, but before I could pour we both turned toward a sudden stir. Richard Russell, the United States senator, swept into the room. He shook half a dozen hands, quickly surveyed the surroundings, and then made a beeline for the bar. He dipped his chin at Rose; without taking his eyes from her he slapped his hand down and ordered: "Bourbon, straight up." From the corner of my eye I could see Dalton; he and Natalie were standing with our old friend Celestine Sibley, the three of them utterly failing to choke back their laughter.

I handed Rose her glass, then reached for another. While I pulled down a bottle of Jack Daniel's, Rose reached in her purse. With Russell's eyes lingering, she withdrew a dollar bill. She dangled it above a brandy snifter that sat on the bar, then she winked and said, "I'll see you a little later." She dropped the bill, turned, and sauntered away.

I poured Russell's drink and shoved the glass forward. "Enjoy yourself, senator." Then I ceded the bar back to a curious tender—and went searching for the lady who'd left the big tip.

Twenty minutes later we chatted with a young advertising man. James Dickey was telling us about a few of the ads he'd written for Coca-Cola and Lay's potato chips. But that wasn't the reason he'd chased me down. He was a wannabe writer desperate to get published. And he begged me to take a look at a few of his poems. McGill approached us; Russell was at his side. "Senator, I'd like you to meet Jack Hall, the editor of the South's finest magazine."

Smiling, Russell extended his hand. "He pours a decent drink too."

●   ●   ●   ●

A dirt road led to Flannery O'Connor's Milledgeville farm.

When I pulled near the house I saw a crooked figure hobble through the door onto the screened porch. From fifty feet I could see her forearms tense as she forced one crutch in front of the other, shuffling to the top of the front-porch stairs. She swung the screen door open and waited, her malformed hip thrust to one side, a dowdy looking, bespectacled hostess graciously coming to greet her caller.

I slammed the car door and walked to the base of three brick stairs.

"Mr. Hall," she said.

I tipped my hat. "Miss O'Connor," I replied. I reached for her hand, which she raised awkwardly, trying to balance the crutch that was wedged into the pit of her right arm. She aimed her chin at a row of wooden rockers. "If you don't mind," she said, "I thought we'd sit here; it's so nice out, and I love the view."

From the front porch of Flannery O'Connor's home you are treated to a panorama of pines that soar to the full limit of human vision, to azaleas that sheathe the north view in a curtain of speckled pink, to peacocks strutting past, screeching, and demanding the attention of every creature within eye and earshot. "Your farm's wonderful," I told her, watching the splashy parade of birds.

She stared at them, the way an artist eyes her own creation. "They're my children, you know." A wily smile crept onto her lips. "They're not much bother during the day, but at night … at night they've been known to cause a stir—especially after I've reminded guests that the insane asylum's just up the road." She inclined an ear in the birds' direction. "Listen." We stood at the door, both of us quiet. One peacock screeched, then came a reply. The author's face brightened. "Sounds just like a stabbed man screaming for help, doesn't it? Might surprise you at midnight, after I've set a hundred lunatics loose in your mind."

I laughed quietly, thinking it all sounded like a scene from one of her stories.

She trudged to the nearest chair and lowered herself clumsily. I watched and wanted to help, but she'd done this before, and didn't seem the type to depend much on others. She leaned the crutches against the wall, turned, straightening her skirt and blouse, putting her hand to an errant strand of hair. Then she reached to the table beside her, and picked up a magazine that Dalton had sent her.

"Your project looks ambitious," she said.

"It is," I replied. "And risky."

She thumbed a few pages. "It's time we had a magazine like this—the South, I mean." She paused at the Sam Phillips story and scanned a few lines. "You'll do well," she mused. She flipped another page. "It's all very polite, all very well mannered, but it's not pulling punches, either." She rested the magazine on her lap. "I was telling a bunch of college kids the other day—it might've been a month ago—that writers need to tell the truth; they've got to be bold, to reveal hard, cold reality. You can't whisper to the deaf, I told them, if you expect them to hear."

She lifted a corner of the magazine. "You're not screaming like one of my stabbed peacocks out there, but you're not exactly whispering, either. I think the tone's just right."

I bowed my head appreciatively. "We're glad you're willing to help."

She turned another page. "As long as you give me plenty of time," she said. "And as I told Mr. Dorsey, so long as I get to choose the books I review."

"We don't have any problem with that."

The front door squealed open. A woman stepped outside, carrying a tray with two glasses and a pitcher of tea.

O'Connor introduced me to her mother, Regina.

I stood and bowed slightly. "A pleasure. "

She motioned for me to sit, welcomed me to her home, and poured the tea. "I'll bring lunch out in a little while," she told her daughter. And then quietly disappeared.

O'Connor reached for the sugar bowl. "So," she began, "Mr. Dorsey said you had a few ideas about essays."

"Well, one in particular," I said. I grabbed a copy of the magazine with Beauchamp's picture. "You've looked through this so you know we're writing for people who love the South. It's for people who live here, who are proud of it, who identify with it, who—"

"Who are tired of pompous Yankees telling us how to do everything better?" O'Connor quipped.

I laughed, "Well, yeah."

She rocked easily, admiring the birds that paraded the length of her front lawn. "That's a chore I'm probably up for," she said.

I settled back in the chair, growing more comfortable, the tempo of my rocker keeping pace with hers. "We don't want to get too highbrow," I said. "But we could use a more literary feel—just a touch of *Harper's* or *Esquire* with a decidedly Southern flavor.

"Yes," O'Connor said distractedly, browsing the magazine again.

"And I know this probably sounds strange," I said, "but one of the things that makes the South so Southern is her writers." I paused, waiting for her to look up. "We might want to remind the pompous Yankees that we've got some."

She folded the magazine closed. "Maybe so." She closed her eyes for a second, thinking, or perhaps just tired. "I've always thought that one of the reasons our writers are good is because there are so many of us," she said. She stirred the tea with her finger. "We're all scared to death we won't measure up. We lie awake at night worrying about everybody who's better.... And of course we all hate Faulkner. He's always looming, this omnipresent reminder of what none of us will ever be." She let loose of a sigh. "He scares the daylights out of everybody."

"I've read *Wise Blood*," I replied, trying to sound soothing. "I don't think you've got much to worry about."

"Oh no, Mr. Hall, you're wrong there." She cut her eyes quickly to mine; they laughed brightly, but there was, I thought, the trace of a wound. "I've got the reviews to prove it."

"Well, I liked it. And the other night, knowing that we'd be together, I reread *A Good Man Is Hard to Find*. I think there must be plenty of writers who hate you," I said smiling.

"Well," she said, "I take it you want me to do something about writing."

I looked out at the pines and azaleas, at the meadow and the birds, at this scene of picture-perfect Southern living. "I was reading something the other day," I told her. "I think it was in the *Atlantic Monthly*, about 'the Southern School's penchant for grotesque characters....'"

O'Connor couldn't contain an amused twitter.

"The author was pondering the Southern imagination—speculating on what fuels it—prattling on about the effects of being so isolated from the rest of the country."

"Some condescending Yankee thinks he knows better," O'Connor teased, but with the sheen of umbrage.

"Yeah," I said with a laugh, "I guess so. I was thinking you might write a reply; that you might explain why our writers create these bizarre personalities."

"Like Hazel Motes?" she ventured.

"He does comes to mind," I confessed, smiling.

She rested her head on the back of the chair. "It's a subject I'm a little weary of," she said.

"Yeah, I guess that doesn't surprise me. But that doesn't mean the subject's tired." I sipped from the tea, rocking easily. "And you know, this might be our best chance to give the Yankees a little writing lesson."

The birds called back and forth raucously. They strutted and preened before us, refusing to go unnoticed. "Well …" she said, "since you put it like that." Then, more sternly, she added, "But when I'm finished, I don't want you coming back here telling me to tone it down."

I gestured toward the magazine, "Do I strike you as a man who tones things down?"

"No," she replied, "… not yet."

Regina O'Connor backed through the door. She set a lunch tray on the table between us. "You all enjoy," she said. "And if you need me, I'll be right inside."

I thanked her and handed a plate to Flannery O'Connor.

"All right," I said, balancing the other plate on my knees. "You've piqued my interest. Why would I want to tone you down? Do I need a heads-up on what's coming?"

She spread a napkin across her lap. "The reason we create oddballs, Mr. Hall, is because we still recognize one when we see him." She folded her hands, like a child about to pray. "Our friends up North have lost perspective. They don't understand the freak because they don't have any idea of what's normal; they couldn't recognize a whole man if he were standing two feet in front of them."

"And Southern novelists have some finer-tuned insight into human nature? Is that what you're saying?"

"Yes," she said. She stared away for a moment, out past her birds, all the way to the tree line and continued, "... though I expect it's fading." She dragged her fork through a mound of potato salad. "We still have a notion of man that's theological. We remember the story of creation, of Adam's fall, of the all-pervasive consequences.... There's still some begrudging belief that it's true."

She rocked again, shifting uncomfortably. "The freakish character doesn't make much sense unless you have some concept of what we were meant to be." She squirmed, searching for a comfortable position. "We are, to be sure, not a Christ-centered region," O'Connor continued, "but He haunts our every move. He's still here, at least at the fringe of our imagination, looking on, shaping the way we see the world...." She picked up her napkin and balled it in her hand. "Southerners live in this constant fear that we might in fact be created in the image of God, that we might actually be here to serve some exalted, unselfish purpose.... Hazel Motes and the other freaks of Southern fiction—they're a picture of fallen man; they're a reminder that none of us is what God intended...." Flannery O'Connor searched the distance again. "That's why these odd characters add depth to our literature. That's why you don't see them coming out of New York or Boston. It's why the *Atlantic Monthly* couldn't possibly understand: Our problem isn't that we're too isolated from the rest of the country, it's that we're not isolated enough."

I smiled. The pace of my rocker quickened. And this sense of deep satisfaction, coupled with a brimming joy, welled up inside me.

"We need three thousand words," I told her.

"I'll check my schedule," she replied.

Chapter 10

As the world eased its way into the next decade, its inhabitants were at peace, the United States of America prospered, and the circulation of *Down South* had soared passed 125,000 copies. Our magazine vanished from newsstands faster than Houdini from center stage. In Atlanta, Charlotte, Richmond, and Raleigh—as far west as Dallas, and as far north as D.C.—readers were like kids with a new box of Cracker Jacks, plunging down deep to discover new treasures.

A more spacious office now swarmed with graduates from Emory, Georgia, and Mercer—kids who wanted to breathe the air of ideas, who savored words, who worshipped Faulkner and Hemingway. They typed and answered phones. They ran errands and proofed copy. They read through a five-foot stack of manuscripts—eyes glazed by the work of kooks and hacks from a thousand miles around—in search of the next Eudora Welty.

Our friends at the paper still glowed green with envy, and there wasn't a writer south of Baltimore who wouldn't pen his best work for free, just to see his byline in our publication. Advertisers were paying any price we asked: Delta Air Lines, Coca-Cola, the big three car companies; Ivory, Oxydol, and Cheer; Lucky Strike, L&M, and Kent—they all appeared in every issue, and we had to expand the magazine from eighty to ninety-six pages, and then to a hundred and four—just to keep pace with the surging number of new ads.

We lived up to every promise Alan had ever made. We made new rules with every edition, and we broke ground that no journalist had dared to turn. We were, Ralph McGill told me every time I saw him, "the boldest thing to blow through town since Sherman."

"But," I always parried, "we've come to build the place up, not tear it down."

In those days Peachtree Street brimmed with vigor. Energy gushed from the new buildings, spilling out into new businesses, the arts, and politics. While King plotted and planned and preached nonviolent action, Atlanta grew and prospered. We sensed our place in the emerging New South. We looked north and saw little we envied, but much we could improve.

Dalton, Alan, and I eyed the *Atlantic Monthly,* the *New Yorker,* and *Harper's.* We had them all in the crosshairs, and we knew, with the writers around us, that we could be better.

• • • •

In January 1960, Patsy Cline became a member of the Grand Ole Opry.

I had stumbled across the news—it hadn't been more than a paragraph in the Saturday paper—and thought back to the first time I'd heard her. Rose and I were cuddled on the couch—this might have been two or three years earlier—watching *Arthur Godfrey's*

Talent Scouts. I remembered the precise moment—when this nervous young girl began to sing *Walkin' after Midnight.* Three lines into the song I'd sat up and leaned forward, toward the television, thinking that I'd never heard a human sound so fresh and unspoiled. Her voice, I thought, belonged more to the realm of nature than to man—more in a category with mountain streams or lapping waves or to songbirds or the patter of rain on a tin roof.

The song became a hit, and over the next few months I'd occasionally see her on *Arthur Godfrey and Friends* or *ABC's Country Music Jubilee.* But then, as quickly as she had appeared, Patsy Cline seemed to have vanished—until January 1960.

When I read the article I thought: This makes sense; it's the beginning a new decade, the world's refreshed and invigorated, the country's drooling over John Kennedy, and the next generation's taking the stage.

There was—and I think everyone had at least a vague sense of it—a budding new sound in Southern music. It had begun with Phillips and Presley—this melding of rock, hillbilly, and country—and Patsy Cline was the vanguard of change. She, along with Johnny Cash, Hank Williams, Skeeter Davis, Marty Robbins, the Everly Brothers—they possessed a sound that soothed us; that made us laugh and love and grieve—that expressed every emotion we'd ever known—raw and unfiltered—from undiluted joy, to warm satisfaction, all the way to suicidal despair.

We've all felt alone and abandoned—but who's captured these common woes with more empathy than Patsy Cline? "I stopped to see a weeping willow / Crying on his pillow, maybe he's crying for me ... I go out walking after midnight out in the moonlight...."

And what about the thrill of young love—the kind that gushes from every pore, that won't stay contained, that was never meant to stay trapped within a single human heart? Has anyone ever brought the indescribable joy of a first kiss back to mind with more pleasure than Phil and Don Everly? "How did I exist until I kissed you / Never had you on my mind / Now you're there all the time / Never knew what I missed 'til I kissed you...."

Johnny Cash sang about cowboys and mothers grieving the lives of reckless sons. He sang about prison and regret, and every man's longing for a better life: "And I ain't seen the sunshine since I don't know when / I'm stuck in Folsom prison, and time keeps draggin' on / But that train keeps a rollin' on down to San Antone..."

Marty Robbins captured the mystique of forbidden love: "Blacker than night were the eyes of Felina / Wicked and evil while casting a spell / My love was deep for this Mexican maiden; I was in love but in vain, I could tell...."

Everywhere, Southern musicians were creating and reconfiguring, taking the music that had been made before, adding their own flavors and spices, and handing back a new genre—created for working men and women—that was picturesque and memorable and fun— and in every imaginable way, pure Southern.

Hazel Bryan glared down from the wall. King loomed in the wings on Auburn Avenue, readying his next crusade. Faubus and Blossom still nipped at our heels—everyone, in his own way, contending for the South's soul. I glanced at the fifty-word article about Patsy Cline, wondering if this was one more way to head them off at the pass.

This was a project Chris would relish, and one that might ease his mother's angst-ridden mind, and so I asked him to tag along. On our first morning in Nashville—it was Saturday, February 12—we had some time to kill. "Why don't we explore downtown?" I said. "See what kind of trouble we can find over there?"

There'd been a heavy snow the night before. Nashville was carpeted in a soft and seamless white. The weekend bustle seemed subdued, and the city moved tenuously, as if afraid it might disturb this unexpected calm.

We strolled through the Arcade, a marketplace that slices through a two-story building and is open to the street at either end. We were bundled up and ambling through the man-made tunnel, our path lined with small shops that lured customers with trinkets and souvenirs. I picked up a Nashville Vols baseball cap. "You ought to get one of these," I told Chris. I squared the hat onto my head and checked it out in the mirror. "And you know what else? We need to get out to Sulphur Dell … that ballpark's weirder than ours."

"Uh-huh," Chris mumbled. He sounded distracted and preoccupied.

I glanced over, curious. Chris stood in the middle of an aisle. He stared out the end of the Arcade toward Fifth Avenue. Others had clustered nearby, the whole crowd captivated by the scene outside.

"What is it?" I asked.

Chris raised a finger, pointing. "There must be a hundred colored guys," he said. "They're marching like soldiers."

I hurried beside him, my eyes following the path of his finger. "What the …?" I tossed the cap back where I'd found it and clapped his shoulder. "Come on," I said, breaking into a jog. "Let's check this out."

We hustled outside, to where a column of young Negroes—men and women—marched in perfect formation. They were lined up in pairs—fifty or sixty deep—all of 'em as neat as Jehovah's Witnesses. I bundled my coat tight to my chest, suddenly chilled, not so much by the weather as by an unexpected wave of nervous expectations.

Was this King? I wondered. Was this something he hadn't told me?

We stayed parallel, trailing the Negroes down Fifth Avenue. As they neared Kress, a company of them—maybe fifteen or twenty—swerved left, through the double doors, into the store.

Methodically, as if they'd practiced the drill a hundred times, a second batch filed into Woolworth's; then a third group swooped into McClellan's.

I pointed at Woolworth's. "Let's stick with them," I told Chris.

Customers and salesclerks stood silently, wide-eyed and watching. The Negroes broke right and left, quietly circulating through the store. They picked up handkerchiefs, notebooks, and small tubes of toothpaste, and then carried them to the nearest cashier.

"What are they doing?" Chris asked.

I shrugged, "Shopping?"

They gathered at the foot of the stairs leading to the second floor. Chris and I watched as they paired off again, and then, two-by-two, made the climb.

"I know what this is about," I muttered to Chris.

He smiled, happier than some schmuck on *The Millionaire* who's just greeted Michael Anthony. "I do too," he said: "It's a sit-in."

It had been less than two weeks since four colored students in Greensboro, North Carolina, had staged a similar event. Their demonstration had been a spur-of-the-moment thing, an impulsive and isolated event that had, through a chain of inexplicable events, sparked a wildfire of protests. Other students at North Carolina A&T were drawn to the rally. White students from neighboring schools came alongside, and on the second day, nineteen students joined the original four at the downtown Woolworth's. The next day the number swelled to eight-five.

The news burned across North Carolina, and later that week, as if by spontaneous combustion, sit-ins flared up in Durham and Raleigh. Now, the fire had migrated west, to Nashville.

Images of Montgomery sprang to mind. I recalled the spirit that had bound those people together, the invisible force that propelled them—that had inspired them to sacrifice for so long for the sake of a lousy bus seat. In the next instant I thought about King's frustration; about his inability to duplicate the intensity of that fervor. And then, in the instant after that one, it occurred to me that this movement—like an embryonic hurricane—might be gathering new force; that Chris and I were witnessing the birth of the next storm.

We hustled upstairs. The colored students calmly took seats at the counter, leaving empty spaces between them. A few customers were already there, nibbling at burgers and the Saturday blue-plate special. They followed the action, looking mystified, curious, and frightened. A waitress backed out from the kitchen balancing a pair of plates along each arm. She turned and stopped. Her eyes raced up and down the counter. Then she slowly moved to her left, depositing the plates before a quartet of nervous customers. She peered up and then down. She reached beneath the register for a washrag and, without a word, wiped the counter clean.

A second waitress burst through the same door. She too stopped and stood as still as Andrew Jackson's statue. Then, under her breath, she gasped, "Oh my...."

Both women were fortyish. They both seemed neighborly enough, and I couldn't detect a trace of anger in either of them. More than anything else they seemed baffled by the peculiar sight before them.

One of the Negro men—I remember, he wore a pale blue suit— asked if they could please be served. The waitress nearest to him pulled at her hairnet. She steadied her gaze and in a calm voice replied, "Well, we don't serve niggers here."

One of the white customers tossed his napkin on top of the counter; he cleared his throat, rose, and quietly walked away. Another followed close behind him. Everyone sat nervously. The waitresses refilled glasses; they rang up sales and made change, glancing fretfully to either side. The Negroes sat patiently, facing forward, hands clasped on blue paper placemats. Within seconds a third woman pushed through the kitchen door. She was dressed like a clerk or secretary, and she carried a piece of poster board that had been crudely torn to a ten-inch square. In blue Magic Marker someone had neatly scrawled "Counter Closed." She held it in full view of the Negro students, then slid it between a napkin holder and a sugar dispenser. The overhead lights went dark, and the waitresses, cooks, and busboy dutifully trudged away.

I put a hand on Chris's shoulder. "Hold on," I whispered. "Let's see what happens." The colored kids swapped glances, then they quietly reached for textbooks and notebooks, and began to read by the natural light that streamed through the tall glass windows.

The counter at that particular Woolworth's is perched on a

balcony overlooking the first floor, giving diners a view of the store beneath them. A crowd had gathered below, staring up, wondering where this story would go.

I guided Chris down the stairs, took out my pad and pen, and sidled up beside a thirty-five-year-old white woman. "So, what do you make of this?" I asked. She gazed up at the black faces above her. Two, maybe three seconds passed. Finally, in an anxious, breathy tone she said, "It's like a science fiction movie ..." her eyes stayed locked on the scene above as she continued, "it's like we've been stricken with frogs or locusts."

Behind us, a small crowd of white boys broke from the crowd and rushed upstairs. Chris and I were right behind them. They fanned out behind the colored kids, ambling up and down the length of the counter. "What the hell are you doing here?" one of them demanded.

There was no reply.

I searched the building, looking for photographers and TV cameras.

The white kids formed up, arms clamped across their chests, a human wall blocking the colored students from the only exit. "Why don't you niggers just get on home?" the white boy said.

The Negroes kept their eyes straight ahead, as silent as saltshakers.

Ten seconds passed in as taut a silence as I've ever known. Then the gang leader pawed the air, disgusted. He turned, muttering to himself, leading his pack back to the main floor.

Nervous glances traveled up and down the counter. And a dozen chests heaved with relief. I jotted a few notes, searched again for cameras and reporters, and then turned to Chris. "Come on," I said. "Let's check out the other stores."

We hurried down Fifth Avenue to the Kress, where we found a carbon copy of the same scene. Negro students spread down the length of a closed counter, in the dark, alone, reading silently while a bewildered white crowd looked on.

We rushed to McClellan's and found the same scene, now in triplicate. A young Negro woman sat at the end of the counter. "Have you talked to anybody?" I asked her. "Has the store manager been here to see you?"

She stared straight ahead, dumb as a block of granite.

I flashed my press credentials. "I'm with *Down South* magazine," I told her. "Maybe we could talk later?"

She studied the press card and then reached for a pen. She scratched out a few words on a sheet of notebook paper and pushed it down the counter. It read: "First Baptist Church—6:15."

I nodded and jammed the note in my pocket.

Chris and I headed back to our hotel. "We'll stop by this church on our way to the Opry," I told him, "We can talk with a few of these kids and still have time to catch the show."

I looked at Chris, thinking: *His mother is going to kill me.*

From the First Baptist parking lot we heard music and laughter and the blur of sounds that comes with celebration. We pushed through a side door, trailing the noise. We twisted down one corridor and turned right into another. I looked back at Chris and said, "Sounds like New Year's Eve." We came to our final turn, veered left, and found ourselves face-to-face with sheer jubilation. They were just kids—the whole crowd of 'em, eighteen and nineteen years old. Their bright smiles flooded the room, and on every exultant face I saw an expression I'd seen a thousand times before—in locker rooms after the big game—when the taste of victory is sweeter than all the tea in Georgia.

We roamed the periphery, catching an occasional wary glare, but no threat to quell the festivities. I spotted the young woman I'd seen at McClellan's. I watched her for a moment, from a distance. Her straight black hair flowed to the tops of her shoulders, her skin was light and flawless, her eyes and teeth were beacons … bright and inviting. She stepped up to greet me and, as she extended her hand, I understood why these people followed Diane Nash.

"That was a quite a show today," I began.

She laughed, as delighted as if she'd just pulled off a surprise party for Martin Luther King. "And we've got more coming," she informed me, her eyes dancing over the revelry. "We've targeted six lunch counters, and we're gonna keep coming till they serve us."

"That might take a while," I replied.

"Yes sir," she said. "I suppose it could."

That night Diane Nash told me how she and a man named Jim Lawson had been planning the event for months, that they'd been teaching kids about Gandhi, blending the principles of nonviolence and Christian love. "Then the Greensboro thing broke," she said. "We weren't expecting that; nobody saw it coming, but the right moment had suddenly arrived." She took a deep breath, still gazing over the crowd. "We couldn't have asked for a better day."

"They sure didn't see you coming," I noted. "It looked to me like you caught everybody by surprise."

Diane Nash couldn't smother a laugh. "I swear, that waitress at McClellan's—she must have dropped ten plates she was so nervous."

The young colored girl basked in the memory. "Poor woman did not know what to make of us," she said. And then, more pensively, "She was as scared as I was."

A young woman who'd overhead us stepped into the conversation. "We went into the 'white only' restroom," she said. "There was an old woman in there, and when she saw us … " the colored girl's hands suddenly clutched at her chest. "She grabbed at her heart like she was about to die; she started crying out, 'Oh, nigras, nigras everywhere.'" The girl's hands fluttered in the air, mocking the frightened white woman. "She ran out of there like the place had caught fire."

The black girl's chuckle lingered—not only with the memory, but also, I suspect, with relief—that the day was done, and they'd come through unscathed.

I turned back to Diane Nash. "You know, you're not going to surprise anybody next time," I said. "They're all talking right now, the store managers are on the phone to New York and Atlanta; they'll have a plan next time. The whole city's going to read the paper tomorrow morning; they'll be expecting you. The police will too."

Her smile dimmed, but only slightly. "I know," she said. She tried to muster one more measure of courage, but the reservoir might have run dry. "We'll be ready." Her voice trilled nervously and I saw, for the first time, that she was afraid. I scanned the room, marveling again at the youth, the current of energy, the hovering presence of shared purpose.

"We do workshops here," she explained. "We practice and role play. We'll be fine." She stared out at her friends. "When they're ready for us, when they come after us … that's when people'll take notice;

that's when they'll actually look at us, when they'll truly see us for the first time."

I felt my music story fading from the spotlight. "And if a reporter wanted to truly see you," I said, resigning myself to what was coming, "when and where would he be?"

"I don't know just yet," she replied coyly. "But I suspect there'll be something going on next week. Maybe Thursday? Maybe through the weekend?"

I flipped my pad closed. "Well, be careful."

She smiled, dipped her chin, and disappeared into the throng.

Chris had found the young man in the powder blue suit. I noticed now that he had a strong, square face, thick lips, and close-cropped hair. And, like Diane Nash, he savored the taste of victory. Chris introduced me to his new friend, John Lewis.

We shook hands and exchanged greetings. And then I tapped on my watch. "We gotta go," I told Chris; "I'm supposed to meet Johnny Cash in twenty minutes."

Chris reached for his new friend's hand. He grasped it firmly and there was, in the strength of the grip, a message conveyed. "I'll see you next Saturday," Chris said.

John returned a taut nod. "All right," he replied, "you'll need to be here early for the training."

"Yeah," Chris said, "I know."

We walked out to the parking lot. I stared at Chris like he'd just grown horns: "You'll meet him here next Saturday? You mind telling me what that's about?"

Chris looked down; he put a hand to the back of his neck and rubbed slowly. "Well..." he said, "a few white kids are coming next week. They just want to show a little support...." He forked off to the passenger side of the car. "I want to be with 'em."

Chris looked at me—the way a politician looks when he's trying to make a preposterous idea sound plausible. "I was thinking, I could give firsthand reports to the magazine—you know—a look from inside the movement, the view from the Woolworth's lunch counter." He slid into the car. "I can type up the first draft; you can clean it up later."

I stared at my son like he'd suggested a trip to the Belgian Congo, not about to admit—despite my fears, despite my frustration with this foiled plan—that I kind of liked the idea. "I don't know," I told him, "we'll need to think about it." I pictured Rose Marie after our last discussion about Percy Jackson—echoes of slammed doors and crashing plates suddenly flooding my mind. "Your mother'll never go along with this."

"Yeah," he said, "I know." We turned out of the parking lot and into the flow of traffic. "I'm not trying to make her mad," Chris said, "but I'm going to do this. These people ..." his voice drifted off into a web of still-forming thoughts, "I don't know anybody like them. They've got something I don't." He glanced off in the distance. "There's something about them, something I don't understand. I'd like to find out what it is."

There he sat, in the front seat of my car, just outside the parking lot of a Negro church: a picture of questioning, searching, prying, curious youth. "Sounds like your buddy John gives a pretty good pep talk," I said.

"Yeah," Chris said with a chuckle. "I guess. I just want to figure out what's going on with these guys, that's all."

"It's more than a seat at the lunch counter, huh?"

"Yeah," Chris said, his voice quiet but certain.

"So what else'd John tell you?" I asked.

A shy grin creased the boy's lips. He formed quote marks his fingers and said, "He thinks they're moving with the 'Spirit of History.'" He shrugged, his mind sorting and sifting new thoughts. "I don't know, maybe he's right." Chris gazed out the window again and said, "He was just so excited. He was scared and nervous, but he was determined, too. I mean … he's going to see this thing through. He doesn't care what it costs."

"We'll see," I replied. "That's easy to say now."

We idled at a stoplight, the car now filled with an eerie glow of lights from the dash, the street, and the traffic signal swaying above. "But you might be right," I said. "That gal I talked to—I didn't see any quit in her, either." A beat or two passed in silence. "Look, we've got a few days to think about this. I'll talk to Dalton, to see what he thinks. I'm afraid this is going to be a big story. When you put this together with Greensboro and all the little brushfires that've been flaring up in North Carolina—there's something cooking here. We need to be the ones who shape the story, who influence the way people think about it."

Chris bobbed his head. "I understand," he said, "and I think I can help."

The light changed and I pulled forward. The Ryman Auditorium was just a few blocks ahead. "And you know what else?" Chris said, "Ansley will want to help too."

Oh geez, I thought, my heart suddenly sinking faster than the *Bismarck. Dalton is going to shoot me.* I swung the car into the parking lot. I knew I wasn't going to stop Chris. I knew nobody was about to stop Diane Nash or John Lewis, or the hundreds of Negro students with them. *I've got to get a handle on this thing—fast.*

Chris and I hurried through the stage door.

We wandered behind the scenes in search of Johnny Cash, and I could have sworn that we'd been transported to another world: One minute we were with hundreds of Negro students who'd gathered to protest, who'd banded together to right wrongs and to boldly point to injustice. Now, we roamed around fantasyland—where life was carefree, where laughter reigned, and where, for at least a little while, music provided an escape from every thought that wasn't pleasant.

Around us musicians strummed and tuned. Stagehands set up microphones and shoved props around the stage. Minnie Pearl rushed by, hatless and all business. Kitty Wells, dressed as if there weren't a cow within a thousand miles, swapped laughs with a banjo player. Chris thumped my shoulder and pointed across the stage. "That's Skeeter Davis," he whispered. Later that night she'd sing "Set Him Free," the song that had won the only Grammy nomination a country singer had ever earned. Lefty Frizzel was perched on a haystack, alone, quietly rehearsing, mouthing the words: "Ten years ago on a cold dark night / There was someone killed 'neath the town hall light … That the slayer who ran looked a lot like me."

We must've looked like bumpkins in New York City—dumbstruck, gazing at new sights with gape-mouthed awe.

I pulled out my notes and checked my outline. I was curious about Cash. I'd seen him on television; like most everybody in America I knew the words to "Folsom Prison Blues"; and I liked to sing along on the chorus of "Cry, Cry, Cry." I couldn't help but to perk at the sound of his voice—the depth of it and the razor-strap timbre that conjured this sense of smoldering power. He'd been hailed as a challenger to Elvis, but Sam Phillips had scoffed at the thought of it. "That's about as apples-to-oranges as it gets," he'd told me. Presley was mischievous and fun; he tantalized star-struck teens with songs about teddy bears and hound dogs and the pain of lost young love. Cash brooded. He sang about hard work, the land, railroads, and the kind of gut-deep sorrow that wouldn't heal for a thousand years.

According to Sam Phillips, neither man posed any threat to the other.

Lost in thought, I didn't hear the footsteps behind me. But I quickened when a voice that sounded a lot like God's declared: "I'm Johnny Cash."

I turned, and there, dressed in trademark black, stood country music's biggest star.

We wandered back to his dressing room; I trailed a half step behind, taking note of his hair, swooped back in the pompadour. He seemed shy, and he looked as though he rather be anywhere than with me, pretending to be interested in questions he'd heard who-knows-how-many times before.

It was Phillips who'd discovered Cash, who'd given him his start, and who'd produced his first hit songs. It was Phillips and his producer, Jack Clement, who'd created the sparse and unadorned "Johnny Cash sound." Those early songs—the bass and lead guitar—they're barely more than a musical bed for Cash's voice to lie in. They're there to augment—to garnish Cash's vocal chords—and not much more.

Cash was one of a kind. And yet, in a lot of ways, he was a throwback—the musical descendant of Jimmie Rodgers, Vernon Dalhart, and Hank Williams. It seemed to me that he had started with them and their music. Then, somewhere along the way, he'd taken a turn no one else had ever made. And this new sound was pure Johnny Cash.

The man could turn a song so sad it'd make lumberjacks cry. The sparse music, the unflinching words, and Cash's voice—each ingredient was blood raw and cut to bone—one was the perfect companion to the other, and somehow it blended to this twangy, siren sound.

That's where I wanted to start—with the music—with the things that touched a million hearts. With Diane Nash in mind—with the week's worth of news that I knew was coming—I wanted to know what made Cash such a powerful magnet.

A lot of critics, it seemed to me, had been too eager to find fault. They'd complained about Cash's guitar skills; some had called Marshall Grant, the band's string bass player "average at best," and one newspaper had referred to Luther Perkins, the Tennessee Two's step-off guitarist, as "no better than a rank amateur." The term "lead guitar," Dalton had once quipped, "had to be the punch line to a joke that hadn't yet been written."

But these guys had missed the point. They failed to see—and hear—where Cash was going. That night, in his dressing room at the Grand Ole Opry, I tiptoed up to the question: "Would your songs be as good if somebody else played them?" I asked.

Cash laughed. He'd read the same stories; he'd heard every complaint that had ever been made. "Oh, I guess it's true," he allowed. "We're not as good as a lot of bands—if that's what you're getting at—but I like our music. We may not be fancy, but we're real, and the music—it's just right for the songs we sing."

He propped his guitar on his knee and strummed.

"So, tell me about the songs," I said. "You're kinda going your own way there, aren't you? Maybe exploring a few different themes?"

"Oh, I don't know," Cash said. "I'm just singing what comes to mind. We're just trying to take real life and hand it back to the people living it, to the folks who build calluses, who do what's gotta be done to keep a family going." He shrugged, and in Cash's eyes I could see that he knew the subject firsthand; that the words sprang from his poverty-stricken days in Arkansas, from desperate work in frightful times, from a deep shaft poured full of sadness. I poked around there for a while, asking about his childhood, and what effect it had on his music.

"I s'pose I've picked more than my fair share of cotton," Cash told me. "I've chopped wood, lugged water out to field hands...." He strummed again, his mind wandering—perhaps to memories of Jack, the brother who'd died when Cash was only twelve. "There were plenty of hard times, but we knew good times too."

His left hand traveled the neck of the guitar. "You know," he said, "life's got to be for living, for doing what you can with the time God gave you. But if you're a singer, if you're going to play at the Opry or the *Hayride*, if you're going to make the honky-tonk circuit—well then, life's got to be for singing, too." He strummed a few chords that sounded familiar. "You gotta tell people that what they do matters, that they're important, that they're the ones who keep the world spinning. Life's good," Cash told me. "But Lord knows, it ain't easy. And it sure ain't fair."

I gestured toward the guitar. "That music, it's off your gospel album, isn't it?"

Cash nodded and played some more. And then, without ever answering, he sang: "Well a man walked down by Galilee so the Holy Book does say / And a great multitude was gathered there without a thing to eat for days / Up stepped a little boy with the basket please take it Lord he said /And with just a five loaves and two little fishes five thousand had fish and bread...."

Chris, who'd been sitting quietly to the side, chimed in with the echo: "It was Jesus," he sang.

"Who was it everybody?"

"It was Jesus."

"Who was it everybody?"

"It was Jesus."

"It was Jesus Christ our Lord ..."

Cash polished off the verse with a flourish. He pointed at Chris, grinning, and with a wink and a smile he said, "Appreciate the backup there, partner."

I sat forward, the pink eraser clamped between my teeth, and wondered out loud: "You sing gospel for the same reason? It's part of this earthy, gritty sound you got going?"

He laid the guitar in its case. "Let me tell you something: When one day's harder'n the next, when there's no end in sight, and things look like they're always moving from bad to worse—a man's got to have some hope. You know, one of the reasons I left Sam was because he didn't want to do gospel; he just didn't think it'd sell. But the folks where I come from ... they got to know that a better day's coming, they got to know that one of these days the Lord's gonna put things right." The singer bunched his lips in a corner. "Part of my job's to pass on a little hope."

"So who's it coming for?" I asked, "… this better day?" Diane Nash hovered at the forefront of my mind, joined now by King, Abernathy, and Chester Burnett.

"The poor," Cash said, "the oppressed, the forgotten.…" He shrugged awkwardly, the look of a man who'd rather sing than talk. "I don't know, maybe for those who don't have much of a voice in this world."

I sat back, the eraser back between my teeth. "The Indians?" I asked, a couple of Cash's lesser-known songs now coming to mind.

"Yes," Cash told me. "We haven't been good to those people. We've cheated them and stole from them; run them off their own land." Cash reached down for his guitar. "You think about who they were, how they lived, what they did …" he plucked at the strings, and in a soft, low voice he sang: "Old Apache squaw how many hungry kids you saw / How many bloody warriors runnin' to the sea, fleein' to the sea … He said the next white man that sees my face is gonna be a dead white man.…"

"So you're out to do a little protesting," I said, "to get a few things set right?"

Cash gave this little hitch of the shoulders, "Maybe," he replied, "at least get people thinking about a few things."

"Anybody buying songs like that?"

He smiled, shaking his head no. "Not too many," he replied, "but I think we can get away with one every now and then. Songs like that, you got to care about the people, not the money."

"The record labels can't survive without the money," I said.

"Yeah, that's one thing I know," Cash answered. "And neither can this place."

I cocked my head, wondering if I'd stirred something sour. "There a problem between you and the Opry?"

Cash shook his head, "No," he said, "not really." He put the guitar back again where it'd come from. "Listen, fellas, it's about time for me to get ready."

Chris and I shook hands with Johnny Cash. We'd hold this story, I thought. We'd wait until Lewis and Nash were page-five news. And then, on the pages of our magazine, we'd make Johnny Cash the conscience of the New South.

•   •   •   •

We were back at the kitchen table early Sunday morning. The trees out our back window remained spindly looking and skeletal. Stripped of their leaves, they reminded me of fragile men who'd been withered by age. But in two weeks, I thought, they'd be reborn. In two weeks, maybe three, we'd feel the first whispers of warmth; we'd see cotton-puff clouds sailing through a seductive blue sky; there'd be embryonic buds on the dogwoods and willows; robins and blue jays would be back at work, gathering raw materials for new nests and singing from the rail of our deck outside.

In a matter of weeks, the world would give hints of a new season, of change, and of things to look forward to. But inside, I knew that the iciness between Rose and Chris could only grow colder. For five years "the Negro situation" had relentlessly wedged its way deeper and further between them. The nonstop talk of civil rights had hacked like a dull-edged cleaver, splitting this pair in two, at times with a vengeance. I had umpired the bouts as best I could, trying to protect the emotions of both, and desperate to preserve the mother-son bond that had always made me marvel. But Chris's "twisted thoughts" on race had plunged Rose into alternating states of despair and rage. And her "stone-age thinking" had hardened Chris's resolve to see, from his still callow perspective, a just society where colored and white lived together in his notion of King's "beloved community." They had yelled and screamed and used words they both regretted. Rose had smashed dishes and hurled books. Chris had stormed out of rooms, slammed doors, and muttered thoughts that should have been kept secret.

When I told Rose about Nashville and about Chris's plans for the coming weekend, she buried her head in both hands. "Well, of course he is," she groaned. "Why would we expect anything different?" She gazed out the sliding glass door, her thumbs tapping at the table restlessly. Then, with no further comment, she moved to the kitchen sink, to busy herself with dirty dishes and musty-smelling rags.

She had, with more regret than a good woman should have to carry, raised the white flag. But that didn't mean she wouldn't suffer. It didn't mean she wouldn't fret and pray and agonize over how a son of hers—a boy she'd raised right—could betray so much of what she'd taught him.

"Look," I told her, "I've talked with Dalton, and I think we've got a plan."

Rose plunged a dish into the lukewarm water.

"We're going to send Chris and Ansley on an undercover assignment," I said.

Her hands came still; her head cocked, as if I'd suddenly changed the subject, as if she'd walked into the middle of some entirely different conversation.

"We're going to have them do a story for the magazine," I explained. "It'll be something like 'The View from Inside the Movement.'"

Her head tilted ten degrees more, like a cat's at the sound of a sudden creak. "You're encouraging this?" she said. "You're … you're … you're what—you're going to send him into this dangerous place, to screw up everything we've always known, to pal around with communists and … and … who knows what kind of weirdoes are behind all this." Her stare persisted, beseeching me for a sentence—just one—that resembled some kind of reasonable explanation.

I stepped beside her and took her hand. "They hardly need encouragement," I said. "They're eighteen years old; they're going to do this whether we want them to or not. This way we can keep an eye on them. We've got a reason to talk to them." I squeezed her hand and said, "This gives me a reason to stay close."

She turned back to the sink. Her chest rose and fell with a sigh of resignation. "All right," she muttered, "at least it's an excuse; it gives me something I can tell our friends at church."

I moved a hand to Rose's shoulder. "We can let 'em do what they need to do," I told her. "They can sit with the colored kids for a couple of days if they want to—get this out of their system—and then, I'm hoping they'll move on."

Rose wiped at another dish, her mind struggling to piece this time in her life together. "So, where do I fit in to any of this?" she wondered. "You and Dalton and the kids—you go traipsing off on all these adventures, doing all these fancy assignments …" Her hands came still. "I'm not even a part of his life anymore, and when I am, I'm the worst part."

I draped an arm over her shoulder. "Look," I said, "you raised this kid. You're the one who's poured your life into him, who's given him every decent quality he's got. He's a good kid, Rose, and you're the reason why." I tightened my grip on her. "Let me carry the load for a little while and then, when we get to the next stage, you'll be right back where you've always been. And I'll be standing there, off to the side again, gazing in wonder at how much a mother and her grown-up son still love one another."

"I don't know," Rose said, her wound splayed wide open. "It seems like he's been gone for a long time, and there's no guarantee he'll be back."

I rubbed her back gently. "No," I replied, "there isn't. But this is as good a bet as I've ever seen."

• • • •

On my desk a nine-by-twelve manila envelope lay at the bottom of four-inch stack of mail. The return address was Milledgeville, Georgia.

I tossed my coat over the back of a chair and tore it open. Quickly, I flipped through nine pages of double-spaced typing, my eyes grazing over the words, slowing just enough for the gist of a topic sentence or two. Then I fell into my chair, leaned over the desk, and began to read—syllable-by-syllable and word-by-word.

Flannery O'Connor talked about writing as a vocation. She believed that every author was confined by the limits of his own talent and imagination. "And while it's true," she conceded, "that the writer always chooses his subjects, he can't add one more drop of ingenuity. There are characters, scenes, and stories that come to life through the power of his conception, but beyond these," she said, "he's impotent to produce more. There is dialog he creates, plots he assembles, tension that comes to a climax in his exceedingly capable hands—but even Faulkner has his limits."

The Southern writer, she went on, unlike those from other regions, has this unique capacity for the deformed. It just comes naturally, she said, and so of course he'd rather create a lively, grotesque character than a dreary, whole one.

"Our critics," she wrote—and I could practically see the sneer— "see these characters as the fruit of a crippled imagination, as the byproducts of the odd, little lives we must lead—all alone, fanning ourselves in parlors and sipping tea, deprived of the vibrant cultures that thrive in New York, Boston, and Philadelphia." But then, with devilry that was barely concealed, she mused: "And yet, for some reason, most Southern writers believe seclusion is their greatest ally."

I turned to the next page, where O'Connor pressed the argument further, noting that Southerners, being secluded, still tend to believe in God and to trust their Bibles. "It is more likely," she suggested, "that writers who perceive the world through this lens, have a sharper eye for what's truly bizarre. This view," she said, "gives them a sensibility through which they see the perverse. And though we, like others, are tempted to separate the sacred from the secular, to divide that which is observable from that which remains mysterious—we are far more likely to comprehend the world's inescapable need for redemption."

Yankees, O'Connor scoffed, just can't seem to grasp the fact that redemption is meaningless unless its need is pressing—unless we see it now, in the mundane events of Monday, Tuesday, and Wednesday morning. Their fiction, she grumbled, along with their art and television and film—assumes this pie-in-the sky posture. It presumes that life is good, that the whole world prospers, and that no one, anywhere, has cause for so much as the slightest angst.

In a fairy-tale world, she wondered, who—or what—has any need of redemption?

I turned another page, and settled back in my chair. "The novelist," O'Connor declared, "especially now, as the world hurtles into its most modern decade, must see the distortions. He must recognize what is repugnant, identify it, and then make it repugnant to his readers." That, she contended, is the novelist's job in the twentieth century.

These days, she lamented, we have become dull to our imperfections and blind to our own afflictions. Which means, if the novelist is to accomplish anything worthwhile, he has no choice but to shock his readers. "To the deaf," she echoed what she told me earlier, "you shout. And for the blind, you draw large, outrageous figures."

The Southern writer, O'Connor explained, is best equipped for the task because he, unlike his Northern counterparts, is so faithfully wed to his region. Dixie, she said, is an indivisible part of him, no less than blood, bone, and muscle. And this union, like one to a beautiful yet flawed bride, begets an awkward and inescapable self-awareness. Through this intimacy, the Southern writer understands, in a way no Northerner could, that self-knowledge reveals imperfection.

Our bizarre characters, she explained, are a picture of how we—as individuals, as a region, as a society—fall short. They are an illustration of what we lack and, at the same time, of what we yearn for.

This Southern self-awareness, she continued, runs against the grain of almost every modern notion. Today, the scientific polls assure us that we're thriving and happy, and that life has never been better. The critics, therefore, insist that literature should reflect our pervasive joy; they demand that writers take their cue from Mr. Gallup's findings and produce books that mirror our cheery lives.

"Have we become that shallow?" she wondered, her disdain almost audible. "Does anybody actually believe that the measure of mankind is now found in polls—in findings that fluctuate as fast as the weather? In a thing so fleeting as a man's good mood?"

I pictured her on the front porch, rocking, agitated, working herself further and further into a state of irritable disbelief. "We must be measured," she wrote, "against ultimate and unchangeable Truth. And against that Truth, we can't help but to see deficiency. Self-awareness," O'Connor wrote, "of a person or a region or even an institution—must, in the final analysis, bring humility."

I was on page six, impressed by her transitions, by the logic, and by how she'd stacked one argument on top of the last one. "All novelists," she now argued, "are seers of the real world." They describe that which exists, which has substance and being. But, she said, reality for some remains mystical.

She spent a paragraph telling us that over the past two centuries "the spirit of each succeeding age" has promised that all would soon be well, and that every ailment must soon surrender to the progress of science. When a novelist is swayed by that breeze, she said, when his life is shaped by what he sees, when it's the result of some plain and determinable factor—then he depicts the natural forces that, in his view, shape his destiny.

But, when the writer believes that life is more mysterious—when he sees man as a being who exists within a created order—when he believes that order has structure and laws that we, as an integral part of it, freely respond to—then the things he sees, the things that are visible in this world, that lay bare on the surface ... they only stir the imagination. They compel him to search further, to experience the mystery that lies deeper.... "This writer," O'Connor insisted, "pushes back the boundaries, pursuing the limits of mystery itself—and his characters have no choice but to follow."

To the modern mind, she surmised, these characters seem pathetic or naive, like one more Quixote tilting at windmills. But, they serve an indispensable purpose.

In this pie-in-the-sky world, she explained, the novelist is expected to show compassion. He's expected to understand human failings— they are, after all, human. And that, no doubt, is why, on the front flap of every new book jacket, we're now promised a sympathetic view of some common malady. But such wholesale compassion makes it impossible to call a thing wrong or evil or just plain stupid. And that, she declared, is why we need the grotesque characters of Southern fiction. They make moral judgment implicit. They show us the distance between what is and what ought to be. By their presence, a moral verdict trumps the soggier and shallow emotions. "It is through these characters," O'Connor concluded, "that the novelist assumes his proper role as prophet."

My eyes popped wide at her last claim, as I'm sure she intended.

The Southern writer, she was quick to explain, sees the inadequacies and imperfections—and beyond them, he understands the full extent of their meaning. He brings things close that remain far away. He is, ultimately, "a realist of distance." And there, she said, in this land of concrete reality, you find the most vivid examples of misshapen Southern characters. "We need them," O'Connor would tell our readers, "because they keep us mindful, despite the trendy polls, that the world isn't right, and that it—and we—are in need of repair."

I took a breath and smiled, knowing that *Down South*, with this essay, would become a stronger and truer voice for the region we were wed to. I reached for the first eight pages, to begin reading a second time, when Dalton popped his head inside. "Is it any good?" he asked.

I looked up, thoughts still swirling. "Yeah," I said quietly.

He stepped inside. "Mind if I have a look?"

I pitched the article to the edge of the desk.

He gave it a quick scan and headed for the door. "I'll bring it back in a few minutes," he said.

I swiveled toward the window, thinking to myself—half jokingly—that I hated this job—because this, I thought, is where every event of the last five years has led me. On a summer night in 1954 my home was bombed, and from that day to this one, I've wondered why. Now, here I was, in the opening days of a new decade, gazing out on Broad Street up toward Marietta, two years into a new enterprise, and already confronted by this improbable cast who were all compelled to close some gap between what is and what ought to be.

Sam Phillips believed that blacks and whites had something

to offer one another, and that our lives would be richer if, at least through music, they were mingled together.

Johnny Cash had seen injustice in a neighborhood where hardly anyone even looked anymore, and he'd brought his talent to bear on the problem.

Martin Luther King foresaw some kind of "beloved community." He'd dedicated every minute of his waking life to bring it into being— a decision that had been costly to him and his young family.

Diane Nash and John Lewis, inspired by King's vision, had energized hundreds of Negro students, who, it seemed to Chris and me, were willing to pay a steep price to make that vision real at a Woolworth's in downtown Nashville.

Flannery O'Connor, as she looked past the peacocks at Andalusia, suffering from a degenerated hip that made the simplest movement painful, saw a world in desperate need. Using the tools she'd been given, including an imagination that had given birth to Hazel Motes, she held out the Bible's promise that one day it would all be better.

It was no accident, I thought, that these were the people who'd crossed my path, that this was the journey that began that night in 1954, that I, having so dramatically witnessed our imperfections, would be one to hasten their repair.

Dalton rapped at the door, breaking the reverie. He strolled in, a ream of paper tucked under one arm, wrapped in rubber bands to hold it together. He pitched O'Connor's piece on my desk. "I made a couple of notes," he said, "but overall, I'd say that's a pretty good piece of work."

"You think?" I parried sarcastically. But then, more seriously, I asked: "What do you make of her premise—about the way Southern writers see the world—that whole redemption thing?"

Dalton slid into a chair. "Believe it or not," he said, "I'm with her on that, and it's not just about novelists. I think that's the job …" he formed quote marks with his fingers, "of being an artist." He eased back, cradling the ream of paper. "I'm not saying every book and movie's got to have some deep message; I'm the first guy to go for a little light entertainment, but in the long run, I buy the argument."

He cut his eyes back to the article. "That stuff about being a prophet, about seeing things …" he picked up the article, "how'd she put it, that bit about the extended meaning and moral judgment.… That's the stuff we need to play up, those are the pull-quotes, the stuff that makes us different than New York, and a heck of a lot better."

I swiveled back and forth, the chair creaking beneath my weight. Outside there was a steady whoosh of traffic, the blare of an occasional horn, the squeal of worn brakes. "So are we artists?" I asked.

Dalton batted the question back with a big grin. "What you really want to know," he said, "is, are we prophets?"

"All right," I said with a shrug, "are we prophets? Are we here to point out the difference between what is and what ought to be? Is it our job to expose this all-encompassing need for redemption?"

Dalton stood; he flipped the chair around and straddled it backwards, looking me in the eye. "Sometimes, it is," he said, "and sometimes.…"

"You waffling?" I asked.

"No," he replied. He rested his chin on the back on the chair. "I think we have the same role; we have the same responsibility—ultimately. But we fulfill it in a different context. We publish ten-thousand-word articles, she writes short stories and novels. We have advertisers. We have young readers and old ones; rich and poor; some of them like sports, others are into politics or books or movies. We have investors who expect a return; we've got a staff, we hire writers and typesetters and designers and photographers—a lot of people depend on us."

"Which means we can turn a blind eye—just occasionally—in order to make a buck?"

"No," Dalton said, "that's not what I'm saying. It means we have to apply a few principles that novelists don't. We have to put the story about the colored musicians underneath the main story. We have to suggest and prod. We employ a touch of nuance...."

"O'Connor shocks people with the bizarre and violent," I offered. "She shouts at the deaf, draws big for the blind. But we whisper. We write small."

"Yeah, at least some of the time." Dalton rubbed his hand along his chin. "I don't know," he said, "maybe there's some blend of prophet and businessman. The businessman leads, the prophet confronts. The businessman nudges here and there, the prophet proclaims. Businessmen insinuate, prophets declare ..." he said as he shrugged in surrender. "I don't know. It'd be interesting to get Alan's take."

"The businessman stays in business," I said. "The prophet doesn't much care."

"I don't think I'd go that far," Dalton countered. "If nobody buys their books, they don't get published, and if they don't get published, they're not proclaiming anything to anybody. We all gotta stay in business."

He stood and picked up a copy of the magazine. "Don't sell us short," he said. "Not everybody's here to do the same thing, or to do it the same way." He held the magazine higher. "And it might be good to remember that more people have read our magazines than have read *Wise Blood*."

"Yeah," I said, "I know."

"Every morning," Dalton reminded me, "you and me and Alan—we come here to make the world just a little bit better. Especially the part that's right here around us." And then he turned to go.

"Hey, what's that?" I hollered after him. I pointed to the stack of paper he carried.

"Geez," he said, "I almost forgot. "A PR guy at J. B. Lippincott sent this over. It's a novel they've got coming out pretty soon; he thought we'd be the perfect place to review it." Dalton plopped the manuscript on top of my desk. "Some gal from Alabama wrote it— her first book. I thought it was pretty good."

I glanced at the title page: *To Kill a Mockingbird* by Harper Lee. "What's it about?" I asked.

"The South," Dalton replied. "And the distance between what is and what ought to be."

He upholds the cause of the
oppressed and gives food to the hungry.
The LORD sets prisoners free.
—Psalm 146:7

Chapter 11

I was back in Nashville.

Thursday's sit-ins had been a repeat episode of the drama I'd seen the week before. About two hundred colored kids marched from the First Baptist Church to the downtown restaurants. Within minutes the counters calmly closed; the students sat and read—alone and in the dark—and then quietly returned home.

But everybody knew the pattern couldn't hold. Waitresses were edgy, clerks fumed, everyday shoppers looked on, more gingerly than they had the week before, and in some—particularly those who were younger—resentment was beginning to fester.

Store managers felt the blow to their bottom line—not just at the lunch counters, but throughout their stores—and across the whole of downtown Nashville.

I had reserved rooms for Chris and Ansley at my hotel. We met for five minutes in the lobby—it was late Friday afternoon—I was rushing downtown to interview the manager of Kress; they were headed to the First Baptist Church.

"So, what's going on down there?" I asked.

"Some kind of briefing," Chris said. "I think they're just laying out a plan for tomorrow."

"And they're giving newcomers a crash course on nonviolence," Ansley added. She slid a typewritten page across the table. "Chris got this in the mail."

"They're wanting kids who haven't been through the workshops to spend some time with this Lawson guy," Chris said. He gestured toward the page and said, "To make sure we know the drill."

I scanned the document. In the left margin, in all caps it said DO NOT: and then, listed down the page were instructions not to strike back or curse, not to laugh or hold conversations with the floor walker, not to leave your seat, not to block entrances to the stores outside or to the aisles inside....

Halfway down the page, in all caps again, it said DO: and there, to the right of the imperative, were instructions to show yourself friendly and courteous at all times, to sit straight and always face the counter, to report serious incidents, to refer information seekers to the leader, and to remember the teachings of Jesus Christ, Mahatma Gandhi, and Martin Luther King. At the bottom of the page there was a final reminder that "love and nonviolence is the way."

I shoved the paper back to Ansley, observing my son carefully. He was two inches taller than just about everybody. He could bench press more than any three people in the room, combined. And on football fields across the South, he was not known for his nonviolent ways. "You think you can do this?" I asked him. "When some dope calls you a nigger lover, when a little twerp wants to know why you're betraying your own kind, you just gonna sit there and 'show yourself friendly and courteous at all times'?"

Ansley grabbed his arm, tugging him close beside her. "I'll keep an eye on him," she said.

"Uh-huh," I muttered, my gaze lingering on Chris, still waiting for his reply.

"Look," he said, "this is different. It's like Dr. King says, we're not doing this just so Negroes can sit at a lunch counter. We're doing it for the twerps and dopes too—because they don't know what justice is, because they're the products of an unjust and unfair society." He looked down sheepishly, recognizing that he might've parroted a few words that weren't exactly his.

"All right," I told him. Then I looked to Ansley. "You guys'll probably be out late. Why don't we meet here for breakfast, say … seven thirty?"

"Seven thirty?" Ansley sounded startled.

"All right," I said. "How about eight?"

•   •   •   •

They were sipping their second cup of coffee when I arrived at 7:50.

Neither had gotten much sleep, and they both looked antsier than the Vanderbilt football team ten minutes before the Georgia game. But these kids were more than nervous, they were scared. They were plagued by the doubts that always hound momentous choices, wondering ten thousand times: "What have I done?"

"I'd ask how you slept," I said, "but I'm pretty sure I know the answer."

Ansley twirled a knife between her fingers; she tapped it against the table, then twirled it some more. "How was your evening?" she asked. "Did you learn anything new?"

I held my coffee cup out to a passing waitress. "Yeah," I said. "I learned that you guys need to be extra careful. The cops are gonna be all over the place—which is probably good—they'll keep things under control. But I got a hunch somebody's going to jail today, and I don't want it to be you."

Chris nodded, but neither he nor Ansley looked surprised.

"It's the weekend," I reminded them. "Nobody's at school or work today, and every white man who's got an ax to grind—it's a good bet they'll be waiting for you."

"Yes sir," Ansley replied. "We've heard."

They began the procession late that morning, just as the lunch crowds began to gather. As they neared the Arcade the police came alive, quickly but inconspicuously keeping watch from the sidelines. White shoppers parted before the Negro crowd. They glared as the students passed, quietly seething.

Before the black column traveled three city blocks, taunts began to retch from the watching white throng: "Go home, niggers!" "Get back to the Africa."

I kept pace with the parade, keeping close watch on Chris and Ansley. The crowd's temperature was climbing. White kids suddenly knifed in and out of Negro territory—pushing the students, dragging them out of line, screaming.

Earlier they'd been content to mock the colored marchers—to taunt and ridicule—but derision had given way to anger, and anger, it appeared, had just given birth to violence.

The Negro protestors approached the first of the five-and-dime stores. Chris and Ansley, along with twenty others, peeled off the main formation and swept through Woolworth's doors. I broke through the crowd, jogged across the street, and shoved my way inside. A crowd waited. The moment the first Negro's foot crossed the threshold they erupted in chants of "No niggers here! No niggers here!"

I watched as Chris sucked in all the air his lungs could hold. He straightened his back, stretching to every bit of his six feet three inches, scoping the crowd in search of a suitable challenger.

Ansley placed a hand to his back and rubbed gently, infusing calmness back into his system.

There are two lunch counters at the Nashville Woolworth's, one upstairs and one down. Chris and Ansley veered left, to the restaurant on the main floor. As they pushed forward, cries of "chicken" and "coward" mixed with the racial slurs. You could feel a shift in the character of the crowd. One man's anger fueled another's, and the jeering throng was transforming itself, one by one, into a vengeful mob.

They wanted blood.

The colored students took their seats, spreading down the length of the lunch counter, leaving spaces between them. The mob skulked at the fringes, each member weighing his next move. Suddenly—and seemingly from out of nowhere—a kid bolted from the pack. He plowed into a colored student, throwing a bone-hard forearm, like a pulling guard leading a sweep around left end. The young Negro flew off the stool. Both men landed hard, sprawled across the black-and-white tile floor. The student gazed up, astonished but unhurt. Slowly, his antagonist came to his feet. He straddled the colored kid's half-prone body, hands on his hips, breath labored. "Get on out of here, nigger." He stared down, his revulsion unmasked and unrestrained. "Just get out of here!"

Ansley moved a hand to Chris's shoulder. Her muscles tightened as she pressed down.

Emboldened, others struck. They pushed and pulled, dragging Negro students off their stools and tossing them aside like garbage. Ugly taunts spewed from every direction.

The colored kids remained silent as stones. They dusted off their hands, remounted their stools, and spun around to face forward— without uttering a word.

The upstairs contingent raced down. They hurried to fill the empty seats, hoping to draw the white mob's fire, and to provide a respite for their friends. John Lewis, Chris's new pal, hurried to the stool on Ansley's left.

A white man, pencil thin and in his midthirties, slithered up before him. "We're sick of you stinking niggers," he declared. His eyes lingered on Lewis's hair, nose, and lips. He sneered. And then, with menacing deliberation, he pulled his fist back. He narrowed his eyes, pressed his lips to a crease, then punched Lewis square in the ribs. The colored man doubled over; he gasped and dropped like a sack of wet cement, writhing in pain.

"Good one, Buck!" a voiced cheered from the crowd.

Chris shot up like a flare. He towered over this thug, his biceps tensed and bulging.

"Sit!" John screamed. Lewis, moaning in pain, ordered Chris to "please sit down." He staggered to his feet, crawled back onto the stool, and braced himself against the counter.

Ansley grabbed Chris's hand. "Easy," she murmured, "just let it go."

Chris scorched the man with eyes that would've set oily rags blazing. But Buck now knew there'd be no retaliation. He swelled up with a coward's courage—the kind that comes with no threat of consequences. He flicked his cigarette into Chris's face. "Judas Iscariot is what you are," he snarled.

A soft moan came from somewhere in the crowd, a cry of sympathy and pain.

I kept my eyes on Chris. Every muscle in the boy's body rippled. I knew every instinct screamed to lash back.

Ansley tugged at the back of his shirt, gently pulling him onto the stool. Chris sat and slowly spun to face the front of the counter.

From six seats away there was a sudden burst of laughter. A pack of white kids had clustered together, gleeful as they watched a new episode unfold. Their leader, dressed in jeans and a black sweatshirt, held a plastic mustard container high overhead. He stood before a Negro student. "You like mustard, boy?" he asked. "Because if you want to be served here, I'll serve you." Slowly, his eyes traveled the length of his arm—from his shoulder past his elbow, to his forearm, to his hands and fingers, to the dreaded yellow container. "Yeah ..." he said, "if you'd like a little mustard, you've come to the right place." He inched closer, looping the container round and round in sinister circles. He checked back with his friends, "What do you think, Billy? You think this boy'd like some mustard?"

"I believe a little yellow'd go good with that Brillo pad he's got for hair," Billy answered.

The white kid crept closer, the container poised like a knife above him. He came to within inches of the young Negro. "You know," he said to Billy, "I believe it would."

And then he squeezed.

Mustard spurted over the colored boy's head. It dripped to his left ear and onto his shoulder. It fell to his eyebrows and trickled down his neck.

The crowd exploded in laughter. The kid squeezed a second time. He shook the container up and down, and then squeezed a third time and then a fourth. And then he pitched the tube toward a second Negro. With gaping, jovial eyes he said, "You want some too?"

The victim of this humiliation pulled a few napkins from a nearby dispenser. He wiped at his forehead, neck, and ears, and then—without a word—he turned to face forward.

Up and down the counter whites cursed and yelled like drill sergeants, making sure the Negroes knew that mustard wasn't the worst of what they had in store.

I watched as one man put his face to within inches of a student's. He pulled a cigarette from his lips and blew smoke into the black man's face. And then, with lips curled to a wicked snarl, he stabbed the butt into the back of the Negro's hand.

The student flinched wildly; he lunged for the ice in a nearby glass and rubbed it onto the burn. He glared at the attacker, cradling the wounded hand, and then he too turned in silence.

A television crew had recorded every movement and sound. And soon the world would have yet another glimpse of a South that had turned ugly. I groaned silently, wishing they'd go away, wishing that everybody here would go back where they'd come from—wishing that somebody somewhere would turn the clock back and put the world right again.

"So, you just gonna sit there?"

It was Buck, the guy who'd tested Chris five minutes earlier, back for round two.

Chris didn't turn or reply. He simply looked down at the counter.

Ansley stared back at the man, wordlessly pleading with him to leave.

"You know, I just don't understand," the man said. He seared holes through Ansley, now addressing her. "I mean, how the hell do white people sit with niggers like this?" He turned back to Chris and shoved at the back of his shoulder. "Pair of lousy traitors is what you are," he said, his voice rough as gravel. "And cowards to boot."

I looked on quietly, determined not to intervene, intent on not committing Benjamin Fine's sin of inserting myself into the story. Chris could end this with one punch. In ten seconds, he could have this guy on his knees begging to serve lunch to every colored kid in Nashville. And he could do it right now.

"What's it going to take for you to get off your butt?" the man growled. He turned to the crowd and shrugged, as if confused. Then he took three steps back; he looked around again, begging for the mob's attention. Then, with a running start, he slammed into Chris, folding the boy in half over the top of the counter. He backed away, grabbed Chris, and spun him round—turned him face-to-face.

The television cameras were ten feet away and rolling. *His mother's going to see this,* I thought, *and she is going to die.*

"Big boy like you," Buck said, "you just gonna watch your nigger friends get the hell beat out of 'em; that what nigger lovers do?"

Chris swiveled back to face forward.

Buck grabbed at his collar, spun him around, faced him eye-to-eye again. "I'm talking to you," he screamed. "You look at a man when he's talking to you, you understand?"

For the third time Chris turned away, and for the third time his adversary reached for him. This time Buck reared back and punched my son square on the jaw. The blow knocked him into the counter.

From out of the crowd a voice screamed, "No!" I turned and searched the mob, but couldn't find the first trace of sympathy.

Chris rubbed his face; he worked his jaw back and forth, testing the bones and muscles. Ansley buried her face in her hands, tears now streaming, as the cameras moved in for a close-up of the pretty white girl.

I fought every instinct to intervene. *This was the worst idea I'd ever had,* I thought to myself. I looked at Chris, eyes imploring him to act. *You can end this with one punch,* I thought; *do not let this guy hit you again.*

Chris sat up straight and faced Buck, silently.

Buck baited him again. "Come on, big boy," he pulled his fist back and dangled it in the air, taunting the boy. "You ain't gonna let me hit you again, are you?"

The television camera watched as Buck pounced again. This time Chris raised his hands and turned, but the punch found its target, and Chris's nose erupted like Vesuvius.

A cry came from the crowd again—a woman's voice shrieking,

"Stop!" And then—from her hiding place in the middle of this mob—Rose Marie charged forward.

Buck struck again, landing a punch to Chris's chin, and then a third to his ribs.

With a burst of adrenaline-fueled strength Rose Marie shoved the assailant aside. She threw her body over her son's, wailing, "Leave him alone." Sobbing, she wrapped herself around Chris, covering him like a blanket, inserting her body between his and the punk who'd attacked him.

I broke out of the crowd. "Rose!" I screamed.

Buck looked on, gape-mouthed. Then he burst out laughing. "First you sit with niggers, now you got a woman doing your fighting for you." He shook his head, "You are one pathetic white man."

Rose grabbed a handful of napkins, quickly plugging her son's bleeding nose. "Lean your head back," she said urgently. "Let me look at this."

To my great relief Chris smiled. He hugged his mother. "I'll be okay," he assured her. He looked to Ansley and then to me; he rubbed his chin and touched the wound at the side of his head. "It's going to be fine," he said. Then, turning back to Rose Marie, but in a voice loud enough for Buck to hear, he said, "I've been hit harder than that by cheerleaders."

Rose ran her hand over Chris's face, down to his chin, inspecting her son's injuries. She turned to her right, to a young colored girl sitting beside her. "I need you to scoot down," she told her. Then, with the flair Southern women bring to climactic events, Rose sat. She folded her arms, eyeing Buck, her gaze drenched with contempt.

"I'm sitting with the niggers too," she sneered. "What are you going to do about it?"

Before Buck could reply, there was a commotion at the back of the store. The crowd turned to watch five cops race inside.

Swell, I thought, *they're just in time.*

They stormed past Buck, past the kid who'd transformed mustard into a weapon, past the guy who'd committed assault with a cigarette, past everyone who'd shoved and pushed and cursed the silent Negro students. They fanned out along the length of the counter, the television camera still rolling. "Who's in charge here?" a cop barked.

"I am," John Lewis answered.

The cop ambled John's way. "You're going to have to leave," he declared.

"We'd like to be served," John replied.

The cop returned a weary look. "You're not going to be served here," he told John. "You and your friends, you need to leave right now."

"I'm sorry," John said, "but we can't do that."

The cop shifted his weight and folded his arms, perturbed that his day wasn't going to get easier. "You understand that if you don't leave we're going to arrest you?"

"Yes sir," John said.

The cop tried again and there was, I think, a hint of sympathy this time. "If you don't leave right now, we're going to take y'all to jail; we're going to lock everybody up."

"Yes sir," John repeated, "I understand."

The policeman shrugged. His gaze traveled from cop to cop, and he dipped his chin, silently ordering them to proceed.

"I'm a reporter," I called. "What's the charge against them?"

He tossed off an indifferent frown. "Disorderly conduct," he replied.

The cop grabbed John above the elbow of his left arm, lifted, and said, "You're under arrest." Chris and Ansley stood at the same time. As the cop led John away they followed, joining the students who filed out of the restaurant in an orderly, single-file line.

Suddenly, Rose leaped from her stool; she rushed forward and grabbed Chris's hand, and then reached behind, taking Ansley's, too, falling in with the column of Negro prisoners.

As they neared the front door the entire procession, as if on some telepathic cue, burst into song. In perfect unison they filled the air with the solemn sound of, "We shall overcome / we shall overcome / we shall overcome some day."

I watched John's lips move with the words. I saw Chris's mouth form the same lyrics. And my wife sang too.

They exited the store, moving into the chilly air. As Chris approached the paddy wagon the cop brushed him aside. He reached past Rose Marie, past Ansley—grabbing at John Lewis's arm, and hoisting the black man into the car. Chris took his girlfriend's hand; he draped an arm over his mother's shoulder—the three of them singing together, "Deep in my heart / I do believe we shall overcome some day."

A cop slammed the door. He shoved a padlock through its receptacle, snapping the lock closed. Then, looping his hand in the air, he signaled the driver to pull away.

I walked up beside Chris and Rose and Ansley. I didn't run. I did not rush to Rose Marie's side. I approached her with something more like reverence than joy. I hugged her and held on—the way you hold things that are precious and fragile.

"What are you doing?" I asked her. "Why in the world are you here?"

My wife put a hand to her face, wiping at damp eyes. She gave a stuttering, confused laugh. "I don't have any idea," she said. "I was just too worried to stay home. I couldn't be there by myself." She laced her arm around Chris's and leaned in, pressing against him. "I couldn't stand not knowing." She wiped at another tear; she tightened her grasp on her son's arm. "We've got to get you to the emergency room," she declared. "Somebody's got a take a look at your nose."

"It's all right," Chris said. "It was just bloody, that's all."

"This is no time to be a hero," Ansley scolded. She grabbed his chin, turning his head to examine the second injury. "That's gonna take a few stitches."

"It's gonna have to wait," Chris replied. "Right now, we got to get down to the jail."

Fifteen cops barked a hundred different orders. They fingerprinted and processed an endless stream of new prisoners, and struggled to corral the swelling black crowd.

In the midst of the bedlam the prisoners smiled triumphantly. They showed no anger, they claimed no rights, they made no assertions of innocence or mistreatment. There was, among the eighty or so offenders, only the presence of quiet exultation.

There's a passage in the Bible that talks about "a peace that passes understanding." When I looked at these kids marching off to jail, singing the old spirituals, beaming smiles back and forth to one another, I knew—in a way I hadn't known before—the meaning of that phrase. They possessed a tranquility I'd not owned in quite the same way, and for a moment—for something just shy of a split second—I envied them. And I was, for as long as I was in their presence, drawn by the spirit they shared.

The police had no time for reflection. They were vastly out-numbered and, it now appeared, they'd been outsmarted as well. At Woolworth's, McClellan's, and Kress the colored kids kept coming. As soon as one paddy wagon pulled away, twenty new kids instantly appeared, then twenty more, and then twenty more after that—wave after wave were flooding into all six stores.

Already, jail cells built for six prisoners were stuffed with thirty, and the flow wasn't about to be dammed.

The scene was almost comical. Colored kids were everywhere—in hallways and offices. "Good grief," I said to a cop, "what are you going to do with 'em?"

He rolled his eyes, unamused and desperate.

The bigwigs huddled together, frantic for a solution. And before long we got word that bail had been dropped to a token five dollars. With a wink toward justice, the cops had made a gambit to clear the jail, but the students refused to play along. As soon as the rumor reached Lewis, Nash, and Lawson, they trumped the cops' best card. A chant suddenly rose and began to travel. It sped from one cell to the next—into waiting rooms and storerooms, out to the parking lot—boisterous protesters all proclaiming: "Jail without bail. Jail without bail."

The cops had not only run out of room, they were out of ideas, and now, they were out of options. They had no choice but to set their prisoners free.

As the Negro students straggled out of the jail I turned to Rose and Ansley. "Why don't you get him to the emergency room?" I said, gesturing toward Chris. "I'll catch up with you back at the hotel. I need a half hour to follow up on this."

Chris wanted to stick with me; he and Ansley both wanted to be part of whatever came next, but the pain was getting serious. So the three of them went one way; I went another.

The students had been released into the custody of Stephen Wright, the president of Fisk University. They were free to leave, the cops had explained, if they promised to go home and stay there. But, like a football team who'd just beaten its fiercest rival, the students needed time to savor the win, and they longed for time together.

By a hundred different routes, they migrated back to First Baptist Church, where a throng of their biggest fans waited. I watched from a distance. The kids regaled one another with war stories. They sang more songs. They laughed. And none of them wanted to leave.

"I see you made it." Diane Nash moseyed up beside me.

I raised my glass and smiled. My eyes skimmed over the crowd. "Quite a celebration," I replied.

She surveyed the festivities. "Well," she said, "I s'pose it is."

"So what'd you win?" I asked. "Has anything really changed?"

"Oh, I suspect a few attitudes might have changed," she replied, "a little bit anyway. We might've won a little respect, maybe some sympathy."

"How do you figure that?" I prodded.

"We've been seen," Diane Nash replied, "and we've been heard. In fact, I think we delivered a pretty clear message."

"And what was that?" I asked.

"We were jailed for disorderly conduct," she said. "But we weren't the ones who rioted. We weren't the ones who disturbed the peace. We weren't the ones who assaulted anybody. And tomorrow, in newspapers and on television, everybody'll see the truth."

"You think that's going to change anybody's mind?"

Diane Nash bobbed her head. "Yes," she replied. "It has to, eventually." She sipped from a cup of water, then glanced up from beneath curious brows. "You were there," she said. "You watched. You heard. It changed you, didn't it?"

"I'm a reporter," I replied, "I have to stay objective."

"Nobody's objective," she scoffed. "Not about this." Then she smiled, "Evasive maybe, but not objective."

"So why didn't you pay the fines?" I asked, changing the subject. "I know you're not exactly flush with cash, but five bucks? I thought that was pretty decent of the cops to offer."

"There was nothing decent about it." She shook her head, as if she couldn't believe I'd tried to pass that off on her. "They weren't trying to help us with our problem; they were just trying to solve theirs."

"You were the ones in jail," I pointed out.

"And now we're out," she replied. Then, smiling, she added, "And besides, jail's not a problem for us."

"Is that right?" I said.

She raised the cup to her lips again. "Our problem's a segregated, unjust society. It's a system that produces inequality.... If we'd paid the fines we'd have become a part of the system, which means we'd be perpetuating the injustice. Now that wouldn't make any sense, would it?"

Behind Diane Nash three hundred colored students sang and laughed and reveled in one another's company. And I wondered, for the second time in the past couple of hours: *How in the world does persecution bring peace?*

• • • •

Chris, Ansley, Rose Marie, and I sat in the lobby late that night and into the first hours of the next morning. A smile that I hadn't seen in years looked to be permanently affixed to Rose Marie's face, and her joy radiated for a hundred feet in every direction.

She and Chris and Ansley wallowed in memories of their adventure—reliving and retelling the story of how Rose had shoved Buck aside and dared "that little twerp" to strike again. Despite the hour, the three of them couldn't surrender each other's company. They lived in a moment they longed to preserve, Chris and Rose savoring not only a memory, but their long-awaited reconciliation.

I sat quietly, marveling at the transformation, grateful, and wondering what it was, exactly, that had happened. But the clock had crept near three, and fatigue, finally, had forced us all upstairs—the kids to their rooms, Rose and me to mine.

On the elevator, when it was just the two of us, I simply said, "What happened, Rose?"

She glanced up, watching the numbers climb from two to three. "I don't know. I just couldn't sit still. I was going stir-crazy, dreaming up the worst, thinking all kinds of horrible thoughts…." She bowed her head. "Then I got here; I snuck in behind the crowd and things were so much worse than anything I'd imagined. I don't know, Jack, I haven't changed my mind about anything. I don't want my son going to a mixed school. I don't want him going to dances with colored girls. It's still like I've always said: When coloreds and whites mix together, it brings out the worst in both of us." She stared at the numbers again. "But those people we saw today, the things they said and did … I don't think I've ever been so ashamed. And then, when that fool hit my boy … I just ran in there. I didn't think about it. I didn't really care about what he might … Oh Jack, I don't know, after that I had to pick a side." She reached back and squeezed my hand, "And I had to take Chris's."

I squeezed Rose's hand, but in my mind's eye Diane Nash appeared, smiling slyly and saying: "You were there. You watched, you heard—and you were changed."

*"Mockingbirds don't do but one thing
... sing their hearts out for us.
That's why it's a sin to kill a mockingbird."
—Miss Maudie, To Kill a Mockingbird*

Chapter 12

Atlanta, Georgia. Two weeks later.

Dalton wrote a beautiful review of Harper Lee's novel.

He prefaced his critique with a short explanation of how the book came into existence, and that story, in and of itself, gives Lee's work a mystical quality.

Nelle Lee, a young woman from Monroeville, Alabama, had moved to New York with dreams of becoming a writer. She was shy, and in her first few months there, she naturally trailed in the wake of her famous childhood friend, Truman Capote. With him, she discovered a colony of Southern artists—this outpost of writers, musicians, and painters who, drawn together by the South's irresistible pull, found refuge in one another's company. Lee hovered at the fringe—more tolerated than embraced by the artsy crowd—with one exception: She'd felt an instant rapport with Michael Martin Brown, a musician-songwriter, and his wife, Joy, a former ballerina.

As their friendship blossomed, Lee confided in the Browns. In a thousand late-night conversations she told them everything, and with as much fire as a bashful girl can summon, she poured out her hopes to one day write a novel. But, like fledgling artists everywhere, Lee struggled to pay the rent and electric bill. And so she slogged through the day selling tickets for BOAC, the British airline. At five o'clock she'd hurry home, nibble at pizza or Chinese, and start all over again—at her typewriter gulping coffee, straining to tap out a few hundred well-ordered words for as long as her eyes would stay open. On Saturdays and Sundays she'd start by midmorning and hope to knock out a thousand more.

The Browns had detected wisps of talent. But, as clear as the Empire State Building, they'd seen her struggle to make time to pursue her dream.

The story skipped forward, to December 1954. Nelle had planned to spend Christmas at home in Alabama. But, with the crush of holiday business, the airline couldn't give her the extra time off. Michael and Joy knew she'd be lonely. They insisted that Nelle spend Christmas Eve with them, stay overnight, and celebrate the following morning.

Reluctantly, but gratefully, Nelle accepted the invitation.

Christmas morning, the whole house was up by seven—the Browns' young daughter as eager as any kid—and this year with good reason. Nineteen fifty-four had been good to her father. And just a few weeks earlier, to top off an already prosperous year, Michael had finished a musical comedy starring Roddy McDowell. That alone had earned him a small fortune and padded the pile that waited beneath the tree.

After breakfast, after singing a few carols, after holding off the Browns' little girl for as long as possible, the time had come to open presents. For Nelle's sake, the adults had agreed to exchange "something little, that's just fun and inexpensive." Still, Nelle was excited about the presents she'd found. For Michael, she'd discovered a portrait of Sydney Smith, the founder of the once-noble *Edinburgh Review*, which, on more than one occasion, had wormed its way into their headier, bourbon-inspired conversations. It cost thirty-five cents. For Joy, Nelle had stumbled across the perfect gift. She'd found it in a used bookstore—a complete set of every word ever uttered by Lady Margot Asquith. Joy relished the dry British wit. And when she'd get in certain moods, when circumstances so clearly called for it, she could, with all the right gestures, strike with the perfect Asquith stinger: "Oh, I'll always cherish the false image I had of you." Or, "She tells enough white lies to ice a wedding cake." Or one of her favorites: "He's clever, but sometimes his brains go to his head."

No gift, at any price, could have delighted Joy more.

Nelle had been thrilled to give the Browns these newfound treasures. But then, as Dalton relayed the story, there was a cumbersome pause—as if Michael and Joy had forgotten, as if they hadn't bothered with a gift for Nelle. Michael seemed content to let the awkwardness dangle. No one spoke; no one made even the slightest move to retrieve a box or package. Then, with a coy smile, Michael lifted his chin toward the tree. "There's something there for you," he told Nelle.

A small envelope remained clothespinned to one of the branches. Nelle, deeply puzzled, stood and walked to the tree. She opened the envelope, and inside—in this small, nearly overlooked bit of folded and glued paper—she discovered a gift that would bless the entire world forever. In the envelope there was a hand-scrawled note. It read:

"You have one year. Your job is to write whatever you please. Merry Christmas."

Lee stared at the note, baffled. "What does that mean?" she asked.

"Exactly what it says," Michael answered. He then explained that he and Joy were giving her a year's salary, but that the gift came with one condition: that she quit her job and spend every day of the next twelve months writing.

And that's what she did.

When you know the background, even these few lines of the story, it is impossible to believe that Harper Lee's book is not a part of some grand and purposeful scheme. I mean, what are the odds—that Lee and Capote, writers of the highest order, just so happened to be next-door neighbors in a backwater Alabama town; that they just so happened to live in New York at the same moment in history; that Lee just so happened to meet Michael Brown; that he and his wife became cherished friends of a shy girl who was new to a city of nearly eight million souls …?

Think just a little further: About Nelle Lee's holiday plans—foiled just weeks after Michael Brown sold his big-ticket comedy. Do the math and figure the odds—that Nelle would spend *that* Christmas with loving and generous friends? And then, armed with that knowledge, tell me: Who doesn't believe that Michael and Joy Brown were instruments in the hands of one hilarious God who—from the day of Harper Lee's birth—orchestrated this improbable and delicious plan?

To Kill a Mockingbird was, of course, an instant success. And Nelle Lee, from Monroeville, Alabama—a girl who hadn't written much of anything ever before—walked away with a Pulitzer Prize.

Dalton, as much he admired the book, was peeved. I've never known anybody to covet a thing more than Dalton and McGill coveted a Pulitzer Prize. But unlike anything Dalton or I had ever written, Lee's book was perfect. The story, the characters, the plot and themes … they could not have been one bit better.

In 1960, through a sequence of inexplicable events, and by the hand of a most unlikely writer, America was gifted with the book it needed.

We were, as we made our entrance into a new decade, on the brink of an era that was filled with promise. But we were a lot like Scout, childlike and blind to so much of what was around us. And like the protagonist of Lee's story, we couldn't stay that way for long. Confronted by Martin King and Elizabeth Eckford and John Lewis and Diane Nash—and watching the world's reaction to them—we'd have no choice but to face new facts and to deal with what was before us.

The pivotal line in Lee's book belongs to Miss Maudie, the Finches' neighbor. She tells Scout, "Mockingbirds don't do but one thing … sing their hearts out for us. That's why it's a sin to kill a mockingbird."

Mockingbirds—the innocents who only sing—are scattered throughout the novel: Jem and Dill are both wounded by malevolent forces. At the story's climax, Tom Robinson, the Negro laborer who's falsely accused, is killed while trying to escape from prison. His death, Mr. Underwood tells us, was like "the senseless slaughter of songbirds."

When I came to the end of Lee's story my mind wandered back to Montgomery—to the old woman I'd met there, the one who'd looked me up and down—suspicious and wary—who'd confessed, that "my feet may be tired, but my soul is rested." I pictured King in the Holt Street pulpit; I closed my eyes and listened again, as if for the first time, to the irresistible cadence, "There comes a time when people get tired of being plunged across the abyss of humiliation...."

Like scenes in a slide show, Elizabeth Eckford popped into my mind, hounded by kids and parents who snarled with a rabid fury I'd seen too many times—this young girl, raised in the Christ-haunted South, whose only salvation that day came from a New York Jew.

The South was slowly being flooded with quiet and kindly creatures who—if one took King at his word—were singing a song for our common good. But, unlike Tom Robinson and Boo Radley, they had no reason to be naive. Now, in this new decade, they knew what was coming. Now—after Montgomery, after Little Rock, after Greensboro and Nashville—Martin King would send out disciples, instructing them with Jesus' own words, "Be as shrewd as snakes and as innocent as doves."

Being shrewd, they knew what to expect. And being innocent, they'd refuse to lash back. They'd turn the other cheek, and one day, if the world was truly on the side of justice, they'd transform enemies into friends—and form a single "beloved community."

Down South, I liked to think, would play the part of Atticus Finch. We would confront evil. And, like Atticus, we would grant others a measure of grace. Like the Maycomb lawyer we wouldn't overlook or excuse what was wicked. We'd condemn it when necessary. And engage it when we could—sometimes with a shout, other times with a whisper—we'd be gracious, drawing others near, leading them to the place where they could see, with less obstruction, a better way. With words and pictures, we'd make our patch of ground just a little bit better.

I thumbed the pages of Harper Lee's book and thought about Flannery O'Connor. Lee's book was tamer; her characters were not nearly so odd. But like O'Connor, Lee drew big, forcing even the blind to take notice. Lee knew, as O'Connor did—as King and Lewis and Nash did, as Johnny Cash and Sam Phillips knew, as Dalton and Alan and I knew too—that in 1960, the most grotesque thing to come to most of our neighbors' minds was a community where we loved one another.

I reread the last few lines, then laid Lee's book aside. I closed my eyes and thought about the world where we lived, and I knew ... it'd be some time before I'd see another day's rest.

... a little more ...

When a delightful concert comes to an end,

the orchestra might offer an encore.

When a fine meal comes to an end,

it's always nice to savor a bit of dessert.

When a great story comes to an end,

we think you may want to linger.

And so, we offer ...

AfterWords—just a little something more after you

have finished a David C. Cook novel.

We invite you to stay awhile in the story.

Thanks for reading!

Turn the page for ...

- **Discussion Questions**
- **An Interview with the Author**
- **Fact and Fiction**

Discussion Questions

Use these questions to discuss *Crossing the Lines* in a reading group or simply to explore the story from a new perspective.

1. Describe the emotional "ride" you took as you read *Crossing the Lines.* What surprised you most as you read the story?

2. In what ways did you identify with Jack? With Rose Marie? Chris?

3. How did the story inspire you? Challenge you?

4. What about the characters or story made you angry or upset?

5. Although the novel is fiction, it's based on true events and real people. How does this impact your reaction to *Crossing the Lines*?

6. How did the main characters grow as the story progressed? Who grew the most? What were the events that prompted that growth?

7. Which of the iconic characters in the novel did you find most compelling? According to the novel, what are some of the lasting effects of their influence? How does this compare to what you know of their actual stories?

8. What was your reaction to the ending of the story?

9. How did this story affect your view of the South during that turbulent time?

10. In what ways (if any) has this story changed you?

An Interview with the Author

Your first novel, *Safe at Home*, dealt with the racial tension of the early 1950s in the setting of minor league baseball. This one follows that story chronologically, but is not set directly in the world of sports. What is it about this era in American history that keeps drawing you back?

This was a time when the country was fundamentally changed—when we saw righteousness confront evil—and righteousness won. It was a time when the courage of humble, anonymous, and powerless people overcame the self-interest of entrenched power. And it was the era when our understanding of justice was challenged and redefined.

In the Gettysburg Address Abraham Lincoln talked about a "new birth of freedom." In many respects the civil rights era was, for people of every color, exactly that.

Both books feature "cameos" by historical figures. How did you go about researching their stories so you could present them in a believable light?

Well, I live in Martin Luther King's hometown. I've been to his boyhood home several times, as well as to the civil rights museum that's right down the road. I've roamed around Ebenezer Baptist Church, where King and his father were copastors. I've been to Dexter Avenue Baptist and to the manse on South Jackson Street in Montgomery. These places are full of books, papers, documentary presentations, and important artifacts from the era.

We have access to King's speeches, sermons, and books. With a couple of clicks on YouTube, you can hear him speak, study his mannerisms, and be captivated by the rhythm of his oratory.

So many of the people involved in this story left a thorough and very personal record. We have the columns and books written by Ralph McGill and Harry Ashmore—their firsthand testimony through which we sense the tension of the times.

This is one of the most thoroughly documented periods of American history, and I live within a few miles of the research library at Emory University where, it seems, every article ever written is at your fingertips.

What surprised you most as you did your research for *Crossing the Lines?*

I came away from the research and writing with enormous gratitude for the way Martin Luther King Jr. changed the hearts and minds of America's white population. Here are a couple episodes that illustrate what I mean:

Early in the book, when Jack asks King about the purpose of the Montgomery bus boycott, King tells him that he hopes to awaken a sense of moral shame. He explains that the effort is ultimately about fellowship. The aftermath of it, he tells Jack, is redemption and reconciliation—a redeeming goodwill for all men.

Most people, I suspect, think of "the movement" as being about rights for black people. I was surprised to learn that it was—thoroughly and from the very beginning—about justice for everyone. King's concern was for a society in which every human could flourish. This twenty-six-year-old pastor recognized, in a thoroughly biblical way, the need for cross-cultural fellowship. He recognized that whites were just as impoverished as blacks by a segregated society. King saw that white people—especially those in power—needed to be freed from the restraints of a segregated society.

There's a point in the story where King tells Chris Hall that he's not interested in ending segregation. The goal, he says, is integration—the creation of a "beloved community" of all God's children. King was always mindful that no one could thrive until everyone had equal opportunity.

Toward the end of the book, in Nashville, we see jailed black protesters refuse to pay bail, even after it's been lowered to a token five dollars. Diane Nash, one of the black leaders, explains to Jack that their goal wasn't to get out of jail; it was to transform an inequitable society. To pay bail, she pointed out, would be to participate in—and thereby perpetuate—an inherently evil system.

Here again, the objective was all-encompassing. It was never about winning rights for a few, but rather, creating a righteous society for all.

I was surprised by the nobility of the movement, and by the courage of the people who took part. Looking back, I see something very Christlike about the whole campaign. There was an intentional way in which these people suffered on behalf of those who persecuted them. They were beaten, arrested, and verbally abused for the sake of their enemies. To win freedom for everyone, they strove to enrich the lives of those who hated them.

It's interesting; this movement so thoroughly transformed American society, and yet it never insisted on a single fundamental change. Rather, it called on the country to embrace the principles of freedom and equality that it had always proclaimed. It simply asked

Americans to be fully American. It didn't demand that the church change; rather, it called on the church to embody the truths of Christ-centered community that it already preached. In other words, it asked the Christian church to become more Christian.

To the extent that we still view this in black-white terms, it's clear that white people were the primary beneficiaries. While the movement changed conditions for black people, it changed the hearts and minds of white people. Which gives us more to celebrate, and more to be grateful for.

Many writers talk about novel writing as something of a discovery process—claiming the characters often take on a life of their own as they write. Did this happen for any of your characters, or did you know from the start how they would grow and respond throughout the story?

I don't think any of the characters took on a life of their own, but I will say that character development in this story was … different. Fictional characters, like real ones, are defined by what they love and want most. We build characters around a single driving force and the tensions it naturally causes. But in this story the characters find themselves in this awkward, embarrassing in-between time. They're proud Southerners, they have a stake in the "Southern way of life," but the foundation's cracking beneath them. They know that change is coming, but no one's sure how to navigate through it.

There's an episode where Flannery O'Connor talks about the "grotesque characters" of Southern fiction. She explains that Southern writers live in this chimerical, Christ-haunted territory—this place where they're forever confronted with the region's failings. As a result,

O'Connor explains, they, unlike writers from other regions, see the distance between "what is" and "what ought to be." These characters embody that distance; they illustrate our deficiencies—as well as our longings.

The grotesque character of this story is racial segregation. I hope, through what's depicted here, readers see our still-lingering biases, as well as an always-emerging hope for the "beloved community."

The novel doesn't hide the ugly truths and the frequent missteps that marked the beginning of the civil rights movement, but it also presents a different picture of the South—a hopeful, culture-rich picture. What inspired you to capture both of these aspects of the South in the 1950s?

I needed to capture both because there's a direct connection between them. And in the connection, there's a vivid picture of our humanness: we're brilliant, creative, and high-minded one moment—evil, oppressive, and hypocritical the next.

It's hard to believe that in the same era (generally speaking) when Faulkner was crafting works of genius, Martin Luther King Jr. was pleading for racial reconciliation. During the days when Sam Phillips was inventing rock and roll, when he was introducing the blues to a whole new audience, producing the music of B. B. King, Howlin' Wolf Burnett, Ike Turner, Jackie Brenston, Johnny Cash, and Elvis Presley—black students were being jailed for ordering coffee at the Woolworth's lunch counter. As Flannery O'Connor penned enduring works of fiction, Georgia governor Marvin Griffin was vowing to stop the 1956 Sugar Bowl, to prevent Georgia Tech from playing a Pittsburgh team that fielded one "Negro" player.

This was an era when Southerners were, at the same time, creating the very best of the world's culture—and the worst. And the fact is, we'd have never had the one without the other. We now realize that:

- It is because of our once segregated society that we now know the thoughts and theology of Martin Luther King Jr.
- It was a long history of racial oppression that gave birth to the blues.
- Without a history of racial strife, we would never be enriched by the "Christ-haunted" and guilt-inspired fiction of so many great Southern writers.

The worst of Southern culture spawned the best. This is the paradox that sends Jack Hall down a career path he never envisioned.

What do you hope readers walk away with after reading *Crossing the Lines*?

I always want people to walk away with an enjoyable reading experience. I want them to be delighted with the language—with its power to draw us into a story and stir our emotions.

Beyond that, I hope readers come away admiring the courage of Martin Luther King Jr., Ralph Abernathy, John Lewis, Diane Nash, and hundreds of others who were responsible for the civil rights movement. And I hope they come away inspired—eager to create in their own neighborhoods and cities, with whatever tools are at hand—something that comes close to the biblical ideal of the "beloved community."

Will you be revisiting the Hall family in any future novels? What writing plans and dreams do you have now that *Crossing the Lines* is on the bookshelves?

I don't have any plans to revisit the Halls, but … you never say never. Right now I'm working on a story about a young woman—a singer from rural Georgia—who's forced to contemplate the purpose of her extraordinary talent; to figure out why it's been given to her, how it's to be used, and the implications of fame and celebrity. We'll see where it goes.

Fact and Fiction

In the first few pages Jack Hall, the protagonist, falls under the influence of Ralph McGill, the gutsy editor of *The Atlanta Constitution*. My depiction of McGill is based on the content of his columns, many of which are found in *The Best of Ralph McGill* by Henry Davis and Jeff Strickland. It is also drawn from McGill's books, *Southern Encounters: Southerners of Note in Ralph McGill's South, A Church, a School,* and *The South and the Southerner.* Two biographies were also helpful: *Ralph Emerson McGill: Voice of the Southern Conscience* by Leonard Ray Teel and *Ralph McGill, a Biography* by Barbara Clowse.

Jack's conscience is further troubled when he befriends Martin Luther King Jr. King's fictional conversations are largely a patchwork of words and concepts culled from his speeches, sermons, and his book: *Stride Toward Freedom.* While I've taken some "chronological liberty" with King's thoughts, suspecting that a few of the ideas he expressed in the early and mid-1960s might have been percolating earlier on, be assured, any substantive idea he expresses here, he expressed during his lifetime.

In the early chapters, the 1956 Sugar Bowl is cause for angst, not only in the Hall household, but also throughout the South. My account of the game and the events surrounding it is cobbled together from articles and editorials in *The Atlanta Constitution* and the *Atlanta Journal.*

Jack's life takes a dramatic turn in 1957, in Little Rock, Arkansas. The scenes that unfold at Central High School are, I believe, accurate portrayals of real events and of the people involved. A few incidents, particularly court cases, have been collapsed into a tighter timeframe, and I haven't always distinguished between district, state, and federal cases.

During their time in Little Rock, Jack and his partner have several conversations with historical figures, including Harry Ashmore, Orval Faubus, Virgil Blossom, Jim Johnson, and Amis Guthridge. These discussions describe actual events and they capture—as best as I could discern from written accounts—the suspicions and fears of the people who took part.

There are dozens of books that describe and interpret the integration of Central High School. I relied most heavily on *Turn Away Thy Son: Little Rock, the Crisis that Shocked a Nation* by Elizabeth Jacoway.

In Little Rock, two young women take center stage for a time: Elizabeth Eckford, a black student who, on the day described, hoped to enroll at the all-white Central High School. And Hazel Bryan, a white girl who cruelly harassed her. Their picture, captured by *Arkansas Gazette* photographer Will Counts, is an iconic image of this event and of the civil rights movement. Bryan (her last name has since changed) has, for that one instant of poor judgment, been vilified for a lifetime. You should know that Hazel Bryan has personally apologized to Eckford. As an adult, she's spent considerable time working with inner-city kids, helping to educate and nurture them. And she, like others throughout the South, has turned from one way of life and embraced another.

During the Little Rock episode readers will also encounter Benjamin Fine, a reporter who plays a minor but poignant role. Fine's actions at Central High have been widely noted, but perhaps most vividly by Gene Roberts and Hank Klibanoff in their book, *The Race Beat: The Press, the Civil Rights Struggle, and the Awakening of a Nation.*

I need to apologize to Nippy Jones and his family. In my recreation of a play from game four of the 1957 World Series I took Jones out of the game and substituted Percy Jackson, a fictional character. The incident described—an odd play in the bottom of the tenth inning at County Stadium in Milwaukee—is essentially true. But the central character was Jones, not Jackson.

Jack's encounters with legendary record producer Sam Phillips cause him to reflect on his life and work. My depiction of Phillips and the musicians he worked with (Elvis Presley, Scotty Moore, Bill Black, Ike Turner, Jackie Brenston, B. B. King, Howlin' Wolf [Chester Burnett], and Johnny Cash) is based on several magazine articles, a visit to Sun Studios in Memphis, and two books: *Good Rockin' Tonight: Sun Records and the Birth of Rock 'n' Roll* by Colin Escott and Martin Hawkins, and *Rock and Roll Is Here to Stay,* edited by William McKeen.

Beginning on page 330 readers eavesdrop on a conversation between Jack and the famous writer Flannery O'Connor. And later, Jack and a friend discuss a fictional O'Connor essay. The author's words, ideas, and opinions are based on actual essays and speeches, chiefly "The Fiction Writer and His Country," "The Church and the Fiction Writer," "Some Aspects of the Grotesque in Southern Fiction," "The Catholic Novelist in the Protestant South," and "The Regional Writer."

From O'Connor's farm in Milledgeville, Georgia, the story moves to Nashville, where you'll experience a disturbing episode in the lives of civil rights heroes John Lewis and Diane Nash. The depiction of these events is based on newspaper stories and, more substantively, on Lewis's memoir, *Walking with the Wind: A Memoir of the Movement*.

In the final few pages you'll read a delightful story about Harper Lee and the creation of *To Kill a Mockingbird*. It's true. My rendering is informed by Charles Shields's description, given in his book *Mockingbird: A Portrait of Harper Lee*.

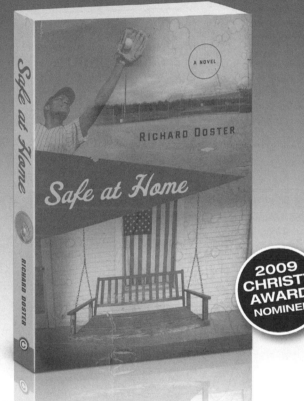

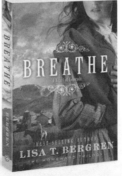